UP FROM SLAVERY

The New York Public Library Collector's Editions are illustrated with original art and handwritten letters, diaries, and manuscripts from the collections of the Library. They are designed to evoke the world of the writer and the book, and to enhance the pleasure of reading the great works of literature.

Booker T. Washington

THE NEW YORK PUBLIC LIBRARY

*Collector's
Edition*

UP FROM SLAVERY

BY

BOOKER T. WASHINGTON

AND OTHER EARLY BLACK NARRATIVES

DOUBLEDAY

New York   London   Toronto

Sydney   Auckland

FRONTISPIECE: Photograph of Booker T. Washington in the 1880s, photographer unknown.

PUBLISHED BY DOUBLEDAY
a division of Bantam Doubleday Dell Publishing Group, Inc.
1540 Broadway, New York, New York 10036

D O U B L E D A Y and the portrayal of an anchor with a dolphin
are trademarks of Doubleday, a division of
Bantam Doubleday Dell Publishing Group, Inc.

Book design by Marysarah Quinn

ISBN 0-385-48729-0

Up from Slavery first published 1901

ACKNOWLEDGMENTS

This volume was created with the participation of many people throughout The New York Public Library. For their help in developing *Up from Slavery and Other Early Black Narratives*, we are grateful for the contributions of the curators and staffs of the Schomburg Center for Research in Black Culture. Special recognition and thanks go to Tonya Bolden and Diana Lachatanere for writing and research; Anne Skillion, Series Editor; and Karen Van Westering, Manager of Publications.

The New York Public Library wishes to extend thanks to its trustees Catherine Marron and Marshall Rose, as well as to Morton Janklow, for their early support and help in initiating this project.

Paul LeClerc, President

Michael Zavelle, Senior Vice President

CONTENTS

ABOUT
BOOKER T. WASHINGTON

In all likelihood, the first time his name appeared in print was in 1861, in the inventory of his late owner, James Burroughs:

1 negro boy (Booker)

This boy of six or seven with no last name was valued at four hundred dollars.

Forty years later, Booker Taliaferro Washington's name appeared in print in a far more dynamic way with *Up from Slavery*, the story of his journey from bondsman in Virginia to master builder of Alabama's Tuskegee Institute.

When published by Doubleday, Page & Company in March 1901, *Up from Slavery* was an instant bestseller. "One of the great books of the year," proclaimed William T. Harris, the U.S. Commissioner of Education, adding that *Up from Slavery* was to the "problems left us by that civil war" what Harriet Beecher Stowe's *Uncle Tom's Cabin* was to its start. "Every white man in the South should read it, and every negro man should study it as an inspiration," hailed C. P. J. Mooney, editor of a Memphis weekly newspaper. The book received kudos from many in the Northern white press as well, including *The*

New York Times and the *Atlantic Monthly.* Again and again, *Up from Slavery* was compared with *The Autobiography of Benjamin Franklin.* It has been called a "Horatio Alger myth in black."

The root of the spectacular rise of this man born seven years before the Emancipation Proclamation, in 1856 (not in 1858 or 1859 as Washington guessed), was his childhood hunger for education. As we read in the early pages of *Up from Slavery:*

> I had no schooling whatever while I was a slave, though I remembered on several occasions I went as far as the school-house door with one of my young mistresses to carry her books. The picture of several dozen boys and girls in a schoolroom engaged in study made a deep impression upon me, and I had the feeling that to get into a schoolhouse and study in this way would be about the same as getting into paradise.

And so it was that this lad, a few months free, began schooling himself with a used copy of Noah Webster's *Elementary Spelling-Book.* While laboring at a West Virginia salt furnace and later a coal mine, he snatched time to attend a makeshift school. Word of a "great school for the coloured people somewhere in Virginia" prompted him to leave home in 1872, with his meager belongings in a satchel and less than two dollars in his pocket. Sixteen-year-old Booker T. Washington had set out on a five-hundred-mile trek to Hampton Normal and Agricultural Institute, where he earned admittance by the vigor with which he cleaned a classroom, paid his way primarily through janitorial work, and graduated with honors in 1875.

Nothing at Hampton captivated him more than the school's founder, General Samuel Chapman Armstrong. Born in 1819 on Hawaii's Maui Island, where his Presbyterian father did missionary work and for a time served as Hawaiian minister of education, Armstrong joined the Union army immediately after graduating from Williams College. A job with the Freedmen's Bureau brought him to the village of Hampton, where he founded a school in 1868 and emerged as a leading proponent of vocational education for black people and a firm believer that self-reliance and industry were the keys to the race's advancement. Armstrong found no more faithful disciple than Booker T. Washington. After teaching a few seasons in his hometown of Malden, West Virginia, and then flirting with the study of law and with the seminary, Washington returned to his alma mater to teach. With him came his hometown sweetheart, Fannie Norton Smith, whose studies at Hampton had been interrupted (probably for lack of money), and whom Washington would wed in 1882. Their daughter, Portia, was born in 1883.

It was on General Armstrong's recommendation that in 1881 Washington was handed the job of starting a school in Tuskegee, Alabama, "in a broken down shanty and an old hen house," as he was fond of saying. The mission of the Tuskegee Normal and Industrial Institute was to train schoolteachers and masters of various crafts and trades. Only a few of the school's graduates were ever expected to pursue a college education.

"The individual who can do something that the world wants done will in the end, make his way regardless of race," was a primary precept Principal Washington instilled in his students. "Nothing ever comes to one, that is worth having, except as a result of hard work" was another. Having students make the very bricks with which they would construct their school buildings was just one way Tuskegee put its teachings on industry and self-reliance into practice.

Helping Washington with fundraising and other aspects of Tuskegee's survival and growth was teacher and Lady Principal, Olivia America Davidson, whom Washington would marry in 1885, about a year after Fannie's death, possibly from injuries suffered in a fall from a wagon. The couple would have two sons, and their strong teamwork on behalf of Tuskegee would continue. Sadly, this ideal match did not last long: On a February night in 1889, when Washington was on the road fundraising, a fire broke out in the Washington home, sending the family out into the cold, and Olivia into collapse.

Washington had her taken North, to Massachusetts General Hospital in Boston, but she never recovered, dying on May 9, 1889. "Olivia's death left [him] destitute, not only emotionally but financially," Washington's biographer, Louis R. Harlan, tells us. "He had spent so long at her bedside, forgetting all else, that he barely had money to bring her body home to Tuskegee." Though he was now a father of three, Washington did not rush to remarry. When he did take another wife, he made a logical choice: Margaret James Murray, Tuskegee's Lady Principal since 1890. They married in 1892 (the date 1893 in *Up from Slavery* is presumably a misprint).

One wonders how Washington coped with his personal griefs and family obligations during Tuskegee's first decade, given the pressure he was under to make Tuskegee a viable institution. He knew the outside world was watching closely to see, as he wrote, "whether or not it was possible for Negroes to build up and control the affairs of a large educational institution." This was truly a feat in post-Reconstruction America, especially in the deep South, where with the withdrawal of Federal troops in 1877 there ensued a reign of terror, with the wholesale theft of black property and white-on-black violence reaching all-time highs, and with the torching of schools for "nigras" a frequent night riders' sport. Fully aware what savage reckoning could befall a black man seen as "uppity," Washington could do nothing but "wear the mask" as he worked tirelessly, ceaselessly, and with great success to procure white patronage and protection for his school.

And so it was that Tuskegee became a beacon and Washington a Moses to multitudes striving to move up from a myriad of desolations rooted in the legacy of slavery. People such as these gained strength from the life story of Booker T. Washington, who became known as "the Sage of Tuskegee."

But *Up from Slavery*'s core story of an awesome overcoming was not its sole attraction for many white readers. Equally appealing for them was Washington's implicit and explicit advocacy of the social philosophy of "accommodation." This philosophy earned him high

Washington with his third wife, Margaret; his sons, Ernest Davidson (far left) and Booker T., Jr.; and his daughter, Portia Marshall, around 1899. In 1904 the Washingtons adopted Margaret's very young orphaned niece, Laura Murray. By all accounts Washington did his best to be a good, attentive father to all four children.

ADDRESS

OF

BOOKER T. WASHINGTON,

Principal Tuskegee Normal and Industrial Institute,

Tuskegee, Ala.,

DELIVERED AT THE OPENING OF THE

ATLANTA COTTON STATES

AND

INTERNATIONAL EXPOSITION,

September 18, 1895.

The back cover of this pamphlet of Washington's "Atlanta Compromise" speech reads: "The calls for copies of this address are so numerous from all parts of the country that it has been decided to put it into this form for general distribution."

praise from powerful white Americans on September 18, 1895, the opening day of the Cotton States and International Exposition in Atlanta, Georgia, where before an interracial audience Washington delivered the address now known as the "Atlanta Compromise." In this speech, Washington denounced the black emigration movement in general and black flight from the South in particular (which would have deprived the South of much cheap labor) with the slogan "Cast down your bucket where you are." Later on, he seemingly gave his blessing to segregation with the now equally famous words: "In all things that are purely social we can be as separate as the five fingers, yet one as the hand in all things essential to mutual progress." (But as many scholars have pointed out, this statement was one many black nationalists could cheer.) Civil rights activists abandoned all hope of help from Washington when they heard of his assertion that "the wisest among my race understand that the agitation of questions of social equality is the extremest folly."

The speech drew tremendous praise from diverse quarters. Washington's future rival and critic W. E. B. Du Bois congratulated him by letter on his "phenomenal success," calling the speech "a word fitly spoken." People on both sides of the color line likened Washington to Frederick Douglass, who had died in February 1895. Not surprisingly, progressives found this comparison obscene, no doubt recalling Douglass's famous dictum "Power concedes nothing without a demand." The statement by African Methodist Episcopal Church Bishop Henry McNeal Turner that Washington would "have to live a long time to undo the harm he has done to our race" was among the more subdued expressions of displeasure with the Atlanta address.

What Bishop Turner or any other black person thought didn't much matter, because with this address influential white Americans summarily glorified Washington as *the* spokesman for his race. "The speech stamps Booker T. Washington as a wise counselor and a safe leader" was the way an *Atlanta Constitution* editorial put it. With this perception abounding, Booker T. Washington went on to become the most prominent and powerful black man in pre–World War I America.

It was hardly a stroke of brilliance, but just plain common sense, that Washington included his Atlanta address in *Up from Slavery,* a book born of anything but serendipity.

In the wake of his Atlanta address, many urged Washington to write his autobiography, among them Walter Hines Page of the Boston publisher Houghton, Mifflin and Company. Washington needed little convincing that an autobiography was in order, but Page would not be the editor to acquire it. At some point in 1897 Washington sent a book proposal to the subscription house J. L. Nichols, in Naperville, Illinois. To expedite things, he chose as his collaborator a black journalist, Edgar Webber.

The Story of My Life and Work (1900) was the autobiography that came of Webber and Washington's collaboration. According to Harlan, Webber was "both lazy and incompetent" and J. L. Nichols was "notorious for shoddy copy-editing and book-making"; the end result was "a thoroughly bad book." Flaws and all, however, *The Story of My Life and Work* sold briskly among blacks, no doubt because of the huge hunger in the black community for books by anyone black, especially one as idolized as Washington.

In his determination to produce a good autobiography, Washington engaged the services of Max Bennett Thrasher, a white journalist who would soon become an ad hoc publicist for Tuskegee Institute. According to Harlan, Thrasher was everything that Webber was not; but as he also tells us, Washington "kept an unusually tight rein" on Thrasher and was intensely involved in this book. *"Up from Slavery* . . . bears unmistakably the marks of Washington's style and personality,"* Harlan assures us, and "manuscript fragments in Washington's own hand . . . suggest that [it] was largely the work of Washington's own mind and purpose."

Washington's mind was on Tuskegee Institute; his purpose was raising money. We find evidence of this in a letter of September 22, 1900, to J. L. Nichols's general manager, apparently written to halt a charge of breach of contract or trust. "[T]he work which I am to do for the other people," wrote Washington, "will have as its main advantage the bringing of this institution before a class of people who have money and to whom I must look for money for endowments and other purposes." Near the end of the letter, Washington stressed that the book he was doing for "the other people" would not hurt sales of *The Story of My Life and Work:* "In proportion as I can get money . . . and keep this institution in a prosperous condition, in the same degree will there be a sale for your book. If this institution were to go down tomorrow, your book would at once become dead property on your hands, so you see it is important that we work wisely and sympathetically together."

"The other people" were Doubleday, Page & Company, with "Page" being Walter Hines Page. In 1899, Doubleday, McClure and Company had offered Washington a book contract, which Washington did not immediately accept. By the time he was ready to take the company up on the offer, the firm had been reorganized. The company's interest in Washington's autobiography was even stronger now that Page was a partner: In a letter to Washington dated January 5, 1900, Page wrote: "In my eyes and in yours, the principal element of success is, of course the effect it will have on public opinion and its influence in furthering the good cause. But incidentally I think it stands a pretty good chance, too, of reaching a very considerable financial success."

Setting the stage for the book's success was its serialization, from November 3, 1900, to February 23, 1901, in *The Outlook* magazine, which had a circulation of more than 100,000. Installments of *Up from Slavery* appeared in very interesting company, including "An Interview with Count Tolstoi" by Edward Steiner; the short story "The Queen's Twins" by Sarah Orne Jewett; and "Some Emerson Memories" by a man who had glimpsed Washington's potential at Hampton's commencement exercises of 1875, Edward Everett Hale, the

TUSKEGEE NORMAL AND INDUSTRIAL INSTITUTE.

(INCORPORATED)

FOR THE TRAINING OF COLORED YOUNG MEN AND WOMEN

Tuskegee, Ala., Feb. 28 190 1

Miss Emily Howland,
Sherwood, N. Y.

Dear Miss Howland:

I thank you very much for your kind letter of recent date and for your kind word regarding my articles in The Outlook. I am surprised at the wide reading which these articles have been given. I have just written the publishers, Doubleday, Page & Co., 34 Union Square, New York, who are to publish these articles in book form, to forward a copy of the book to Mrs. Rebecca Moore. This book will likely appear the first or second week in March.

I should write more fully, but I am just on the eve of taking a train for the North.

Yours truly
Booker T. Washington

In this letter to Tuskegee donor Emily Howland, Washington thanks her for her "kind word regarding my articles [i.e., the installments of Up from Slavery] *in* The Outlook" *and adds, "I am surprised at the wide reading which these articles have been given."*

clergyman and writer best remembered for his 1863 story about the Civil War, "The Man Without a Country."

As Washington had hoped, *Up from Slavery* did bring Tuskegee new benefactors. There was E. Julia Emery, an American living in England, who showed her appreciation for Washington's work with a check for one thousand dollars. A gift of five thousand dollars came from millionaire-inventor George Eastman, creator of roll film and the Kodak camera. The biggest benefactor the book attracted was industrialist Andrew Carnegie, whom Doubleday, Page & Company's co-founder Frank N. Doubleday had coaxed into reading *Up from Slavery* during a game of golf. Carnegie became a staunch supporter of Tuskegee. His early gifts included a Carnegie Library, $600,000 in U.S. Steel bonds, and the proclamation that "the serious race question of the South is to be solved wisely, only by following Booker T. Washington's policy."

Not so, said many members of the black intelligentsia. And those who deemed accommodation an anathema likewise deemed *Up from Slavery* a disservice to the race. In the vanguard was the Harvard graduate William Monroe Trotter, publisher of the newspaper the *Guardian* and leader of the anti–Booker T. Washington faction in black Boston. The most often cited criticism of the book came from another Harvard man, W. E. B. Du Bois, whose views had evolved quite a bit since he applauded Washington on his Atlanta address.

"It is as though Nature must needs make men a little narrow to give them force." This is how Du Bois opened his review of *Up from Slavery* in the July 16, 1901, issue of *The Dial*, a turn-of-the-century "little magazine." Du Bois took Washington to task for soft-pedaling the horrors of slavery, for promoting stereotypes about blacks, for being less than honest about the racism he had encountered. Du Bois's best-known critique of Washington would come in his essay "Of Mr. Booker T. Washington and Others," collected in *The Souls of Black Folk* (1903). Here, Du Bois even more firmly decried Washington's accommodationist position as contributing to black disenfranchisement, *de jure* segregation (as a result of *Plessy v. Ferguson*),

Portrait of Booker T. Washington by Alfred Houghton Clark and (opposite) the first page of the first installment of Up from Slavery *as they appeared together in* The Outlook, *November 3, 1900.*

UP FROM SLAVERY[1]

An Autobiography

BY BOOKER T. WASHINGTON

Chapter I.—A Slave Among Slaves

I WAS born a slave on a plantation in Franklin County, Virginia. I am not quite sure of the exact place or exact date of my birth, but at any rate I suspect I must have been born somewhere and at some time. As nearly as I have been able to learn, I was born near a cross-roads post-office called Hale's Ford, and the year was 1858 or 1859. I do not know the month or the day. The earliest impressions I can now recall are of the plantation and the slave quarters—the latter being the part of the plantation where the slaves had their cabins.

My life had its beginning in the midst of the most miserable, desolate, and discouraging surroundings. This was so, however, not because my owners were especially cruel, for they were not, as compared with many others. I was born in a typical log cabin, about fourteen by sixteen feet square. In this cabin I lived with my mother and a brother and sister till after the Civil War, when we were all declared free.

Of my ancestry I know almost nothing. In the slave quarters, and even later, I heard whispered conversations among the colored people of the tortures which the slaves, including, no doubt, my ancestors on my mother's side, suffered in the middle passage of the slave ship while being conveyed from Africa to America. I have been unsuccessful in securing any information that would throw any accurate light upon the history of my family beyond my mother. She, I remember, had a half-brother and a half-sister. In the days of slavery not very much attention was given to family history and family records—that is, black family records. My mother, I suppose, attracted the attention of a purchaser who was afterward my owner and hers. Her addition to the slave family attracted about as much attention as the purchase of a new horse or cow. Of my father I know even less than of my mother. I do not even know his name. I have heard reports to the effect that he was a white man who lived on one of the near-by plantations. Whoever he was, I never heard of his taking the least interest in me or providing in any way for my rearing. But I do not find especial fault with him. He was simply another unfortunate victim of the institution which the Nation unhappily had engrafted upon it at that time.

The cabin was not only our living-place, but was also used as the kitchen for the plantation. My mother was the plantation cook. The cabin was without glass windows; it had only openings in the side which let in the light, and also the cold, chilly air of winter. There was a door to the cabin—that is, something that was called a door—but the uncertain hinges by which it was hung, and the large cracks in it, to say nothing of the fact that it was too small, made the room a very uncomfortable one. In addition to these openings there was, in the lower right-hand corner of the room, the "cat-hole," a contrivance which almost every mansion or cabin in Virginia possessed during the ante-bellum period. The "cat-hole" was a square opening, about seven by eight inches, provided for the purpose of letting the cat pass in and out of the house at will during the night. In the case of our particular cabin I could never understand the necessity for this convenience, since there were at least a half-dozen other places in the cabin that would have accommodated the cats. There was no wooden floor in our cabin, the naked earth being used as a floor. In the center of the earthen floor there was a large, deep opening covered with boards, which was

[1] Copyright, 1900, by Booker T. Washington.

and the "steady withdrawal" of funds from predominantly black colleges and universities. Du Bois further asserted that Booker T. Washington's program "practically accepts the alleged inferiority of blacks" and absolved white America of all responsibility for the plight of so many among the nation's ten million black souls.

Reproach from a few intellectuals had little or no effect on Washington's popularity or that of *Up from Slavery*. By 1903 the book's sales had reached 30,000 copies and were steadily rising (as were those of *The Story of My Life and Work,* which allegedly outsold *Up from Slavery* at one point). What's more, by 1903, there were more than a dozen translations of *Up from Slavery* in progress (from Arabic to Zulu, literally) and a Braille edition was already out. The book was a major boost to Booker T. Washington's ambitions, and opened important doors to him, including those of the White House.

About six months after the publication of *Up from Slavery,* on October 16, 1901, Washington dined at the White House with President Theodore Roosevelt, who was eager to consult with him on political appointments and assorted race matters. Though this infuriated many white people in both the North and South, ultimately it increased Washington's fame and power, enabling him to expand his network, dubbed "the Tuskegee Machine" by Du Bois, who also may have been the one to dub Washington "the Wizard."

As the undisputed "boss" of black America, Washington could make or break people's careers and institutions. As an adviser not only to Theodore Roosevelt but also to President William Howard Taft, he secured political appointments for black men loyal to his philosophy, as well as determined the fate of a few white men seeking office. He steered philanthropists to dozens of black schools he deemed worthy and diverted funds from those of which he did not approve. Countering the myth that he was categorically opposed to higher education for blacks, he sent his own children to college, and served as a trustee of both Fisk and Howard universities and helped both connect with major philanthropists.

Given his prominence, many activists were furious with Washington for not speaking out vociferously against white mob violence, Jim Crow, and other injustices. Even today there are those who cannot forgive him his official silence on such things, though it is now more widely known that Washington secretly orchestrated and funded several test cases against Jim Crow laws, and supported other efforts regarded as militant in his day.

Washington virtually controlled the black press—driving into ruination more than a few who published dissent and winning the allegiance of some newspapers and magazines through carrot, through stick, and even through secret ownership. And he could be vicious against those who challenged his program. One notorious example followed what Washington called the "Boston Riot," which was more like a little ruckus, between pro- and anti-Bookerites on July 30, 1903, at a Boston church where Washington was speaking. William Monroe Trotter was there, but he had not instigated the trouble; nevertheless, Washington manipulated his arrest and conviction for conspiracy to disturb the peace, and Trotter spent thirty days in jail. After the incident, according to Harlan, Washington embarked on an intense persecution of Trotter and his supporters, blackballing Du Bois from a job at Atlanta University, for example. He was also known to plant spies within organizations he opposed. Among the organizations he kept tabs on and tried to sabotage was one Du Bois helped found in 1909, the National Association for the Advancement of Colored People (NAACP).

Washington's political actions were, for the most part, either unknown to or overlooked by average black people, for Washington brought many good things into their lives. There was the Tuskegee Negro Conference (started in 1892), an annual gathering of hundreds who, as Washington described it, "come to spend a day in finding out what the actual industrial, mental, and moral conditions of the people are, and in forming plans for improvement." There was the Jesup Wagon, an agricultural school on wheels launched in 1904 for the purpose of going out into the countryside with news and information that would help small farmers increase their productivity. In 1900,

Washington founded the National Negro Business League, an idea appropriated from Du Bois. This organization, over which he presided until his death, provided him with another means of enlisting and controlling supporters (especially in the North), but it also helped foster black entrepreneurship. He also sponsored National Negro Health Week in March 1915, designed to bring money and energies to bear on issues of sanitation, hygiene, and disease prevention among the poor.

Meanwhile, Washington was attracting and maintaining tremendous backing for Tuskegee from such sources as John D. Rockefeller, Jr.; Henry H. Rogers, an early partner in Standard Oil; investment banker Jacob Schiff; the Phelps Stokes family; and Julius Rosenwald, president of Sears, Roebuck, and Company. As a result, when Washington died in 1915, Tuskegee Institute had more than one hundred well-equipped buildings, a faculty of nearly two hundred men and women offering instruction in some forty trades and professions, and an endowment of roughly two million dollars. Considering what Washington had to start with, Tuskegee had certainly come a very long way. On the foundation Washington laid stands Tuskegee University (since 1985), offering forty-five undergraduate majors in the liberal arts and sciences, twenty-one master's programs, and a doctorate in veterinary medicine.

But Washington's accomplishments took a tremendous toll on his health. Occasionally he heeded the urgings of his wife, close friends, and physicians to take a vacation, but he never really knew what it was to take it easy. Diabetes was just one ailment he suffered in his later years. Sheer exhaustion was another.

While up North in early November 1915, Washington was admitted to St. Luke's Hospital in New York City. Among other things, his kidneys were weak and his blood pressure dangerously high. When doctors advised him that death was imminent, Washington did not fight it. He did, however, resist dying in the North. To doctors' counsel that he would probably not survive the trip to Tuskegee, Washington responded: "I was born in the South, I have lived in the

Booker T. Washington toward the end of his life.

South, and I expect to die and be buried in the South." And so it was that on November 12, Margaret Washington boarded a southbound train with her husband. They arrived at their home, The Oaks, on the night of November 13. The next morning, a little before five, Booker T. Washington died.

Shortly thereafter, J. L. Nichols was hawking *Booker T. Washington's Own Story of His Life and Work,* "the original autobiography brought up to date with a complete account of Dr. Washington's sickness and death," allegedly containing "the only photos of the funeral and burial." Washington's glory had begun to dim when the Republicans lost the White House in 1912 and as black and white support grew for Du Bois and other progressive minds; still, Washington's life story was a viable product.

"The Age of Booker T. Washington" is how some chroniclers have labeled black history from 1881 to 1915 because, as John Hope Franklin summed it up in *From Slavery to Freedom,* "the ascendancy of this man is one of the most dramatic and significant episodes in the history of American education and race relations."

But was he the best thing that happened to black America in the post-Reconstruction era, or, in the long run, was his ascendancy something to bemoan? This is the continuing question, one posed perhaps nowhere more memorably than in a novel by a man who attended Tuskegee Institute in the 1930s, Ralph Ellison. The moment comes early on in *Invisible Man:* the nameless protagonist is recalling his days at a school in the South presided over by the ultimate Uncle Tom, and he muses over the bronze statue of the college's founder, "the cold Father symbol, his hands outstretched in the breathtaking gesture of lifting a veil that flutters in hard, metallic folds above the face of a kneeling slave; and I am standing puzzled, unable to decide whether the veil is really being lifted, or lowered more firmly in place; whether I am witnessing a revelation or a more efficient blinding."

However one judges Washington, the fact remains that he is unforgettable. Inescapable, too, for those seeking insight on the black experience in the early twentieth century as well as the heritage of many racial issues in these post–Second Reconstruction days. And where better to start than with the touchstone of his sagacity and wizardry, *Up from Slavery*, never out of print since its first publication nearly a century ago.

ABOUT THIS EDITION

The photographs, letters, illustrations, and other material that adorn this Collector's Edition of *Up from Slavery and Other Early Black Narratives* are drawn from the collections of the Schomburg Center for Research in Black Culture, a national research library devoted to collecting, preserving, and providing access to resources documenting the experiences of peoples of African descent throughout the world. The Center's collections first won international acclaim in 1926, when the personal collection of the distinguished Puerto Rican–born black scholar and bibliophile Arturo Alfonso Schomburg was added to the Division of Negro Literature, History and Prints of the 135th Street Branch of The New York Public Library. Schomburg himself served as curator from 1932 until his death in 1938. Renamed in his honor in 1940, the collection has grown steadily through the years. In 1972 it was designated as one of The Research Libraries of The New York Public Library and was renamed the Schomburg Center for Research in Black Culture. Today, the center contains over five million items.

PHOTOGRAPHS AND PRINTS FROM EARLY EDITIONS OF *UP FROM SLAVERY*

Of particular interest in this Collector's Edition are the reproductions from the earliest published versions of *Up from Slavery* and its predecessor autobiography, *The Story of My Life and Work*—including the serialized appearance of *Up from Slavery* in *The Outlook* (November 3, 1900 to February 23, 1901) and Doubleday, Page & Company's 1901 first edition (as well as a few images from its fiftieth anniversary edition of 1951). These illustrations show Washington at various stages of his life, along with members of his family, and benefactors, faculty, staff, and students of Tuskegee Normal and Industrial Institute. Among these are images that bring into quick focus the great leaps he made in life: the cabin in which he believed he was born and the graceful Queen Anne–style house built some forty years later that served as his Tuskegee residence; the school's early makeshift facilities—the outbuildings on a ramshackle plantation—and Porter Hall, the school's stately first building.

The Outlook magazine was founded in 1870 as *The Christian Union* by social reformer Reverend Henry Ward Beecher, son of the founder of the American Bible Society, Lyman Beecher, and brother of Harriet Beecher Stowe, author of *Uncle Tom's Cabin*. *The Christian Union* became *The Outlook* in 1893. The issues that featured *Up from Slavery* included affecting photographs from Washington's life, illustrating his beginnings, his early jobs and schooling, and the Tuskegee Institute—its buildings and students in classes in its earliest years. It also included in the first installment a reproduction of a portrait of Booker T. Washington drawn from life for *The Outlook* by Alfred Houghton Clark. At the end of this installment was the poem "Booker T. Washington" by the most celebrated black poet of the day, Paul Laurence Dunbar. The last four lines of this poem captured Washington's single-mindedness: "Straight on he goes, nor turns to look behind/Where hot the hounds come baying at his hip;/With one idea foremost in his mind,/Like the keen prow of some on-forging ship."

The Doubleday, Page & Company first edition of *Up from Slavery* featured a frontispiece portrait of Washington by renowned photographer and artist Gertrude Käsebier, and we have used it in the same way here. The Schomburg Center's copy bears two important autographs: Washington's own, and Schomburg's, with the inscription "Gift—For exhibition purposes."

The Story of My Life and Work is chiefly valuable today as an artifact of Washington's life, especially for the photographs it includes, which add to the visual documentation of Tuskegee Institute.

ORIGINAL HANDWRITTEN MATERIALS AND OTHER MEMENTOS OF WASHINGTON'S LIFE

The two letters to Emily Howland (one in Washington's hand, the other in the hand of an assistant) reproduced in this edition come from the Schomburg Center's collection of Washington's letters, primarily to donors and supporters of Tuskegee, and serve as examples of the manner that Washington used to such good effect in raising funds and cultivating donor relations.

That Washington was able to get support for his school from some of the wealthiest Americans of his day is a major aspect of his wizardry. But before checks for thousands and hundreds of thousands of dollars began arriving, there were smaller donations. Some of these undoubtedly came in response to brochures like the one that illustrates this volume. Another "souvenir" marks the event that catapulted Washington to his first fame: the title page of the Atlanta address in pamphlet form, issued with the entire rave review of the speech by Clark Howell, the editor of the *Atlanta Constitution*, which ran in the September 19, 1895, edition of the *New York World*, and from which Washington quotes in *Up from Slavery*.

Gertrude Käsebier's frontispiece portrait of Washington and (opposite) the title page from Doubleday, Page & Company's first edition of Up from Slavery.

UP FROM SLAVERY

AN AUTOBIOGRAPHY

BY

BOOKER T. WASHINGTON

AUTHOR OF "THE FUTURE OF THE AMERICAN NEGRO"

NEW YORK

DOUBLEDAY, PAGE & CO.

1901

Booker T. Washington's autograph nameplate from the Library's copy of the first edition of Up from Slavery.

The Other Early Black Narratives in This Edition

In *Up from Slavery,* Booker T. Washington does not dwell on his own relatively brief personal experience of slavery, preferring instead to chronicle his struggle to go beyond it. But other writers much less well known than Washington have chronicled the experience itself and its aftermath, offering perspective and background to Washington's story. For this Collector's Edition, the Library has selected some moving and fascinating excerpts from the narratives of six other early black writers—four women and two men—that we hope will enrich this special volume.

Slave narratives emerged during the antebellum era. Dictated or written by slaves who had escaped to freedom, they were autobiographical writings intended at one and the same time to leave records for relatives and historians and to raise awareness and support for the

The Library's copy of the first edition of Up from Slavery *was a gift, with his inscription, from Arturo Alfonso Schomburg, the great book collector whose legacy formed the foundation of the Schomburg Center for Research in Black Culture.*

abolitionist cause. Ignored by some scholars who believed they were either written or edited by abolitionists and thus of questionable authenticity, slave narratives regained credibility in the 1970s through the work of historians John Blassingame, Eugene Genovese, and others. Since then, historical and literary scholarship examining slave narratives has increased, and the narratives are being reprinted for new generations of readers.

Slave narratives formed an important part of Arturo Alfonso Schomburg's original collection of books and other materials, which became the core of the Schomburg Collection. Accepted unquestioningly by Mr. Schomburg as autobiographical writings, these works were also valued for their documentary evidence of the heroism of black men and women. In addition, they were prized as examples of the early literary production of black writers.

The History of Mary Prince, A West Indian Slave (1831): *The History of Mary Prince* is unique, the first known narrative by an enslaved woman in the Americas and the first (and one of the few) British female slave narratives ever published. British slaves and ex-slaves were usually written about in the antislavery newspapers, since the slave narrative as a genre was not as well developed in England as in the United States. Scenes like the harrowing ones in which Mary is ruthlessly beaten for a minor infraction were presented in all the slave narratives to inform and remind readers of the brutality of the system.

The Life of Josiah Henson, Formerly a Slave, Now an Inhabitant of Canada, as Narrated by Himself (1849): Reportedly the model for Harriet Beecher Stowe's "Uncle Tom" of *Uncle Tom's Cabin*, Josiah Henson ostensibly was a "good" slave. Despite being shunted from one master to another, suffering beatings and other cruel treatment, he was industrious, efficient, and able to induce other slaves to work hard. He was made the overseer on plantations in Maryland and Kentucky, and was a preacher of the African Methodist Episcopal Church. As proof of his pious character, he did not escape despite the opportunity afforded him when he traveled through free territory. Eventually, however, he did escape into Canada and assisted other slaves to escape there. Later he spoke out against slavery on lecture tours in England.

Dictated to Samuel Eliot, Josiah Henson's narrative was published almost twenty years after he ran away. The scene he relates of his sale and separation from his mother when he was only three years old, and of his mother's anguish and pleading to be sold with her child, was a common one, experienced by many slave parents, grandparents, and children, and mentioned by all the slave narrators. Although described almost dispassionately by Henson, this dramatic scene could not fail to bring tears to the eyes of the "dear readers" of Henson's narrative, and to further condemn an inhumane system and gain adherents for the antislavery struggle.

The Life of Josiah Henson, among the best-known slave narratives and one that gained a certain notoriety, was quite popular, selling roughly six thousand copies in its first three years of publication. Sales increased in the 1850s, when Henson became an international sensation thanks to Harriet Beecher Stowe, author of the most devastating piece of literature for proslavery forces, *Uncle Tom's Cabin.* In *The Key to Uncle Tom's Cabin* (1853), her apologia of her famous novel, Stowe cited Henson's narrative among her sources. From this reference was born the rumor and then the legend that Josiah Henson was the original "Uncle Tom." Henson let the legend live, and like Booker T. Washington, for the sake of the work he was trying to do for his people, he took advantage of the publicity.

In 1858 the same firm that published *The Key to Uncle Tom's Cabin* released a revised edition of Henson's life story under the title *Truth Stranger Than Fiction: Father Henson's Story of His Own Life,* with an introduction by Stowe, and an engraved portrait of Henson (reproduced in this volume). Between 1876 and 1879, subsequent editions of the book appeared, with *Mrs. Harriet Beecher Stowe's "Uncle Tom"* or just plain *"Uncle Tom"* added, in parentheses, to the titles. When the last Henson memoir was published, Henson was in his eighties. The year was 1881, the same year Booker T. Washington opened Tuskegee Institute.

Running a Thousand Miles for Freedom: or, The Escape of William and Ellen Craft from Slavery (1860): William and Ellen Craft participated in one of the more daring escapes by fugitive slaves. William disguised his fair-skinned wife as his sick master, while he played the part of the faithful servant. Ellen used a pair of dark glasses and a muffler to hide her face and put her arm in a sling to avoid having to sign hotel registers. To cover their flight, the Crafts got permission from their owners to leave Macon, where they lived, during the Christmas season. Traveling north by train and steamer, they encountered few problems until they arrived in Baltimore, the last slave city on their journey. There, according to Maryland law, a master was required to post a bond for any slave going North. William was able to convince the station master that "his master" was in desperate need of medical care and was too sick to sign. Fellow passengers, who had seen "Master" Ellen feigning illness, supported William's claim, and they were allowed to complete their trip to Philadelphia.

In his preface to the narrative, William Craft noted that the book would merely be an account of their escape, unlike other narratives that provided details about the slave experience. The excitement of their adventure made this one of the more popular narratives.

The Narrative of Bethany Veney, a Slave Woman (1889): Bethany Veney's narrative was published some thirty years after she became a free woman (1858), thanks to a Mr. G. J. Adams, of Providence, Rhode Island, who purchased her and for whose family she worked for a time. Veney, called "Aunt Betty" by some, was well past seventy when she dictated her narrative, probably to the resident of East Greenwich, Rhode Island, known only by the initials M.W.G. The excerpt included in this Collector's Edition tells the wrenching tale of Veney's marriage torn asunder during slavery.

Memories of Childhood's Slavery Days (1909): The high-spirited and disarming Annie L. Burton was a child when liberated by the Union army, and remained in the South until 1879, supporting herself at various times as a chambermaid, cook, laundress, and housekeeper. Eventually Boston became her home, and there she ran a restaurant. One of the oft-cited highlights of Burton's life was her ability to put a nephew through Hampton Institute.

UP FROM SLAVERY

This volume is dedicated to my Wife

MRS. MARGARET JAMES WASHINGTON

And to my Brother

MR. JOHN H. WASHINGTON

*Whose patience, fidelity, and hard work have gone far
to make the work at Tuskegee successful*

PREFACE

This volume is the outgrowth of a series of articles, dealing with incidents in my life, which were published consecutively in the *Outlook*. While they were appearing in that magazine I was constantly surprised at the number of requests which came to me from all parts of the country, asking that the articles be permanently preserved in book form. I am most grateful to the *Outlook* for permission to gratify these requests.

I have tried to tell a simple, straightforward story, with no attempt at embellishment. My regret is that what I have attempted to do has been done so imperfectly. The greater part of my time and strength is required for the executive work connected with the Tuskegee Normal and Industrial Institute, and in securing the money necessary for the support of the institution. Much of what I have said has been written on board trains, or at hotels or railroad stations while I have been waiting for trains, or during the moments that I could spare from my work while at Tuskegee. Without the painstaking and generous assistance of Mr. Max Bennett Thrasher I could not have succeeded in any satisfactory degree.

CONTENTS

CHAPTER I

A Slave Among Slaves

I was born a slave on a plantation in Franklin County, Virginia. I am not quite sure of the exact place or exact date of my birth, but at any rate I suspect I must have been born somewhere and at some time. As nearly as I have been able to learn, I was born near a cross-roads post-office called Hale's Ford, and the year was 1858 or 1859. I do not know the month or the day. The earliest impressions I can now recall are of the plantation and the slave quarters—the latter being the part of the plantation where the slaves had their cabins.

My life had its beginning in the midst of the most miserable, desolate, and discouraging surroundings. This was so, however, not because my owners were especially cruel, for they were not, as compared with many others. I was born in a typical log cabin, about fourteen by sixteen feet square. In this cabin I lived with my mother and a brother and sister till after the Civil War, when we were all declared free.

Of my ancestry I know almost nothing. In the slave quarters, and even later, I heard whispered conversations among the coloured people of the tortures which the slaves, including, no doubt, my ancestors on my mother's side, suffered in the middle passage of the slave ship while being conveyed from Africa to America. I have been unsuccessful in securing any information that would throw any accurate light upon the history of my family beyond my mother. She, I remember, had a half-brother and a half-sister. In the days of slavery not very much attention was given to family history and family records—that is, black family records. My mother, I suppose, attracted the attention of a purchaser who was afterward my owner and hers. Her addition to the slave family attracted about as much attention as the purchase of a new horse or cow. Of my father I know even less than of my mother. I do not even know his name. I have heard reports to the effect that he was a white man who lived on one of the near-by plantations. Whoever he was, I never heard of his taking the least interest in me or providing in any way for my rearing. But I do not find especial fault with him. He was simply another unfortunate victim of the institution which the Nation unhappily had engrafted upon it at that time.

The cabin was not only our living-place, but was also used as the kitchen for the plantation. My mother was the plantation cook. The cabin was without glass windows; it had only openings in the side which let in the light, and also the cold, chilly air of winter. There was a door to the cabin—that is, something that was called a door—but the uncertain hinges by which it was hung, and the large cracks in it, to say nothing of the fact that it was too small, made the room a very uncomfortable one. In addition to these openings there was, in the lower right-hand corner of the room, the "cat-hole,"—a contrivance which almost every mansion or cabin in Virginia possessed during the ante-bellum period. The "cat-hole" was a square opening, about seven by eight inches, provided for the purpose of letting the cat pass in and out of the house at will during the night. In the case of our particular cabin I could never understand the necessity for this convenience, since there were at least a half-dozen other places in the cabin that would have accommodated the cats. There was no wooden floor in our cabin, the naked earth being used as a floor. In the centre of the earthen floor there was a large, deep opening covered with boards, which was used as a place in which to store sweet potatoes

This is the cabin in which Washington believed he was born.

during the winter. An impression of this potato-hole is very distinctly engraved upon my memory, because I recall that during the process of putting the potatoes in or taking them out I would often come into possession of one or two, which I roasted and thoroughly enjoyed. There was no cooking-stove on our plantation, and all the cooking for the whites and slaves my mother had to do over an open fireplace, mostly in pots and "skillets." While the poorly built cabin caused us to suffer with cold in the winter, the heat from the open fireplace in summer was equally trying.

The early years of my life, which were spent in the little cabin, were not very different from those of thousands of other slaves. My mother, of course, had little time in which to give attention to the training of her children during the day. She snatched a few moments for our care in the early morning before her work began, and at night after the day's work was done. One of my earliest recollections is that of my mother cooking a chicken late at night, and awakening her children for the purpose of feeding them. How or where she got it I do not know. I presume, however, it was procured from our owner's farm. Some people may call this theft. If such a thing were to happen now, I should condemn it as theft myself. But taking place at the time it did, and for the reason that it did, no one could ever make me believe that my mother was guilty of thieving. She was simply a victim of the system of slavery. I cannot remember having slept in a bed until after our family was declared free by the Emancipation Proclamation. Three children—John, my older brother, Amanda, my sister, and myself—had a pallet on the dirt floor, or, to be more correct, we slept in and on a bundle of filthy rags laid upon the dirt floor.

I was asked not long ago to tell something about the sports and pastimes that I engaged in during my youth. Until that question was asked it had never occurred to me that there was no period of my life that was devoted to play. From the time that I can remember anything, almost every day of my life has been occupied in some kind of labour; though I think I would now be a more useful man if I had

had time for sports. During the period that I spent in slavery I was not large enough to be of much service, still I was occupied most of the time in cleaning the yards, carrying water to the men in the fields, or going to the mill, to which I used to take the corn, once a week, to be ground. The mill was about three miles from the plantation. This work I always dreaded. The heavy bag of corn would be thrown across the back of the horse, and the corn divided about evenly on each side; but in some way, almost without exception, on these trips, the corn would so shift as to become unbalanced and would fall off the horse, and often I would fall with it. As I was not strong enough to reload the corn upon the horse, I would have to wait, sometimes for many hours, till a chance passer-by came along who would help me out of my trouble. The hours while waiting for some one were usually spent in crying. The time consumed in this way made me late in reaching the mill, and by the time I got my corn ground and reached home it would be far into the night. The road was a lonely one, and often led through dense forests. I was always frightened. The woods were said to be full of soldiers who had deserted from the army, and I had been told that the first thing a deserter did to a Negro boy when he found him alone was to cut off his ears. Besides, when I was late in getting home I knew I would always get a severe scolding or a flogging.

I had no schooling whatever while I was a slave, though I re-member on several occasions I went as far as the schoolhouse door with one of my young mistresses to carry her books. The picture of several dozen boys and girls in a schoolroom engaged in study made a deep impression upon me, and I had the feeling that to get into a schoolhouse and study in this way would be about the same as getting into paradise.

So far as I can now recall, the first knowledge that I got of the fact that we were slaves, and that freedom of the slaves was being discussed, was early one morning before day, when I was awakened by my mother kneeling over her children and fervently praying that Lincoln and his armies might be successful, and that one day she and her children might be free. In this connection I have never been able to understand how the slaves throughout the South, completely ignorant as were the masses so far as books or newspapers were concerned, were able to keep themselves so accurately and completely informed about the great National questions that were agitating the country. From the time that Garrison, Lovejoy, and others began to agitate for freedom, the slaves throughout the South kept in close touch with the progress of the movement. Though I was a mere child during the preparation for the Civil War and during the war itself, I now recall the many late-at-night whispered discussions that I heard my mother and the other slaves on the plantation indulge in. These discussions showed that they understood the situation, and that they kept themselves informed of events by what was termed the "grapevine" telegraph.

During the campaign when Lincoln was first a candidate for the Presidency, the slaves on our far-off plantation, miles from any railroad or large city or daily newspaper, knew what the issues involved were. When war was begun between the North and the South, every slave on our plantation felt and knew that, though other issues were discussed, the primal one was that of slavery. Even the most ignorant members of my race on the remote plantations felt in their hearts, with a certainty that admitted of no doubt, that the freedom of the slaves would be the one great result of the war, if the Northern armies conquered. Every success of the Federal armies and every defeat of the Confederate forces was watched with the keenest and most intense interest. Often the slaves got knowledge of the results of great battles before the white people received it. This news was usually gotten from the coloured man who was sent to the post-office for the mail. In our case the post-office was about three miles from the plantation, and the mail came once or twice a week. The man who was sent to the office would linger about the place long enough to get the drift of the conversation from the group of white people who naturally congregated there, after receiving their mail, to discuss the latest news. The mail-carrier on his way back to our master's house would as naturally retail the news that he had secured among the slaves, and in this way they often heard of important events before the white people at the "big house," as the master's house was called.

I cannot remember a single instance during my childhood or early boyhood when our entire family sat down to the table together, and God's blessing was asked, and the family ate a meal in a civilized manner. On the plantation in Virginia, and even later, meals were gotten by the children very much as dumb animals get theirs. It was a piece of bread here and a scrap of meat there. It was a cup of milk at one time and some potatoes at another. Sometimes a portion of our family would eat out of the skillet or pot, while some one else would eat from a tin plate held on the knees, and often using nothing but the hands with which to hold the food. When I had grown to sufficient size, I was required to go to the "big house" at meal-times to fan the flies from the table by means of a large set of paper fans operated by a pulley. Naturally much of the conversation of the white people turned upon the subject of freedom and the war, and I absorbed a good deal of it. I remember that at one time I saw two of my young mistresses and some lady visitors eating ginger-cakes, in the yard. At that time those cakes seemed to me to be absolutely the most tempting and desirable things that I had ever seen; and I then and there resolved that, if I ever got free, the height of my ambition would be reached if I could get to the point where I could secure and eat ginger-cakes in the way that I saw those ladies doing.

Of course as the war was prolonged the white people, in many cases, often found it difficult to secure food for themselves. I think the slaves felt the deprivation less than the whites, because the usual diet for the slaves was corn bread and pork, and these could be raised on the plantation; but coffee, tea, sugar, and other articles which the whites had been accustomed to use could not be raised on the plantation, and the conditions brought about by the war frequently made it impossible to secure these things. The whites were often in great straits. Parched corn was used for coffee, and a kind of black molasses was used instead of sugar. Many times nothing was used to sweeten the so-called tea and coffee.

The first pair of shoes that I recall wearing were wooden ones. They had rough leather on the top, but the bottoms, which were about an inch thick, were of wood. When I walked they made a fearful noise, and besides this they were very inconvenient, since there was no yielding to the natural pressure of the foot. In wearing them one presented an exceedingly awkward appearance. The most trying ordeal that I was forced to endure as a slave boy, however, was the wearing of a flax shirt. In the portion of Virginia where I lived it was common to use flax as part of the clothing for the slaves. That part of the flax from which our clothing was made was largely the refuse, which of course was the cheapest and roughest part. I can scarcely imagine any torture, except, perhaps, the pulling of a tooth, that is equal to that caused by putting on a new flax shirt for the first time. It is almost equal to the feeling that one would experience if he had a dozen or more chestnut burrs, or a hundred small pin-points, in contact with his flesh. Even to this day I can recall accurately the tortures that I underwent when putting on one of these garments. The fact that my flesh was soft and tender added to the pain. But I had no choice. I had to wear the flax shirt or none; and had it been left to me to choose, I should have chosen to wear no covering. In connection with the flax shirt, my brother John, who is several years older than I am, performed one of the most generous acts that I ever heard of one slave relative doing for another. On several occasions when I was being forced to wear a new flax shirt, he generously agreed to put it on in my stead and wear it for several days, till it was "broken in." Until I had grown to be quite a youth this single garment was all that I wore.

One may get the idea, from what I have said, that there was bitter feeling toward the white people on the part of my race, because of the fact that most of the white population was away fighting in a war which would result in keeping the Negro in slavery if the South was successful. In the case of the slaves on our place this was not true, and it was not true of any large portion of the slave population in the South where the Negro was treated with anything like decency. During the Civil War one of my young masters was killed, and two were severely wounded. I recall the feeling of sorrow which existed among the slaves when they heard of the death of "Mars' Billy." It was no sham sorrow, but real. Some of the slaves had nursed "Mars' Billy"; others had played with him when he was a child. "Mars' Billy" had begged for mercy in the case of others when the overseer or master was thrashing them. The sorrow in the slave quarter was only second to that in the "big house." When the two young masters were brought home wounded, the sympathy of the slaves was shown in many ways. They were just as anxious to assist in the nursing as the family relatives of the wounded. Some of the slaves would even beg for the privilege of sitting up at night to nurse their wounded masters. This tenderness and sympathy on the part of those held in bondage was a result of their kindly and generous nature. In order to defend and protect the women and children who were left on the plantations when the white males went to war, the slaves would have laid down their lives. The slave who was selected to sleep in the "big house" during the absence of the males was considered to have the place of honour. Any one attempting to harm "young Mistress" or "old Mistress" during the night would have had to cross the dead body of the slave to do so. I do not know how many have noticed it, but I think that it will be found to be true that there are few instances, either in slavery or freedom, in which a member of my race has been known to betray a specific trust.

As a rule, not only did the members of my race entertain no feelings of bitterness against the whites before and during the war, but there are many instances of Negroes tenderly caring for their former masters and mistresses who for some reason have become poor and dependent since the war. I know of instances where the former masters of slaves have for years been supplied with money by their former slaves to keep them from suffering. I have known of still other cases in which the former slaves have assisted in the education of the descendants of their former owners. I know of a case on a large plantation in the South in which a young white man, the son of the former owner of the estate, has become so reduced in purse and self-control by reason of drink that he is a pitiable creature; and yet, notwithstanding the poverty of the coloured people themselves on this plantation, they have for years supplied this young white man with the necessities of life. One sends him a little coffee or sugar, another a little meat, and so on. Nothing that the coloured people possess is too good for the son of "old Mars' Tom," who will perhaps never be permitted to suffer while any remain on the place who knew directly or indirectly of "old Mars' Tom."

I have said that there are few instances of a member of my race betraying a specific trust. One of the best illustrations of this which I know of is in the case of an ex-slave from Virginia whom I met not long ago in a little town in the state of Ohio. I found that this man had made a contract with his master, two or three years previous to the Emancipation Proclamation, to the effect that the slave was to be permitted to buy himself, by paying so much per year for his body; and while he was paying for himself, he was to be permitted to labour where and for whom he pleased. Finding that he could secure better wages in Ohio, he went there. When freedom came, he was still in debt to his master some three hundred dollars. Notwithstanding that the Emancipation Proclamation freed him from any obligation to his master, this black man walked the greater portion of the distance back to where his old master lived in Virginia, and placed the last dollar, with interest, in his hands. In talking to me about this, the man told me that he knew that he did not have to pay the debt, but that he had given his word to his master, and his word he had never broken. He felt that he could not enjoy his freedom till he had fulfilled his promise.

From some things that I have said one may get the idea that some of the slaves did not want freedom. This is not true. I have never seen one who did not want to be free, or one who would return to slavery.

I pity from the bottom of my heart any nation or body of people that is so unfortunate as to get entangled in the net of slavery. I have long since ceased to cherish any spirit of bitterness against the Southern white people on account of the enslavement of my race. No one section of our country was wholly responsible for its introduction, and, besides, it was recognized and protected for years by the General Government. Having once got its tentacles fastened on to the economic and social life of the Republic, it was no easy matter for the country to relieve itself of the institution. Then, when we rid ourselves of prejudice, or racial feeling, and look facts in the face, we must acknowledge that, notwithstanding the cruelty and moral wrong of slavery, the ten million Negroes inhabiting this country, who themselves or whose ancestors went through the school of American slavery, are in a stronger and more hopeful condition, materially, intellectually, morally, and religiously, than is true of an equal number of black people in any other portion of the globe. This is so to such an extent that Negroes in this country, who themselves or whose forefathers went through the school of slavery, are constantly returning to Africa as missionaries to enlighten those who remained in the fatherland. This I say, not to justify slavery—on the other hand, I condemn it as an institution, as we all know that in America it was established for selfish and financial reasons, and not from a missionary motive—but to call attention to a fact, and to show how Providence so often uses men and institutions to accomplish a purpose. When persons ask me in these days how, in the midst of what sometimes seem hopelessly discouraging conditions, I can have such faith in the future of my race in this country, I remind them of the wilderness through which and out of which, a good Providence has already led us.

Ever since I have been old enough to think for myself, I have entertained the idea that, notwithstanding the cruel wrongs inflicted upon us, the black man got nearly as much out of slavery as the white man did. The hurtful influences of the institution were not by any means confined to the Negro. This was fully illustrated by the life upon our own plantation. The whole machinery of slavery was so constructed as to cause labour, as a rule, to be looked upon as a badge of degradation, of inferiority. Hence labour was something that both races on the slave plantation sought to escape. The slave system on our place, in a large measure, took the spirit of self-reliance and self-help out of the white people. My old master had many boys and girls, but not one, so far as I know, ever mastered a single trade or special line of productive industry. The girls were not taught to cook, sew, or to take care of the house. All of this was left to the slaves. The slaves, of course, had little personal interest in the life of the plantation, and their ignorance prevented them from learning how to do things in the most improved and thorough manner. As a result of the system, fences were out of repair, gates were hanging half off the hinges, doors creaked, window-panes were out, plastering had fallen but was not replaced, weeds grew in the yard. As a rule, there was food for whites and blacks, but inside the house, and on the dining-room table, there was wanting that delicacy and refinement of touch and finish which can make a home the most convenient, comfortable, and attractive place in the world. Withal there was a waste of food and other materials which was sad. When freedom came, the slaves were almost as well fitted to begin life anew as the master, except in the matter of book-learning and ownership of property. The slave owner and his sons had mastered no special industry. They unconsciously had imbibed the feeling that manual labour was not the proper thing for them. On the other hand, the slaves, in many cases, had mastered some handicraft, and none were ashamed, and few unwilling, to labour.

Finally the war closed, and the day of freedom came. It was a momentous and eventful day to all upon our plantation. We had been expecting it. Freedom was in the air, and had been for months. Deserting soldiers returning to their homes were to be seen every day. Others who had been discharged, or whose regiments had been paroled, were constantly passing near our place. The "grape-vine telegraph" was kept busy night and day. The news and mutterings of great events were swiftly carried from one plantation to another. In the fear of "Yankee" invasions, the silverware and other valuables were taken from the "big house," buried in the woods, and guarded by trusted slaves. Woe be to any one who would have attempted to disturb the buried treasure. The slaves would give the Yankee soldiers food, drink, clothing—anything but that which had been specifically intrusted to their care and honour. As the great day drew nearer, there was more singing in the slave quarters than usual. It was bolder, had more ring, and lasted later into the night. Most of the verses of the plantation songs had some reference to freedom. True, they had sung those same verses before, but they had been careful to explain that the "freedom" in these songs referred to the next world, and had no connection with life in this world. Now they gradually threw off the mask, and were not afraid to let it be known that the "freedom" in their songs meant freedom of the body in this world. The night before the eventful day, word was sent to the slave quarters to the effect that something unusual was going to take place at the "big house" the next morning. There was little, if any, sleep that night. All was excitement and expectancy. Early the next morning word was sent to all the slaves, old and young, to gather at the house. In company with my mother, brother, and sister, and a large number of other slaves, I went to the master's house. All of our master's family were either standing or seated on the veranda of the house, where they could see what was to take place and hear what was said. There was a feeling of deep interest, or perhaps sadness, on their faces, but not bitterness. As I now recall the impression they made upon me, they did not at the moment seem to be sad because of the loss of property, but rather because of parting with those whom they had reared and who were in many ways very close to them. The most distinct thing that I now recall in connection with the scene was that some man who seemed to be a stranger (a United States officer, I presume) made a little speech and then read a rather long paper—the Emancipation Proclamation, I think. After the reading we were told that we were all free, and could go when and where we pleased. My mother, who was standing by my side, leaned over and kissed her children, while tears of joy ran down her cheeks. She explained to us what it all meant, that this was the day for which she had been so long praying, but fearing that she would never live to see.

For some minutes there was great rejoicing, and thanksgiving, and wild scenes of ecstasy. But there was no feeling of bitterness. In fact, there was pity among the slaves for our former owners. The wild rejoicing on the part of the emancipated coloured people lasted but for a brief period, for I noticed that by the time they returned to their cabins there was a change in their feelings. The great responsibility of being free, of having charge of themselves, of having to think and plan for themselves and their children, seemed to take possession of them. It was very much like suddenly turning a youth of ten or twelve years out into the world to provide for himself. In a few hours the great questions with which the Anglo-Saxon race had been grappling for centuries had been thrown upon these people to be solved. These were the questions of a home, a living, the rearing of children, education, citizenship, and the establishment and support of churches. Was it any wonder that within a few hours the wild rejoicing ceased and a feeling of deep gloom seemed to pervade the slave quarters? To some it seemed that, now that they were in actual possession of it, freedom was a more serious thing than they had expected to find it. Some of the slaves were seventy or eighty years old; their best days were gone. They had no strength with which to earn a living in a strange place and among strange people, even if they had been sure where to find a new place of abode. To this class the problem seemed especially hard. Besides, deep down in their hearts there was a strange and peculiar attachment to "old Marster" and "old Missus," and to their children, which they found it hard to think of breaking off. With these they had spent in some cases nearly a half-century, and it was no light thing to think of parting. Gradually, one by one, stealthily at first, the older slaves began to wander from the slave quarters back to the "big house" to have a whispered conversation with their former owners as to the future.

CHAPTER II

Boyhood Days

After the coming of freedom there were two points upon which practically all the people on our place were agreed, and I find that this was generally true throughout the South: that they must change their names, and that they must leave the old plantation for at least a few days or weeks in order that they might really feel sure that they were free.

In some way a feeling got among the coloured people that it was far from proper for them to bear the surname of their former owners, and a great many of them took other surnames. This was one of the first signs of freedom. When they were slaves, a coloured person was simply called "John" or "Susan." There was seldom occasion for more than the use of the one name. If "John" or "Susan" belonged to a white man by the name of "Hatcher," sometimes he was called "John Hatcher," or as often "Hatcher's John." But there was a feeling that "John Hatcher" or "Hatcher's John" was not the proper title by which to denote a freeman; and so in many cases "John Hatcher" was changed to "John S. Lincoln" or "John S. Sherman," the initial "S" standing for no name, it being simply a part of what the coloured man proudly called his "entitles."

As I have stated, most of the coloured people left the old plantation for a short while at least, so as to be sure, it seemed, that they could leave and try their freedom on to see how it felt. After they had remained away for a time, many of the older slaves, especially, returned to their old homes and made some kind of contract with their former owners by which they remained on the estate.

My mother's husband, who was the stepfather of my brother John and myself, did not belong to the same owners as did my mother. In fact, he seldom came to our plantation. I remember seeing him there perhaps once a year, that being about Christmas time. In some way, during the war, by running away and following the Federal soldiers, it seems, he found his way into the new state of West Virginia. As soon as freedom was declared, he sent for my mother to come to the Kanawha Valley, in West Virginia. At that time a journey from Virginia over the mountains to West Virginia was rather a tedious and in some cases a painful undertaking. What little clothing and few household goods we had were placed in a cart, but the children walked the greater portion of the distance, which was several hundred miles.

I do not think any of us ever had been very far from the plantation, and the taking of a long journey into another state was quite an event. The parting from our former owners and the members of our own race on the plantation was a serious occasion. From the time of our parting till their death we kept up a correspondence with the older members of the family, and in later years we have kept in touch with those who were the younger members. We were several weeks making the trip, and most of the time we slept in the open air and did our cooking over a log fire out-of-doors. One night I recall that we camped near an abandoned log cabin, and my mother decided to build a fire in that for cooking, and afterward to make a "pallet" on the floor for our sleeping. Just as the fire had gotten well started a large black snake fully a yard and a half long dropped down the chimney and ran out on the floor. Of course we at once abandoned that cabin. Finally we reached our destination—a little town called Malden, which is about five miles from Charleston, the present capital of the state.

At that time salt-mining was the great industry in that part of West Virginia, and the little town of Malden was right in the midst of the salt-furnaces. My stepfather had already secured a job at a salt-furnace, and he had also secured a little cabin for us to live in. Our new house was no better than the one we had left on the old plantation in Virginia. In fact, in one respect it was worse. Notwithstanding the poor condition of our plantation cabin, we were at all times sure of pure air. Our new home was in the midst of a cluster of cabins crowded closely together, and as there were no sanitary regulations, the filth about the cabins was often intolerable. Some of our neighbours were coloured people, and some were the poorest and most ignorant and degraded white people. It was a motley mixture. Drinking, gambling, quarrels, fights, and shockingly immoral practices were frequent. All who lived in the little town were in one way or another connected with the salt business. Though I was a mere child, my stepfather put me and my brother at work in one of the furnaces. Often I began work as early as four o'clock in the morning.

The first thing I ever learned in the way of book knowledge was while working in this salt-furnace. Each salt-packer had his barrels marked with a certain number. The number allotted to my stepfather was "18." At the close of the day's work the boss of the packers would come around and put "18" on each of our barrels, and I soon learned to recognize that figure wherever I saw it, and after a while got to the point where I could make that figure, though I knew nothing about any other figures or letters.

From the time that I can remember having any thoughts about anything, I recall that I had an intense longing to learn to read. I determined, when quite a small child, that, if I accomplished nothing else in life, I would in some way get enough education to enable me to read common books and newspapers. Soon after we got settled in some manner in our new cabin in West Virginia, I induced my mother to get hold of a book for me. How or where she got it I do not know, but in some way she procured an old copy of Webster's "blue-back" spelling-book, which contained the alphabet, followed

Washington was about nine years old when he began working in West Virginia's Kanawha Valley salt-furnace, near Saltville, Virginia, where this lithograph of two freedmen processing salt is set.

by such meaningless words as "ab," "ba," "ca," "da." I began at once to devour this book, and I think that it was the first one I ever had in my hands. I had learned from somebody that the way to begin to read was to learn the alphabet, so I tried in all the ways I could think of to learn it,—all of course without a teacher, for I could find no one to teach me. At that time there was not a single member of my race anywhere near us who could read, and I was too timid to approach any of the white people. In some way, within a few weeks, I mastered the greater portion of the alphabet. In all my efforts to learn to read my mother shared fully my ambition, and sympathized with me and aided me in every way that she could. Though she was totally ignorant, so far as mere book knowledge was concerned, she had high ambitions for her children, and a large fund of good, hard, common sense which seemed to enable her to meet and master every situation. If I have done anything in life worth attention, I feel sure that I inherited the disposition from my mother.

In the midst of my struggles and longing for an education, a young coloured boy who had learned to read in the state of Ohio came to Malden. As soon as the coloured people found out that he could read, a newspaper was secured, and at the close of nearly every day's work this young man would be surrounded by a group of men and women who were anxious to hear him read the news contained in the papers. How I used to envy this man! He seemed to me to be the one young man in all the world who ought to be satisfied with his attainments.

About this time the question of having some kind of a school opened for the coloured children in the village began to be discussed by members of the race. As it would be the first school for Negro children that had ever been opened in that part of Virginia, it was, of course, to be a great event, and the discussion excited the widest interest. The most perplexing question was where to find a teacher. The young man from Ohio who had learned to read the papers was considered, but his age was against him. In the midst of the discussion about a teacher, another young coloured man from Ohio, who had been a soldier, in some way found his way into town. It was soon learned that he possessed considerable education, and he was engaged by the coloured people to teach their first school. As yet no free schools had been started for coloured people in that section, hence each family agreed to pay a certain amount per month, with the understanding that the teacher was to "board 'round"—that is, spend a day with each family. This was not bad for the teacher, for each family tried to provide the very best on the day the teacher was to be its guest. I recall that I looked forward with an anxious appetite to the "teacher's day" at our little cabin.

This experience of a whole race beginning to go to school for the first time, presents one of the most interesting studies that has ever occurred in connection with the development of any race. Few people who were not right in the midst of the scenes can form any exact idea of the intense desire which the people of my race showed for an education. As I have stated, it was a whole race trying to go to school. Few were too young, and none too old, to make the attempt to learn. As fast as any kind of teachers could be secured, not only were day-schools filled, but night-schools as well. The great ambition of the older people was to try to learn to read the Bible before they died. With this end in view, men and women who were fifty or seventy-five years old would often be found in the night-school. Sunday-schools were formed soon after freedom, but the principal book studied in the Sunday-school was the spelling-book. Day-school, night-school, Sunday-school, were always crowded, and often many had to be turned away for want of room.

The opening of the school in the Kanawha Valley, however, brought to me one of the keenest disappointments that I ever experienced. I had been working in a salt-furnace for several months, and my stepfather had discovered that I had a financial value, and so, when the school opened, he decided that he could not spare me from my work. This decision seemed to cloud my every ambition. The disappointment was made all the more severe by reason of the fact that my place of work was where I could see the happy children passing to and from school, mornings and afternoons. Despite this disappointment, however, I determined that I would learn something, anyway. I applied myself with greater earnestness than ever to the mastering of what was in the "blue-back" speller.

My mother sympathized with me in my disappointment, and sought to comfort me in all the ways she could, and to help me find a way to learn. After a while I succeeded in making arrangements with the teacher to give me some lessons at night, after the day's work was done. These night lessons were so welcome that I think I learned more at night than the other children did during the day. My own experiences in the night-school gave me faith in the night-school idea, with which, in after years, I had to do both at Hampton and Tuskegee. But my boyish heart was still set upon going to the day-school, and I let no opportunity slip to push my case. Finally I won, and was permitted to go to the school in the day for a few months, with the understanding that I was to rise early in the morning and work in the furnace till nine o'clock, and return immediately after school closed in the afternoon for at least two more hours of work.

The schoolhouse was some distance from the furnace, and as I had to work till nine o'clock, and the school opened at nine, I found myself in a difficulty. School would always be begun before I reached it, and sometimes my class had recited. To get around this difficulty I yielded to a temptation for which most people, I suppose, will condemn me; but since it is a fact, I might as well state it. I have great faith in the power and influence of facts. It is seldom that anything is permanently gained by holding back a fact. There was a large clock in a little office in the furnace. This clock, of course, all the hundred or more workmen depended upon to regulate their hours of beginning and ending the day's work. I got the idea that the way for me to reach school on time was to move the clock hands from half-past eight up to the nine o'clock mark. This I found myself doing morning after morning, till the furnace "boss" discovered that something was wrong, and locked the clock in a case. I did not mean to inconvenience anybody. I simply meant to reach that schoolhouse in time.

When, however, I found myself at the school for the first time, I also found myself confronted with two other difficulties. In the first place, I found that all of the other children wore hats or caps on their heads, and I had neither hat nor cap. In fact, I do not remember that up to the time of going to school I had ever worn any kind of covering upon my head, nor do I recall that either I or anybody else had even thought anything about the need of covering for my head. But, of course, when I saw how all the other boys were dressed, I began to feel quite uncomfortable. As usual, I put the case before my mother, and she explained to me that she had no money with which to buy a "store hat," which was a rather new institution at that time among the members of my race and was considered quite the thing for young and old to own, but that she would find a way to help me out of the difficulty. She accordingly got two pieces of "homespun" (jeans) and sewed them together, and I was soon the proud possessor of my first cap.

The lesson that my mother taught me in this has always remained with me, and I have tried as best I could to teach it to others. I have always felt proud, whenever I think of the incident, that my mother had strength of character enough not to be led into the temptation of seeming to be that which she was not—of trying to impress my schoolmates and others with the fact that she was able to buy me a "store hat" when she was not. I have always felt proud that she refused to go into debt for that which she did not have the money to pay for. Since that time I have owned many kinds of caps and hats, but never one of which I have felt so proud as of the cap made of the two pieces of cloth sewed together by my mother. I have noted the fact, but without satisfaction, I need not add, that several of the boys who began their careers with "store hats" and who were my school-mates and used to join in the sport that was made of me because I had only a "homespun" cap, have ended their careers in the penitentiary, while others are not able now to buy any kind of hat.

My second difficulty was with regard to my name, or rather *a* name. From the time when I could remember anything, I had been called simply "Booker." Before going to school it had never occurred to me that it was needful or appropriate to have an additional name. When I heard the school-roll called, I noticed that all of the children had at least two names, and some of them indulged in what seemed to me the extravagance of having three. I was in deep perplexity, because I knew that the teacher would demand of me at least two names, and I had only one. By the time the occasion came for the enrolling of my name, an idea occurred to me which I thought would make me equal to the situation; and so, when the teacher asked me what my full name was, I calmly told him "Booker Washington," as if I had been called by that name all my life; and by that name I have since been known. Later in my life I found that my mother had given me the name of "Booker Taliaferro" soon after I was born, but in some way that part of my name seemed to disappear and for a long while was forgotten, but as soon as I found out about it I revived it, and made my full name "Booker Taliaferro Washington." I think there are not many men in our country who have had the privilege of naming themselves in the way that I have.

More than once I have tried to picture myself in the position of a boy or man with an honoured and distinguished ancestry which I could trace back through a period of hundreds of years, and who had not only inherited a name, but fortune and a proud family homestead; and yet I have sometimes had the feeling that if I had inherited these, and had been a member of a more popular race, I should have been inclined to yield to the temptation of depending upon my ancestry and my colour to do that for me which I should do for myself. Years ago I resolved that because I had no ancestry myself I would leave a record of which my children would be proud, and which might encourage them to still higher effort.

The world should not pass judgment upon the Negro, and especially the Negro youth, too quickly or too harshly. The Negro boy has obstacles, discouragements, and temptations to battle with that are little known to those not situated as he is. When a white boy undertakes a task, it is taken for granted that he will succeed. On the other hand, people are usually surprised if the Negro boy does not fail. In a word, the Negro youth starts out with the presumption against him.

The influence of ancestry, however, is important in helping forward any individual or race, if too much reliance is not placed upon it. Those who constantly direct attention to the Negro youth's moral weaknesses, and compare his advancement with that of white youths, do not consider the influence of the memories which cling about the old family homesteads. I have no idea, as I have stated elsewhere, who my grandmother was. I have, or have had, uncles and aunts and cousins, but I have no knowledge as to where most of them are. My case will illustrate that of hundreds of thousands of black people in every part of our country. The very fact that the white boy is conscious that, if he fails in life, he will disgrace the whole family record, extending back through many generations, is of tremendous value in helping him to resist temptations. The fact that the individual has behind and surrounding him proud family history and connection serves as a stimulus to help him to overcome obstacles when striving for success.

The time that I was permitted to attend school during the day was short, and my attendance was irregular. It was not long before I had to stop attending day-school altogether, and devote all of my time again to work. I resorted to the night-school again. In fact, the greater part of the education I secured in my boyhood was gathered through the night-school after my day's work was done. I had difficulty often in securing a satisfactory teacher. Sometimes, after I had secured some one to teach me at night, I would find, much to my disappointment, that the teacher knew but little more than I did. Often I would have to walk several miles at night in order to recite my night-school lessons. There was never a time in my youth, no matter how dark and discouraging the days might be, when one resolve did not continually remain with me, and that was a determination to secure an education at any cost.

Soon after we moved to West Virginia, my mother adopted into our family, notwithstanding our poverty, an orphan boy, to whom afterward we gave the name of James B. Washington. He has ever since remained a member of the family.

After I had worked in the salt-furnace for some time, work was secured for me in a coal-mine which was operated mainly for the purpose of securing fuel for the salt-furnace. Work in the coal-mine I always dreaded. One reason for this was that any one who worked in a coal-mine was always unclean, at least while at work, and it was a very hard job to get one's skin clean after the day's work was over. Then it was fully a mile from the opening of the coal-mine to the face of the coal, and all, of course, was in the blackest darkness. I do not believe that one ever experiences anywhere else such darkness as he does in a coal-mine. The mine was divided into a large number of different "rooms" or departments, and, as I never was able to learn the location of all these "rooms," I many times found myself lost in the mine. To add to the horror of being lost, sometimes my light would go out, and then, if I did not happen to have a match, I would wander about in the darkness until by chance I found some one to give me a light. The work was not only hard, but it was dangerous. There was always the danger of being blown to pieces by a premature explosion of powder, or of being crushed by falling slate. Accidents from one or the other of these causes were frequently occurring, and this kept me in constant fear. Many children of the tenderest years were compelled then, as is now true, I fear, in most coal-mining districts, to spend a large part of their lives in these coal-mines, with little opportunity to get an education; and, what is worse, I have often noted that, as a rule, young boys who begin life in a coal-mine are often physically and mentally dwarfed. They soon lose ambition to do anything else than to continue as a coal-miner.

In those days, and later as a young man, I used to try to picture in my imagination the feelings and ambitions of a white boy with absolutely no limit placed upon his aspirations and activities. I used to envy the white boy who had no obstacles placed in the way of his becoming a Congressman, Governor, Bishop, or President by reason of the accident of his birth or race. I used to picture the way that I would act under such circumstances; how I would begin at the bottom and keep rising until I reached the highest round of success.

In later years, I confess that I do not envy the white boy as I once did. I have learned that success is to be measured not so much by the position that one has reached in life as by the obstacles which he has overcome while trying to succeed. Looked at from this standpoint, I almost reach the conclusion that often the Negro boy's birth and connection with an unpopular race is an advantage, so far as real life is concerned. With few exceptions, the Negro youth must work harder and must perform his tasks even better than a white youth in order to secure recognition. But out of the hard and unusual struggle through which he is compelled to pass, he gets a strength, a confidence, that one misses whose pathway is comparatively smooth by reason of birth and race.

From any point of view, I had rather be what I am, a member of the Negro race, than be able to claim membership with the most favoured of any other race. I have always been made sad when I have heard members of any race claiming rights and privileges, or certain badges of distinction, on the ground simply that they were members of this or that race, regardless of their own individual worth or attainments. I have been made to feel sad for such persons because I am conscious of the fact that mere connection with what is known as a superior race will not permanently carry an individual forward unless he has individual worth, and mere connection with what is regarded as an inferior race will not finally hold an individual back if he possesses intrinsic, individual merit. Every persecuted individual and race should get much consolation out of the great human law, which is universal and eternal, that merit, no matter under what skin found, is, in the long run, recognized and rewarded. This I have said here, not to call attention to myself as an individual, but to the race to which I am proud to belong.

CHAPTER III

The Struggle for an Education

One day, while at work in the coal-mine, I happened to overhear two miners talking about a great school for coloured people somewhere in Virginia. This was the first time that I had ever heard anything about any kind of school or college that was more pretentious than the little coloured school in our town.

In the darkness of the mine I noiselessly crept as close as I could to the two men who were talking. I heard one tell the other that not only was the school established for the members of my race, but that opportunities were provided by which poor but worthy students could work out all or a part of the cost of board, and at the same time be taught some trade or industry.

As they went on describing the school, it seemed to me that it must be the greatest place on earth, and not even Heaven presented more attractions for me at that time than did the Hampton Normal and Agricultural Institute in Virginia, about which these men were talking. I resolved at once to go to that school, although I had no idea where it was, or how many miles away, or how I was going to reach it; I remembered only that I was on fire constantly with one ambition, and that was to go to Hampton. This thought was with me day and night.

HAMPTON NORMAL AGRICULTURAL INSTITUTE.
est. 1868
HAMPTON, VA.

". . . but the first sight of the large, three-story, brick school building seemed to have rewarded me for all that I had undergone in order to reach the place. . . . I felt that I had reached the promised land . . ."

After hearing of the Hampton Institute, I continued to work for a few months longer in the coal-mine. While at work there, I heard of a vacant position in the household of General Lewis Ruffner, the owner of the salt-furnace and coal-mine. Mrs. Viola Ruffner, the wife of General Ruffner, was a "Yankee" woman from Vermont. Mrs. Ruffner had a reputation all through the vicinity for being very strict with her servants, and especially with the boys who tried to serve her. Few of them had remained with her more than two or three weeks. They all left with the same excuse: she was too strict. I decided, however, that I would rather try Mrs. Ruffner's house than remain in the coal-mine, and so my mother applied to her for the vacant position. I was hired at a salary of $5 per month.

I had heard so much about Mrs. Ruffner's severity that I was almost afraid to see her, and trembled when I went into her presence. I had not lived with her many weeks, however, before I began to understand her. I soon began to learn that, first of all, she wanted everything kept clean about her, that she wanted things done promptly and systematically, and that at the bottom of everything she wanted absolute honesty and frankness. Nothing must be sloven or slipshod; every door, every fence, must be kept in repair.

I cannot now recall how long I lived with Mrs. Ruffner before going to Hampton, but I think it must have been a year and a half. At any rate, I here repeat what I have said more than once before, that the lessons that I learned in the home of Mrs. Ruffner were as valuable to me as any education I have ever gotten anywhere since. Even to this day I never see bits of paper scattered around a house or in the street that I do not want to pick them up at once. I never see a filthy yard that I do not want to clean it, a paling off of a fence that I do not want to put it on, an unpainted or unwhitewashed house that I do not want to paint or whitewash it, or a button off one's clothes, or a grease-spot on them or on a floor, that I do not want to call attention to it.

From fearing Mrs. Ruffner I soon learned to look upon her as one of my best friends. When she found that she could trust me she did so implicitly. During the one or two winters that I was with her she gave me an opportunity to go to school for an hour in the day during a portion of the winter months, but most of my studying was done at night, sometimes alone, sometimes under some one whom I could hire to teach me. Mrs. Ruffner always encouraged and sympathized with me in all my efforts to get an education. It was while living with her that I began to get together my first library. I secured a dry-goods box, knocked out one side of it, put some shelves in it, and began putting into it every kind of book that I could get my hands upon, and called it my "library."

Notwithstanding my success at Mrs. Ruffner's I did not give up the idea of going to the Hampton Institute. In the fall of 1872 I determined to make an effort to get there, although, as I have stated, I had no definite idea of the direction in which Hampton was, or of what it would cost to go there. I do not think that any one thoroughly sympathized with me in my ambition to go to Hampton unless it was my mother, and she was troubled with a grave fear that I was starting out on a "wild-goose chase." At any rate, I got only a half-hearted consent from her that I might start. The small amount of money that I had earned had been consumed by my stepfather and the remainder of the family, with the exception of a very few dollars, and so I had very little with which to buy clothes and pay my travelling expenses. My brother John helped me all that he could, but of course that was not a great deal, for his work was in the coal-mine, where he did not earn much, and most of what he did earn went in the direction of paying the household expenses.

Perhaps the thing that touched and pleased me most in connection with my starting for Hampton was the interest that many of the older coloured people took in the matter. They had spent the best days of their lives in slavery, and hardly expected to live to see the time when they would see a member of their race leave home to attend a boarding-school. Some of these older people would give me a nickel, others a quarter, or a handkerchief.

Finally the great day came, and I started for Hampton. I had only a small, cheap satchel that contained what few articles of clothing I could get. My mother at the time was rather weak and broken in health. I hardly expected to see her again, and thus our parting was all the more sad. She, however, was very brave through it all. At that time there were no through trains connecting that part of West Virginia with eastern Virginia. Trains ran only a portion of the way, and the remainder of the distance was travelled by stage-coaches.

The distance from Malden to Hampton is about five hundred miles. I had not been away from home many hours before it began to grow painfully evident that I did not have enough money to pay my fare to Hampton. One experience I shall long remember. I had been travelling over the mountains most of the afternoon in an old-fashioned stage-coach, when, late in the evening, the coach stopped for the night at a common, unpainted house called a hotel. All the other passengers except myself were whites. In my ignorance I supposed that the little hotel existed for the purpose of accommodating the passengers who travelled on the stage-coach. The difference that the colour of one's skin would make I had not thought anything about. After all the other passengers had been shown rooms and were getting ready for supper, I shyly presented myself before the man at the desk. It is true I had practically no money in my pocket with which to pay for bed or food, but I had hoped in some way to beg my way into the good graces of the landlord, for at that season in the mountains of Virginia the weather was cold, and I wanted to get indoors for the night. Without asking as to whether I had any money, the man at the desk firmly refused to even consider the matter of providing me with food or lodging. This was my first experience in finding out what the colour of my skin meant. In some way I managed to keep warm by walking about, and so got through the night. My whole soul was so bent upon reaching Hampton that I did not have time to cherish any bitterness toward the hotel-keeper.

By walking, begging rides both in wagons and in the cars, in some way, after a number of days, I reached the city of Richmond, Virginia, about eighty-two miles from Hampton. When I reached there, tired, hungry, and dirty, it was late in the night. I had never been in a large city, and this rather added to my misery. When I reached Richmond, I was completely out of money. I had not a single acquaintance in the place, and, being unused to city ways, I did not know where to go. I applied at several places for lodging, but they all wanted money, and that was what I did not have. Knowing nothing else better to do, I walked the streets. In doing this I passed by many food-stands where fried chicken and half-moon apple pies were piled high and made to present a most tempting appearance. At that time it seemed to me that I would have promised all that I expected to possess in the future to have gotten hold of one of those chicken legs or one of those pies. But I could not get either of these, nor anything else to eat.

I must have walked the streets till after midnight. At last I became so exhausted that I could walk no longer. I was tired, I was hungry, I was everything but discouraged. Just about the time when I reached extreme physical exhaustion, I came upon a portion of a street where the board sidewalk was considerably elevated. I waited for a few minutes, till I was sure that no passers-by could see me, and then crept under the sidewalk and lay for the night upon the ground, with my satchel of clothing for a pillow. Nearly all night I could hear the tramp of feet over my head. The next morning I found myself some-what refreshed, but I was extremely hungry, because it had been a long time since I had had sufficient food. As soon as it became light enough for me to see my surroundings I noticed that I was near a large ship, and that this ship seemed to be unloading a cargo of pig iron. I went at once to the vessel and asked the captain to permit me to help unload the vessel in order to get money for food. The captain, a white man, who seemed to be kind-hearted, consented. I worked long enough to earn money for my breakfast, and it seems to me, as I remember it now, to have been about the best breakfast that I have ever eaten.

My work pleased the captain so well that he told me if I desired I could continue working for a small amount per day. This I was very glad to do. I continued working on this vessel for a number of days. After buying food with the small wages I received there was not much left to add to the amount I must get to pay my way to Hampton. In order to economize in every way possible, so as to be sure to reach Hampton in a reasonable time, I continued to sleep under the same sidewalk that gave me shelter the first night I was in Richmond. Many years after that the coloured citizens of Richmond very kindly tendered me a reception at which there must have been two thousand people present. This reception was held not far from the spot where I slept the first night I spent in that city, and I must confess that my mind was more upon the sidewalk that first gave me shelter than upon the reception, agreeable and cordial as it was.

When I had saved what I considered enough money with which to reach Hampton, I thanked the captain of the vessel for his kindness, and started again. Without any unusual occurrence I reached Hampton, with a surplus of exactly fifty cents with which to begin my education. To me it had been a long, eventful journey; but the first sight of the large, three-story, brick school building seemed to have rewarded me for all that I had undergone in order to reach the place. If the people who gave the money to provide that building could appreciate the influence the sight of it had upon me, as well as upon thousands of other youths, they would feel all the more encouraged to make such gifts. It seemed to me to be the largest and most beautiful building I had ever seen. The sight of it seemed to give me new life. I felt that a new kind of existence had now begun—that life would now have a new meaning. I felt that I had reached the promised land, and I resolved to let no obstacle prevent me from putting forth the highest effort to fit myself to accomplish the most good in the world.

As soon as possible after reaching the grounds of the Hampton Institute, I presented myself before the head teacher for assignment to a class. Having been so long without proper food, a bath, and change of clothing, I did not, of course, make a very favourable impression upon her, and I could see at once that there were doubts in her mind about the wisdom of admitting me as a student. I felt that I could hardly blame her if she got the idea that I was a worthless loafer or tramp. For some time she did not refuse to admit me, neither did she decide in my favour, and I continued to linger about her, and to impress her in all the ways I could with my worthiness. In the meantime I saw her admitting other students, and that added greatly to my discomfort, for I felt, deep down in my heart, that I could do as well as they, if I could only get a chance to show what was in me.

After some hours had passed, the head teacher said to me: "The adjoining recitation-room needs sweeping. Take the broom and sweep it."

It occurred to me at once that here was my chance. Never did I receive an order with more delight. I knew that I could sweep, for Mrs. Ruffner had thoroughly taught me how to do that when I lived with her.

I swept the recitation-room three times. Then I got a dusting-cloth and I dusted it four times. All the woodwork around the walls, every bench, table, and desk, I went over four times with my dusting-cloth. Besides, every piece of furniture had been moved and every closet and corner in the room had been thoroughly cleaned. I had the feeling that in a large measure my future depended upon the impression I made upon the teacher in the cleaning of that room. When I was through, I reported to the head teacher. She was a "Yankee" woman who knew just where to look for dirt. She went into the room and inspected the floor and closets; then she took her handkerchief and rubbed it on the woodwork about the walls, and over the table and benches. When she was unable to find one bit of dirt on the floor, or a particle of dust on any of the furniture, she quietly remarked, "I guess you will do to enter this institution."

I was one of the happiest souls on earth. The sweeping of that room was my college examination, and never did any youth pass an examination for entrance into Harvard or Yale that gave him more genuine satisfaction. I have passed several examinations since then, but I have always felt that this was the best one I ever passed.

I have spoken of my own experience in entering the Hampton Institute. Perhaps few, if any, had anything like the same experience that I had, but about that same period there were hundreds who found their way to Hampton and other institutions after experiencing something of the same difficulties that I went through. The young men and women were determined to secure an education at any cost.

The sweeping of the recitation-room in the manner that I did it seems to have paved the way for me to get through Hampton. Miss Mary F. Mackie, the head teacher, offered me a position as janitor. This, of course, I gladly accepted, because it was a place where I could work out nearly all the cost of my board. The work was hard and taxing, but I stuck to it. I had a large number of rooms to care for, and had to work late into the night, while at the same time I had to rise by four o'clock in the morning, in order to build the fires and have a little time in which to prepare my lessons. In all my career at Hampton, and ever since I have been out in the world, Miss Mary F. Mackie, the head teacher to whom I have referred, proved one of my strongest and most helpful friends. Her advice and encouragement were always helpful and strengthening to me in the darkest hour.

I have spoken of the impression that was made upon me by the buildings and general appearance of the Hampton Institute, but I have not spoken of that which made the greatest and most lasting impression upon me, and that was a great man—the noblest, rarest human being that it has ever been my privilege to meet. I refer to the late General Samuel C. Armstrong.

It has been my fortune to meet personally many of what are called great characters, both in Europe and America, but I do not hesitate to say that I never met any man who, in my estimation, was the equal of General Armstrong. Fresh from the degrading influences of the slave plantation and the coal-mines, it was a rare privilege for me to be permitted to come into direct contact with such a character as General Armstrong. I shall always remember that the first time I went into his presence he made the impression upon me of being a perfect man; I was made to feel that there was something about him that was superhuman. It was my privilege to know the General personally from the time I entered Hampton till he died, and the more I saw of him the greater he grew in my estimation. One might have removed from Hampton all the buildings, class-rooms, teachers, and industries, and given the men and women there the opportunity of coming into daily contact with General Armstrong, and that alone would have been a liberal education. The older I grow, the more I am convinced that there is no education which one can get from books and costly apparatus that is equal to that which can be gotten from contact with great men and women. Instead of studying books so constantly, how I wish that our schools and colleges might learn to study men and things!

General Armstrong spent two of the last six months of his life in my home at Tuskegee. At that time he was paralyzed to the extent that he had lost control of his body and voice in a very large degree. Notwithstanding his affliction, he worked almost constantly night and day for the cause to which he had given his life. I never saw a man who so completely lost sight of himself. I do not believe he ever had a selfish thought. He was just as happy in trying to assist some other institution in the South as he was when working for Hampton. Although he fought the Southern white man in the Civil War, I never heard him utter a bitter word against him afterward. On the other hand, he was constantly seeking to find ways by which he could be of service to the Southern whites.

It would be difficult to describe the hold that he had upon the students at Hampton, or the faith they had in him. In fact, he was worshipped by his students. It never occurred to me that General Armstrong could fail in anything that he undertook. There is almost no request that he could have made that would not have been complied with. When he was a guest at my home in Alabama, and was so badly paralyzed that he had to be wheeled about in an invalid's chair,

General Samuel Chapman Armstrong, founder of Hampton Institute. Washington said of him: "It was my privilege to know the General personally from the time I entered Hampton till he died, and the more I saw of him the greater he grew in my estimation."

I recall that one of the General's former students had occasion to push his chair up a long, steep hill that taxed his strength to the utmost. When the top of the hill was reached, the former pupil, with a glow of happiness on his face, exclaimed, "I am so glad that I have been permitted to do something that was real hard for the General before he dies!" While I was a student at Hampton, the dormitories became so crowded that it was impossible to find room for all who wanted to be admitted. In order to help remedy the difficulty, the General conceived the plan of putting up tents to be used as rooms. As soon as it became known that General Armstrong would be pleased if some of the older students would live in the tents during the winter, nearly every student in school volunteered to go.

I was one of the volunteers. The winter that we spent in those tents was an intensely cold one, and we suffered severely—how much I am sure General Armstrong never knew, because we made no complaints. It was enough for us to know that we were pleasing General Armstrong, and that we were making it possible for an additional number of students to secure an education. More than once, during a cold night, when a stiff gale would be blowing, our tent was lifted bodily, and we would find ourselves in the open air. The General would usually pay a visit to the tents early in the morning, and his earnest, cheerful, encouraging voice would dispel any feeling of despondency.

I have spoken of my admiration for General Armstrong, and yet he was but a type of that Christlike body of men and women who went into the Negro schools at the close of the war by the hundreds to assist in lifting up my race. The history of the world fails to show a higher, purer, and more unselfish class of men and women than those who found their way into those Negro schools.

Life at Hampton was a constant revelation to me; was constantly taking me into a new world. The matter of having meals at regular hours, of eating on a tablecloth, using a napkin, the use of the bathtub and of the tooth-brush, as well as the use of sheets upon the bed, were all new to me.

I sometimes feel that almost the most valuable lesson I got at the Hampton Institute was in the use and value of the bath. I learned there for the first time some of its value, not only in keeping the body healthy, but in inspiring self-respect and promoting virtue. In all my travels in the South and elsewhere since leaving Hampton I have always in some way sought my daily bath. To get it sometimes when I have been the guest of my own people in a single-roomed cabin has not always been easy to do, except by slipping away to some stream in the woods. I have always tried to teach my people that some provision for bathing should be a part of every house.

For some time, while a student at Hampton, I possessed but a single pair of socks, but when I had worn these till they became soiled, I would wash them at night and hang them by the fire to dry, so that I might wear them again the next morning.

The charge for my board at Hampton was ten dollars per month. I was expected to pay a part of this in cash and to work out the remainder. To meet this cash payment, as I have stated, I had just fifty cents when I reached the institution. Aside from a very few dollars that my brother John was able to send me once in a while, I had no money with which to pay my board. I was determined from the first to make my work as janitor so valuable that my services would be indispensable. This I succeeded in doing to such an extent that I was soon informed that I would be allowed the full cost of my board in return for my work. The cost of tuition was seventy dollars a year. This, of course, was wholly beyond my ability to provide. If I had been compelled to pay the seventy dollars for tuition, in addition to providing for my board, I would have been compelled to leave the Hampton school. General Armstrong, however, very kindly got Mr. S. Griffitts Morgan, of New Bedford, Mass., to defray the cost of my tuition during the whole time that I was at Hampton. After I finished the course at Hampton and had entered upon my lifework at Tuskegee, I had the pleasure of visiting Mr. Morgan several times.

After having been for a while at Hampton, I found myself in difficulty because I did not have books and clothing. Usually, however, I got around the trouble about books by borrowing from those who were more fortunate than myself. As to clothes, when I reached Hampton I had practically nothing. Everything that I possessed was in a small hand satchel. My anxiety about clothing was increased because of the fact that General Armstrong made a personal inspection of the young men in ranks, to see that their clothes were clean. Shoes had to be polished, there must be no buttons off the clothing, and no grease-spots. To wear one suit of clothes continually, while at work and in the schoolroom, and at the same time keep it clean, was rather a hard problem for me to solve. In some way I managed to get on till the teachers learned that I was in earnest and meant to succeed, and then some of them were kind enough to see that I was partly supplied with second-hand clothing that had been sent in barrels from the North. These barrels proved a blessing to hundreds of poor but deserving students. Without them I question whether I should ever have gotten through Hampton.

When I first went to Hampton I do not recall that I had ever slept in a bed that had two sheets on it. In those days there were not many buildings there, and room was very precious. There were seven other boys in the same room with me; most of them, however, students who had been there for some time. The sheets were quite a puzzle to me. The first night I slept under both of them, and the second night I slept on top of both of them; but by watching the other boys I learned my lesson in this, and have been trying to follow it ever since and to teach it to others.

I was among the youngest of the students who were in Hampton at that time. Most of the students were men and women—some as old as forty years of age. As I now recall the scene of my first year, I do not believe that one often has the opportunity of coming into contact with three or four hundred men and women who were so tremendously in earnest as these men and women were. Every hour was occupied in study or work. Nearly all had had enough actual contact with the world to teach them the need of education. Many of the older ones were, of course, too old to master the text-books very

Washington was around seventeen and well on course at Hampton when this photograph was taken in 1873.

thoroughly, and it was often sad to watch their struggles; but they made up in earnestness much of what they lacked in books. Many of them were as poor as I was, and, besides having to wrestle with their books, they had to struggle with a poverty which prevented their having the necessities of life. Many of them had aged parents who were dependent upon them, and some of them were men who had wives whose support in some way they had to provide for.

The great and prevailing idea that seemed to take possession of every one was to prepare himself to lift up the people at his home. No one seemed to think of himself. And the officers and teachers, what a rare set of human beings they were! They worked for the students night and day, in season and out of season. They seemed happy only when they were helping the students in some manner. Whenever it is written—and I hope it will be—the part that the Yankee teachers played in the education of the Negroes immediately after the war will make one of the most thrilling parts of the history of this country. The time is not far distant when the whole South will appreciate this service in a way that it has not yet been able to do.

CHAPTER IV

Helping Others

At the end of my first year at Hampton I was confronted with another difficulty. Most of the students went home to spend their vacation. I had no money with which to go home, but I had to go somewhere. In those days very few students were permitted to remain at the school during vacation. It made me feel very sad and homesick to see the other students preparing to leave and starting for home. I not only had no money with which to go home, but I had none with which to go anywhere.

In some way, however, I had gotten hold of an extra, second-hand coat which I thought was a pretty valuable coat. This I decided to sell, in order to get a little money for travelling expenses. I had a good deal of boyish pride, and I tried to hide, as far as I could, from the other students the fact that I had no money and nowhere to go. I made it known to a few people in the town of Hampton that I had this coat to sell, and, after a good deal of persuading, one coloured man promised to come to my room to look the coat over and consider the matter of buying it. This cheered my drooping spirits considerably. Early the next morning my prospective customer appeared. After looking the garment over carefully, he asked me how much I wanted for it. I told him I thought it was worth three dollars. He seemed to agree with me as to price, but remarked in the most matter-of-fact way: "I tell you what I will do; I will take the coat, and I will pay you five cents, cash down, and pay you the rest of the money just as soon as I can get it." It is not hard to imagine what my feelings were at the time.

With this disappointment I gave up all hope of getting out of the town of Hampton for my vacation work. I wanted very much to go where I might secure work that would at least pay me enough to purchase some much-needed clothing and other necessities. In a few days practically all the students and teachers had left for their homes, and this served to depress my spirits even more.

After trying for several days in and near the town of Hampton, I finally secured work in a restaurant at Fortress Monroe. The wages, however, were very little more than my board. At night, and between meals, I found considerable time for study and reading; and in this direction I improved myself very much during the summer.

When I left school at the end of my first year, I owed the institution sixteen dollars that I had not been able to work out. It was my greatest ambition during the summer to save money enough with which to pay this debt. I felt that this was a debt of honour, and that I could hardly bring myself to the point of even trying to enter school again till it was paid. I economized in every way that I could think of—did my own washing, and went without necessary garments—but still I found my summer vacation ending and I did not have the sixteen dollars.

One day, during the last week of my stay in the restaurant, I found under one of the tables a crisp, new ten-dollar bill. I could hardly contain myself, I was so happy. As it was not my place of business I felt it to be the proper thing to show the money to the proprietor. This I did. He seemed as glad as I was, but he coolly explained to me that, as it was his place of business, he had a right to keep the money, and he proceeded to do so. This, I confess, was another pretty hard blow to me. I will not say that I became discouraged, for as I now look back over my life I do not recall that I ever became discouraged over anything that I set out to accomplish. I have begun everything with the idea that I could succeed, and I never had much patience with the multitudes of people who are always ready to explain why one cannot succeed. I have always had a high regard for the man who could tell me how to succeed. I determined to face the situation just as it was. At the end of the week I went to the treasurer of the Hampton Institute, General J. F. B. Marshall, and told him frankly my condition. To my gratification he told me that I could reënter the institution, and that he would trust me to pay the debt when I could. During the second year I continued to work as a janitor.

The education that I received at Hampton out of the text-books was but a small part of what I learned there. One of the things that impressed itself upon me deeply, the second year, was the unselfishness of the teachers. It was hard for me to understand how any individuals could bring themselves to the point where they could be so happy in working for others. Before the end of the year, I think I began learning that those who are happiest are those who do the most for others. This lesson I have tried to carry with me ever since.

I also learned a valuable lesson at Hampton by coming into contact with the best breeds of live stock and fowls. No student, I think, who has had the opportunity of doing this could go out into the world and content himself with the poorest grades.

Perhaps the most valuable thing that I got out of my second year was an understanding of the use and value of the Bible. Miss Nathalie Lord, one of the teachers, from Portland, Me., taught me how to use and love the Bible. Before this I had never cared a great deal about it, but now I learned to love to read the Bible, not only for the spiritual help which it gives, but on account of it as literature. The lessons taught me in this respect took such a hold upon me that at the present time, when I am at home, no matter how busy I am, I always make it a rule to read a chapter or a portion of a chapter in the morning, before beginning the work of the day.

Whatever ability I may have as a public speaker I owe in a

measure to Miss Lord. When she found out that I had some inclination in this direction, she gave me private lessons in the matter of breathing, emphasis, and articulation. Simply to be able to talk in public for the sake of talking has never had the least attraction for me. In fact, I consider that there is nothing so empty and unsatisfactory as mere abstract public speaking; but from my early childhood I have had a desire to do something to make the world better, and then to be able to speak to the world about that thing.

The debating societies at Hampton were a constant source of delight to me. These were held on Saturday evening; and during my whole life at Hampton I do not recall that I missed a single meeting. I not only attended the weekly debating society, but was instrumental in organizing an additional society. I noticed that between the time when supper was over and the time to begin evening study there were about twenty minutes which the young men usually spent in idle gossip. About twenty of us formed a society for the purpose of utilizing this time in debate or in practice in public speaking. Few persons ever derived more happiness or benefit from the use of twenty minutes of time than we did in this way.

At the end of my second year at Hampton, by the help of some money sent me by my mother and brother John, supplemented by a small gift from one of the teachers at Hampton, I was enabled to return to my home in Malden, West Virginia, to spend my vacation. When I reached home I found that the salt-furnaces were not running, and that the coal-mine was not being operated on account of the miners being out on a "strike." This was something which, it seemed, usually occurred whenever the men got two or three months ahead in their savings. During the strike, of course, they spent all that they had saved, and would often return to work in debt at the same wages, or would move to another mine at considerable expense. In either case, my observations convinced me that the miners were worse off at the end of a strike. Before the days of strikes in that section of the country, I knew miners who had considerable money in the bank, but as soon as the professional labour agitators got control, the savings of even the more thrifty ones began disappearing.

My mother and the other members of the family were, of course, much rejoiced to see me and to note the improvement that I had made during my two years' absence. The rejoicing on the part of all classes of the coloured people, and especially the older ones, over my return, was almost pathetic. I had to pay a visit to each family and take a meal with each, and at each place tell the story of my experiences at Hampton. In addition to this I had to speak before the church and Sunday-school, and at various other places. The thing that I was most in search of, though, work, I could not find. There was no work on account of the strike. I spent nearly the whole of the first month of my vacation in an effort to find something to do by which I could earn money to pay my way back to Hampton and save a little money to use after reaching there.

Toward the end of the first month, I went to a place a considerable distance from my home, to try to find employment. I did not succeed, and it was night before I got started on my return. When I had gotten within a mile or so of my home I was so completely tired out that I could not walk any farther, and I went into an old, abandoned house to spend the remainder of the night. About three o'clock in the morning my brother John found me asleep in this house, and broke to me, as gently as he could, the sad news that our dear mother had died during the night.

This seemed to me the saddest and blankest moment in my life. For several years my mother had not been in good health, but I had no idea, when I parted from her the previous day, that I should never see her alive again. Besides that, I had always had an intense desire to be with her when she did pass away. One of the chief ambitions which spurred me on at Hampton was that I might be able to get to be in a position in which I could better make my mother comfortable and happy. She had so often expressed the wish that she might be permitted to live to see her children educated and started out into the world.

In a very short time after the death of my mother our little home was in confusion. My sister Amanda, although she tried to do the best she could, was too young to know anything about keeping house, and my stepfather was not able to hire a housekeeper. Sometimes we had food cooked for us, and sometimes we did not. I remember that more than once a can of tomatoes and some crackers constituted a meal. Our clothing went uncared for, and everything about our home was soon in a tumble-down condition. It seems to me that this was the most dismal period of my life.

My good friend Mrs. Ruffner, to whom I have already referred, always made me welcome at her home, and assisted me in many ways during this trying period. Before the end of the vacation she gave me some work, and this, together with work in a coal-mine at some distance from my home, enabled me to earn a little money.

At one time it looked as if I would have to give up the idea of returning to Hampton, but my heart was so set on returning that I determined not to give up going back without a struggle. I was very anxious to secure some clothes for the winter, but in this I was disappointed, except for a few garments which my brother John secured for me. Notwithstanding my need of money and clothing, I was very happy in the fact that I had secured enough money to pay my travelling expenses back to Hampton. Once there, I knew that I could make myself so useful as a janitor that I could in some way get through the school year.

Three weeks before the time for the opening of the term at Hampton, I was pleasantly surprised to receive a letter from my good friend Miss Mary F. Mackie, the lady principal, asking me to return to Hampton two weeks before the opening of the school, in order that I might assist her in cleaning the buildings and getting things in order for the new school year. This was just the opportunity I wanted. It gave me a chance to secure a credit in the treasurer's office. I started for Hampton at once.

During these two weeks I was taught a lesson which I shall never forget. Miss Mackie was a member of one of the oldest and most cultured families of the North, and yet for two weeks she worked by my side cleaning windows, dusting rooms, putting beds in order, and what not. She felt that things would not be in condition for the opening of school unless every window-pane was perfectly clean, and she took the greatest satisfaction in helping to clean them herself. The work which I have described she did every year that I was at Hampton.

It was hard for me at this time to understand how a woman of her education and social standing could take such delight in performing such service, in order to assist in the elevation of an unfortunate race. Ever since then I have had no patience with any school for my race in the South which did not teach its students the dignity of labour.

During my last year at Hampton every minute of my time that was not occupied with my duties as janitor was devoted to hard study. I was determined, if possible, to make such a record in my class as would cause me to be placed on the "honour roll" of Commencement speakers. This I was successful in doing. It was June of 1875 when I finished the regular course of study at Hampton. The greatest benefits that I got out of my life at the Hampton Institute, perhaps, may be classified under two heads:—

First was contact with a great man, General S. C. Armstrong, who, I repeat, was, in my opinion, the rarest, strongest, and most beautiful character that it has ever been my privilege to meet.

Second, at Hampton, for the first time, I learned what education was expected to do for an individual. Before going there I had a good deal of the then rather prevalent idea among our people that to secure an education meant to have a good, easy time, free from all necessity for manual labour. At Hampton I not only learned that it was not a disgrace to labour, but learned to love labour, not alone for its financial value, but for labour's own sake and for the independence and self-reliance which the ability to do something which the world wants done brings. At that institution I got my first taste of what it meant to live a life of unselfishness, my first knowledge of the fact that the happiest individuals are those who do the most to make others useful and happy.

I was completely out of money when I graduated. In company with other Hampton students, I secured a place as a table waiter in a summer hotel in Connecticut, and managed to borrow enough money with which to get there. I had not been in this hotel long before I found out that I knew practically nothing about waiting on a hotel table. The head waiter, however, supposed that I was an accomplished waiter. He soon gave me charge of a table at which there sat four or five wealthy and rather aristocratic people. My ignorance of how to wait upon them was so apparent that they scolded me in such a severe manner that I became frightened and left their table, leaving them sitting there without food. As a result of this I was reduced from the position of waiter to that of a dish-carrier.

But I determined to learn the business of waiting, and did so within a few weeks and was restored to my former position. I have had the satisfaction of being a guest in this hotel several times since I was a waiter there.

At the close of the hotel season I returned to my former home in Malden, and was elected to teach the coloured school at that place. This was the beginning of one of the happiest periods of my life. I now felt that I had the opportunity to help the people of my home town to a higher life. I felt from the first that mere book education was not all that the young people of that town needed. I began my work at eight o'clock in the morning, and, as a rule, it did not end until ten o'clock at night. In addition to the usual routine of teaching, I taught the pupils to comb their hair, and to keep their hands and faces clean, as well as their clothing. I gave special attention to teaching them the proper use of the tooth-brush and the bath. In all my teaching I have watched carefully the influence of the tooth-brush, and I am convinced that there are few single agencies of civilization that are more far-reaching.

There were so many of the older boys and girls in the town, as well as men and women, who had to work in the daytime but still were craving an opportunity for some education, that I soon opened a night-school. From the first, this was crowded every night, being about as large as the school that I taught in the day. The efforts of some of the men and women, who in many cases were over fifty years of age, to learn, were in some cases very pathetic.

My day and night school work was not all that I undertook. I established a small reading-room and a debating society. On Sundays I taught two Sunday-schools, one in the town of Malden in the afternoon, and the other in the morning at a place three miles distant from Malden. In addition to this, I gave private lessons to several young men whom I was fitting to send to the Hampton Institute. Without regard to pay and with little thought of it, I taught any one who wanted to learn anything that I could teach him. I was supremely happy in the opportunity of being able to assist somebody else. I did receive, however, a small salary from the public fund, for my work as a public-school teacher.

During the time that I was a student at Hampton my older brother, John, not only assisted me all that he could, but worked all of the time in the coal-mines in order to support the family. He willingly neglected his own education that he might help me. It was my earnest wish to help him to prepare to enter Hampton, and to save money to assist him in his expenses there. Both of these objects I was successful in accomplishing. In three years my brother finished the course at Hampton, and he is now holding the important position of Superintendent of Industries at Tuskegee. When he returned from Hampton, we both combined our efforts and savings to send our adopted brother, James, through the Hampton Institute. This we succeeded in doing, and he is now the postmaster at the Tuskegee Institute. The year 1877, which was my second year of teaching in Malden, I spent very much as I did the first.

It was while my home was at Malden that what was known as the

"During the time that I was a student at Hampton my older brother, John . . . willingly neglected his own education that he might help me."

"Ku Klux Klan" was in the height of its activity. The "Ku Klux" were bands of men who had joined themselves together for the purpose of regulating the conduct of the coloured people, especially with the object of preventing the members of the race from exercising any influence in politics. They corresponded somewhat to the "patrollers" of whom I used to hear a great deal during the days of slavery, when I was a small boy. The "patrollers" were bands of white men—usually young men—who were organized largely for the purpose of regulating the conduct of the slaves at night in such matters as preventing the slaves from going from one plantation to another without passes, and for preventing them from holding any kind of meetings without permission and without the presence at these meetings of at least one white man.

Like the "patrollers" the "Ku Klux" operated almost wholly at night. They were, however, more cruel than the "patrollers." Their objects, in the main, were to crush out the political aspirations of the Negroes, but they did not confine themselves to this, because schoolhouses as well as churches were burned by them, and many innocent persons were made to suffer. During this period not a few coloured people lost their lives.

As a young man, the acts of these lawless bands made a great impression upon me. I saw one open battle take place at Malden between some of the coloured and white people. There must have been not far from a hundred persons engaged on each side; many on both sides were seriously injured, among them being General Lewis Ruffner, the husband of my friend Mrs. Viola Ruffner. General Ruffner tried to defend the coloured people, and for this he was knocked down and so seriously wounded that he never completely recovered. It seemed to me as I watched this struggle between members of the two races, that there was no hope for our people in this country. The "Ku Klux" period was, I think, the darkest part of the Reconstruction days.

I have referred to this unpleasant part of the history of the South simply for the purpose of calling attention to the great change that

"*As a young man, the acts of these lawless bands made a great impression upon me. . . . The 'Ku Klux' period was, I think, the darkest part of the Reconstruction days.*"

has taken place since the days of the "Ku Klux." To-day there are no such organizations in the South, and the fact that such ever existed is almost forgotten by both races. There are few places in the South now where public sentiment would permit such organizations to exist.

CHAPTER V

The Reconstruction Period

The years from 1867 to 1878 I think may be called the period of Reconstruction. This included the time that I spent as a student at Hampton and as a teacher in West Virginia. During the whole of the Reconstruction period two ideas were constantly agitating the minds of the coloured people, or, at least, the minds of a large part of the race. One of these was the craze for Greek and Latin learning, and the other was a desire to hold office.

It could not have been expected that a people who had spent generations in slavery, and before that generations in the darkest heathenism, could at first form any proper conception of what an education meant. In every part of the South, during the Reconstruction period, schools, both day and night, were filled to overflowing with people of all ages and conditions, some being as far along in age as sixty and seventy years. The ambition to secure an education was most praiseworthy and encouraging. The idea, however, was too prevalent that, as soon as one secured a little education, in some unexplainable way he would be free from most of the hardships of the world, and, at any rate, could live without manual labour. There was a further feeling that a knowledge, however little, of the Greek and Latin languages would make one a very superior human being, something bordering almost on the supernatural. I remember that the first coloured man whom I saw who knew something about foreign languages impressed me at that time as being a man of all others to be envied.

Naturally, most of our people who received some little education became teachers or preachers. While among these two classes there were many capable, earnest, godly men and women, still a large proportion took up teaching or preaching as an easy way to make a living. Many became teachers who could do little more than write their names. I remember there came into our neighbourhood one of this class, who was in search of a school to teach, and the question arose while he was there as to the shape of the earth and how he would teach the children concerning this subject. He explained his position in the matter by saying that he was prepared to teach that the earth was either flat or round, according to the preference of a majority of his patrons.

The ministry was the profession that suffered most—and still suffers, though there has been great improvement—on account of not only ignorant but in many cases immoral men who claimed that they were "called to preach." In the earlier days of freedom almost every coloured man who learned to read would receive "a call to preach" within a few days after he began reading. At my home in West Virginia the process of being called to the ministry was a very interesting one. Usually the "call" came when the individual was sitting in church. Without warning the one called would fall upon the floor as if struck by a bullet, and would lie there for hours, speechless and motionless. Then the news would spread all through the neighbourhood that this individual had received a "call." If he were inclined to resist the summons, he would fall or be made to fall a second or third time. In the end he always yielded to the call. While I wanted an education badly, I confess that in my youth I had a fear that when I had learned to read and write well I would receive one of these "calls"; but, for some reason, my call never came.

When we add the number of wholly ignorant men who preached

or "exhorted" to that of those who possessed something of an education, it can be seen at a glance that the supply of ministers was large. In fact, some time ago I knew a certain church that had a total membership of about two hundred, and eighteen of that number were ministers. But, I repeat, in many communities in the South the character of the ministry is being improved, and I believe that within the next two or three decades a very large proportion of the unworthy ones will have disappeared. The "calls" to preach, I am glad to say, are not nearly so numerous now as they were formerly, and the calls to some industrial occupation are growing more numerous. The improvement that has taken place in the character of the teachers is even more marked than in the case of the ministers.

During the whole of the Reconstruction period our people throughout the South looked to the Federal Government for everything, very much as a child looks to its mother. This was not unnatural. The central government gave them freedom, and the whole Nation had been enriched for more than two centuries by the labour of the Negro. Even as a youth, and later in manhood, I had the feeling that it was cruelly wrong in the central government, at the beginning of our freedom, to fail to make some provision for the general education of our people in addition to what the states might do, so that the people would be the better prepared for the duties of citizenship.

It is easy to find fault, to remark what might have been done, and perhaps, after all, and under all the circumstances, those in charge of the conduct of affairs did the only thing that could be done at the time. Still, as I look back now over the entire period of our freedom, I cannot help feeling that it would have been wiser if some plan could have been put in operation which would have made the possession of a certain amount of education or property, or both, a test for the exercise of the franchise, and a way provided by which this test should be made to apply honestly and squarely to both the white and black races.

Though I was but little more than a youth during the period of

Reconstruction, I had the feeling that mistakes were being made, and that things could not remain in the condition that they were in then very long. I felt that the Reconstruction policy, so far as it related to my race, was in a large measure on a false foundation, was artificial and forced. In many cases it seemed to me that the ignorance of my race was being used as a tool with which to help white men into office, and that there was an element in the North which wanted to punish the Southern white men by forcing the Negro into positions over the heads of the Southern whites. I felt that the Negro would be the one to suffer for this in the end. Besides, the general political agitation drew the attention of our people away from the more fundamental matters of perfecting themselves in the industries at their doors and in securing property.

The temptations to enter political life were so alluring that I came very near yielding to them at one time, but I was kept from doing so by the feeling that I would be helping in a more substantial way by assisting in the laying of the foundation of the race through a generous education of the hand, head, and heart. I saw coloured men who were members of the state legislatures, and county officers, who, in some cases, could not read or write, and whose morals were as weak as their education. Not long ago, when passing through the streets of a certain city in the South, I heard some brick-masons calling out, from the top of a two-story brick building on which they were working, for the "Governor" to "hurry up and bring up some more bricks." Several times I heard the command, "Hurry up, Governor!" "Hurry up, Governor!" My curiosity was aroused to such an extent that I made inquiry as to who the "Governor" was, and soon found that he was a coloured man who at one time had held the position of Lieutenant-Governor of his state.

But not all the coloured people who were in office during Reconstruction were unworthy of their positions, by any means. Some of them, like the late Senator B. K. Bruce, Governor Pinchback, and many others, were strong, upright, useful men. Neither were all the class designated as carpetbaggers dishonourable men. Some of them, like ex-Governor Bullock, of Georgia, were men of high character and usefulness.

Of course the coloured people, so largely without education, and wholly without experience in government, made tremendous mistakes, just as any people similarly situated would have done. Many of the Southern whites have a feeling that, if the Negro is permitted to exercise his political rights now to any degree, the mistakes of the Reconstruction period will repeat themselves. I do not think this would be true, because the Negro is a much stronger and wiser man than he was thirty-five years ago, and he is fast learning the lesson that he cannot afford to act in a manner that will alienate his Southern white neighbours from him. More and more I am convinced that the final solution of the political end of our race problem will be for each state that finds it necessary to change the law bearing upon the franchise to make the law apply with absolute honesty, and without opportunity for double dealing or evasion, to both races alike. Any other course my daily observation in the South convinces me, will be unjust to the Negro, unjust to the white man, and unfair to the rest of the states in the Union, and will be, like slavery, a sin that at some time we shall have to pay for.

In the fall of 1878, after having taught school in Malden for two years, and after I had succeeded in preparing several of the young men and women, besides my two brothers, to enter the Hampton Institute, I decided to spend some months in study at Washington, D.C. I remained there for eight months. I derived a great deal of benefit from the studies which I pursued, and I came into contact with some strong men and women. At the institution I attended there was no industrial training given to the students, and I had an opportunity of comparing the influence of an institution with no industrial training with that of one like the Hampton Institute, that emphasized the industries. At this school I found the students, in most cases, had more money, were better dressed, wore the latest style of all manner of clothing, and in some cases were more brilliant mentally. At

Hampton it was a standing rule that, while the institution would be responsible for securing some one to pay the tuition for the students, the men and women themselves must provide for their own board, books, clothing, and room wholly by work, or partly by work and partly in cash. At the institution at which I now was, I found that a large proportion of the students by some means had their personal expenses paid for them. At Hampton the student was constantly making the effort through the industries to help himself, and that very effort was of immense value in character-building. The students at the other school seemed to be less self-dependent. They seemed to give more attention to mere outward appearances. In a word, they did not appear to me to be beginning at the bottom, on a real, solid foundation, to the extent that they were at Hampton. They knew more about Latin and Greek when they left school, but they seemed to know less about life and its conditions as they would meet it at their homes. Having lived for a number of years in the midst of comfortable surroundings, they were not as much inclined as the Hampton students to go into the country districts of the South, where there was little of comfort, to take up work for our people, and they were more inclined to yield to the temptation to become hotel waiters and Pullman-car porters as their life-work.

During the time I was a student in Washington the city was crowded with coloured people, many of whom had recently come from the South. A large proportion of these people had been drawn to Washington because they felt that they could lead a life of ease there. Others had secured minor government positions, and still another large class was there in the hope of securing Federal positions. A number of coloured men—some of them very strong and brilliant—were in the House of Representatives at that time, and one, the Hon. B. K. Bruce, was in the Senate. All this tended to make Washington an attractive place for members of the coloured race. Then, too, they knew that at all times they could have the protection of the law in the District of Columbia. The public schools in Washington for coloured people were better then than they were elsewhere. I took great interest in studying the life of our people there closely at that time. I found that while among them there was a large element of substantial, worthy citizens, there was also a superficiality about the life of a large class that greatly alarmed me. I saw young coloured men who were not earning more than four dollars a week spend two dollars or more for a buggy on Sunday to ride up and down Pennsylvania Avenue in, in order that they might try to convince the world that they were worth thousands. I saw other young men who received seventy-five or one hundred dollars per month from the Government, who were in debt at the end of every month. I saw men who but a few months previous were members of Congress, then without employment and in poverty. Among a large class there seemed to be a dependence upon the Government for every conceivable thing. The members of this class had little ambition to create a position for themselves, but wanted the Federal officials to create one for them. How many times I wished then, and have often wished since, that by some power of magic I might remove the great bulk of these people into the country districts and plant them upon the soil, upon the solid and never deceptive foundation of Mother Nature, where all nations and races that have ever succeeded have gotten their start,—a start that at first may be slow and toilsome, but one that nevertheless is real.

In Washington I saw girls whose mothers were earning their living by laundrying. These girls were taught by their mothers, in rather a crude way it is true, the industry of laundrying. Later, these girls entered the public schools and remained there perhaps six or eight years. When the public-school course was finally finished, they wanted more costly dresses, more costly hats and shoes. In a word, while their wants had been increased, their ability to supply their wants had not been increased in the same degree. On the other hand, their six or eight years of book education had weaned them away from the occupation of their mothers. The result of this was in too many cases that the girls went to the bad. I often thought how much wiser it would have been to give these girls the same amount of mental training—and I favour any kind of training, whether in the languages or mathematics, that gives strength and culture to the mind—but at the same time to give them the most thorough training in the latest and best methods of laundrying and other kindred occupations.

CHAPTER VI

Black Race and Red Race

During the year that I spent in Washington, and for some little time before this, there had been considerable agitation in the state of West Virginia over the question of moving the capital of the state from Wheeling to some other central point. As a result of this, the Legislature designated three cities to be voted upon by the citizens of the state as the permanent seat of government. Among these cities was Charleston, only five miles from Malden, my home. At the close of my school year in Washington I was very pleasantly surprised to receive, from a committee of white people in Charleston, an invitation to canvass the state in the interests of that city. This invitation I accepted, and spent nearly three months in speaking in various parts of the state. Charleston was successful in winning the prize, and is now the permanent seat of government.

The reputation that I made as a speaker during this campaign induced a number of persons to make an earnest effort to get me to enter political life, but I refused, still believing that I could find other service which would prove of more permanent value to my race. Even then I had a strong feeling that what our people most needed was to get a foundation in education, industry, and property, and for this I felt that they could better afford to strive than for political preferment. As for my individual self, it appeared to me to be reasonably certain that I could succeed in political life, but I had a feeling that it would be a rather selfish kind of success—individual success at the cost of failing to do my duty in assisting in laying a foundation for the masses.

At this period in the progress of our race a very large proportion of the young men who went to school or to college did so with the expressed determination to prepare themselves to be great lawyers, or Congressmen, and many of the women planned to become music teachers; but I had a reasonably fixed idea, even at that early period in my life, that there was need for something to be done to prepare the way for successful lawyers, Congressmen, and music teachers.

I felt that the conditions were a good deal like those of an old coloured man, during the days of slavery, who wanted to learn how to play on the guitar. In his desire to take guitar lessons he applied to one of his young masters to teach him; but the young man, not having much faith in the ability of the slave to master the guitar at his age, sought to discourage him by telling him: "Uncle Jake, I will give you guitar lessons; but, Jake, I will have to charge you three dollars for the first lesson, two dollars for the second lesson, and one dollar for the third lesson. But I will charge you only twenty-five cents for the last lesson."

Uncle Jake answered: "All right, boss, I hires you on dem terms. But, boss! I wants yer to be sure an' give me dat las' lesson first."

Soon after my work in connection with the removal of the capital was finished, I received an invitation which gave me great joy and which at the same time was a very pleasant surprise. This was a letter from General Armstrong, inviting me to return to Hampton at the next Commencement to deliver what was called the "post-graduate address." This was an honour which I had not dreamed of receiving. With much care I prepared the best address that I was capable of. I chose for my subject "The Force That Wins."

As I returned to Hampton for the purpose of delivering this address, I went over much of the same ground—now, however, covered entirely by railroad—that I had traversed nearly six years before, when I first sought entrance into Hampton Institute as a student. Now I was able to ride the whole distance in the train. I was constantly contrasting this with my first journey to Hampton. I think I may say, without seeming egotism, that it is seldom that five years have wrought such a change in the life and aspirations of an individual.

At Hampton I received a warm welcome from teachers and students. I found that during my absence from Hampton the institute each year had been getting closer to the real needs and conditions of our people; that the industrial teaching, as well as that of the academic department, had greatly improved. The plan of the school was not modelled after that of any other institution then in existence, but every improvement was made under the magnificent leadership of General Armstrong solely with the view of meeting and helping the needs of our people as they presented themselves at the time. Too often, it seems to me, in missionary and educational work among undeveloped races, people yield to the temptation of doing that which was done a hundred years before, or is being done in other communities a thousand miles away. The temptation often is to run each individual through a certain educational mould, regardless of the condition of the subject or the end to be accomplished. This was not so at Hampton Institute.

The address which I delivered on Commencement Day seems to have pleased every one, and many kind and encouraging words were spoken to me regarding it. Soon after my return to my home in West Virginia, where I had planned to continue teaching, I was again surprised to receive a letter from General Armstrong, asking me to return to Hampton partly as a teacher and partly to pursue some supplementary studies. This was in the summer of 1879. Soon after I began my first teaching in West Virginia I had picked out four of the brightest and most promising of my pupils, in addition to my two brothers, to whom I have already referred, and had given them special attention, with the view of having them go to Hampton. They had gone there, and in each case the teachers had found them so well prepared that they entered advanced classes. This fact, it seems, led to my being called back to Hampton as a teacher. One of the young men that I sent to Hampton in this way is now Dr. Samuel E. Courtney, a successful physician in Boston, and a member of the School Board of that city.

About this time the experiment was being tried for the first time, by General Armstrong, of educating Indians at Hampton. Few people then had any confidence in the ability of the Indians to receive education and to profit by it. General Armstrong was anxious to try the experiment systematically on a large scale. He secured from the reservations in the Western states over one hundred wild and for the most part perfectly ignorant Indians, the greater proportion of whom were young men. The special work which the General desired me to do was to be a sort of "house father" to the Indian young men—that is, I was to live in the building with them and have the charge of their discipline, clothing, rooms, and so on. This was a very tempting offer, but I had become so much absorbed in my work in West Virginia that I dreaded to give it up. However, I tore myself away from it. I did not know how to refuse to perform any service that General Armstrong desired of me.

On going to Hampton, I took up my residence in a building with about seventy-five Indian youths. I was the only person in the building who was not a member of their race. At first I had a good deal of doubt about my ability to succeed. I knew that the average Indian felt himself above the white man, and, of course, he felt himself far above the Negro, largely on account of the fact of the Negro having submitted to slavery—a thing which the Indian would never do. The Indians, in the Indian Territory, owned a large number of slaves during the days of slavery. Aside from this, there was a general feeling that the attempt to educate and civilize the red men at Hampton would be a failure. All this made me proceed very cautiously, for I felt keenly the great responsibility. But I was determined to succeed. It was not long before I had the complete confidence of the

Indians, and not only this, but I think I am safe in saying that I had their love and respect. I found that they were about like any other human beings; that they responded to kind treatment and resented ill-treatment. They were continually planning to do something that would add to my happiness and comfort. The things that they disliked most, I think, were to have their long hair cut, to give up wearing their blankets, and to cease smoking; but no white American ever thinks that any other race is wholly civilized until he wears the white man's clothes, eats the white man's food, speaks the white man's language, and professes the white man's religion.

When the difficulty of learning the English language was subtracted, I found that in the matter of learning trades and in mastering academic studies there was little difference between the coloured and Indian students. It was a constant delight to me to note the interest which the coloured students took in trying to help the Indians in every way possible. There were a few of the coloured students who felt that the Indians ought not to be admitted to Hampton, but these were in the minority. Whenever they were asked to do so, the Negro students gladly took the Indians as room-mates, in order that they might teach them to speak English and to acquire civilized habits.

I have often wondered if there was a white institution in this country whose students would have welcomed the incoming of more than a hundred companions of another race in the cordial way that these black students at Hampton welcomed the red ones. How often I have wanted to say to white students that they lift themselves up in proportion as they help to lift others, and the more unfortunate the race, and the lower in the scale of civilization, the more does one raise one's self by giving the assistance.

This reminds me of a conversation which I once had with the Hon. Frederick Douglass. At one time Mr. Douglass was travelling in the state of Pennsylvania, and was forced, on account of his colour, to ride in the baggage-car, in spite of the fact that he had paid the same price for his passage that the other passengers had paid. When some of the white passengers went into the baggage-car to console Mr. Douglass, and one of them said to him: "I am sorry, Mr. Douglass, that you have been degraded in this manner," Mr. Douglass straightened himself up on the box upon which he was sitting, and replied: "They cannot degrade Frederick Douglass. The soul that is within me no man can degrade. I am not the one that is being degraded on account of this treatment, but those who are inflicting it upon me."

In one part of our country, where the law demands the separation of the races on the railroad trains, I saw at one time a rather amusing instance which showed how difficult it sometimes is to know where the black begins and the white ends.

There was a man who was well known in his community as a Negro, but who was so white that even an expert would have hard work to classify him as a black man. This man was riding in the part of the train set aside for the coloured passengers. When the train conductor reached him, he showed at once that he was perplexed. If the man was a Negro, the conductor did not want to send him into the white people's coach; at the same time, if he was a white man, the conductor did not want to insult him by asking him if he was a Negro. The official looked him over carefully, examining his hair, eyes, nose, and hands, but still seemed puzzled. Finally, to solve the difficulty, he stooped over and peeped at the man's feet. When I saw the conductor examining the feet of the man in question, I said to myself, "That will settle it;" and so it did, for the trainman promptly decided that the passenger was a Negro, and let him remain where he was. I congratulated myself that my race was fortunate in not losing one of its members.

My experience has been that the time to test a true gentleman is to observe him when he is in contact with individuals of a race that is less fortunate than his own. This is illustrated in no better way than by observing the conduct of the old-school type of Southern gentleman when he is in contact with his former slaves or their descendants.

An example of what I mean is shown in a story told of George

Washington, who, meeting a coloured man in the road once, who politely lifted his hat, lifted his own in return. Some of his white friends who saw the incident criticised Washington for his action. In reply to their criticism George Washington said: "Do you suppose that I am going to permit a poor, ignorant, coloured man to be more polite than I am?"

While I was in charge of the Indian boys at Hampton, I had one or two experiences which illustrate the curious workings of caste in America. One of the Indian boys was taken ill, and it became my duty to take him to Washington, deliver him over to the Secretary of the Interior, and get a receipt for him, in order that he might be returned to his Western reservation. At that time I was rather ignorant of the ways of the world. During my journey to Washington, on a steamboat, when the bell rang for dinner, I was careful to wait and not enter the dining room until after the greater part of the passengers had finished their meal. Then, with my charge, I went to the dining saloon. The man in charge politely informed me that the Indian could be served, but that I could not. I never could understand how he knew just where to draw the colour line, since the Indian and I were of about the same complexion. The steward, however, seemed to be an expert in this matter. I had been directed by the authorities at Hampton to stop at a certain hotel in Washington with my charge, but when I went to this hotel the clerk stated that he would be glad to receive the Indian into the house, but said that he could not accommodate me.

An illustration of something of this same feeling came under my observation afterward. I happened to find myself in a town in which so much excitement and indignation were being expressed that it seemed likely for a time that there would be a lynching. The occasion of the trouble was that a dark-skinned man had stopped at the local hotel. Investigation, however, developed the fact that this individual was a citizen of Morocco, and that while travelling in this country he spoke the English language. As soon as it was learned that he was not an American Negro, all the signs of indignation disappeared. The man who was the innocent cause of the excitement, though, found it prudent after that not to speak English.

At the end of my first year with the Indians there came another opening for me at Hampton, which, as I look back over my life now, seems to have come providentially, to help to prepare me for my work at Tuskegee later. General Armstrong had found out that there was quite a number of young coloured men and women who were intensely in earnest in wishing to get an education, but who were prevented from entering Hampton Institute because they were too poor to be able to pay any portion of the cost of their board, or even to supply themselves with books. He conceived the idea of starting a night-school in connection with the Institute, into which a limited number of the most promising of these young men and women would be received, on condition that they were to work for ten hours during the day, and attend school for two hours at night. They were to be paid something above the cost of their board for their work. The greater part of their earnings was to be reserved in the school's treasury as a fund to be drawn on to pay their board when they had become students in the day-school, after they had spent one or two years in the night-school. In this way they would obtain a start in their books and a knowledge of some trade or industry, in addition to the other far-reaching benefits of the institution.

General Armstrong asked me to take charge of the night-school, and I did so. At the beginning of this school there were about twelve strong, earnest men and women who entered the class. During the day the greater part of the young men worked in the school's saw-mill, and the young women worked in the laundry. The work was not easy in either place, but in all my teaching I never taught pupils who gave me such genuine satisfaction as these did. They were good students, and mastered their work thoroughly. They were so much in earnest that only the ringing of the retiring-bell would make them stop studying, and often they would urge me to continue the lessons after the usual hour for going to bed had come.

These students showed so much earnestness, both in their hard work during the day, as well as in their application to their studies at night, that I gave them the name of "The Plucky Class"—a name which soon grew popular and spread throughout the institution. After a student had been in the night-school long enough to prove what was in him, I gave him a printed certificate which read something like this:—

"This is to certify that James Smith is a member of The Plucky Class of the Hampton Institute, and is in good and regular standing."

The students prized these certificates highly, and they added greatly to the popularity of the night-school. Within a few weeks this department had grown to such an extent that there were about twenty-five students in attendance. I have followed the course of many of these twenty-five men and women ever since then, and they are now holding important and useful positions in nearly every part of the South. The night-school at Hampton, which started with only twelve students, now numbers between three and four hundred, and is one of the permanent and most important features of the institution.

CHAPTER VII

Early Days at Tuskegee

During the time that I had charge of the Indians and the night-school at Hampton, I pursued some studies myself, under the direction of the instructors there. One of these instructors was the Rev. Dr. H. B. Frissell, the present Principal of the Hampton Institute, General Armstrong's successor.

In May, 1881, near the close of my first year in teaching the night-school, in a way that I had not dared expect, the opportunity opened for me to begin my life-work. One night in the chapel, after the usual chapel exercises were over, General Armstrong referred to the fact that he had received a letter from some gentlemen in Alabama asking him to recommend some one to take charge of what was to be a normal school for the coloured people in the little town of Tuskegee in that state. These gentlemen seemed to take it for granted that no coloured man suitable for the position could be secured, and they were expecting the General to recommend a white man for the place. The next day General Armstrong sent for me to come to his office, and, much to my surprise, asked me if I thought I could fill the position in Alabama. I told him that I would be willing to try. Accordingly, he wrote to the people who had applied to him for the information, that he did not know of any white man to suggest, but if they would be willing to take a coloured man, he had one whom he could recommend. In this letter he gave them my name.

Several days passed before anything more was heard about the matter. Some time afterward, one Sunday evening during the chapel exercises, a messenger came in and handed the General a telegram. At the end of the exercises he read the telegram to the school. In substance, these were its words: "Booker T. Washington will suit us. Send him at once."

There was a great deal of joy expressed among the students and teachers, and I received very hearty congratulations. I began to get ready at once to go to Tuskegee. I went by way of my old home in West Virginia, where I remained for several days, after which I proceeded to Tuskegee. I found Tuskegee to be a town of about two thousand inhabitants, nearly one-half of whom were coloured. It was in what was known as the Black Belt of the South. In the county in which Tuskegee is situated the coloured people outnumbered the whites by about three to one. In some of the adjoining and near-by counties the proportion was not far from six coloured persons to one white.

I have often been asked to define the term "Black Belt." So far as I can learn, the term was first used to designate a part of the country which was distinguished by the colour of the soil. The part of the country possessing this thick, dark, and naturally rich soil was, of course, the part of the South where the slaves were most profitable, and consequently they were taken there in the largest numbers. Later, and especially since the war, the term seems to be used wholly in a political sense—that is, to designate the counties where the black people outnumber the white.

Before going to Tuskegee I had expected to find there a building and all the necessary apparatus ready for me to begin teaching. To my disappointment, I found nothing of the kind. I did find, though, that which no costly building and apparatus can supply,—hundreds of hungry, earnest souls who wanted to secure knowledge.

Tuskegee seemed an ideal place for the school. It was in the midst of the great bulk of the Negro population, and was rather secluded, being five miles from the main line of railroad, with which it was connected by a short line. During the days of slavery, and since, the town had been a centre for the education of the white people. This was an added advantage, for the reason that I found the white people possessing a degree of culture and education that is not surpassed by many localities. While the coloured people were ignorant, they had not, as a rule, degraded and weakened their bodies by vices such as are common to the lower class of people in the large cities. In general, I found the relations between the two races pleasant. For example, the largest, and I think at that time the only hardware store in the town was owned and operated jointly by a coloured man and a white man. This copartnership continued until the death of the white partner.

I found that about a year previous to my going to Tuskegee some of the coloured people who had heard something of the work of education being done at Hampton had applied to the state Legislature, through their representatives, for a small appropriation to be used in starting a normal school in Tuskegee. This request the Legislature had complied with to the extent of granting an annual appropriation of two thousand dollars. I soon learned, however, that this money could be used only for the payment of the salaries of the instructors, and that there was no provision for securing land, buildings, or apparatus. The task before me did not seem a very encouraging one. It seemed much like making bricks without straw. The coloured people were overjoyed, and were constantly offering their services in any way in which they could be of assistance in getting the school started.

My first task was to find a place in which to open the school. After looking the town over with some care, the most suitable place that could be secured seemed to be a rather dilapidated shanty near the coloured Methodist church, together with the church itself as a sort of assembly-room. Both the church and the shanty were in about as bad condition as was possible. I recall that during the first months of school that I taught in this building it was in such poor repair that, whenever it rained, one of the older students would very kindly leave his lessons and hold an umbrella over me while I heard the recitations of the others. I remember, also, that on more than one occasion my landlady held an umbrella over me while I ate breakfast.

At the time I went to Alabama the coloured people were taking considerable interest in politics, and they were very anxious that I should become one of them politically, in every respect. They seemed to have a little distrust of strangers in this regard. I recall that one man, who seemed to have been designated by the others to look after my political destiny, came to me on several occasions and said, with a good deal of earnestness: "We wants you to be sure to vote jes' like we votes. We can't read de newspapers very much, but we knows how to vote, an' we wants you to vote jes' like we votes." He added: "We watches de white man, and we keeps watching de white man till we finds out which way de white man's gwine to vote; an' when we finds out which way de white man's gwine to vote, den we votes 'xactly de other way. Den we knows we's right."

I am glad to add, however, that at the present time the disposition to vote against the white man merely because he is white is largely disappearing, and the race is learning to vote from principle, for what the voter considers to be for the best interests of both races.

I reached Tuskegee, as I have said, early in June, 1881. The first month I spent in finding accommodations for the school, and in travelling through Alabama, examining into the actual life of the people, especially in the country districts, and in getting the school advertised among the class of people that I wanted to have attend it. The most of my travelling was done over the country roads, with a mule and a cart or a mule and a buggy wagon for conveyance. I ate and slept with the people, in their little cabins. I saw their farms, their schools, their churches. Since, in the case of the most of these visits, there had been no notice given in advance that a stranger was expected, I had the advantage of seeing the real, everyday life of the people.

In the plantation districts I found that, as a rule, the whole family slept in one room, and that in addition to the immediate family there sometimes were relatives, or others not related to the family, who slept in the same room. On more than one occasion I went outside the house to get ready for bed, or to wait until the family had gone to bed. They usually contrived some kind of a place for me to sleep, either on the floor or in a special part of another's bed. Rarely was there any place provided in the cabin where one could bathe even the face and hands, but usually some provision was made for this outside the house, in the yard.

The common diet of the people was fat pork and corn bread. At times I have eaten in cabins where they had only corn bread and "black-eye peas" cooked in plain water. The people seemed to have no other idea than to live on this fat meat and corn bread,—the meat, and the meal of which the bread was made, having been bought at a high price at a store in town, notwithstanding the fact that the land all about the cabin homes could easily have been made to produce nearly every kind of garden vegetable that is raised anywhere in the country. Their one object seemed to be to plant nothing but cotton; and in many cases cotton was planted up to the very door of the cabin.

In these cabin homes I often found sewing-machines which had been bought, or were being bought, on instalments, frequently at a cost of as much as sixty dollars, or showy clocks for which the occupants of the cabins had paid twelve or fourteen dollars. I remember that on one occasion when I went into one of these cabins for dinner, when I sat down to the table for a meal with the four members of the family, I noticed that, while there were five of us at the table, there was but one fork for the five of us to use. Naturally there was an awkward pause on my part. In the opposite corner of that same cabin was an organ for which the people told me they were paying sixty dollars in monthly instalments. One fork, and a sixty-dollar organ!

In most cases the sewing-machine was not used, the clocks were so worthless that they did not keep correct time—and if they had, in nine cases out of ten there would have been no one in the family who could have told the time of day—while the organ, of course, was rarely used for want of a person who could play upon it.

In the case to which I have referred, where the family sat down to the table for the meal at which I was their guest, I could see plainly that this was an awkward and unusual proceeding, and was done in my honour. In most cases, when the family got up in the morning, for example, the wife would put a piece of meat in a frying-pan and put a lump of dough in a "skillet," as they called it. These utensils would be placed on the fire, and in ten or fifteen minutes breakfast would be ready. Frequently the husband would take his bread and meat in his hand and start for the field, eating as he walked. The mother would sit down in a corner and eat her breakfast, perhaps from a plate and perhaps directly from the "skillet" or frying-pan, while the children would eat their portion of the bread and meat while running about the yard. At certain seasons of the year, when meat was scarce, it was rarely that the children who were not old enough or strong enough to work in the fields would have the luxury of meat.

The breakfast over, and with practically no attention given to the house, the whole family would, as a general thing, proceed to the cotton-field. Every child that was large enough to carry a hoe was put to work, and the baby—for usually there was at least one baby—would be laid down at the end of the cotton row, so that its mother could give it a certain amount of attention when she had finished chopping her row. The noon meal and the supper were taken in much the same way as the breakfast.

All the days of the family would be spent after much this same routine, except Saturday and Sunday. On Saturday the whole family would spend at least half a day, and often a whole day, in town. The idea in going to town was, I suppose, to do shopping, but all the shopping that the whole family had money for could have been attended to in ten minutes by one person. Still, the whole family remained in town for most of the day, spending the greater part of the time in standing on the streets, the women, too often, sitting about somewhere smoking or dipping snuff. Sunday was usually spent in going to some big meeting. With few exceptions, I found that the crops were mortgaged in the counties where I went, and that the most of the coloured farmers were in debt. The state had not been able to build schoolhouses in the country districts, and, as a rule, the schools were taught in churches or in log cabins. More than once, while on my journeys, I found that there was no provision made in the house used for school purposes for heating the building during the winter, and consequently a fire had to be built in the yard, and teacher and pupils passed in and out of the house as they got cold or warm. With few exceptions, I found the teachers in these country schools to be miserably poor in preparation for their work, and poor in moral character. The schools were in session from three to five months. There was practically no apparatus in the schoolhouses, except that occasionally there was a rough blackboard. I recall that one day I went into a schoolhouse—or rather into an abandoned log cabin that was being used as a schoolhouse—and found five pupils who were studying a lesson from one book. Two of these, on the front seat, were using the book between them; behind these were two others peeping over the shoulders of the first two, and behind the four was a fifth little fellow who was peeping over the shoulders of all four.

What I have said concerning the character of the schoolhouses and teachers will also apply quite accurately as a description of the church buildings and the ministers.

I met some very interesting characters during my travels. As illustrating the peculiar mental processes of the country people, I remember that I asked one coloured man, who was about sixty years old, to tell me something of his history. He said that he had been born in Virginia, and sold into Alabama in 1845. I asked him how many were sold at the same time. He said, "There were five of us; myself and brother and three mules."

In giving all these descriptions of what I saw during my month of travel in the country around Tuskegee, I wish my readers to keep in mind the fact that there were many encouraging exceptions to the conditions which I have described. I have stated in such plain words what I saw, mainly for the reason that later I want to emphasize the encouraging changes that have taken place in the community, not wholly by the work of the Tuskegee school, but by that of other institutions as well.

CHAPTER VIII

Teaching School in a Stable and a Hen-House

I confess that what I saw during my month of travel and investigation left me with a very heavy heart. The work to be done in order to lift these people up seemed almost beyond accomplishing. I was only one person, and it seemed to me that the little effort which I could put forth could go such a short distance toward bringing about results. I wondered if I could accomplish anything, and if it were worth while for me to try.

Of one thing I felt more strongly convinced than ever, after spending this month in seeing the actual life of the coloured people, and that was that, in order to lift them up, something must be done more than merely to imitate New England education as it then existed. I saw more clearly than ever the wisdom of the system which General Armstrong had inaugurated at Hampton. To take the children of such people as I had been among for a month, and each day give them a few hours of mere book education, I felt would be almost a waste of time.

After consultation with the citizens of Tuskegee, I set July 4, 1881, as the day for the opening of the school in the little shanty and church which had been secured for its accommodation. The white people, as well as the coloured, were greatly interested in the starting

The Tuskegee Institute "campus" in its infancy.

of the new school, and the opening day was looked forward to with much earnest discussion. There were not a few white people in the vicinity of Tuskegee who looked with some disfavour upon the project. They questioned its value to the coloured people, and had a fear that it might result in bringing about trouble between the races. Some had the feeling that in proportion as the Negro received education, in the same proportion would his value decrease as an economic factor in the state. These people feared the result of education would be that the Negroes would leave the farms, and that it would be difficult to secure them for domestic service.

The white people who questioned the wisdom of starting this new school had in their minds pictures of what was called an educated Negro, with a high hat, imitation gold eye-glasses, a showy walking-stick, kid gloves, fancy boots, and what not—in a word, a man who was determined to live by his wits. It was difficult for these people to see how education would produce any other kind of a coloured man.

In the midst of all the difficulties which I encountered in getting the little school started, and since then through a period of nineteen years, there are two men among all the many friends of the school in Tuskegee upon whom I have depended constantly for advice and guidance; and the success of the undertaking is largely due to these men, from whom I have never sought anything in vain. I mention them simply as types. One is a white man and an ex-slaveholder, Mr. George W. Campbell; the other is a black man and an ex-slave, Mr. Lewis Adams. These were the men who wrote to General Armstrong for a teacher.

Mr. Campbell is a merchant and banker, and had had little experience in dealing with matters pertaining to education. Mr. Adams was a mechanic, and had learned the trades of shoemaking, harness-making, and tinsmithing during the days of slavery. He had never been to school a day in his life, but in some way he had learned to read and write while a slave. From the first, these two men saw clearly what my plan of education was, sympathized with me, and supported me in every effort. In the days which were darkest financially for the school, Mr. Campbell was never appealed to when he was not willing to extend all the aid in his power. I do not know two men, one an ex-slaveholder, one an ex-slave, whose advice and judgment I would feel more like following in everything which concerns the life and development of the school at Tuskegee than those of these two men.

I have always felt that Mr. Adams, in a large degree, derived his unusual power of mind from the training given his hands in the process of mastering well three trades during the days of slavery. If one goes to-day into any Southern town, and asks for the leading and most reliable coloured man in the community, I believe that in five cases out of ten he will be directed to a Negro who learned a trade during the days of slavery.

On the morning that the school opened, thirty students reported for admission. I was the only teacher. The students were about equally divided between the sexes. Most of them lived in Macon County, the county in which Tuskegee is situated, and of which it is the county-seat. A great many more students wanted to enter the school, but it had been decided to receive only those who were above fifteen years of age, and who had previously received some education. The greater part of the thirty were public-school teachers, and some of them were nearly forty years of age. With the teachers came some of their former pupils, and when they were examined it was amusing to note that in several cases the pupil entered a higher class than did his former teacher. It was also interesting to note how many big books some of them had studied, and how many high-sounding subjects some of them claimed to have mastered. The bigger the book and the longer the name of the subject, the prouder they felt of their accomplishment. Some had studied Latin, and one or two Greek. This they thought entitled them to special distinction.

In fact, one of the saddest things I saw during the month of travel which I have described was a young man, who had attended some high school, sitting down in a one-room cabin, with grease on his clothing, filth all around him, and weeds in the yard and garden, engaged in studying a French grammar.

The students who came first seemed to be fond of memorizing long and complicated "rules" in grammar and mathematics, but had little thought or knowledge of applying these rules to the everyday affairs of their life. One subject which they liked to talk about, and tell me that they had mastered, in arithmetic, was "banking and discount," but I soon found out that neither they nor almost any one in the neighbourhood in which they lived had ever had a bank account. In registering the names of the students, I found that almost every one of them had one or more middle initials. When I asked what the "J" stood for, in the name of John J. Jones, it was explained to me that this was a part of his "entitles." Most of the students wanted to get an education because they thought it would enable them to earn more money as school-teachers.

Notwithstanding what I have said about them in these respects, I have never seen a more earnest and willing company of young men and women than these students were. They were all willing to learn the right thing as soon as it was shown them what was right. I was determined to start them off on a solid and thorough foundation, so far as their books were concerned. I soon learned that most of them had the merest smattering of the high-sounding things that they had studied. While they could locate the Desert of Sahara or the capital of China on an artificial globe, I found out that the girls could not locate the proper places for the knives and forks on an actual dinner-table, or the places on which the bread and meat should be set.

I had to summon a good deal of courage to take a student who had been studying cube root and "banking and discount," and explain to him that the wisest thing for him to do first was thoroughly to master the multiplication table.

The number of pupils increased each week, until by the end of the first month there were nearly fifty. Many of them, however, said that, as they could remain only for two or three months, they wanted to enter a high class and get a diploma the first year if possible.

At the end of the first six weeks a new and rare face entered the school as a co-teacher. This was Miss Olivia A. Davidson, who later became my wife. Miss Davidson was born in Ohio, and received her preparatory education in the public schools of that state. When little more than a girl, she heard of the need of teachers in the South. She went to the state of Mississippi and began teaching there. Later she taught in the city of Memphis. While teaching in Mississippi, one of her pupils became ill with smallpox. Every one in the community was so frightened that no one would nurse the boy. Miss Davidson closed her school and remained by the bedside of the boy night and day until he recovered. While she was at her Ohio home on her vacation, the worst epidemic of yellow fever broke out in Memphis, Tenn., that perhaps has ever occurred in the South. When she heard of this, she at once telegraphed the Mayor of Memphis, offering her services as a yellow-fever nurse, although she had never had the disease.

Miss Davidson's experience in the South showed her that the people needed something more than mere book-learning. She heard of the Hampton system of education, and decided that this was what she wanted in order to prepare herself for better work in the South. The attention of Mrs. Mary Hemenway, of Boston, was attracted to her rare ability. Through Mrs. Hemenway's kindness and generosity, Miss Davidson, after graduating at Hampton, received an opportunity to complete a two years' course of training at the Massachusetts State Normal School at Framingham.

Before she went to Framingham, some one suggested to Miss Davidson that, since she was so very light in colour, she might find it more comfortable not to be known as a coloured woman in this school in Massachusetts. She at once replied that under no circumstances and for no considerations would she consent to deceive any one in regard to her racial identity.

Soon after her graduation from the Framingham institution, Miss Davidson came to Tuskegee, bringing into the school many valuable and fresh ideas as to the best methods of teaching, as well as a rare moral character and a life of unselfishness that I think has seldom been equalled. No single individual did more toward laying the foun-

"Decision of Character" was the title of graduate Olivia America Davidson's address at Hampton's 1879 commencement exercises, where Booker T. Washington, the postgraduate speaker, delivered "The Force That Wins."

dations of the Tuskegee Institute so as to insure the successful work that has been done there than Olivia A. Davidson.

Miss Davidson and I began consulting as to the future of the school from the first. The students were making progress in learning books and in developing their minds; but it became apparent at once that, if we were to make any permanent impression upon those who had come to us for training, we must do something besides teach them mere books. The students had come from homes where they had had no opportunities for lessons which would teach them how to care for their bodies. With few exceptions, the homes in Tuskegee in which the students boarded were but little improvement upon those from which they had come. We wanted to teach the students how to bathe; how to care for their teeth and clothing. We wanted to teach them what to eat, and how to eat it properly, and how to care for their rooms. Aside from this, we wanted to give them such a practical knowledge of some one industry, together with the spirit of industry, thrift, and economy, that they would be sure of knowing how to make a living after they had left us. We wanted to teach them to study actual things instead of mere books alone.

We found that the most of our students came from the country districts, where agriculture in some form or other was the main dependence of the people. We learned that about eighty-five per cent of the coloured people in the Gulf states depended upon agriculture for their living. Since this was true, we wanted to be careful not to educate our students out of sympathy with agricultural life, so that they would be attracted from the country to the cities, and yield to the temptation of trying to live by their wits. We wanted to give them such an education as would fit a large proportion of them to be teachers, and at the same time cause them to return to the plantation districts and show the people there how to put new energy and new ideas into farming, as well as into the intellectual and moral and religious life of the people.

All these ideas and needs crowded themselves upon us with a seriousness that seemed well-nigh overwhelming. What were we to do? We had only the little old shanty and the abandoned church which the good coloured people of the town of Tuskegee had kindly loaned us for the accommodation of the classes. The number of students was increasing daily. The more we saw of them, and the more we travelled through the country districts, the more we saw that our efforts were reaching, to only a partial degree, the actual needs of the people whom we wanted to lift up through the medium of the students whom we should educate and send out as leaders.

The more we talked with the students, who were then coming to us from several parts of the state, the more we found that the chief ambition among a large proportion of them was to get an education so that they would not have to work any longer with their hands.

This is illustrated by a story told of a coloured man in Alabama, who, one hot day in July, while he was at work in a cotton-field, suddenly stopped, and, looking toward the skies, said: "O Lawd, de cotton am so grassy, de work am so hard, and the sun am so hot dat I b'lieve dis darky am called to preach!"

About three months after the opening of the school, and at the time when we were in the greatest anxiety about our work, there came into the market for sale an old and abandoned plantation which was situated about a mile from the town of Tuskegee. The mansion house—or "big house," as it would have been called—which had been occupied by the owners during slavery, had been burned. After making a careful examination of this place, it seemed to be just the location that we wanted in order to make our work effective and permanent.

But how were we to get it? The price asked for it was very little—only five hundred dollars—but we had no money, and we were strangers in the town and had no credit. The owner of the land agreed to let us occupy the place if we could make a payment of two hundred and fifty dollars down, with the understanding that the remaining two hundred and fifty dollars must be paid within a year.

Although five hundred dollars was cheap for the land, it was a large sum when one did not have any part of it.

In the midst of the difficulty I summoned a great deal of courage and wrote to my friend General J. F. B. Marshall, the Treasurer of the Hampton Institute, putting the situation before him and beseeching him to lend me the two hundred and fifty dollars on my own personal responsibility. Within a few days a reply came to the effect that he had no authority to lend me money belonging to the Hampton Institute, but that he would gladly lend me the amount needed from his own personal funds.

I confess that the securing of this money in this way was a great surprise to me, as well as a source of gratification. Up to that time I never had had in my possession so much money as one hundred dollars at a time, and the loan which I had asked General Marshall for seemed a tremendously large sum to me. The fact of my being responsible for the repaying of such a large amount of money weighed very heavily upon me.

I lost no time in getting ready to move the school on to the new farm. At the time we occupied the place there were standing upon it a cabin, formerly used as the dining room, an old kitchen, a stable, and an old hen-house. Within a few weeks we had all of these structures in use. The stable was repaired and used as a recitation-room, and very presently the hen-house was utilized for the same purpose.

I recall that one morning, when I told an old coloured man who lived near, and who sometimes helped me, that our school had grown so large that it would be necessary for us to use the hen-house for school purposes, and that I wanted him to help me give it a thorough cleaning out the next day, he replied, in the most earnest manner: "What you mean, boss? You sholy ain't gwine clean out de hen-house in de *day*-time?"

Nearly all the work of getting the new location ready for school purposes was done by the students after school was over in the afternoon. As soon as we got the cabins in condition to be used, I determined to clear up some land so that we could plant a crop. When I explained my plan to the young men, I noticed that they did not seem to take to it very kindly. It was hard for them to see the connection between clearing land and an education. Besides, many of them had been school-teachers, and they questioned whether or not clearing land would be in keeping with their dignity. In order to relieve them from any embarrassment, each afternoon after school I took my axe and led the way to the woods. When they saw that I was not afraid or ashamed to work, they began to assist with more enthusiasm. We kept at the work each afternoon, until we had cleared about twenty acres and had planted a crop.

In the meantime Miss Davidson was devising plans to repay the loan. Her first effort was made by holding festivals, or "suppers." She made a personal canvass among the white and coloured families in the town of Tuskegee, and got them to agree to give something, like a cake, a chicken, bread, or pies, that could be sold at the festival. Of course the coloured people were glad to give anything that they could spare, but I want to add that Miss Davidson did not apply to a single white family, so far as I now remember, that failed to donate something; and in many ways the white families showed their interest in the school.

Several of these festivals were held, and quite a little sum of money was raised. A canvass was also made among the people of both races for direct gifts of money, and most of those applied to gave small sums. It was often pathetic to note the gifts of the older coloured people, most of whom had spent their best days in slavery. Sometimes they would give five cents, sometimes twenty-five cents. Sometimes the contribution was a quilt, or a quantity of sugarcane. I recall one old coloured woman, who was about seventy years of age, who came to see me when we were raising money to pay for the farm. She hobbled into the room where I was, leaning on a cane. She was clad in rags; but they were clean. She said: "Mr. Washin'ton, God knows I spent de bes' days of my life in slavery. God knows I's ignorant an' poor; but," she added, "I knows what you an' Miss

Davidson is tryin' to do. I knows you is tryin' to make better men an' better women for de coloured race. I ain't got no money, but I wants you to take dese six eggs, what I's been savin' up, an' I wants you to put dese six eggs into de eddication of dese boys an' gals."

Since the work at Tuskegee started, it has been my privilege to receive many gifts for the benefit of the institution, but never any, I think, that touched me so deeply as this one.

CHAPTER IX

Anxious Days and Sleepless Nights

The coming of Christmas, that first year of our residence in Alabama, gave us an opportunity to get a farther insight into the real life of the people. The first thing that reminded us that Christmas had arrived was the "foreday" visits of scores of children rapping at our doors, asking for "Chris'mus gifts! Chris'mus gifts!" Between the hours of two o'clock and five o'clock in the morning I presume that we must have had a half-hundred such calls. This custom prevails throughout this portion of the South to-day.

During the days of slavery it was a custom quite generally observed throughout all the Southern states to give the coloured people a week of holiday at Christmas, or to allow the holiday to continue as long as the "yule log" lasted. The male members of the race, and often the female members, were expected to get drunk. We found that for a whole week the coloured people in and around Tuskegee dropped work the day before Christmas, and that it was difficult to get any one to perform any service from the time they stopped work until after the New Year. Persons who at other times did not use strong drink thought it quite the proper thing to indulge in it rather freely during the Christmas week. There was a widespread hilarity, and a free use of guns, pistols, and gunpowder generally. The sacredness of the season seemed to have been almost wholly lost sight of.

During this first Christmas vacation I went some distance from the town to visit the people on one of the large plantations. In their poverty and ignorance it was pathetic to see their attempts to get joy out of the season that in most parts of the country is so sacred and so dear to the heart. In one cabin I noticed that all that the five children had to remind them of the coming of Christ was a single bunch of firecrackers, which they had divided among them. In another cabin, where there were at least a half-dozen persons, they had only ten cents' worth of ginger-cakes, which had been bought in the store the day before. In another family they had only a few pieces of sugar-cane. In still another cabin I found nothing but a new jug of cheap, mean whiskey, which the husband and wife were making free use of, notwithstanding the fact that the husband was one of the local ministers. In a few instances I found that the people had gotten hold of some bright-coloured cards that had been designed for advertising purposes, and were making the most of those. In other homes some member of the family had bought a new pistol. In the majority of cases there was nothing to be seen in the cabin to remind one of the coming of the Saviour, except that the people had ceased work in the fields and were lounging about their homes. At night, during Christmas week, they usually had what they called a "frolic," in some cabin on the plantation. This meant a kind of rough dance, where there was likely to be a good deal of whiskey used, and where there might be some shooting or cutting with razors.

While I was making this Christmas visit I met an old coloured man who was one of the numerous local preachers, who tried to convince me, from the experience Adam had in the Garden of Eden, that God had cursed all labour, and that, therefore, it was a sin for any man to work. For that reason this man sought to do as little work as possible. He seemed at that time to be supremely happy, because he was living, as he expressed it, through one week that was free from sin.

In the school we made a special effort to teach our students the meaning of Christmas, and to give them lessons in its proper observance. In this we have been successful to a degree that makes me feel safe in saying that the season now has a new meaning, not only through all that immediate region, but, in a measure, wherever our graduates have gone.

At the present time one of the most satisfactory features of the Christmas and Thanksgiving seasons at Tuskegee is the unselfish and beautiful way in which our graduates and students spend their time in administering to the comfort and happiness of others, especially the unfortunate. Not long ago some of our young men spent a holiday in rebuilding a cabin for a helpless coloured woman who is about seventy-five years old. At another time I remember that I made it known in chapel, one night, that a very poor student was suffering from cold, because he needed a coat. The next morning two coats were sent to my office for him.

I have referred to the disposition on the part of the white people in the town of Tuskegee and vicinity to help the school. From the first, I resolved to make the school a real part of the community in which it was located. I was determined that no one should have the feeling that it was a foreign institution, dropped down in the midst of the people, for which they had no responsibility and in which they had no interest. I noticed that the very fact that they had been asked to contribute toward the purchase of the land made them begin to feel as if it was going to be their school, to a large degree. I noted that just in proportion as we made the white people feel that the institution was a part of the life of the community, and that, while we wanted to make friends in Boston, for example, we also wanted to make white friends in Tuskegee, and that we wanted to make the school of real service to all the people, their attitude toward the school became favourable.

Perhaps I might add right here, what I hope to demonstrate later, that, so far as I know, the Tuskegee school at the present time has no warmer and more enthusiastic friends anywhere than it has among the white citizens of Tuskegee and throughout the state of Alabama and the entire South. From the first, I have advised our people in the South to make friends in every straightforward, manly way with their next-door neighbour, whether he be a black man or a white man. I have also advised them, where no principle is at stake, to consult the interests of their local communities, and to advise with their friends in regard to their voting.

For several months the work of securing the money with which to pay for the farm went on without ceasing. At the end of three months enough was secured to repay the loan of two hundred and fifty dollars to General Marshall, and within two months more we had secured the entire five hundred dollars and had received a deed of the one hundred acres of land. This gave us a great deal of satisfaction. It was not only a source of satisfaction to secure a permanent location for the school, but it was equally satisfactory to know that the greater part of the money with which it was paid for had been gotten from the white and coloured people in the town of Tuskegee. The most of this money was obtained by holding festivals and concerts, and from small individual donations.

Our next effort was in the direction of increasing the cultivation of the land, so as to secure some return from it, and at the same time give the students training in agriculture. All the industries at Tuskegee have been started in natural and logical order, growing out of the needs of a community settlement. We began with farming, because we wanted something to eat.

Many of the students, also, were able to remain in school but a few weeks at a time, because they had so little money with which to pay their board. Thus another object which made it desirable to get an industrial system started was in order to make it available as a means of helping the students to earn money enough so that they might be able to remain in school during the nine months' session of the school year.

The first animal that the school came into possession of was an old blind horse given us by one of the white citizens of Tuskegee.

Perhaps I may add here that at the present time the school owns over two hundred horses, colts, mules, cows, calves, and oxen, and about seven hundred hogs and pigs, as well as a large number of sheep and goats.

The school was constantly growing in numbers, so much so that, after we had got the farm paid for, the cultivation of the land begun, and the old cabins which we had found on the place somewhat repaired, we turned our attention toward providing a large, substantial building. After having given a good deal of thought to the subject, we finally had the plans drawn for a building that was estimated to cost about six thousand dollars. This seemed to us a tremendous sum, but we knew that the school must go backward or forward, and that our work would mean little unless we could get hold of the students in their home life.

One incident which occurred about this time gave me a great deal of satisfaction as well as surprise. When it became known in the town that we were discussing the plans for a new, large building, a Southern white man who was operating a sawmill not far from Tuskegee came to me and said that he would gladly put all the lumber necessary to erect the building on the grounds, with no other guarantee for payment than my word that it would be paid for when we secured some money. I told the man frankly that at the time we did not have in our hands one dollar of the money needed. Notwithstanding this, he insisted on being allowed to put the lumber on the grounds. After we had secured some portion of the money we permitted him to do this.

Miss Davidson again began the work of securing in various ways small contributions for the new building from the white and coloured people in and near Tuskegee. I think I never saw a community of people so happy over anything as were the coloured people over the prospect of this new building. One day, when we were holding a meeting to secure funds for its erection, an old, ante-bellum coloured man came a distance of twelve miles and brought in his ox-cart a large hog. When the meeting was in progress, he rose in the midst of the company and said that he had no money which he could give, but that he had raised two fine hogs, and that he had brought one of them as a contribution toward the expenses of the building. He closed his announcement by saying: "Any nigger that's got any love for his race, or any respect for himself, will bring a hog to the next meeting." Quite a number of men in the community also volunteered to give several days' work, each, toward the erection of the building.

After we had secured all the help that we could in Tuskegee, Miss Davidson decided to go North for the purpose of securing additional funds. For weeks she visited individuals and spoke in churches and before Sunday schools and other organizations. She found this work quite trying, and often embarrassing. The school was not known, but she was not long in winning her way into the confidence of the best people in the North.

The first gift from any Northern person was received from a New York lady whom Miss Davidson met on the boat that was bringing her North. They fell into a conversation, and the Northern lady became so much interested in the effort being made at Tuskegee that before they parted Miss Davidson was handed a check for fifty dollars. For some time before our marriage, and also after it, Miss Davidson kept up the work of securing money in the North and in the South by interesting people by personal visits and through correspondence. At the same time she kept in close touch with the work at Tuskegee, as lady principal and classroom teacher. In addition to this, she worked among the older people in and near Tuskegee, and taught a Sunday school class in the town. She was never very strong, but never seemed happy unless she was giving all of her strength to the cause which she loved. Often, at night, after spending the day in going from door to door trying to interest persons in the work at Tuskegee, she would be so exhausted that she could not undress herself. A lady upon whom she called, in Boston, afterward told me that at one time when Miss Davidson called to see her and sent up her card the lady was detained a little before she could see Miss

Davidson, and when she entered the parlour she found Miss Davidson so exhausted that she had fallen asleep.

While putting up our first building, which was named Porter
Hall, after Mr. A. H. Porter, of Brooklyn, N.Y., who gave a generous
sum toward its erection, the need for money became acute. I had
given one of our creditors a promise that upon a certain day he
should be paid four hundred dollars. On the morning of that day we
did not have a dollar. The mail arrived at the school at ten o'clock,
and in this mail there was a check sent by Miss Davidson for exactly
four hundred dollars. I could relate many instances of almost the
same character. This four hundred dollars was given by two ladies in
Boston. Two years later, when the work at Tuskegee had grown
considerably, and when we were in the midst of a season when we
were so much in need of money that the future looked doubtful and
gloomy, the same two Boston ladies sent us six thousand dollars.
Words cannot describe our surprise, or the encouragement that the
gift brought to us. Perhaps I might add here that for fourteen years
these same friends have sent us six thousand dollars each year.

As soon as the plans were drawn for the new building, the students began digging out the earth where the foundations were to be
laid, working after the regular classes were over. They had not fully
outgrown the idea that it was hardly the proper thing for them to use
their hands, since they had come there, as one of them expressed it,
"to be educated, and not to work." Gradually, though, I noted with
satisfaction that a sentiment in favour of work was gaining ground.
After a few weeks of hard work the foundations were ready, and a
day was appointed for the laying of the corner-stone.

When it is considered that the laying of this corner-stone took
place in the heart of the South, in the "Black Belt," in the centre of
that part of our country that was most devoted to slavery; that at that
time slavery had been abolished only about sixteen years; that only
sixteen years before that no Negro could be taught from books without the teacher receiving the condemnation of the law or of public

As the school's first edifice, Porter Hall necessarily had to be a multipurpose building: in the attic, the "girls'" dormitory; on the second floor, the chapel, reading room, and library; on the first floor, six "recitation rooms," as classrooms were called; and in the basement, the kitchen, dining room, and commissary.

sentiment—when all this is considered, the scene that was witnessed on that spring day at Tuskegee was a remarkable one. I believe there are few places in the world where it could have taken place.

The principal address was delivered by the Hon. Waddy Thompson, the Superintendent of Education for the county. About the corner-stone were gathered the teachers, the students, their parents and friends, the county officials—who were white—and all the leading white men in that vicinity, together with many of the black men and women whom these same white people but a few years before had held a title to as property. The members of both races were anxious to exercise the privilege of placing under the corner-stone some memento.

Before the building was completed we passed through some very trying seasons. More than once our hearts were made to bleed, as it were, because bills were falling due that we did not have the money to meet. Perhaps no one who has not gone through the experience, month after month, of trying to erect buildings and provide equipment for a school when no one knew where the money was to come from, can properly appreciate the difficulties under which we laboured. During the first years at Tuskegee I recall that night after night I would roll and toss on my bed, without sleep, because of the anxiety and uncertainty which we were in regarding money. I knew that, in a large degree, we were trying an experiment—that of testing whether or not it was possible for Negroes to build up and control the affairs of a large educational institution. I knew that if we failed it would injure the whole race. I knew that the presumption was against us. I knew that in the case of white people beginning such an enterprise it would be taken for granted that they were going to succeed, but in our case I felt that people would be surprised if we succeeded. All this made a burden which pressed down on us, sometimes, it seemed, at the rate of a thousand pounds to the square inch.

In all our difficulties and anxieties, however, I never went to a white or a black person in the town of Tuskegee for any assistance that was in their power to render, without being helped according to their means. More than a dozen times, when bills figuring up into the hundreds of dollars were falling due, I applied to the white men of Tuskegee for small loans, often borrowing small amounts from as many as a half-dozen persons, to meet our obligations. One thing I was determined to do from the first, and that was to keep the credit of the school high; and this, I think I can say without boasting, we have done all through these years.

I shall always remember a bit of advice given me by Mr. George W. Campbell, the white man to whom I have referred as the one who induced General Armstrong to send me to Tuskegee. Soon after I entered upon the work Mr. Campbell said to me, in his fatherly way: "Washington, always remember that credit is capital."

At one time when we were in the greatest distress for money that we ever experienced, I placed the situation frankly before General Armstrong. Without hesitation he gave me his personal check for all the money which he had saved for his own use. This was not the only time that General Armstrong helped Tuskegee in this way. I do not think I have ever made this fact public before.

During the summer of 1882, at the end of the first year's work of the school, I was married to Miss Fannie N. Smith, of Malden, W. Va. We began keeping house in Tuskegee early in the fall. This made a home for our teachers, who now had been increased to four in number. My wife was also a graduate of the Hampton Institute. After earnest and constant work in the interests of the school, together with her housekeeping duties, my wife passed away in May, 1884. One child, Portia M. Washington, was born during our marriage.

From the first, my wife most earnestly devoted her thoughts and time to the work of the school, and was completely one with me in every interest and ambition. She passed away, however, before she had an opportunity of seeing what the school was designed to be.

CHAPTER X

A Harder Task Than Making Bricks
Without Straw

From the very beginning, at Tuskegee, I was determined to have the students do not only the agricultural and domestic work, but to have them erect their own buildings. My plan was to have them, while performing this service, taught the latest and best methods of labour, so that the school would not only get the benefit of their efforts, but the students themselves would be taught to see not only utility in labour, but beauty and dignity; would be taught, in fact, how to lift labour up from mere drudgery and toil, and would learn to love work for its own sake. My plan was not to teach them to work in the old way, but to show them how to make the forces of nature— air, water, steam, electricity, horse-power—assist them in their labour.

At first many advised against the experiment of having the buildings erected by the labour of the students, but I was determined to stick to it. I told those who doubted the wisdom of the plan that I knew that our first buildings would not be so comfortable or so complete in their finish as buildings erected by the experienced hands of outside workmen, but that in the teaching of civilization, self-help, and self-reliance, the erection of the buildings by the students themselves would more than compensate for any lack of comfort or fine finish.

I further told those who doubted the wisdom of this plan, that the majority of our students came to us in poverty, from the cabins of the cotton, sugar, and rice plantations of the South, and that while I knew it would please the students very much to place them at once in finely constructed buildings, I felt that it would be following out a more natural process of development to teach them how to construct their own buildings. Mistakes I knew would be made, but these mistakes would teach us valuable lessons for the future.

During the now nineteen years' existence of the Tuskegee school, the plan of having the buildings erected by student labour has been adhered to. In this time forty buildings, counting small and large, have been built, and all except four are almost wholly the product of student labour. As an additional result, hundreds of men are now scattered throughout the South who received their knowledge of mechanics while being taught how to erect these buildings. Skill and knowledge are now handed down from one set of students to another in this way, until at the present time a building of any description or size can be constructed wholly by our instructors and students, from the drawing of the plans to the putting in of the electric fixtures, without going off the grounds for a single workman.

Not a few times, when a new student has been led into the temptation of marring the looks of some building by leadpencil marks or by the cuts of a jack-knife, I have heard an old student remind him: "Don't do that. That is our building. I helped put it up."

In the early days of the school I think my most trying experience was in the matter of brickmaking. As soon as we got the farm work reasonably well started, we directed our next efforts toward the industry of making bricks. We needed these for use in connection with the erection of our own buildings; but there was also another reason for establishing this industry. There was no brickyard in the town, and in addition to our own needs there was a demand for bricks in the general market.

I had always sympathized with the "Children of Israel," in their task of "making bricks without straw," but ours was the task of making bricks with no money and no experience.

In the first place, the work was hard and dirty, and it was difficult to get the students to help. When it came to brickmaking, their distaste for manual labour in connection with book education became especially manifest. It was not a pleasant task for one to stand in the mud-pit for hours, with the mud up to his knees. More than one man became disgusted and left the school.

We tried several locations before we opened up a pit that furnished brick clay. I had always supposed that brickmaking was very simple, but I soon found out by bitter experience that it required special skill and knowledge, particularly in the burning of the bricks. After a good deal of effort we moulded about twenty-five thousand bricks, and put them into a kiln to be burned. This kiln turned out to be a failure, because it was not properly constructed or properly burned. We began at once, however, on a second kiln. This, for some reason, also proved a failure. The failure of this kiln made it still more difficult to get the students to take any part in the work. Several of the teachers, however, who had been trained in the industries at Hampton, volunteered their services, and in some way we succeeded in getting a third kiln ready for burning. The burning of a kiln required about a week. Toward the latter part of the week, when it seemed as if we were going to have a good many thousand bricks in a few hours, in the middle of the night the kiln fell. For the third time we had failed.

The failure of this last kiln left me without a single dollar with which to make another experiment. Most of the teachers advised the abandoning of the effort to make bricks. In the midst of my troubles I thought of a watch which had come into my possession years before. I took this watch to the city of Montgomery, which was not far distant, and placed it in a pawn-shop. I secured cash upon it to the amount of fifteen dollars, with which to renew the brickmaking experiment. I returned to Tuskegee, and, with the help of the fifteen dollars, rallied our rather demoralized and discouraged forces and began a fourth attempt to make bricks. This time, I am glad to say, we were successful. Before I got hold of any money, the time-limit on my watch had expired, and I have never seen it since; but I have never regretted the loss of it.

Brickmaking has now become such an important industry at the school that last season our students manufactured twelve hundred thousand of first-class bricks, of a quality suitable to be sold in any market. Aside from this, scores of young men have mastered the brickmaking trade—both the making of bricks by hand and by machinery—and are now engaged in this industry in many parts of the South.

The making of these bricks taught me an important lesson in regard to the relations of the two races in the South. Many white people who had had no contact with the school, and perhaps no sympathy with it, came to us to buy bricks because they found out that ours were good bricks. They discovered that we were supplying a real want in the community. The making of these bricks caused many of the white residents of the neighbourhood to begin to feel that the education of the Negro was not making him worthless, but that in educating our students we were adding something to the wealth and comfort of the community. As the people of the neighbourhood came to us to buy bricks, we got acquainted with them; they traded with us and we with them. Our business interests became intermingled. We had something which they wanted; they had something which we wanted. This, in a large measure, helped to lay the foundation for the pleasant relations that have continued to exist between us and the white people in that section, and which now extend throughout the South.

Wherever one of our brickmakers has gone in the South, we find that he has something to contribute to the well-being of the community into which he has gone; something that has made the community feel that, in a degree, it is indebted to him, and perhaps, to a certain

Several of the brick buildings constructed by students during the school's early days are still standing and in use today.

extent, dependent upon him. In this way pleasant relations between the races have been stimulated.

My experience is that there is something in human nature which always makes an individual recognize and reward merit, no matter under what colour of skin merit is found. I have found, too, that it is the visible, the tangible, that goes a long ways in softening prejudices. The actual sight of a first-class house that a Negro has built is ten times more potent than pages of discussion about a house that he ought to build, or perhaps could build.

The same principle of industrial education has been carried out in the building of our own wagons, carts, and buggies, from the first. We now own and use on our farm and about the school dozens of these vehicles, and every one of them has been built by the hands of the students. Aside from this, we help supply the local market with these vehicles. The supplying of them to the people in the community has had the same effect as the supplying of bricks, and the man who learns at Tuskegee to build and repair wagons and carts is regarded as a benefactor by both races in the community where he goes. The people with whom he lives and works are going to think twice before they part with such a man.

The individual who can do something that the world wants done will, in the end, make his way regardless of his race. One man may go into a community prepared to supply the people there with an analysis of Greek sentences. The community may not at that time be prepared for, or feel the need of, Greek analysis, but it may feel its need of bricks and houses and wagons. If the man can supply the need for those, then, it will lead eventually to a demand for the first product, and with the demand will come the ability to appreciate it and to profit by it.

About the time that we succeeded in burning our first kiln of bricks we began facing in an emphasized form the objection of the students to being taught to work. By this time it had gotten to be pretty well advertised throughout the state that every student who came to Tuskegee, no matter what his financial ability might be, must learn some industry. Quite a number of letters came from parents protesting against their children engaging in labour while they were in the school. Other parents came to the school to protest in person. Most of the new students brought a written or a verbal request from their parents to the effect that they wanted their children taught nothing but books. The more books, the larger they were, and the longer the titles printed upon them, the better pleased the students and their parents seemed to be.

I gave little heed to these protests, except that I lost no opportunity to go into as many parts of the state as I could, for the purpose of speaking to the parents, and showing them the value of industrial education. Besides, I talked to the students constantly on the subject. Notwithstanding the unpopularity of industrial work, the school continued to increase in numbers to such an extent that by the middle of the second year there was an attendance of about one hundred and fifty, representing almost all parts of the state of Alabama, and including a few from other states.

In the summer of 1882 Miss Davidson and I both went North and engaged in the work of raising funds for the completion of our new building. On my way North I stopped in New York to try to get a letter of recommendation from an officer of a missionary organization who had become somewhat acquainted with me a few years previous. This man not only refused to give me the letter, but advised me most earnestly to go back home at once, and not make an attempt to get money, for he was quite sure that I would never get more than enough to pay my travelling expenses. I thanked him for his advice, and proceeded on my journey.

The first place I went to in the North, was Northampton, Mass., where I spent nearly a half-day in looking for a coloured family with whom I could board, never dreaming that any hotel would admit me. I was greatly surprised when I found that I would have no trouble in being accommodated at a hotel.

We were successful in getting money enough so that on Thanksgiving Day of that year we held our first service in the chapel of Porter Hall, although the building was not completed.

In looking about for some one to preach the Thanksgiving sermon, I found one of the rarest men that it has ever been my privilege to know. This was the Rev. Robert C. Bedford, a white man from Wisconsin, who was then pastor of a little coloured Congregational church in Montgomery, Ala. Before going to Montgomery to look for some one to preach this sermon I had never heard of Mr. Bedford. He had never heard of me. He gladly consented to come to Tuskegee and hold the Thanksgiving service. It was the first service of the kind that the coloured people there had ever observed, and what a deep interest they manifested in it! The sight of the new building made it a day of Thanksgiving for them never to be forgotten.

Mr. Bedford consented to become one of the trustees of the school, and in that capacity, and as a worker for it, he has been connected with it for eighteen years. During this time he has borne the school upon his heart night and day, and is never so happy as when he is performing some service, no matter how humble, for it. He completely obliterates himself in everything, and looks only for permission to serve where service is most disagreeable, and where others would not be attracted. In all my relations with him he has seemed to me to approach as nearly to the spirit of the Master as almost any man I ever met.

A little later there came into the service of the school another man, quite young at the time, and fresh from Hampton, without whose service the school never could have become what it is. This was Mr. Warren Logan, who now for seventeen years has been the treasurer of the Institute, and the acting principal during my absence. He has always shown a degree of unselfishness and an amount of business tact, coupled with a clear judgment, that has kept the school in good condition no matter how long I have been absent from it. During all the financial stress through which the school has passed, his patience and faith in our ultimate success have not left him.

As soon as our first building was near enough to completion so that we could occupy a portion of it—which was near the middle of the second year of the school—we opened a boarding department. Students had begun coming from quite a distance, and in such increasing numbers that we felt more and more that we were merely skimming over the surface, in that we were not getting hold of the students in their home life.

We had nothing but the students and their appetites with which to begin a boarding department. No provision had been made in the new building for a kitchen and dining room; but we discovered that by digging out a large amount of earth from under the building we could make a partially lighted basement room that could be used for a kitchen and dining room. Again I called on the students to volunteer for work, this time to assist in digging out the basement. This they did, and in a few weeks we had a place to cook and eat in, although it was very rough and uncomfortable. Any one seeing the place now would never believe that it was once used for a dining room.

The most serious problem, though, was to get the boarding department started off in running order, with nothing to do with in the way of furniture, and with no money with which to buy anything. The merchants in the town would let us have what food we wanted on credit. In fact, in those earlier years I was constantly embarrassed because people seemed to have more faith in me than I had in myself. It was pretty hard to cook, however, without stoves, and awkward to eat without dishes. At first the cooking was done out-of-doors, in the old-fashioned, primitive style, in pots and skillets placed over a fire. Some of the carpenters' benches that had been used in the construction of the building were utilized for tables. As for dishes, there were too few to make it worth while to spend time in describing them.

No one connected with the boarding department seemed to have any idea that meals must be served at certain fixed and regular hours, and this was a source of great worry. Everything was so out of joint and so inconvenient that I feel safe in saying that for the first two

Washington wanted "to send every graduate out feeling and knowing that labour is dignified and beautiful . . ."

weeks something was wrong at every meal. Either the meat was not done or had been burnt, or the salt had been left out of the bread, or the tea had been forgotten.

Early one morning I was standing near the dining-room door listening to the complaints of the students. The complaints that morning were especially emphatic and numerous, because the whole breakfast had been a failure. One of the girls who had failed to get any breakfast came out and went to the well to draw some water to drink to take the place of the breakfast which she had not been able to get. When she reached the well, she found that the rope was broken and that she could get no water. She turned from the well and said, in the most discouraged tone, not knowing that I was where I could hear her, "We can't even get water to drink at this school." I think no one remark ever came so near discouraging me as that one.

At another time, when Mr. Bedford—whom I have already spoken of as one of our trustees, and a devoted friend of the institution—was visiting the school, he was given a bedroom immediately over the dining room. Early in the morning he was awakened by a rather animated discussion between two boys in the dining room below. The discussion was over the question as to whose turn it was to use the coffee-cup that morning. One boy won the case by proving that for three mornings he had not had an opportunity to use the cup at all.

But gradually, by patience and hard work, we brought order out of chaos, just as will be true of any problem if we stick to it with patience and wisdom and earnest effort.

As I look back now over that part of our struggle, I am glad that we had it. I am glad that we endured all those discomforts and inconveniences. I am glad that our students had to dig out the place for their kitchen and dining room. I am glad that our first boarding-place was in that dismal, ill-lighted, and damp basement. Had we started in a fine, attractive, convenient room, I fear we would have "lost our heads" and become "stuck up." It means a great deal, I think, to start off on a foundation which one has made for one's self.

When our old students return to Tuskegee now, as they often do, and go into our large, beautiful, well-ventilated, and well-lighted dining room, and see tempting, well-cooked food—largely grown by the students themselves—and see tables, neat tablecloths and napkins, and vases of flowers upon the tables, and hear singing birds, and note that each meal is served exactly upon the minute, with no disorder, and with almost no complaint coming from the hundreds that now fill our dining room, they, too, often say to me that they are glad that we started as we did, and built ourselves up year by year, by a slow and natural process of growth.

Tuskegee seniors in a psychology class.

CHAPTER XI

Making Their Beds Before
They Could Lie on Them

A little later in the history of the school we had a visit from
General J. F. B. Marshall, the Treasurer of the Hampton Institute, who had had faith enough to lend us the first two hundred and
fifty dollars with which to make a payment down on the farm. He
remained with us a week, and made a careful inspection of everything. He seemed well pleased with our progress, and wrote back
interesting and encouraging reports to Hampton. A little later Miss
Mary F. Mackie, the teacher who had given me the "sweeping"
examination when I entered Hampton, came to see us, and still later
General Armstrong himself came.

At the time of the visits of these Hampton friends the number of
teachers at Tuskegee had increased considerably, and the most of the
new teachers were graduates of the Hampton Institute. We gave our
Hampton friends, especially General Armstrong, a cordial welcome.
They were all surprised and pleased at the rapid progress that the
school had made within so short a time. The coloured people from
miles around came to the school to get a look at General Armstrong,
about whom they had heard so much. The General was not only
welcomed by the members of my own race, but by the Southern
white people as well.

This first visit which General Armstrong made to Tuskegee gave me an opportunity to get an insight into his character such as I had not before had. I refer to his interest in the Southern white people. Before this I had had the thought that General Armstrong, having fought the Southern white man, rather cherished a feeling of bitterness toward the white South, and was interested in helping only the coloured man there. But this visit convinced me that I did not know the greatness and the generosity of the man. I soon learned, by his visits to the Southern white people, and from his conversations with them, that he was as anxious about the prosperity and the happiness of the white race as the black. He cherished no bitterness against the South, and was happy when an opportunity offered for manifesting his sympathy. In all my acquaintance with General Armstrong I never heard him speak, in public or in private, a single bitter word against the white man in the South. From his example in this respect I learned the lesson that great men cultivate love, and that only little men cherish a spirit of hatred. I learned that assistance given to the weak makes the one who gives it strong; and that oppression of the unfortunate makes one weak.

It is now long ago that I learned this lesson from General Armstrong, and resolved that I would permit no man, no matter what his colour might be, to narrow and degrade my soul by making me hate him. With God's help, I believe that I have completely rid myself of any ill feeling toward the Southern white man for any wrong that he may have inflicted upon my race. I am made to feel just as happy now when I am rendering service to Southern white men as when the service is rendered to a member of my own race. I pity from the bottom of my heart any individual who is so unfortunate as to get into the habit of holding race prejudice.

The more I consider the subject, the more strongly I am convinced that the most harmful effect of the practice to which the people in certain sections of the South have felt themselves compelled to resort, in order to get rid of the force of the Negroes' ballot, is not wholly in the wrong done to the Negro, but in the permanent injury to the morals of the white man. The wrong to the Negro is temporary, but to the morals of the white man the injury is permanent. I have noted time and time again that when an individual perjures himself in order to break the force of the black man's ballot, he soon learns to practise dishonesty in other relations of life, not only where the Negro is concerned, but equally so where a white man is concerned. The white man who begins by cheating a Negro usually ends by cheating a white man. The white man who begins to break the law by lynching a Negro soon yields to the temptation to lynch a white man. All this, it seems to me, makes it important that the whole Nation lend a hand in trying to lift the burden of ignorance from the South.

Another thing that is becoming more apparent each year in the development of education in the South is the influence of General Armstrong's idea of education; and this not upon the blacks alone, but upon the whites also. At the present time there is almost no Southern state that is not putting forth efforts in the direction of securing industrial education for its white boys and girls, and in most cases it is easy to trace the history of these efforts back to General Armstrong.

Soon after the opening of our humble boarding department students began coming to us in still larger numbers. For weeks we not only had to contend with the difficulty of providing board, with no money, but also with that of providing sleeping accommodations. For this purpose we rented a number of cabins near the school. These cabins were in a dilapidated condition, and during the winter months the students who occupied them necessarily suffered from the cold. We charged the students eight dollars a month—all they were able to pay—for their board. This included, besides board, room, fuel, and washing. We also gave the students credit on their board bills for all the work which they did for the school which was of any value to the institution. The cost of tuition, which was fifty dollars a year for each student, we had to secure then, as now, wherever we could.

This small charge in cash gave us no capital with which to start a boarding department. The weather during the second winter of our work was very cold. We were not able to provide enough bed-clothes to keep the students warm. In fact, for some time we were not able to provide, except in a few cases, bedsteads and mattresses of any kind. During the coldest nights I was so troubled about the discomfort of the students that I could not sleep myself. I recall that on several occasions I went in the middle of the night to the shanties occupied by the young men, for the purpose of comforting them. Often I found some of them sitting huddled around a fire, with the one blanket which we had been able to provide wrapped around them, trying in this way to keep warm. During the whole night some of them did not attempt to lie down. One morning, when the night previous had been unusually cold, I asked those of the students in the chapel who thought that they had been frostbitten during the night to raise their hands. Three hands went up. Notwithstanding these experiences, there was almost no complaining on the part of the students. They knew that we were doing the best that we could for them. They were happy in the privilege of being permitted to enjoy any kind of opportunity that would enable them to improve their condition. They were constantly asking what they might do to lighten the burdens of the teachers.

I have heard it stated more than once, both in the North and in the South, that coloured people would not obey and respect each other when one member of the race is placed in a position of authority over others. In regard to this general belief and these statements, I can say that during the nineteen years of my experience at Tuskegee I never, either by word or act, have been treated with disrespect by any student or officer connected with the institution. On the other hand, I am constantly embarrassed by the many acts of thoughtful kindness. The students do not seem to want to see me carry a large book or a satchel or any kind of a burden through the grounds. In such cases more than one always offers to relieve me. I almost never go out of my office when the rain is falling that some student does not come to my side with an umbrella and ask to be allowed to hold it over me.

While writing upon this subject, it is a pleasure for me to add that in all my contact with the white people of the South I have never received a single personal insult. The white people in and near Tuskegee, to an especial degree, seem to count it a privilege to show me all the respect within their power, and often go out of their way to do this.

Not very long ago I was making a journey between Dallas (Texas) and Houston. In some way it became known in advance that I was on the train. At nearly every station at which the train stopped, numbers of white people, including in most cases the officials of the town, came aboard and introduced themselves and thanked me heartily for the work that I was trying to do for the South.

On another occasion, when I was making a trip from Augusta, Georgia, to Atlanta, being rather tired from much travel, I rode in a Pullman sleeper. When I went into the car, I found there two ladies from Boston whom I knew well. These good ladies were perfectly ignorant, it seems, of the customs of the South, and in the goodness of their hearts insisted that I take a seat with them in their section. After some hesitation I consented. I had been there but a few minutes when one of them, without my knowledge, ordered supper to be served to the three of us. This embarrassed me still further. The car was full of Southern white men, most of whom had their eyes on our party. When I found that supper had been ordered, I tried to contrive some excuse that would permit me to leave the section, but the ladies insisted that I must eat with them. I finally settled back in my seat with a sigh, and said to myself, "I am in for it now, sure."

To add further to the embarrassment of the situation, soon after the supper was placed on the table one of the ladies remembered that she had in her satchel a special kind of tea which she wished served, and as she said she felt quite sure the porter did not know how to brew it properly, she insisted upon getting up and preparing and serving it herself. At last the meal was over; and it seemed the longest one that I had ever eaten. When we were through, I decided to get myself out of the embarrassing situation and go into the smoking-room, where most of the men were by that time, to see how the land lay. In the meantime, however, it had become known in some way throughout the car who I was. When I went into the smoking-room I was never more surprised in my life than when each man, nearly every one of them a citizen of Georgia, came up and introduced himself to me and thanked me earnestly for the work that I was trying to do for the whole South. This was not flattery, because each one of these individuals knew that he had nothing to gain by trying to flatter me.

From the first I have sought to impress the students with the idea that Tuskegee is not my institution, or that of the officers, but that it is their institution, and that they have as much interest in it as any of the trustees or instructors. I have further sought to have them feel that I am at the institution as their friend and adviser, and not as their overseer. It has been my aim to have them speak with directness and frankness about anything that concerns the life of the school. Two or three times a year I ask the students to write me a letter criticising or making complaints or suggestions about anything connected with the institution. When this is not done, I have them meet me in the chapel for a heart-to-heart talk about the conduct of the school. There are no meetings with our students that I enjoy more than these, and none are more helpful to me in planning for the future. These meetings, it seems to me, enable me to get at the very heart of all that concerns the school. Few things help an individual more than to place responsibility upon him, and to let him know that you trust him. When I have read of labour troubles between employers and employees, I have often thought that many strikes and similar disturbances might be avoided if the employers would cultivate the habit of getting nearer to their employees, of consulting and advising with them, and letting them feel that the interests of the two are the same. Every individual responds to confidence, and this is not more true of any race than of the Negroes. Let them once understand that you are unselfishly interested in them, and you can lead them to any extent.

It was my aim from the first at Tuskegee to not only have the

The first principle of industrial teaching at Tuskegee was that "the student shall be so educated that he shall be enabled to meet conditions as they exist now, in the part of the South where he lives—in a word, to be able to do the thing which the world wants done . . ."

buildings erected by the students themselves, but to have them make their own furniture as far as was possible. I now marvel at the patience of the students while sleeping upon the floor while waiting for some kind of a bedstead to be constructed, or at their sleeping without any kind of a mattress while waiting for something that looked like a mattress to be made.

In the early days we had very few students who had been used to handling carpenters' tools, and the bedsteads made by the students then were very rough and very weak. Not unfrequently when I went into the students' rooms in the morning I would find at least two bedsteads lying about on the floor. The problem of providing mattresses was a difficult one to solve. We finally mastered this, however, by getting some cheap cloth and sewing pieces of this together so as to make large bags. These bags we filled with the pine straw—or, as it is sometimes called, pine needles—which we secured from the forests near by. I am glad to say that the industry of mattress-making has grown steadily since then, and has been improved to such an extent that at the present time it is an important branch of the work which is taught systematically to a number of our girls, and that the mattresses that now come out of the mattress-shop at Tuskegee are about as good as those bought in the average store. For some time after the opening of the boarding department we had no chairs in the students' bedrooms or in the dining rooms. Instead of chairs we used stools which the students constructed by nailing together three pieces of rough board. As a rule, the furniture in the students' rooms during the early days of the school consisted of a bed, some stools, and sometimes a rough table made by the students. The plan of having the students make the furniture is still followed, but the number of pieces in a room has been increased, and the workmanship has so improved that little fault can be found with the articles now. One thing that I have always insisted upon at Tuskegee is that everywhere there should be absolute cleanliness. Over and over again the students were reminded in those first years—and are reminded now—that people would excuse us for our poverty, for our lack of comforts and conveniences, but that they would not excuse us for dirt.

Another thing that has been insisted upon at the school is the use of the tooth-brush. "The gospel of the tooth-brush," as General Armstrong used to call it, is a part of our creed at Tuskegee. No student is permitted to remain who does not keep and use a tooth-brush. Several times, in recent years, students have come to us who brought with them almost no other article except a tooth-brush. They had heard from the lips of older students about our insisting upon the use of this, and so, to make a good impression, they brought at least a tooth-brush with them. I remember that one morning, not long ago, I went with the lady principal on her usual morning tour of inspection of the girls' rooms. We found one room that contained three girls who had recently arrived at the school. When I asked them if they had tooth-brushes, one of the girls replied, pointing to a brush: "Yes, sir. That is our brush. We bought it together, yesterday." It did not take them long to learn a different lesson.

It has been interesting to note the effect that the use of the toothbrush has had in bringing about a higher degree of civilization among the students. With few exceptions, I have noticed that, if we can get a student to the point where, when the first or second toothbrush disappears, he of his own motion buys another, I have not been disappointed in the future of that individual. Absolute cleanliness of the body has been insisted upon from the first. The students have been taught to bathe as regularly as to take their meals. This lesson we began teaching before we had anything in the shape of a bathhouse. Most of the students came from plantation districts, and often we had to teach them how to sleep at night; that is, whether between the two sheets—after we got to the point where we could provide them two sheets—or under both of them. Naturally I found it difficult to teach them to sleep between two sheets when we were able to supply but one. The importance of the use of the nightgown received the same attention.

For a long time one of the most difficult tasks was to teach the students that all the buttons were to be kept on their clothes, and that there must be no torn places and no grease-spots. This lesson, I am pleased to be able to say, has been so thoroughly learned and so faithfully handed down from year to year by one set of students to another that often at the present time, when the students march out of chapel in the evening and their dress is inspected, as it is every night, not one button is to be found missing.

CHAPTER XII

Raising Money

When we opened our boarding department, we provided rooms in the attic of Porter Hall, our first building, for a number of girls. But the number of students, of both sexes, continued to increase. We could find rooms outside the school grounds for many of the young men, but the girls we did not care to expose in this way. Very soon the problem of providing more rooms for the girls, as well as a larger boarding department for all the students, grew serious. As a result, we finally decided to undertake the construction of a still larger building—a building that would contain rooms for the girls and boarding accommodations for all.

After having had a preliminary sketch of the needed building made, we found that it would cost about ten thousand dollars. We had no money whatever with which to begin; still we decided to give the needed building a name. We knew we could name it, even though we were in doubt about our ability to secure the means for its construction. We decided to call the proposed building Alabama Hall, in honour of the state in which we were labouring. Again Miss Davidson began making efforts to enlist the interest and help of the coloured and white people in and near Tuskegee. They responded willingly, in proportion to their means. The students, as in the case of our first building, Porter Hall, began digging out the dirt in order to allow of the laying of the foundations.

When we seemed at the end of our resources, so far as securing money was concerned, something occurred which showed the greatness of General Armstrong—something which proved how far he was above the ordinary individual. When we were in the midst of great anxiety as to where and how we were to get funds for the new building, I received a telegram from General Armstrong asking me if I could spend a month travelling with him through the North, and asking me, if I could do so, to come to Hampton at once. Of course I accepted General Armstrong's invitation, and went to Hampton immediately. On arriving there I found that the General had decided to take a quartette of singers through the North, and hold meetings for a month in important cities, at which meetings he and I were to speak. Imagine my surprise when the General told me, further, that these meetings were to be held, not in the interests of Hampton, but in the interests of Tuskegee, and that the Hampton Institute was to be responsible for all the expenses.

Although he never told me so in so many words, I found out that General Armstrong took this method of introducing me to the people of the North, as well as for the sake of securing some immediate funds to be used in the erection of Alabama Hall. A weak and narrow man would have reasoned that all the money which came to Tuskegee in this way would be just so much taken from the Hampton Institute; but none of these selfish or short-sighted feelings ever entered the breast of General Armstrong. He was too big to be little, too good to be mean. He knew that the people in the North who gave money gave it for the purpose of helping the whole cause of Negro civilization, and not merely for the advancement of any one school. The General knew, too, that the way to strengthen Hampton was to make it a centre of unselfish power in the working out of the whole Southern problem.

In regard to the addresses which I was to make in the North, I recall just one piece of advice which the General gave me. He said:

"Give them an idea for every word." I think it would be hard to improve upon this advice; and it might be made to apply to all public speaking. From that time to the present I have always tried to keep his advice in mind.

Meetings were held in New York, Brooklyn, Boston, Philadelphia, and other large cities, and at all of these meetings General Armstrong pleaded, together with myself, for help, not for Hampton, but for Tuskegee. At these meetings an especial effort was made to secure help for the building of Alabama Hall, as well as to introduce the school to the attention of the general public. In both these respects the meetings proved successful.

After that kindly introduction I began going North alone to secure funds. During the last fifteen years I have been compelled to spend a large proportion of my time away from the school, in an effort to secure money to provide for the growing needs of the institution. In my efforts to get funds I have had some experiences that may be of interest to my readers. Time and time again I have been asked, by people who are trying to secure money for philanthropic purposes, what rule or rules I followed to secure the interest and help of people who were able to contribute money to worthy objects. As far as the science of what is called begging can be reduced to rules, I would say that I have had but two rules. First, always to do my whole duty regarding making our work known to individuals and organizations; and, second, not to worry about the results. This second rule has been the hardest for me to live up to. When bills are on the eve of falling due, with not a dollar in hand with which to meet them, it is pretty difficult to learn not to worry, although I think I am learning more and more each year that all worry simply consumes, and to no purpose, just so much physical and mental strength that might otherwise be given to effective work. After considerable experience in coming into contact with wealthy and noted men, I have observed that those who have accomplished the greatest results are those who "keep under the body"; are those who never grow excited or lose self-control, but are always calm, self-possessed, patient, and polite. I think that President William McKinley is the best example of a man of this class that I have ever seen.

In order to be successful in any kind of undertaking, I think the main thing is for one to grow to the point where he completely forgets himself; that is, to lose himself in a great cause. In proportion as one loses himself in this way, in the same degree does he get the highest happiness out of his work.

My experience in getting money for Tuskegee has taught me to have no patience with those people who are always condemning the rich because they are rich, and because they do not give more to objects of charity. In the first place, those who are guilty of such sweeping criticisms do not know how many people would be made poor, and how much suffering would result, if wealthy people were to part all at once with any large proportion of their wealth in a way to disorganize and cripple great business enterprises. Then very few persons have any idea of the large number of applications for help that rich people are constantly being flooded with. I know wealthy people who receive as many as twenty calls a day for help. More than once, when I have gone into the offices of rich men, I have found half a dozen persons waiting to see them, and all come for the same purpose, that of securing money. And all these calls in person, to say nothing of the applications received through the mails. Very few people have any idea of the amount of money given away by persons who never permit their names to be known. I have often heard persons condemned for not giving away money, who, to my own knowledge, were giving away thousands of dollars every year so quietly that the world knew nothing about it.

As an example of this, there are two ladies in New York, whose names rarely appear in print, but who, in a quiet way, have given us the means with which to erect three large and important buildings during the last eight years. Besides the gift of these buildings, they have made other generous donations to the school. And they not only help Tuskegee, but they are constantly seeking opportunities to help other worthy causes.

Although it has been my privilege to be the medium through which a good many hundred thousand dollars have been received for the work at Tuskegee, I have always avoided what the world calls "begging." I often tell people that I have never "begged" any money, and that I am not a "beggar." My experience and observation have convinced me that persistent asking outright for money from the rich does not, as a rule, secure help. I have usually proceeded on the principle that persons who possess sense enough to earn money have sense enough to know how to give it away, and that the mere making known of the facts regarding Tuskegee, and especially the facts regarding the work of the graduates, has been more effective than outright begging. I think that the presentation of facts, on a high, dignified plane, is all the begging that most rich people care for.

While the work of going from door to door and from office to office is hard, disagreeable, and costly in bodily strength, yet it has some compensations. Such work gives one a rare opportunity to study human nature. It also has its compensations in giving one an opportunity to meet some of the best people in the world—to be more correct, I think I should say *the best* people in the world. When one takes a broad survey of the country, he will find that the most useful and influential people in it are those who take the deepest interest in institutions that exist for the purpose of making the world better.

At one time, when I was in Boston, I called at the door of a rather wealthy lady, and was admitted to the vestibule and sent up my card. While I was waiting for an answer, her husband came in, and asked me in the most abrupt manner what I wanted. When I tried to explain the object of my call, he became still more ungentlemanly in his words and manner, and finally grew so excited that I left the house without waiting for a reply from the lady. A few blocks from that house I called to see a gentleman who received me in the most cordial manner. He wrote me his check for a generous sum, and then, before I had had an opportunity to thank him, said: "I am so grateful to you, Mr. Washington, for giving me the opportunity to help a

The Tuskegee Normal and Industrial Institute.

Tuskegee, Alabama.

(INCORPORATED.)

LOCATION—In the Black Belt of Alabama, where the colored people outnumber the white, three to one.

STUDENTS, INSTRUCTORS—850 Students, nearly half girls; 86 Instructors; 21 States represented; average age $18\frac{1}{2}$; none under 14, each student is taught a trade or some industry in addition to his class room studies.

COURSE OF STUDY—English education, combined with industrial and religious training; the school is non-sectarian; 26 industries are in constant operation.

VALUE OF PROPERTY—The property consists of 2267 acres of land, 37 buildings, almost wholly built by student labor, is valued at $290,000 and no mortgage.

NEEDS—$50 annually for the education of each Student; ($200 enables a student to finish the course of study; $1,000 creates permanent scholarship. Students pay their own board partly in cash and partly in labor.) Money in any amounts for current expenses, and buildings. Even $1.00 will help us much.

SOME RESULTS—300 graduates and ex-students are now at work in every Southern state as school teachers, farmers, mechanics, housekeepers and leaders along other lines. Besides thousands are reached through the Tuskegee Negro Conference with its various local conferences.

Address,

BOOKER T. WASHINGTON, Principal,

TUSKEGEE, ALABAMA.

A page from a Tuskegee fundraising brochure.

good cause. It is a privilege to have a share in it. We in Boston are constantly indebted to you for doing *our* work." My experience in securing money convinces me that the first type of man is growing more rare all the time, and that the latter type is increasing; that is, that, more and more, rich people are coming to regard men and women who apply to them for help for worthy objects, not as beggars, but as agents for doing their work.

In the city of Boston I have rarely called upon an individual for funds that I have not been thanked for calling, usually before I could get an opportunity to thank the donor for the money. In that city the donors seem to feel, in a large degree, that an honour is being conferred upon them in their being permitted to give. Nowhere else have I met with, in so large a measure, this fine and Christlike spirit as in the city of Boston, although there are many notable instances of it outside that city. I repeat my belief that the world is growing in the direction of giving. I repeat that the main rule by which I have been guided in collecting money is to do my full duty in regard to giving people who have money an opportunity to help.

In the early years of the Tuskegee school I walked the streets or travelled country roads in the North for days and days without receiving a dollar. Often it has happened, when during the week I had been disappointed in not getting a cent from the very individuals from whom I most expected help, and when I was almost broken down and discouraged, that generous help has come from some one who I had had little idea would give at all.

I recall that on one occasion I obtained information that led me to believe that a gentleman who lived about two miles out in the country from Stamford, Conn., might become interested in our efforts at Tuskegee if our conditions and needs were presented to him. On an unusually cold and stormy day I walked the two miles to see him. After some difficulty I succeeded in securing an interview with him. He listened with some degree of interest to what I had to say, but did not give me anything. I could not help having the feeling that, in a measure, the three hours that I had spent in seeing him had been thrown away. Still, I had followed my usual rule of doing my duty. If I had not seen him, I should have felt unhappy over neglect of duty.

Two years after this visit a letter came to Tuskegee from this man, which read like this: "Enclosed I send you a New York draft for ten thousand dollars, to be used in furtherance of your work. I had placed this sum in my will for your school, but deem it wiser to give it to you while I live. I recall with pleasure your visit to me two years ago."

I can hardly imagine any occurrence which could have given me more genuine satisfaction than the receipt of this draft. It was by far the largest single donation which up to that time the school had ever received. It came at a time when an unusually long period had passed since we had received any money. We were in great distress because of lack of funds, and the nervous strain was tremendous. It is difficult for me to think of any situation that is more trying on the nerves than that of conducting a large institution, with heavy financial obligations to meet, without knowing where the money is to come from to meet these obligations from month to month.

In our case I felt a double responsibility, and this made the anxiety all the more intense. If the institution had been officered by white persons, and had failed, it would have injured the cause of Negro education; but I knew that the failure of our institution, officered by Negroes, would not only mean the loss of a school, but would cause people, in a large degree, to lose faith in the ability of the entire race. The receipt of this draft for ten thousand dollars, under all these circumstances, partially lifted a burden that had been pressing down upon me for days.

From the beginning of our work to the present I have always had the feeling, and lose no opportunity to impress our teachers with the same idea, that the school will always be supported in proportion as the inside of the institution is kept clean and pure and wholesome.

The first time I ever saw the late Collis P. Huntington, the great railroad man, he gave me two dollars for our school. The last time I saw him, which was a few months before he died, he gave me fifty thousand dollars toward our endowment fund. Between these two gifts there were others of generous proportions which came every year from both Mr. and Mrs. Huntington.

Some people may say that it was Tuskegee's good luck that brought to us this gift of fifty thousand dollars. No, it was not luck. It was hard work. Nothing ever comes to one, that is worth having, except as a result of hard work. When Mr. Huntington gave me the first two dollars, I did not blame him for not giving me more, but made up my mind that I was going to convince him by tangible results that we were worthy of larger gifts. For a dozen years I made a strong effort to convince Mr. Huntington of the value of our work. I noted that just in proportion as the usefulness of the school grew, his donations increased. Never did I meet an individual who took a more kindly and sympathetic interest in our school than did Mr. Huntington. He not only gave money to us, but took time in which to advise me, as a father would a son, about the general conduct of the school.

More than once I have found myself in some pretty tight places while collecting money in the North. The following incident I have never related but once before, for the reason that I feared that people would not believe it. One morning I found myself in Providence, Rhode Island, without a cent of money with which to buy breakfast. In crossing the street to see a lady from whom I hoped to get some money, I found a bright new twenty-five-cent piece in the middle of the street-car track. I not only had this twenty-five cents for my breakfast, but within a few minutes I had a donation from the lady on whom I had started to call.

At one of our Commencements I was bold enough to invite the Rev. E. Winchester Donald, D.D., rector of Trinity Church, Boston, to preach the Commencement sermon. As we then had no room large enough to accommodate all who would be present, the place of meeting was under a large, improvised arbour, built partly of brush and partly of rough boards. Soon after Dr. Donald had begun speaking, the rain came down in torrents, and he had to stop, while some one held an umbrella over him.

The boldness of what I had done never dawned upon me until I saw the picture made by the rector of Trinity Church standing before that large audience under an old umbrella, waiting for the rain to cease so that he could go on with his address.

It was not very long before the rain ceased and Dr. Donald finished his sermon; and an excellent sermon it was, too, in spite of the weather. After he had gone to his room, and had gotten the wet threads of his clothes dry, Dr. Donald ventured the remark that a large chapel at Tuskegee would not be out of place. The next day a letter came from two ladies who were then travelling in Italy, saying that they had decided to give us the money for such a chapel as we needed.

A short time ago we received twenty thousand dollars from Mr. Andrew Carnegie, to be used for the purpose of erecting a new library building. Our first library and reading-room were in a corner of a shanty, and the whole thing occupied a space about five by twelve feet. It required ten years of work before I was able to secure Mr. Carnegie's interest and help. The first time I saw him, ten years ago, he seemed to take but little interest in our school, but I was determined to show him that we were worthy of his help. After ten years of hard work I wrote him a letter reading as follows:

DECEMBER 15, 1900.

MR. ANDREW CARNEGIE, 5 W. FIFTY-FIRST ST., NEW YORK.

DEAR SIR: Complying with the request which you made of me when I saw you at your residence a few days ago, I now submit in writing an appeal for a library building for our institution.

We have 1100 students, 86 officers and instructors, together with their families, and about 200 coloured people living near the school, all of whom would make use of the library building.

We have over 12,000 books, periodicals, etc., gifts from our friends, but we have no suitable place for them, and we have no suitable reading-room.

Our graduates go to work in every section of the South, and whatever knowledge might be obtained in the library would serve to assist in the elevation of the whole Negro race.

Such a building as we need could be erected for about $20,000. All of the work for the building, such as brickmaking, brick-masonry, carpentry, blacksmithing, etc., would be done by the students. The money which you would give would not only supply the building, but the erection of the building would give a large number of students an opportunity to learn the building trades, and the students would use the money paid to them to keep themselves in school. I do not believe that a similar amount of money often could be made go so far in uplifting a whole race.

If you wish further information, I shall be glad to furnish it.

Yours truly,

Booker T. Washington, Principal.

The next mail brought back the following reply: "I will be very glad to pay the bills for the library building as they are incurred, to the extent of twenty thousand dollars, and I am glad of this opportunity to show the interest I have in your noble work."

I have found that strict business methods go a long way in securing the interest of rich people. It has been my constant aim at Tuskegee to carry out, in our financial and other operations, such business methods as would be approved of by any New York banking house.

I have spoken of several large gifts to the school; but by far the greater proportion of the money that has built up the institution has come in the form of small donations from persons of moderate means. It is upon these small gifts, which carry with them the interest of hundreds of donors, that any philanthropic work must depend largely for its support. In my efforts to get money I have often been surprised at the patience and deep interest of the ministers, who are besieged on every hand and at all hours of the day for help. If no other consideration had convinced me of the value of the Christian life, the Christlike work which the Church of all denominations in America has done during the last thirty-five years for the elevation of the black man would have made me a Christian. In a large degree it has been the pennies, the nickels, and the dimes which have come from the Sunday-schools, the Christian Endeavour societies, and the missionary societies, as well as from the church proper, that have helped to elevate the Negro at so rapid a rate.

This speaking of small gifts reminds me to say that very few Tuskegee graduates fail to send us an annual contribution. These contributions range from twenty-five cents up to ten dollars.

Soon after beginning our third year's work we were surprised to receive money from three special sources, and up to the present time we have continued to receive help from them. First, the State Legislature of Alabama increased its annual appropriation from two thousand dollars to three thousand dollars; I might add that still later it increased this sum to four thousand five hundred dollars a year. The effort to secure this increase was led by the Hon. M. F. Foster, the member of the Legislature from Tuskegee. Second, we received one thousand dollars from the John F. Slater Fund. Our work seemed to please the trustees of this fund, as they soon began increasing their annual grant. This has been added to from time to time until at present we receive eleven thousand dollars annually from this Fund. The other help to which I have referred came in the shape of an allowance from the Peabody Fund. This was at first five hundred dollars, but it has since been increased to fifteen hundred dollars.

The effort to secure help from the Slater and Peabody Funds

brought me into contact with two rare men—men who have had much to do in shaping the policy for the education of the Negro. I refer to the Hon. J. L. M. Curry, of Washington, who is the general agent for these two funds, and Mr. Morris K. Jesup, of New York. Dr. Curry is a native of the South, an ex-Confederate soldier, yet I do not believe there is any man in the country who is more deeply interested in the highest welfare of the Negro than Dr. Curry, or one who is more free from race prejudice. He enjoys the unique distinction of possessing to an equal degree the confidence of the black man and the Southern white man. I shall never forget the first time I met him. It was in Richmond, Va., where he was then living. I had heard much about him. When I first went into his presence, trembling because of my youth and inexperience, he took me by the hand so cordially, and spoke such encouraging words, and gave me such helpful advice regarding the proper course to pursue, that I came to know him then, as I have known him ever since, as a high example of one who is constantly and unselfishly at work for the betterment of humanity.

Mr. Morris K. Jesup, the treasurer of the Slater Fund, I refer to because I know of no man of wealth and large and complicated business responsibilities who gives not only money but his time and thought to the subject of the proper method of elevating the Negro to the extent that is true of Mr. Jesup. It is very largely through his effort and influence that during the last few years the subject of industrial education has assumed the importance that it has, and been placed on its present footing.

CHAPTER XIII

Two Thousand Miles
for a Five-Minute Speech

Soon after the opening of our boarding department, quite a number of students who evidently were worthy, but who were so poor that they did not have any money to pay even the small charges at the school, began applying for admission. This class was composed of both men and women. It was a great trial to refuse admission to these applicants, and in 1884 we established a night-school to accommodate a few of them.

The night-school was organized on a plan similar to the one which I had helped to establish at Hampton. At first it was composed of about a dozen students. They were admitted to the night-school only when they had no money with which to pay any part of their board in the regular day-school. It was further required that they must work for ten hours during the day at some trade or industry, and study academic branches for two hours during the evening. This was the requirement for the first one or two years of their stay. They were to be paid something above the cost of their board, with the understanding that all of their earnings, except a very small part, were to be reserved in the school's treasury, to be used for paying their board in the regular day-school after they had entered that department. The night-school, started in this manner, has grown until there are at present four hundred and fifty-seven students enrolled in it alone.

There could hardly be a more severe test of a student's worth than this branch of the Institute's work. It is largely because it furnishes such a good opportunity to test the backbone of a student that I place such high value upon our night-school. Any one who is willing to work ten hours a day at the brick-yard, or in the laundry, through one or two years, in order that he or she may have the privilege of studying academic branches for two hours in the evening, has enough bottom to warrant being further educated.

After the student has left the night-school he enters the day-school, where he takes academic branches four days in a week, and works at his trade two days. Besides this he usually works at his trade during the three summer months. As a rule, after a student has succeeded in going through the night-school test, he finds a way to finish the regular course in industrial and academic training. No student, no matter how much money he may be able to command, is permitted to go through school without doing manual labour. In fact, the industrial work is now as popular as the academic branches. Some of the most successful men and women who have graduated from the institution obtained their start in the night-school.

While a great deal of stress is laid upon the industrial side of the work at Tuskegee, we do not neglect or overlook in any degree the religious and spiritual side. The school is strictly undenominational, but it is thoroughly Christian, and the spiritual training of the students is not neglected. Our preaching service, prayer-meetings, Sunday-school, Christian Endeavour Society, Young Men's Christian Association, and various missionary organizations, testify to this.

In 1885, Miss Olivia Davidson, to whom I have already referred as being largely responsible for the success of the school during its early history, and I were married. During our married life she continued to divide her time and strength between our home and the work for the school. She not only continued to work in the school at Tuskegee, but also kept up her habit of going North to secure funds.

In 1889 she died, after four years of happy married life and eight years of hard and happy work for the school. She literally wore herself out in her never ceasing efforts in behalf of the work that she so dearly loved. During our married life there were born to us two bright, beautiful boys, Baker Taliaferro and Ernest Davidson. The older of these, Baker, has already mastered the brick-maker's trade at Tuskegee.

I have often been asked how I began the practice of public speaking. In answer I would say that I never planned to give any large part of my life to speaking in public. I have always had more of an ambition to *do* things than merely to talk *about* doing them. It seems that when I went North with General Armstrong to speak at the series of public meetings to which I have referred, the President of the National Educational Association, the Hon. Thomas W. Bicknell, was present at one of those meetings and heard me speak. A few days afterward he sent me an invitation to deliver an address at the next meeting of the Educational Association. This meeting was to be held in Madison, Wis. I accepted the invitation. This was, in a sense, the beginning of my public-speaking career.

On the evening that I spoke before the Association there must have been not far from four thousand persons present. Without my knowing it, there were a large number of people present from Alabama, and some from the town of Tuskegee. These white people afterward frankly told me that they went to this meeting expecting to hear the South roundly abused, but were pleasantly surprised to find that there was no word of abuse in my address. On the contrary, the South was given credit for all the praiseworthy things that it had done. A white lady who was a teacher in a college in Tuskegee wrote back to the local paper that she was gratified, as well as surprised, to note the credit which I gave the white people of Tuskegee for their help in getting the school started. This address at Madison was the first that I had delivered that in any large measure dealt with the general problem of the races. Those who heard it seemed to be pleased with what I said and with the general position that I took.

When I first came to Tuskegee, I determined that I would make it my home, that I would take as much pride in the right actions of the people of the town as any white man could do, and that I would, at the same time, deplore the wrong-doing of the people as much as any white man. I determined never to say anything in a public address in the North that I would not be willing to say in the South. I early learned that it is a hard matter to convert an individual by abusing him, and that this is more often accomplished by giving credit for all the praiseworthy actions performed than by calling attention alone to all the evil done.

While pursuing this policy I have not failed, at the proper time and in the proper manner, to call attention, in no uncertain terms, to the wrongs which any part of the South has been guilty of. I have found that there is a large element in the South that is quick to respond to straightforward, honest criticism of any wrong policy. As a rule, the place to criticise the South, when criticism is necessary, is in the South—not in Boston. A Boston man who came to Alabama to criticise Boston would not effect so much good, I think, as one who had his word of criticism to say in Boston.

In this address at Madison I took the ground that the policy to be pursued with reference to the races was, by every honourable means, to bring them together and to encourage the cultivation of friendly relations, instead of doing that which would embitter. I further contended that, in relation to his vote, the Negro should more and more consider the interests of the community in which he lived, rather than seek alone to please some one who lived a thousand miles away from him and from his interests.

In this address I said that the whole future of the Negro rested largely upon the question as to whether or not he should make himself, through his skill, intelligence, and character, of such undeniable value to the community in which he lived that the community could not dispense with his presence. I said that any individual who learned to do something better than anybody else—learned to do a common thing in an uncommon manner—had solved his problem, regardless of the colour of his skin, and that in proportion as the Negro learned to produce what other people wanted and must have, in the same proportion would he be respected.

I spoke of an instance where one of our graduates had produced two hundred and sixty-six bushels of sweet potatoes from an acre of ground, in a community where the average production had been only forty-nine bushels to the acre. He had been able to do this by reason of his knowledge of the chemistry of the soil and by his knowledge of improved methods of agriculture. The white farmers in the neighbourhood respected him, and came to him for ideas regarding the raising of sweet potatoes. These white farmers honoured and respected him because he, by his skill and knowledge, had added something to the wealth and the comfort of the community in which he lived. I explained that my theory of education for the Negro would not, for example, confine him for all time to farm life—to the production of the best and the most sweet potatoes—but that, if he succeeded in this line of industry, he could lay the foundations upon which his children and grand-children could grow to higher and more important things in life.

Such, in brief, were some of the views I advocated in this first address dealing with the broad question of the relations of the two races, and since that time I have not found any reason for changing my views on any important point.

In my early life I used to cherish a feeling of ill will toward any one who spoke in bitter terms against the Negro, or who advocated measures that tended to oppress the black man or take from him opportunities for growth in the most complete manner. Now, whenever I hear any one advocating measures that are meant to curtail the development of another, I pity the individual who would do this. I know that the one who makes this mistake does so because of his own lack of opportunity for the highest kind of growth. I pity him because I know that he is trying to stop the progress of the world, and because I know that in time the development and the ceaseless advance of humanity will make him ashamed of his weak and narrow position. One might as well try to stop the progress of a mighty railroad train by throwing his body across the track, as to try to stop the growth of the world in the direction of giving mankind more intelligence, more culture, more skill, more liberty, and in the direction of extending more sympathy and more brotherly kindness.

The address which I delivered at Madison, before the National Educational Association, gave me a rather wide introduction in the North, and soon after that opportunities began offering themselves for me to address audiences there.

I was anxious, however, that the way might also be opened for me to speak directly to a representative Southern white audience. A partial opportunity of this kind, one that seemed to me might serve as an entering wedge, presented itself in 1893, when the international meeting of Christian Workers was held at Atlanta, Ga. When this invitation came to me, I had engagements in Boston that seemed to make it impossible for me to speak in Atlanta. Still, after looking over my list of dates and places carefully, I found that I could take a train from Boston that would get me into Atlanta about thirty minutes before my address was to be delivered, and that I could remain in that city about sixty minutes before taking another train for Boston. My invitation to speak in Atlanta stipulated that I was to confine my address to five minutes. The question, then, was whether or not I could put enough into a five-minute address to make it worth while for me to make such a trip.

I knew that the audience would be largely composed of the most influential class of white men and women, and that it would be a rare opportunity for me to let them know what we were trying to do at Tuskegee, as well as to speak to them about the relations of the races. So I decided to make the trip. I spoke for five minutes to an audience of two thousand people, composed mostly of Southern and Northern whites. What I said seemed to be received with favour and enthusiasm. The Atlanta papers of the next day commented in friendly terms on my address, and a good deal was said about it in different parts of the country. I felt that I had in some degree accomplished my object—that of getting a hearing from the dominant class of the South.

The demands made upon me for public addresses continued to increase, coming in about equal numbers from my own people and from Northern whites. I gave as much time to these addresses as I could spare from the immediate work at Tuskegee. Most of the addresses in the North were made for the direct purpose of getting funds with which to support the school. Those delivered before the coloured people had for their main object the impressing upon them of the importance of industrial and technical education in addition to academic and religious training.

I now come to that one of the incidents in my life which seems to have excited the greatest amount of interest, and which perhaps went further than anything else in giving me a reputation that in a sense might be called National. I refer to the address which I delivered at the opening of the Atlanta Cotton states and International Exposition, at Atlanta, Ga., September 18, 1895.

So much has been said and written about this incident, and so many questions have been asked me concerning the address, that perhaps I may be excused for taking up the matter with some detail. The five-minute address in Atlanta, which I came from Boston to deliver, was possibly the prime cause for an opportunity being given me to make the second address there. In the spring of 1895 I received a telegram from prominent citizens in Atlanta asking me to accompany a committee from that city to Washington for the purpose of appearing before a committee of Congress in the interest of securing Government help for the Exposition. The committee was composed of about twenty-five of the most prominent and most influential white men of Georgia. All the members of this committee were white men except Bishop Grant, Bishop Gaines, and myself. The Mayor and several other city and state officials spoke before the committee. They were followed by the two coloured bishops. My name was the last on the list of speakers. I had never before appeared before such a committee, nor had I ever delivered any address in the capital of the Nation. I had many misgivings as to what I ought to say, and as to the impression that my address would make. While I cannot recall in detail what I said, I remember that I tried to impress upon the committee, with all the earnestness and plainness of any language that I could command, that if Congress wanted to do something which would assist in ridding the South of the race question and making friends between the two races, it should, in every proper way, encourage the material and intellectual growth of both races. I said that the Atlanta Exposition would present an opportunity for both races to show what advance they had made since freedom, and would at the same time afford encouragement to them to make still greater progress.

I tried to emphasize the fact that while the Negro should not be deprived by unfair means of the franchise, political agitation alone would not save him, and that back of the ballot he must have property, industry, skill, economy, intelligence, and character, and that no race without these elements could permanently succeed. I said that in granting the appropriation Congress could do something that would prove to be of real and lasting value to both races, and that it was the first great opportunity of the kind that had been presented since the close of the Civil War.

I spoke for fifteen or twenty minutes, and was surprised at the close of my address to receive the hearty congratulations of the Georgia committee and of the members of Congress who were present. The Committee was unanimous in making a favourable report, and in a few days the bill passed Congress. With the passing of this bill the success of the Atlanta Exposition was assured.

Soon after this trip to Washington the directors of the Exposition decided that it would be a fitting recognition of the coloured race to erect a large and attractive building which should be devoted wholly to showing the progress of the Negro since freedom. It was further decided to have the building designed and erected wholly by Negro mechanics. This plan was carried out. In design, beauty, and general finish the Negro Building was equal to the others on the grounds.

After it was decided to have a separate Negro exhibit, the question arose as to who should take charge of it. The officials of the Exposition were anxious that I should assume this responsibility, but I declined to do so, on the plea that the work at Tuskegee at that time demanded my time and strength. Largely at my suggestion, Mr. I. Garland Penn, of Lynchburg, Va., was selected to be at the head of the Negro department. I gave him all the aid that I could. The Negro exhibit, as a whole, was large and creditable. The two exhibits in this department which attracted the greatest amount of attention were those from the Hampton Institute and the Tuskegee Institute. The people who seemed to be the most surprised, as well as pleased, at what they saw in the Negro Building were the Southern white people.

As the day for the opening of the Exposition drew near, the Board of Directors began preparing the programme for the opening exercises. In the discussion from day to day of the various features of this programme, the question came up as to the advisability of putting a member of the Negro race on for one of the opening addresses, since the Negroes had been asked to take such a prominent part in the Exposition. It was argued, further, that such recognition would mark the good feeling prevailing between the two races. Of course there were those who were opposed to any such recognition of the rights of the Negro, but the Board of Directors, composed of men who represented the best and most progressive element in the South, had their way, and voted to invite a black man to speak on the opening day. The next thing was to decide upon the person who was thus to represent the Negro race. After the question had been canvassed for several days, the directors voted unanimously to ask me to deliver one of the opening-day addresses, and in a few days after that I received the official invitation.

The receiving of this invitation brought to me a sense of responsi-

Booker T. Washington. Principal.   Warren Logan. Treasurer

TUSKEGEE NORMAL AND INDUSTRIAL INSTITUTE
(INCORPORATED)

FOR THE TRAINING OF COLORED YOUNG MEN AND WOMEN

Tuskegee, Ala. Sept 4, 95.

Dear Miss Howland:—

I thank you very much for your note regarding the Atlanta speaking. It was a great surprise to me as it has been to the colored people in general to receive such an invitation. No one had dared dream that the Directors would invite a colored man to deliver an address in connection with the main programme and from the same stand as the white speakers. Had your letter not come I should not have been led to emphasize the dignity of labor so much as I now have in mind to do. While the appointment brings

A letter to Emily Howland, written twelve days before Washington's historic Atlanta address, in which he records his surprise at receiving the invitation to speak: "No one had dared dream that the Directors would invite a colored man to deliver an address in connection with the main programme and from the same stand as the white speakers."

bility that it would be hard for any one not placed in my position to appreciate. What were my feelings when this invitation came to me? I remembered that I had been a slave; that my early years had been spent in the lowest depths of poverty and ignorance, and that I had had little opportunity to prepare me for such a responsibility as this. It was only a few years before that time that any white man in the audience might have claimed me as his slave; and it was easily possible that some of my former owners might be present to hear me speak.

I knew, too, that this was the first time in the entire history of the Negro that a member of my race had been asked to speak from the same platform with white Southern men and women on any important National occasion. I was asked now to speak to an audience composed of the wealth and culture of the white South, the representatives of my former masters. I knew, too, that while the greater part of my audience would be composed of Southern people, yet there would be present a large number of Northern whites, as well as a great many men and women of my own race.

I was determined to say nothing that I did not feel from the bottom of my heart to be true and right. When the invitation came to me, there was not one word of intimation as to what I should say or as to what I should omit. In this I felt that the Board of Directors had paid a tribute to me. They knew that by one sentence I could have blasted, in a large degree, the success of the Exposition. I was also painfully conscious of the fact that, while I must be true to my own race in my utterances, I had it in my power to make such an ill-timed address as would result in preventing any similar invitation being extended to a black man again for years to come. I was equally determined to be true to the North, as well as to the best element of the white South, in what I had to say.

The papers, North and South, had taken up the discussion of my coming speech, and as the time for it drew near this discussion became more and more widespread. Not a few of the Southern white papers were unfriendly to the idea of my speaking. From my own race I received many suggestions as to what I ought to say. I prepared myself as best I could for the address, but as the eighteenth of September drew nearer, the heavier my heart became, and the more I feared that my effort would prove a failure and a disappointment.

The invitation had come at a time when I was very busy with my school work, as it was the beginning of our school year. After preparing my address, I went through it, as I usually do with all those utterances which I consider particularly important, with Mrs. Washington, and she approved of what I intended to say. On the sixteenth of September, the day before I was to start for Atlanta, so many of the Tuskegee teachers expressed a desire to hear my address that I consented to read it to them in a body. When I had done so, and had heard their criticisms and comments, I felt somewhat relieved, since they seemed to think well of what I had to say.

On the morning of September 17, together with Mrs. Washington and my three children, I started for Atlanta. I felt a good deal as I suppose a man feels when he is on his way to the gallows. In passing through the town of Tuskegee I met a white farmer who lived some distance out in the country. In a jesting manner this man said: "Washington, you have spoken before the Northern white people, the Negroes in the South, and to us country white people in the South; but in Atlanta, to-morrow, you will have before you the Northern whites, the Southern whites, and the Negroes all together. I am afraid that you have got yourself into a tight place." This farmer diagnosed the situation correctly, but his frank words did not add anything to my comfort.

In the course of the journey from Tuskegee to Atlanta both coloured and white people came to the train to point me out, and discussed with perfect freedom, in my hearing, what was going to take place the next day. We were met by a committee in Atlanta. Almost the first thing that I heard when I got off the train in that city was an expression something like this, from an old coloured man near by: "Dat's de man of my race what's gwine to make a speech at de Exposition to-morrow. I'se sho' gwine to hear him."

Atlanta was literally packed, at the time, with people from all parts of this country, and with representatives of foreign governments, as well as with military and civic organizations. The afternoon papers had forecasts of the next day's proceedings in flaring headlines. All this tended to add to my burden. I did not sleep much that night. The next morning, before day, I went carefully over what I intended to say. I also kneeled down and asked God's blessing upon my effort. Right here, perhaps, I ought to add that I make it a rule never to go before an audience, on any occasion, without asking the blessing of God upon what I want to say.

I always make it a rule to make especial preparation for each separate address. No two audiences are exactly alike. It is my aim to reach and talk to the heart of each individual audience, taking it into my confidence very much as I would a person. When I am speaking to an audience, I care little for how what I am saying is going to sound in the newspapers, or to another audience, or to an individual. At the time, the audience before me absorbs all my sympathy, thought, and energy.

Early in the morning a committee called to escort me to my place in the procession which was to march to the Exposition grounds. In this procession were prominent coloured citizens in carriages, as well as several Negro military organizations. I noted that the Exposition officials seemed to go out of their way to see that all of the coloured people in the procession were properly placed and properly treated. The procession was about three hours in reaching the Exposition grounds, and during all of this time the sun was shining down upon us disagreeably hot. When we reached the grounds, the heat, together with my nervous anxiety, made me feel as if I were about ready to collapse, and to feel that my address was not going to be a success. When I entered the audience-room, I found it packed with humanity from bottom to top, and there were thousands outside who could not get in.

The room was very large, and well suited to public speaking. When I entered the room, there were vigorous cheers from the coloured portion of the audience, and faint cheers from some of the white people. I had been told, while I had been in Atlanta, that while many white people were going to be present to hear me speak, simply out of curiosity, and that others who would be present would be in full sympathy with me, there was a still larger element of the audience which would consist of those who were going to be present for the purpose of hearing me make a fool of myself, or, at least, of hearing me say some foolish thing, so that they could say to the officials who had invited me to speak, "I told you so!"

One of the trustees of the Tuskegee Institute, as well as my personal friend, Mr. William H. Baldwin, Jr. was at the time General Manager of the Southern Railroad, and happened to be in Atlanta on that day. He was so nervous about the kind of reception that I would have, and the effect that my speech would produce, that he could not persuade himself to go into the building, but walked back and forth in the grounds outside until the opening exercises were over.

CHAPTER XIV

The Atlanta Exposition Address

The Atlanta Exposition, at which I had been asked to make an address as a representative of the Negro race, as stated in the last chapter, was opened with a short address from Governor Bullock. After other interesting exercises, including an invocation from Bishop Nelson, of Georgia, a dedicatory ode by Albert Howell, Jr., and addresses by the President of the Exposition and Mrs. Joseph Thompson, the President of the Woman's Board, Governor Bullock introduced me with the words, "We have with us to-day a representative of Negro enterprise and Negro civilization."

When I arose to speak, there was considerable cheering, especially from the coloured people. As I remember it now, the thing that was uppermost in my mind was the desire to say something that would cement the friendship of the races and bring about hearty coöperation between them. So far as my outward surroundings were concerned, the only thing that I recall distinctly now is that when I got up, I saw thousands of eyes looking intently into my face. The following is the address which I delivered:—

Mr. President and Gentlemen of the Board of Directors and Citizens.

One-third of the population of the South is of the Negro race. No enterprise seeking the material, civil, or moral welfare of this section can disregard this element of our population and reach the highest success. I but convey to you, Mr. President and Directors, the sentiment of the masses of my race when I say that in no way have the value and manhood of the American Negro been more fittingly and generously recognized than by the managers of this magnificent Exposition at every stage of its progress. It is a recognition that will do more to cement the friendship of the two races than any occurrence since the dawn of our freedom.

Not only this, but the opportunity here afforded will awaken among us a new era of industrial progress. Ignorant and inexperienced, it is not strange that in the first years of our new life we began at the top instead of at the bottom; that a seat in Congress or the state legislature was more sought than real estate or industrial skill; that the political convention or stump speaking had more attractions than starting a dairy farm or truck garden.

A ship lost at sea for many days suddenly sighted a friendly vessel. From the mast of the unfortunate vessel was seen a signal, "Water, water; we die of thirst!" The answer from the friendly vessel at once came back, "Cast down your bucket where you are." A second time the signal, "Water, water; send us water!" ran up from the distressed vessel, and was answered, "Cast down your bucket where you are." And a third and fourth signal for water was answered, "Cast down your bucket where you are." The captain of the distressed vessel, at last heeding the injunction, cast down his bucket, and it came up full of fresh, sparkling water from the mouth of the Amazon River. To those of my race who depend on bettering their condition in a foreign land or who underestimate the importance of cultivating friendly relations with the Southern white man, who is their next-door neighbour, I would say: "Cast down your bucket where you are"—cast it down in making friends in every manly way of the people of all races by whom we are surrounded.

Cast it down in agriculture, mechanics, in commerce, in domestic service, and in the professions. And in this connection it is well to bear in mind that whatever other sins the South may be called to bear, when it comes to business, pure and simple, it is in the South that the Negro is given a man's chance in the commercial world, and in nothing is this Exposition more eloquent than in emphasizing this chance. Our greatest danger is that in the great leap from slavery to freedom we may overlook the fact that the masses of us are to live by the productions of our hands, and fail to keep in mind that we shall prosper in proportion as we learn to dignify and glorify common labour and put brains and skill into the common occupations of life; shall prosper in proportion as we learn to draw the line between the superficial and the substantial, the ornamental gewgaws of life and the useful. No race can prosper till it learns that there is as much dignity in tilling a field as in writing a poem. It is at the bottom of life we must begin, and not at the top. Nor should we permit our grievances to overshadow our opportunities.

To those of the white race who look to the incoming of those of foreign birth and strange tongue and habits for the prosperity of the South, were I permitted I would repeat what I say to my own race, "Cast down your bucket where you are." Cast it down among the eight millions of Negroes whose habits you know, whose fidelity and love you have tested in days when to have proved treacherous meant the ruin of your firesides. Cast down your bucket among these people who have, without strikes and labour wars, tilled your fields, cleared your forests, builded your railroads and cities, and brought forth treasures from the bowels of the earth, and helped make possible this magnificent representation of the progress of the South. Casting down your bucket among my people, helping and encouraging them as you are doing on these grounds, and to education of head, hand, and heart, you will find that they will buy your surplus land, make blossom the waste places in your fields, and run your factories. While doing this, you can be sure in the future, as in the past, that you and your families will be surrounded by the most patient, faithful, law-abiding, and unresentful people that the world has seen. As we have proved our loyalty to you in the past, in nursing your children, watching by the sick-bed of your mothers and fathers, and often following them with tear-dimmed eyes to their graves, so in the future, in our humble way, we shall stand by you with a devotion that no foreigner can approach, ready to lay down our lives, if need be, in defence of yours, interlacing our industrial, commercial, civil, and religious life with yours in a way that shall make the interests of both races one. In all things that are purely social we can be as separate as the fingers, yet one as the hand in all things essential to mutual progress.

There is no defence or security for any of us except in the highest intelligence and development of all. If anywhere there are efforts tending to curtail the fullest growth of the Negro, let these efforts be turned into stimulating, encouraging, and making him the most useful and intelligent citizen. Effort or means so invested will pay a thousand per cent interest. These efforts will be twice blessed—"blessing him that gives and him that takes."

There is no escape through law of man or God from the inevitable:—

> *The laws of changeless justice bind*
> *Oppressor with oppressed;*
> *And close as sin and suffering joined*
> *We march to fate abreast.*

Nearly sixteen millions of hands will aid you in pulling the load upward, or they will pull against you the load downward. We shall constitute one-third and more of the ignorance and crime of the South, or one-third its intelligence and progress; we shall contribute one-third to the business and industrial prosperity of the South, or we shall prove a veritable body of death, stagnating, depressing, retarding every effort to advance the body politic.

Gentlemen of the Exposition, as we present to you our humble effort at an exhibition of our progress, you must not expect overmuch. Starting thirty years ago with ownership here and there in a few quilts and pumpkins and chickens (gathered from miscellaneous sources), remember the path that has led from these to the inventions and production of agricultural implements, buggies, steam-engines, newspapers, books, statuary, carving, paintings, the management of drug-stores and banks, has not been trodden without contact with thorns and thistles. While we take pride in what we exhibit as a result of our independent efforts, we do not for a moment forget that our part in this exhibition would fall far short of your expectations but for the constant help that has come to our educational life, not only from the Southern states, but especially from Northern philanthropists, who have made their gifts a constant stream of blessing and encouragement.

The wisest among my race understand that the agitation of questions of social equality is the extremest folly, and that progress in the enjoyment of all the privileges that will come to us must be the result of severe and constant struggle rather than of artificial forcing. No race that has anything to contribute to the markets of the world is long in any degree ostracized. It is important and right that all privileges of the law be ours, but it is vastly more important that we be prepared for the exercises of these privileges. The opportunity to earn a dollar in a factory just now is worth infinitely more than the opportunity to spend a dollar in an opera-house.

In conclusion, may I repeat that nothing in thirty years has given us more hope and encouragement, and drawn us so near to you of the white race, as this opportunity offered by the Exposition; and here bending, as it were, over the altar that represents the results of the struggles of your race and mine, both starting practically empty-handed three decades ago, I pledge that in your effort to work out the great and intricate problem which God has laid at the doors of the South, you shall have at all times the patient, sympathetic help of my race; only let this be constantly in mind, that, while from representations in these buildings of the product of field, of forest, of mine, of factory, letters, and art, much good will come, yet far above and beyond material benefits will be that higher good, that, let us pray God, will come, in a blotting out of sectional differences and racial animosities and suspicions, in a determination to administer absolute justice, in a willing obedience among all classes to the mandates of law. This, this, coupled with our material prosperity, will bring into our beloved South a new heaven and a new earth.

The first thing that I remember, after I had finished speaking, was that Governor Bullock rushed across the platform and took me by the hand, and that others did the same. I received so many and such hearty congratulations that I found it difficult to get out of the building. I did not appreciate to any degree, however, the impression which my address seemed to have made, until the next morning, when I went into the business part of the city. As soon as I was recognized, I was surprised to find myself pointed out and surrounded by a crowd of men who wished to shake hands with me. This was kept up on every street on to which I went, to an extent which embarrassed me so much that I went back to my boarding-place. The next morning I returned to Tuskegee. At the station in Atlanta, and at almost all of the stations at which the train stopped between that city and Tuskegee, I found a crowd of people anxious to shake hands with me.

The papers in all parts of the United States published the address in full, and for months afterward there were complimentary editorial references to it. Mr. Clark Howell, the editor of the Atlanta *Constitution,* telegraphed to a New York paper, among other words, the following, "I do not exaggerate when I say that Professor Booker T. Washington's address yesterday was one of the most notable speeches, both as to character and as to the warmth of its reception, ever delivered to a Southern audience. The address was a revelation. The whole speech is a platform upon which blacks and whites can stand with full justice to each other."

The Boston *Transcript* said editorially: "The speech of Booker T. Washington at the Atlanta Exposition, this week, seems to have dwarfed all the other proceedings and the Exposition itself. The sensation that it has caused in the press has never been equalled."

I very soon began receiving all kinds of propositions from lecture bureaus, and editors of magazines and papers, to take the lecture platform, and to write articles. One lecture bureau offered me fifty thousand dollars, or two hundred dollars a night and expenses, if I would place my services at its disposal for a given period. To all these communications I replied that my life-work was at Tuskegee; and that whenever I spoke it must be in the interests of the Tuskegee school and my race, and that I would enter into no arrangements that seemed to place a mere commercial value upon my services.

Some days after its delivery I sent a copy of my address to the President of the United States, the Hon. Grover Cleveland. I received from him the following autograph reply:—

Gray Gables, Buzzard's Bay, Mass.,
October 6, 1895.

Booker T. Washington, Esq.:

My Dear Sir: I thank you for sending me a copy of your address delivered at the Atlanta Exposition.

I thank you with much enthusiasm for making the address. I have read it with intense interest, and I think the Exposition would be fully justified if it did not do more than furnish the opportunity for its delivery. Your words cannot fail to delight and encourage all who wish well for your race; and if our coloured fellow-citizens do not from your utterances gather new hope and form new determinations to gain every valuable advantage offered them by their citizenship, it will be strange indeed.

Yours very truly,

Grover Cleveland.

Later I met Mr. Cleveland, for the first time, when, as President, he visited the Atlanta Exposition. At the request of myself and others he consented to spend an hour in the Negro Building, for the purpose of inspecting the Negro exhibit and of giving the coloured people in attendance an opportunity to shake hands with him. As soon as I met

Mr. Cleveland I became impressed with his simplicity, greatness, and rugged honesty. I have met him many times since then, both at public functions and at his private residence in Princeton, and the more I see of him the more I admire him. When he visited the Negro Building in Atlanta he seemed to give himself up wholly, for that hour, to the coloured people. He seemed to be as careful to shake hands with some old coloured "auntie" clad partially in rags, and to take as much pleasure in doing so, as if he were greeting some millionaire. Many of the coloured people took advantage of the occasion to get him to write his name in a book or on a slip of paper. He was as careful and patient in doing this as if he were putting his signature to some great state document.

Mr. Cleveland has not only shown his friendship for me in many personal ways, but has always consented to do anything I have asked of him for our school. This he has done, whether it was to make a personal donation or to use his influence in securing the donations of others. Judging from my personal acquaintance with Mr. Cleveland, I do not believe that he is conscious of possessing any colour prejudice. He is too great for that. In my contact with people I find that, as a rule, it is only the little, narrow people who live for themselves, who never read good books, who do not travel, who never open up their souls in a way to permit them to come into contact with other souls—with the great outside world. No man whose vision is bounded by colour can come into contact with what is highest and best in the world. In meeting men, in many places, I have found that the happiest people are those who do the most for others; the most miserable are those who do the least. I have also found that few things, if any, are capable of making one so blind and narrow as race prejudice. I often say to our students, in the course of my talks to them on Sunday evenings in the chapel, that the longer I live and the more experience I have of the world, the more I am convinced that, after all, the one thing that is most worth living for—and dying for, if need be—is the opportunity of making some one else more happy and more useful.

The coloured people and the coloured newspapers at first seemed to be greatly pleased with the character of my Atlanta address, as well as with its reception. But after the first burst of enthusiasm began to die away, and the coloured people began reading the speech in cold type, some of them seemed to feel that they had been hypnotized. They seemed to feel that I had been too liberal in my remarks toward the Southern whites, and that I had not spoken out strongly enough for what they termed the "rights" of the race. For a while there was a reaction, so far as a certain element of my own race was concerned, but later these reactionary ones seemed to have been won over to my way of believing and acting.

While speaking of changes in public sentiment, I recall that about ten years after the school at Tuskegee was established, I had an experience that I shall never forget. Dr. Lyman Abbott, then the pastor of Plymouth Church, and also editor of the *Outlook* (then the *Christian Union*), asked me to write a letter for his paper giving my opinion of the exact condition, mental and moral, of the coloured ministers in the South, as based upon my observations. I wrote the letter, giving the exact facts as I conceived them to be. The picture painted was a rather black one—or, since I am black, shall I say "white"? It could not be otherwise with a race but a few years out of slavery, a race which had not had time or opportunity to produce a competent ministry.

What I said soon reached every Negro minister in the country, I think, and the letters of condemnation which I received from them were not few. I think that for a year after the publication of this article every association and every conference or religious body of any kind, of my race, that met, did not fail before adjourning to pass a resolution condemning me, or calling upon me to retract or modify what I had said. Many of these organizations went so far in their resolutions as to advise parents to cease sending their children to Tuskegee. One association even appointed a "missionary" whose duty it was to warn the people against sending their children to Tuskegee. This missionary had a son in the school, and I noticed that, whatever the "missionary" might have said or done with regard to others, he was careful not to take his son away from the institution. Many of the coloured papers, especially those that were the organs of religious bodies, joined in the general chorus of condemnation or demands for retraction.

During the whole time of the excitement, and through all the criticism, I did not utter a word of explanation or retraction. I knew that I was right, and that time and the sober second thought of the people would vindicate me. It was not long before the bishops and other church leaders began to make a careful investigation of the conditions of the ministry, and they found out that I was right. In fact, the oldest and most influential bishop in one branch of the Methodist Church said that my words were far too mild. Very soon public sentiment began making itself felt, in demanding a purifying of the ministry. While this is not yet complete by any means, I think I may say, without egotism, and I have been told by many of our most influential ministers, that my words had much to do with starting a demand for the placing of a higher type of men in the pulpit. I have had the satisfaction of having many who once condemned me thank me heartily for my frank words.

The change of the attitude of the Negro ministry, so far as regards myself, is so complete that at the present time I have no warmer friends among any class than I have among the clergymen. The improvement in the character and life of the Negro ministers is one of the most gratifying evidences of the progress of the race. My experience with them, as well as other events in my life, convince me that the thing to do, when one feels sure that he has said or done the right thing, and is condemned, is to stand still and keep quiet. If he is right, time will show it.

In the midst of the discussion which was going on concerning my Atlanta speech, I received the letter which I give below, from Dr. Gilman, the President of Johns Hopkins University, who had been made chairman of the judges of award in connection with the Atlanta Exposition:—

Johns Hopkins University, Baltimore,
President's Office, September 30, 1895.

Dear Mr. Washington: Would it be agreeable to you to be one of the Judges of Award in the Department of Education at Atlanta? If so, I shall be glad to place your name upon the list. A line by telegraph will be welcomed.

Yours very truly,
D. C. Gilman.

I think I was even more surprised to receive this invitation than I had been to receive the invitation to speak at the opening of the Exposition. It was to be a part of my duty, as one of the jurors, to pass not only upon the exhibits of the coloured schools, but also upon those of the white schools. I accepted the position, and spent a month in Atlanta in performance of the duties which it entailed. The board of jurors was a large one, consisting in all of sixty members. It was about equally divided between Southern white people and Northern white people. Among them were college presidents, leading scientists and men of letters, and specialists in many subjects. When the group of jurors to which I was assigned met for organization, Mr. Thomas Nelson Page, who was one of the number, moved that I be made secretary of that division, and the motion was unanimously adopted. Nearly half of our division were Southern people. In performing my duties in the inspection of the exhibits of white schools I was in every case treated with respect, and at the close of our labours I parted from my associates with regret.

I am often asked to express myself more freely than I do upon the political condition and the political future of my race. These recollections of my experience in Atlanta give me the opportunity to do so briefly. My own belief is, although I have never before said so in so many words, that the time will come when the Negro in the South will be accorded all the political rights which his ability, character, and material possessions entitle him to. I think, though, that the opportunity to freely exercise such political rights will not come in any large degree through outside or artificial forcing, but will be accorded to the Negro by the Southern white people themselves, and that they will protect him in the exercise of those rights. Just as soon as the South gets over the old feeling that it is being forced by "foreigners," or "aliens," to do something which it does not want to do, I believe that the change in the direction that I have indicated is going to begin. In fact, there are indications that it is already beginning in a slight degree.

Let me illustrate my meaning. Suppose that some months before the opening of the Atlanta Exposition there had been a general demand from the press and public platform outside the South that a Negro be given a place on the opening programme, and that a Negro be placed upon the board of jurors of award. Would any such recognition of the race have taken place? I do not think so. The Atlanta officials went as far as they did because they felt it to be a pleasure, as well as a duty, to reward what they considered merit in the Negro race. Say what we will, there is something in human nature which we cannot blot out, which makes one man, in the end, recognize and reward merit in another, regardless of colour or race.

I believe it is the duty of the Negro—as the greater part of the race is already doing—to deport himself modestly in regard to political claims, depending upon the slow but sure influences that proceed from the possession of property, intelligence, and high character for the full recognition of his political rights. I think that the according of the full exercise of political rights is going to be a matter of natural, slow growth, not an over-night, gourd-vine affair. I do not believe that the Negro should cease voting, for a man cannot learn the exercise of self-government by ceasing to vote, any more than a boy can learn to swim by keeping out of the water, but I do believe that in his voting he should more and more be influenced by those of intelligence and character who are his next-door neighbours.

I know coloured men who, through the encouragement, help, and advice of Southern white people, have accumulated thousands of dollars' worth of property, but who, at the same time, would never think of going to those same persons for advice concerning the casting of their ballots. This, it seems to me, is unwise and unreasonable, and should cease. In saying this I do not mean that the Negro should truckle, or not vote from principle, for the instant he ceases to vote from principle he loses the confidence and respect of the Southern white man even.

I do not believe that any state should make a law that permits an ignorant and poverty-stricken white man to vote, and prevents a black man in the same condition from voting. Such a law is not only unjust, but it will react, as all unjust laws do, in time; for the effect of such a law is to encourage the Negro to secure education and property, and at the same time it encourages the white man to remain in ignorance and poverty. I believe that in time, through the operation of intelligence and friendly race relations, all cheating at the ballot-box in the South will cease. It will become apparent that the white man who begins by cheating a Negro out of his ballot soon learns to cheat a white man out of his, and that the man who does this ends his career of dishonesty by the theft of property or by some equally serious crime. In my opinion, the time will come when the South will encourage all of its citizens to vote. It will see that it pays better, from every standpoint, to have healthy, vigorous life than to have that political stagnation which always results when one-half of the population has no share and no interest in the Government.

As a rule, I believe in universal, free suffrage, but I believe that in the South we are confronted with peculiar conditions that justify the protection of the ballot in many of the states, for a while at least, either by an educational test, a property test, or by both combined; but whatever tests are required, they should be made to apply with equal and exact justice to both races.

CHAPTER XV

The Secret of Success in Public Speaking

As to how my address at Atlanta was received by the audience in the Exposition building, I think I prefer to let Mr. James Creelman, the noted war correspondent, tell. Mr. Creelman was present, and telegraphed the following account to the New York *World:*—

ATLANTA, SEPTEMBER 18.

While President Cleveland was waiting at Gray Gables to-day, to send the electric spark that started the machinery of the Atlanta Exposition, a Negro Moses stood before a great audience of white people and delivered an oration that marks a new epoch in the history of the South; and a body of Negro troops marched in a procession with the citizen soldiery of Georgia and Louisiana. The whole city is thrilling to-night with a realization of the extraordinary significance of these two unprecedented events. Nothing has happened since Henry Grady's immortal speech before the New England society in New York that indicates so profoundly the spirit of the New South, except, perhaps, the opening of the Exposition itself.

When Professor Booker T. Washington, Principal of an industrial school for coloured people in Tuskegee, Ala. stood on the platform of the Auditorium, with the sun shining over the heads of his auditors into his eyes, and with his whole face lit up with the fire of prophecy, Clark Howell, the successor of Henry Grady, said to me, "That man's speech is the beginning of a moral revolution in America."

It is the first time that a Negro has made a speech in the South on any important occasion before an audience composed of white men and women. It electrified the audience, and the response was as if it had come from the throat of a whirlwind.

Mrs. Thompson had hardly taken her seat when all eyes were turned on a tall tawny Negro sitting in the front row of the platform. It was Professor Booker T. Washington, President of the Tuskegee (Alabama) Normal and Industrial Institute, who must rank from this time forth as the foremost man of his race in America. Gilmore's Band played the "Star-Spangled Banner," and the audience cheered. The tune changed to "Dixie" and the audience roared with shrill "hi-yis." Again the music changed, this time to "Yankee Doodle," and the clamour lessened.

All this time the eyes of the thousands present looked straight at the Negro orator. A strange thing was to happen. A black man was to speak for his people, with none to interrupt him. As Professor Washington strode to the edge of the stage, the low, descending sun shot fiery rays through the windows into his face. A great shout greeted him. He turned his head to avoid the blinding light, and moved about the platform for relief. Then he turned his wonderful countenance to the sun without a blink of the eyelids, and began to talk.

There was a remarkable figure; tall, bony, straight as a Sioux chief, high forehead, straight nose, heavy jaws, and strong, determined mouth, with big white teeth, piercing eyes, and a commanding manner. The sinews stood out on his bronzed neck, and his muscular right arm swung high in the air, with a lead-pencil grasped in the clinched brown fist. His big feet were planted squarely, with the heels together and the toes turned out. His voice rang out clear and true, and he paused impressively as he made each point. Within ten minutes the multitude was in an uproar of enthusiasm—handkerchiefs were waved, canes were flourished, hats were tossed in the air. The fairest women of Georgia stood up and cheered. It was as if the orator had bewitched them.

And when he held his dusky hand high above his head, with the fingers stretched wide apart, and said to the white people of the South on behalf of his race, "In all things that are purely social we can be as separate as the fingers, yet one as the hand in all things essential to mutual progress," the great wave of sound dashed itself against the walls, and the whole audience was on its feet in a delirium of applause, and I thought at that moment of the night when Henry Grady stood among the curling wreaths of tobacco-smoke in Delmonico's banquet-hall and said, "I am a Cavalier among Roundheads."

I have heard the great orators of many countries, but not even Gladstone himself could have pleaded a cause with more consummate power than did this angular Negro, standing in a nimbus of sunshine, surrounded by the men who once fought to keep his race in bondage. The roar might swell ever so high, but the expression of his earnest face never changed.

A ragged, ebony giant, squatted on the floor in one of the aisles, watched the orator with burning eyes and tremulous face until the supreme burst of applause came, and then the tears ran down his face. Most of the Negroes in the audience were crying, perhaps without knowing just why.

At the close of the speech Governor Bullock rushed across the stage and seized the orator's hand. Another shout greeted this demonstration, and for a few minutes the two men stood facing each other, hand in hand.

So far as I could spare the time from the immediate work at Tuskegee, after my Atlanta address, I accepted some of the invitations to speak in public which came to me, especially those that would take me into territory where I thought it would pay to plead the cause of my race, but I always did this with the understanding that I was to be free to talk about my life-work and the needs of my people. I also had it understood that I was not to speak in the capacity of a professional lecturer, or for mere commercial gain.

In my efforts on the public platform I never have been able to understand why people come to hear me speak. This question I never can rid myself of. Time and time again, as I have stood in the street in front of a building and have seen men and women passing in large numbers into the audience-room where I was to speak, I have felt ashamed that I should be the cause of people—as it seemed to me— wasting a valuable hour of time. Some years ago I was to deliver an address before a literary society in Madison, Wis. An hour before the time set for me to speak, a fierce snow-storm began, and continued for several hours. I made up my mind that there would be no audience, and that I should not have to speak, but, as a matter of duty, I went to the church, and found it packed with people. The surprise gave me a shock that I did not recover from during the whole evening.

People often ask me if I feel nervous before speaking, or else they suggest that, since I speak so often, they suppose that I get used to it. In answer to this question I have to say that I always suffer intensely from nervousness before speaking. More than once, just before I was to make an important address, this nervous strain has been so great that I have resolved never again to speak in public. I not only feel nervous before speaking, but after I have finished I usually feel a sense of regret, because it seems to me as if I had left out of my address the main thing and the best thing that I had meant to say.

There is a great compensation, though, for this preliminary nervous suffering, that comes to me after I have been speaking for about ten minutes, and have come to feel that I have really mastered my audience, and that we have gotten into full and complete sympathy with each other. It seems to me that there is rarely such a combination of mental and physical delight in any effort as that which comes to a public speaker when he feels that he has a great audience completely within his control. There is a thread of sympathy and oneness that connects a public speaker with his audience, that is just as strong as though it was something tangible and visible. If in an audience of a thousand people there is one person who is not in sympathy with my views, or is inclined to be doubtful, cold, or critical, I can pick him out. When I have found him I usually go straight at him, and it is a great satisfaction to watch the process of his thawing out. I find that the most effective medicine for such individuals is administered at first in the form of a story, although I never tell an anecdote simply for the sake of telling one. That kind of thing, I think, is empty and hollow, and an audience soon finds it out.

I believe that one always does himself and his audience an injustice when he speaks merely for the sake of speaking. I do not believe that one should speak unless, deep down in his heart, he feels convinced that he has a message to deliver. When one feels, from the bottom of his feet to the top of his head, that he has something to say that is going to help some individual or some cause, then let him say it; and in delivering his message I do not believe that many of the artificial rules of elocution can, under such circumstances, help him very much. Although there are certain things, such as pauses, breathing, and pitch of voice, that are very important, none of these can take the place of *soul* in an address. When I have an address to deliver, I like to forget all about the rules for the proper use of the English language, and all about rhetoric and that sort of thing, and I like to make the audience forget all about these things, too.

Nothing tends to throw me off my balance so quickly, when I am speaking, as to have some one leave the room. To prevent this, I make up my mind, as a rule, that I will try to make my address so interesting, will try to state so many interesting facts one after another, that no one can leave. The average audience, I have come to believe, wants facts rather than generalities or sermonizing. Most people, I think, are able to draw proper conclusions if they are given the facts in an interesting form on which to base them.

As to the kind of audience that I like best to talk to, I would put at the top of the list an organization of strong, wide-awake, business men, such, for example, as is found in Boston, New York, Chicago, and Buffalo. I have found no other audience so quick to see a point, and so responsive. Within the last few years I have had the privilege of speaking before most of the leading organizations of this kind in the large cities of the United States. The best time to get hold of an organization of business men is after a good dinner, although I think that one of the worst instruments of torture that was ever invented is the custom which makes it necessary for a speaker to sit through a fourteen-course dinner, every minute of the time feeling sure that his speech is going to prove a dismal failure and disappointment.

I rarely take part in one of these long dinners that I do not wish that I could put myself back in the little cabin where I was a slave boy, and again go through the experience there—one that I shall never forget—of getting molasses to eat once a week from the "big house." Our usual diet on the plantation was corn bread and pork, but on Sunday morning my mother was permitted to bring down a little molasses from the "big house" for her three children, and when it was received how I did wish that every day was Sunday! I would get my tin plate and hold it up for the sweet morsel, but I would always shut my eyes while the molasses was being poured out into the plate, with the hope that when I opened them I would be surprised to see how much I had got. When I opened my eyes I would tip the plate in one direction and another, so as to make the molasses spread all over it, in the full belief that there would be more of it and that it would last longer if spread out in this way. So strong are my childish impressions of those Sunday morning feasts that it would be pretty hard for any one to convince me that there is not more molasses on a plate when it is spread all over the plate than when it occupies a little corner—if there is a corner in a plate. At any rate, I have never believed in "cornering" syrup. My share of the syrup was usually about two tablespoonfuls, and those two spoonfuls of molasses were much more enjoyable to me than is a fourteen-course dinner after which I am to speak.

Next to a company of business men, I prefer to speak to an

audience of Southern people, of either race, together or taken separately. Their enthusiasm and responsiveness are a constant delight. The "amens" and "dat's de truf" that come spontaneously from the coloured individuals are calculated to spur any speaker on to his best efforts. I think that next in order of preference I would place a college audience. It has been my privilege to deliver addresses at many of our leading colleges, including Harvard, Yale, Williams, Amherst, Fisk University, the University of Pennsylvania, Wellesley, the University of Michigan, Trinity College in North Carolina, and many others.

It has been a matter of deep interest to me to note the number of people who have come to shake hands with me after an address, who say that this is the first time they have ever called a Negro "Mister."

When speaking directly in the interests of the Tuskegee Institute, I usually arrange, some time in advance, a series of meetings in important centres. This takes me before churches, Sunday-schools, Christian Endeavour Societies, and men's and women's clubs. When doing this I sometimes speak before as many as four organizations in a single day.

Three years ago, at the suggestion of Mr. Morris K. Jesup, of New York, and Dr. J. L. M. Curry, the general agent of the fund, the trustees of the John F. Slater Fund voted a sum of money to be used in paying the expenses of Mrs. Washington and myself while holding a series of meetings among the coloured people in the large centres of Negro population, especially in the large cities of the ex-slaveholding states. Each year during the last three years we have devoted some weeks to this work. The plan that we have followed has been for me to speak in the morning to the ministers, teachers, and professional men. In the afternoon Mrs. Washington would speak to the women alone, and in the evening I spoke to a large mass-meeting. In almost every case the meetings have been attended not only by the coloured people in large numbers, but by the white people. In Chattanooga, Tenn., for example, there was present at the mass-meeting an audience of not less than three thousand persons, and I was informed that eight hundred of these were white. I have done no work that I really enjoyed more than this, or that I think has accomplished more good.

These meetings have given Mrs. Washington and myself an opportunity to get first-hand, accurate information as to the real condition of the race, by seeing the people in their homes, their churches, their Sunday-schools, and their places of work, as well as in the prisons and dens of crime. These meetings also gave us an opportunity to see the relations that exist between the races. I never feel so hopeful about the race as I do after being engaged in a series of these meetings. I know that on such occasions there is much that comes to the surface that is superficial and deceptive, but I have had experience enough not to be deceived by mere signs and fleeting enthusiasms. I have taken pains to go to the bottom of things and get facts, in a cold, business-like manner.

I have seen the statement made lately, by one who claims to know what he is talking about, that, taking the whole Negro race into account, ninety per cent of the Negro women are not virtuous. There never was a baser falsehood uttered concerning a race, or a statement made that was less capable of being proved by actual facts.

No one can come into contact with the race for twenty years, as I have done in the heart of the South, without being convinced that the race is constantly making slow but sure progress materially, educationally, and morally. One might take up the life of the worst element in New York City, for example, and prove almost anything he wanted to prove concerning the white man, but all will agree that this is not a fair test.

Early in the year 1897 I received a letter inviting me to deliver an address at the dedication of the Robert Gould Shaw monument in Boston. I accepted the invitation. It is not necessary for me, I am sure, to explain who Robert Gould Shaw was, and what he did. The monument to his memory stands near the head of Boston Common, facing the State House. It is counted to be the most perfect piece of art of the kind to be found in the country.

The exercises connected with the dedication were held in Music

Hall, in Boston, and the great hall was packed from top to bottom with one of the most distinguished audiences that ever assembled in the city. Among those present there were more persons representing the famous old anti-slavery element than it is likely will ever be brought together in the country again. The late Hon. Roger Wolcott, then Governor of Massachusetts, was the presiding officer, and on the platform with him were many other officials and hundreds of distinguished men. A report of the meeting which appeared in the Boston *Transcript* will describe it better than any words of mine could do:—

The core and kernel of yesterday's great noon meeting in honour of the Brotherhood of Man, in Music Hall, was the superb address of the Negro President of Tuskegee. "Booker T. Washington received his Harvard A. M. last June, the first of his race," said Governor Wolcott, "to receive an honorary degree from the oldest university in the land, and this for the wise leadership of his people." When Mr. Washington rose in the flag-filled, enthusiasm-warmed, patriotic, and glowing atmosphere of Music Hall, people felt keenly that here was the civic justification of the old abolition spirit of Massachusetts; in his person the proof of her ancient and indomitable faith; in his strong thought and rich oratory, the crown and glory of the old war days of suffering and strife. The scene was full of historic beauty and deep significance. "Cold" Boston was alive with the fire that is always hot in her heart for righteousness and truth. Rows and rows of people who are seldom seen at any public function, whole families of those who are certain to be out of town on a holiday, crowded the place to overflowing. The city was at her birthright *fête* in the persons of hundreds of her best citizens, men and women whose names and lives stand for the virtues that make for honourable civic pride.

Battle-music had filled the air. Ovation after ovation, applause warm and prolonged, had greeted the officers and friends of Colonel Shaw, the sculptor, St. Gaudens, the memorial Committee, the Governor and his staff, and the Negro soldiers of the Fifty-fourth Massachusetts as they came upon the platform or entered the hall. Colonel Henry Lee, of Governor Andrew's old staff, had made a noble, simple presentation speech for the committee, paying tribute to Mr. John M. Forbes, in whose stead he served. Governor Wolcott had made his short, memorable speech, saying, "Fort Wagner marked an epoch in the history of a race, and called it into manhood." Mayor Quincy had received the monument for the city of Boston. The story of Colonel Shaw and his black regiment had been told in gallant words, and then, after the singing of

> *Mine eyes have seen the glory*
> *Of the coming of the Lord,*

Booker Washington arose. It was, of course, just the moment for him. The multitude, shaken out of its usual symphony-concert calm, quivered with an excitement that was not suppressed. A dozen times it had sprung to its feet to cheer and wave and hurrah, as one person. When this man of culture and voice and power, as well as a dark skin, began, and uttered the names of Stearns and of Andrew, feeling began to mount. You could see tears glisten in the eyes of soldiers and civilians. When the orator turned to the coloured soldiers on the platform, to the colour-bearer of Fort Wagner, who smilingly bore still the flag he had never lowered even when wounded, and said, "To you, to the scarred and scattered remnants of the Fifty-fourth, who, with empty sleeve and wanting leg, have honoured this occasion with your presence, to you, your commander is not dead. Though Boston erected no monument and history recorded no story, in you and in the loyal race which you represent, Robert Gould Shaw would have a monument which time could not wear away," then came the climax of the emotion of the day and the hour. It was Roger Wolcott, as well as the Governor of Massachusetts, the individual representative of the people's sympathy as well as the chief magistrate, who had sprung first to his feet and cried, "Three cheers to Booker T. Washington!"

Among those on the platform was Sergeant William H. Carney, of New Bedford, Mass., the brave coloured officer who was the colour-bearer at Fort Wagner and held the American flag. In spite of the fact that a large part of his regiment was killed, he escaped, and exclaimed, after the battle was over, "The old flag never touched the ground."

This flag Sergeant Carney held in his hands as he sat on the platform, and when I turned to address the survivors of the coloured regiment who were present, and referred to Sergeant Carney, he rose, as if by instinct, and raised the flag. It has been my privilege to witness a good many satisfactory and rather sensational demonstrations in connection with some of my public addresses, but in dramatic effect I have never seen or experienced anything which equalled this. For a number of minutes the audience seemed to entirely lose control of itself.

In the general rejoicing throughout the country which followed the close of the Spanish-American war, peace celebrations were arranged in several of the large cities. I was asked by President William R. Harper, of the University of Chicago, who was chairman of the committee of invitations for the celebration to be held in the city of Chicago, to deliver one of the addresses at the celebration there. I accepted the invitation, and delivered two addresses there during the Jubilee week. The first of these, and the principal one, was given in the Auditorium, on the evening of Sunday, October 16. This was the largest audience that I have ever addressed, in any part of the country; and besides speaking in the main Auditorium, I also addressed, that same evening, two overflow audiences in other parts of the city.

It was said that there were sixteen thousand persons in the Auditorium, and it seemed to me as if there were as many more on the outside trying to get in. It was impossible for any one to get near the entrance without the aid of a policeman. President William McKinley attended this meeting, as did also the members of his Cabinet, many foreign ministers, and a large number of army and navy officers, many of whom had distinguished themselves in the war which had just closed. The speakers, besides myself, on Sunday evening, were Rabbi Emil G. Hirsch, Father Thomas P. Hodnett, and Dr. John H. Barrows.

The Chicago *Times-Herald,* in describing the meeting, said of my address:—

He pictured the Negro choosing slavery rather than extinction; recalled Crispus Attucks shedding his blood at the beginning of the American Revolution, that white Americans might be free, while black Americans remained in slavery; rehearsed the conduct of the Negroes with Jackson at New Orleans; drew a vivid and pathetic picture of the Southern slaves protecting and supporting the families of their masters while the latter were fighting to perpetuate black slavery; recounted the bravery of coloured troops at Port Hudson and Forts Wagner and Pillow, and praised the heroism of the black regiments that stormed El Caney and Santiago to give freedom to the enslaved people of Cuba, forgetting, for the time being, the unjust discrimination that law and custom make against them in their own country.

In all of these things, the speaker declared, his race had chosen the better part. And then he made his eloquent appeal to the consciences of the white Americans: "When you have gotten the full story of the heroic conduct of the Negro in the Spanish-American war, have heard it from the lips of Northern soldier and Southern soldier, from ex-abolitionist and ex-masters, then decide within yourselves whether a race that is thus willing to die for its country should not be given the highest opportunity to live for its country."

The part of the speech which seemed to arouse the wildest and most sensational enthusiasm was that in which I thanked the President for his recognition of the Negro in his appointments during the Spanish-American war. The President was sitting in a box at the right of the stage. When I addressed him I turned toward the box, and as I finished the sentence thanking him for his generosity, the whole audience rose and cheered again and again, waving handkerchiefs and hats and canes, until the President arose in the box and bowed his acknowledgments. At that the enthusiasm broke out again, and the demonstration was almost indescribable.

One portion of my address at Chicago seemed to have been misunderstood by the Southern press, and some of the Southern papers took occasion to criticise me rather strongly. These criticisms continued for several weeks, until I finally received a letter from the editor of the *Age-Herald*, published in Birmingham, Ala., asking me if I would say just what I meant by this part of my address. I replied to him in a letter which seemed to satisfy my critics. In this letter I said that I had made it a rule never to say before a Northern audience anything that I would not say before an audience in the South. I said that I did not think it was necessary for me to go into extended explanations; if my seventeen years of work in the heart of the South had not been explanation enough, I did not see how words could explain. I said that I made the same plea that I had made in my address at Atlanta, for the blotting out of race prejudice in "commercial and civil relations." I said that what is termed social recognition was a question which I never discussed, and then I quoted from my Atlanta address what I had said there in regard to that subject.

In meeting crowds of people at public gatherings, there is one type of individual that I dread. I mean the crank. I have become so accustomed to these people now that I can pick them out at a distance when I see them elbowing their way up to me. The average crank has a long beard, poorly cared for, a lean, narrow face, and wears a black coat. The front of his vest and coat are slick with grease, and his trousers bag at the knees.

In Chicago, after I had spoken at a meeting, I met one of these fellows. They usually have some process for curing all of the ills of the world at once. This Chicago specimen had a patent process by which he said Indian corn could be kept through a period of three or four years, and he felt sure that if the Negro race in the South would, as a whole, adopt his process, it would settle the whole race question. It mattered nothing that I tried to convince him that our present problem was to teach the Negroes how to produce enough corn to last them through one year. Another Chicago crank had a scheme by which he wanted me to join him in an effort to close up all the National banks in the country. If that was done, he felt sure it would put the Negro on his feet.

The number of people who stand ready to consume one's time, to no purpose, is almost countless. At one time I spoke before a large audience in Boston in the evening. The next morning I was awakened by having a card brought to my room, and with it a message that some one was anxious to see me. Thinking that it must be something very important, I dressed hastily and went down. When I reached the hotel office I found a blank and innocent-looking individual waiting for me, who coolly remarked: "I heard you talk at a meeting last night. I rather liked your talk, and so I came in this morning to hear you talk some more."

I am often asked how it is possible for me to superintend the work at Tuskegee and at the same time be so much away from the school. In partial answer to this I would say that I think I have learned, in some degree at least, to disregard the old maxim which says, "Do not get others to do that which you can do yourself." My motto, on the other hand, is, "Do not do that which others can do as well."

One of the most encouraging signs in connection with the Tuskegee school is found in the fact that the organization is so thorough that the daily work of the school is not dependent upon the presence of any one individual. The whole executive force, including instructors and clerks, now numbers eighty-six. This force is so organized and subdivided that the machinery of the school goes on day by day like clockwork. Most of our teachers have been connected with the institution for a number of years, and are as much interested in it as I am. In my absence, Mr. Warren Logan, the treasurer, who has been at the school seventeen years, is the executive. He is efficiently supported by Mrs. Washington, and by my faithful secretary, Mr. Emmett J. Scott, who handles the bulk of my correspondence and keeps me in daily touch with the life of the school, and who also keeps me informed of whatever takes place in the South that concerns the race. I owe more to his tact, wisdom, and hard work than I can describe.

The main executive work of the school, whether I am at Tuskegee or not, centres in what we call the executive council. This council meets twice a week, and is composed of the nine persons who are at the head of the nine departments of the school. For example: Mrs. B. K. Bruce, the Lady Principal, the widow of the late ex-senator Bruce, is a member of the council, and represents in it all that pertains to the life of the girls at the school. In addition to the executive council there is a financial committee of six, that meets every week and decides upon the expenditures for the week. Once a month, and sometimes oftener, there is a general meeting of all the instructors. Aside from these there are innumerable smaller meetings, such as that of the instructors in the Phelps Hall Bible Training School, or of the instructors in the agricultural department.

In order that I may keep in constant touch with the life of the institution, I have a system of reports so arranged that a record of the school's work reaches me every day in the year, no matter in what part of the country I am. I know by these reports even what students are excused from school, and why they are excused—whether for reasons of ill health or otherwise. Through the medium of these reports I know each day what the income of the school in money is; I know how many gallons of milk and how many pounds of butter come from the dairy; what the bill of fare for the teachers and students is; whether a certain kind of meat was boiled or baked, and whether certain vegetables served in the dining room were bought from a store or procured from our own farm. Human nature I find to be very much the same the world over, and it is sometimes not hard to yield to the temptation to go to a barrel of rice that has come from the store—with the grain all prepared to go into the pot—rather than to take the time and trouble to go to the field and dig and wash one's own sweet potatoes, which might be prepared in a manner to take the place of the rice.

Emmett J. Scott came to Tuskegee at the age of twenty-four in 1897 and for close to twenty years served Washington as private secretary, confidant, and "vice-president" of the Tuskegee Machine.

I am often asked how, in the midst of so much work, a large part of which is before the public, I can find time for any rest or recreation, and what kind of recreation or sports I am fond of. This is rather a difficult question to answer. I have a strong feeling that every individual owes it to himself, and to the cause which he is serving, to keep a vigorous, healthy body, with the nerves steady and strong, prepared for great efforts and prepared for disappointments and trying positions. As far as I can, I make it a rule to plan for each day's work—not merely to go through with the same routine of daily duties, but to get rid of the routine work as early in the day as possible, and then to enter upon some new or advance work. I make it a rule to clear my desk every day, before leaving my office, of all correspondence and memoranda, so that on the morrow I can begin a *new* day of work. I make it a rule never to let my work drive me, but to so master it, and keep it in such complete control, and to keep so far ahead of it, that I will be the master instead of the servant. There is a physical and mental and spiritual enjoyment that comes from a consciousness of being the absolute master of one's work, in all its details, that is very satisfactory and inspiring. My experience teaches me that, if one learns to follow this plan, he gets a freshness of body and vigour of mind out of work that goes a long way toward keeping him strong and healthy. I believe that when one can grow to the point where he loves his work, this gives him a kind of strength that is most valuable.

When I begin my work in the morning, I expect to have a successful and pleasant day of it, but at the same time I prepare myself for unpleasant and unexpected hard places. I prepare myself to hear that one of our school buildings is on fire, or has burned, or that some disagreeable accident has occurred, or that some one has abused me in a public address or printed article, for something that I have done or omitted to do, or for something that he had heard that I had said—probably something that I had never thought of saying.

In nineteen years of continuous work I have taken but one vacation. That was two years ago, when some of my friends put the money into my hands and forced Mrs. Washington and myself to spend three months in Europe. I have said that I believe it is the duty of every one to keep his body in good condition. I try to look after the little ills, with the idea that if I take care of the little ills the big ones will not come. When I find myself unable to sleep well, I know that something is wrong. If I find any part of my system the least weak, and not performing its duty, I consult a good physician. The ability to sleep well, at any time and in any place, I find of great advantage. I have so trained myself that I can lie down for a nap of fifteen or twenty minutes, and get up refreshed in body and mind.

I have said that I make it a rule to finish up each day's work before leaving it. There is, perhaps, one exception to this. When I have an unusually difficult question to decide—one that appeals strongly to the emotions—I find it a safe rule to sleep over it for a night, or to wait until I have had an opportunity to talk it over with my wife and friends.

As to my reading; the most time I get for solid reading is when I am on the cars. Newspapers are to me a constant source of delight and recreation. The only trouble is that I read too many of them. Fiction I care little for. Frequently I have to almost force myself to read a novel that is on every one's lips. The kind of reading that I have the greatest fondness for is biography. I like to be sure that I am reading about a real man or a real thing. I think I do not go too far when I say that I have read nearly every book and magazine article that has been written about Abraham Lincoln. In literature he is my patron saint.

Out of the twelve months in a year I suppose that, on an average, I spend six months away from Tuskegee. While my being absent from the school so much unquestionably has its disadvantages, yet there are at the same time some compensations. The change of work brings a certain kind of rest. I enjoy a ride of a long distance on the cars, when I am permitted to ride where I can be comfortable. I get rest on the cars, except when the inevitable individual who seems to be on every train approaches me with the now familiar phrase: "Isn't this Booker Washington? I want to introduce myself to you." Absence from the school enables me to lose sight of the unimportant details of the work, and study it in a broader and more comprehensive manner than I could do on the grounds. This absence also brings me into contact with the best work being done in educational lines, and into contact with the best educators in the land.

But, after all this is said, the time when I get the most solid rest and recreation is when I can be at Tuskegee, and, after our evening meal is over, can sit down, as is our custom, with my wife and Portia and Baker and Davidson, my three children, and read a story, or each take turns in telling a story. To me there is nothing on earth equal to that, although what is nearly equal to it is to go with them for an hour or more, as we like to do on Sunday afternoons, into the woods, where we can live for a while near the heart of nature, where no one can disturb or vex us, surrounded by pure air, the trees, the shrubbery, the flowers, and the sweet fragrance that springs from a hundred plants, enjoying the chirp of the crickets and the songs of the birds. This is solid rest.

My garden, also, what little time I can be at Tuskegee, is another source of rest and enjoyment. Somehow I like, as often as possible, to touch nature, not something that is artificial or an imitation, but the real thing. When I can leave my office in time so that I can spend thirty or forty minutes in spading the ground, in planting seeds, in digging about the plants, I feel that I am coming into contact with something that is giving me strength for the many duties and hard places that await me out in the big world. I pity the man or woman who has never learned to enjoy nature and to get strength and inspiration out of it.

Aside from the large number of fowls and animals kept by the school, I keep individually a number of pigs and fowls of the best grades, and in raising these I take a great deal of pleasure. I think the pig is my favourite animal. Few things are more satisfactory to me than a high-grade Berkshire or Poland China pig.

Games I care little for. I have never seen a game of football. In cards I do not know one card from another. A game of old-fashioned marbles with my two boys, once in a while, is all I care for in this direction. I suppose I would care for games now if I had had any time in my youth to give to them, but that was not possible.

CHAPTER XVI

Europe

In 1893 I was married to Miss Margaret James Murray, a native of Mississippi, and a graduate of Fisk University, in Nashville, Tenn., who had come to Tuskegee as a teacher several years before, and at the time we were married was filling the position of Lady Principal. Not only is Mrs. Washington completely one with me in the work directly connected with the school, relieving me of many burdens and perplexities, but aside from her work on the school grounds, she carries on a mothers' meeting in the town of Tuskegee, and a plantation work among the women, children, and men who live in a settlement connected with a large plantation about eight miles from Tuskegee. Both the mothers' meeting and the plantation work are carried on, not only with a view to helping those who are directly reached, but also for the purpose of furnishing object-lessons in these two kinds of work that may be followed by our students when they go out into the world for their own life-work.

Aside from these two enterprises, Mrs. Washington is also largely responsible for a woman's club at the school which brings together, twice a month, the women who live on the school grounds and those who live near, for the discussion of some important topic. She is also the President of what is known as the Federation of Southern Col-

In addition to her role at Tuskegee, Margaret James Murray Washington was a dynamo in the Negro Women's Club Movement. She served as co-founder, first vice president, and second president of the National Federation of Afro-American Women and co-founder and fifth president of the premier black women's organization of the early twentieth century, the National Association of Colored Women.

oured Women's Clubs, and is Chairman of the Executive Committee of the National Federation of Coloured Women's Clubs.

Portia, the oldest of my three children, has learned dressmaking. She has unusual ability in instrumental music. Aside from her studies at Tuskegee, she has already begun to teach there.

Baker Taliaferro is my next oldest child. Young as he is, he has already nearly mastered the brick-mason's trade. He began working at this trade when he was quite small, dividing his time between this and class work; and he has developed great skill in the trade and a fondness for it. He says that he is going to be an architect and brickmason. One of the most satisfactory letters that I have ever received from any one came to me from Baker last summer. When I left home for the summer, I told him that he must work at his trade half of each day, and that the other half of the day he could spend as he pleased. When I had been away from home two weeks, I received the following letter from him:

TUSKEGEE, ALABAMA.

MY DEAR PAPA: Before you left home you told me to work at my trade half of each day. I like my work so much that I want to work at my trade all day. Besides, I want to earn all the money I can, so that when I go to another school I shall have money to pay my expenses.

Your son,
BAKER.

My youngest child, Ernest Davidson Washington, says that he is going to be a physician. In addition to going to school, where he studies books and has manual training, he regularly spends a portion of his time in the office of our resident physician, and has already learned to do many of the duties which pertain to a doctor's office.

The thing in my life which brings me the keenest regret is that my work in connection with public affairs keeps me for so much of the time away from my family, where, of all places in the world, I

Washington's Tuskegee residence, The Oaks, was designed by the first black graduate of M.I.T., Robert Robertson Taylor, and built, in 1899, by Tuskegee students and faculty with materials produced on campus. The Oaks was restored by the National Park Service in 1981.

delight to be. I always envy the individual whose life-work is so laid that he can spend his evenings at home. I have sometimes thought that people who have this rare privilege do not appreciate it as they should. It is such a rest and relief to get away from crowds of people, and handshaking, and travelling, and get home, even if it be for but a very brief while.

Another thing at Tuskegee out of which I get a great deal of pleasure and satisfaction is in the meeting with our students, and teachers, and their families, in the chapel for devotional exercises every evening at half-past eight, the last thing before retiring for the night. It is an inspiring sight when one stands on the platform there and sees before him eleven or twelve hundred earnest young men and women; and one cannot but feel that it is a privilege to help to guide them to a higher and more useful life.

In the spring of 1899 there came to me what I might describe as almost the greatest surprise of my life. Some good ladies in Boston arranged a public meeting in the interests of Tuskegee, to be held in the Hollis Street Theatre. This meeting was attended by large numbers of the best people of Boston, of both races. Bishop Lawrence presided. In addition to an address made by myself, Mr. Paul Lawrence Dunbar read from his poems, and Dr. W. E. B. Du Bois read an original sketch.

Some of those who attended this meeting noticed that I seemed unusually tired, and some little time after the close of the meeting, one of the ladies who had been interested in it asked me in a casual way if I had ever been to Europe. I replied that I never had. She asked me if I had ever thought of going, and I told her no; that it was something entirely beyond me. This conversation soon passed out of my mind, but a few days afterward I was informed that some friends in Boston, including Mr. Francis J. Garrison, had raised a sum of money sufficient to pay all the expenses of Mrs. Washington and myself during a three or four months' trip to Europe. It was added with emphasis that we *must* go. A year previous to this Mr. Garrison had attempted to get me to promise to go to Europe for a summer's rest, with the understanding that he would be responsible for raising the money among his friends for the expenses of the trip. At that time such a journey seemed so entirely foreign to anything that I should ever be able to undertake that I confess I did not give the matter very serious attention; but later Mr. Garrison joined his efforts to those of the ladies whom I have mentioned, and when their plans were made known to me Mr. Garrison not only had the route mapped out, but had, I believe, selected the steamer upon which we were to sail.

The whole thing was so sudden and so unexpected that I was completely taken off my feet. I had been at work steadily for eighteen years in connection with Tuskegee, and I had never thought of anything else but ending my life in that way. Each day the school seemed to depend upon me more largely for its daily expenses, and I told these Boston friends that, while I thanked them sincerely for their thoughtfulness and generosity, I could not go to Europe, for the reason that the school could not live financially while I was absent. They then informed me that Mr. Henry L. Higginson, and some other good friends who I know do not want their names made public, were then raising a sum of money which would be sufficient to keep the school in operation while I was away. At this point I was compelled to surrender. Every avenue of escape had been closed.

Deep down in my heart the whole thing seemed more like a dream than like reality, and for a long time it was difficult for me to make myself believe that I was actually going to Europe. I had been born and largely reared in the lowest depths of slavery, ignorance, and poverty. In my childhood I had suffered for want of a place to sleep, for lack of food, clothing, and shelter. I had not had the privilege of sitting down to a dining-table until I was quite well grown. Luxuries had always seemed to me to be something meant for white people, not for my race. I had always regarded Europe, and London, and Paris, much as I regard heaven. And now could it be that I was actually going to Europe? Such thoughts as these were constantly with me.

Two other thoughts troubled me a good deal. I feared that people who heard that Mrs. Washington and I were going to Europe might not know all the circumstances, and might get the idea that we had become, as some might say, "stuck up," and were trying to "show off." I recalled that from my youth I had heard it said that too often, when people of my race reached any degree of success, they were inclined to unduly exalt themselves; to try and ape the wealthy, and in so doing to lose their heads. The fear that people might think this of us haunted me a good deal. Then, too, I could not see how my conscience would permit me to spare the time from my work and be happy. It seemed mean and selfish in me to be taking a vacation while others were at work, and while there was so much that needed to be done. From the time I could remember, I had always been at work, and I did not see how I could spend three or four months in doing nothing. The fact was that I did not know how to take a vacation.

Mrs. Washington had much the same difficulty in getting away, but she was anxious to go because she thought that I needed the rest. There were many important National questions bearing upon the life of the race which were being agitated at that time, and this made it all the harder for us to decide to go. We finally gave our Boston friends our promise that we would go, and then they insisted that the date of our departure be set as soon as possible. So we decided upon May 10. My good friend Mr. Garrison kindly took charge of all the details necessary for the success of the trip, and he, as well as other friends, gave us a great number of letters of introduction to people in France and England, and made other arrangements for our comfort and convenience abroad. Good-bys were said at Tuskegee, and we were in New York May 9, ready to sail the next day. Our daughter Portia, who was then studying in South Framingham, Mass., came to New York to see us off. Mr. Scott, my secretary, came with me to New York, in order that I might clear up the last bit of business before I left. Other friends also came to New York to see us off. Just before we went on board the steamer another pleasant surprise came to us in the form of a letter from two generous ladies, stating that they had decided to give us the money with which to erect a new building to be used in properly housing all our industries for girls at Tuskegee.

We were to sail on the *Friesland*, of the Red Star Line, and a beautiful vessel she was. We went on board just before noon, the hour of sailing. I had never before been on board a large ocean steamer, and the feeling which took possession of me when I found myself there is rather hard to describe. It was a feeling, I think, of awe mingled with delight. We were agreeably surprised to find that the captain, as well as several of the other officers, not only knew who we were, but was expecting us and gave us a pleasant greeting. There were several passengers whom we knew, including Senator Sewell, of New Jersey, and Edward Marshall, the newspaper correspondent. I had just a little fear that we would not be treated civilly by some of the passengers. This fear was based upon what I had heard other people of my race, who had crossed the ocean, say about unpleasant experiences in crossing the ocean in American vessels. But in our case, from the captain down to the most humble servant, we were treated with the greatest kindness. Nor was this kindness confined to those who were connected with the steamer; it was shown by all the passengers also. There were not a few Southern men and women on board, and they were as cordial as those from other parts of the country.

As soon as the last good-bys were said, and the steamer had cut loose from the wharf, the load of care, anxiety, and responsibility which I had carried for eighteen years began to lift itself from my shoulders at the rate, it seemed to me, of a pound a minute. It was the first time in all those years that I had felt, even in a measure, free from care; and my feeling of relief it is hard to describe on paper. Added to this was the delightful anticipation of being in Europe soon. It all seemed more like a dream than like a reality.

Mr. Garrison had thoughtfully arranged to have us have one of the most comfortable rooms on the ship. The second or third day out

I began to sleep, and I think that I slept at the rate of fifteen hours a day during the remainder of the ten days' passage. Then it was that I began to understand how tired I really was. These long sleeps I kept up for a month after we landed on the other side. It was such an unusual feeling to wake up in the morning and realize that I had no engagements; did not have to take a train at a certain hour; did not have an appointment to meet some one, or to make an address, at a certain hour. How different all this was from some of the experiences that I have been through when travelling, when I have sometimes slept in three different beds in a single night!

When Sunday came, the captain invited me to conduct the religious services, but, not being a minister, I declined. The passengers, however, began making requests that I deliver an address to them in the dining-saloon some time during the voyage, and this I consented to do. Senator Sewell presided at this meeting. After ten days of delightful weather, during which I was not seasick for a day, we landed at the interesting old city of Antwerp, in Belgium.

The next day after we landed happened to be one of those numberless holidays which the people of those countries are in the habit of observing. It was a bright, beautiful day. Our room in the hotel faced the main public square, and the sights there—the people coming in from the country with all kinds of beautiful flowers to sell, the women coming in with their dogs drawing large, brightly polished cans filled with milk, the people streaming into the cathedral—filled me with a sense of newness that I had never before experienced.

After spending some time in Antwerp, we were invited to go with a party of a half-dozen persons on a trip through Holland. This party included Edward Marshall and some American artists who had come over on the same steamer with us. We accepted the invitation, and enjoyed the trip greatly. I think it was all the more interesting and instructive because we went for most of the way on one of the slow, old-fashioned canal-boats. This gave us an opportunity of seeing and studying the real life of the people in the country districts. We went in this way as far as Rotterdam, and later went to The Hague, where the Peace Conference was then in session, and where we were kindly received by the American representatives.

The thing that impressed itself most on me in Holland was the thoroughness of the agriculture and the excellence of the Holstein cattle. I never knew, before visiting Holland, how much it was possible for people to get out of a small plot of ground. It seemed to me that absolutely no land was wasted. It was worth a trip to Holland, too, just to get a sight of three or four hundred fine Holstein cows grazing in one of those intensely green fields.

From Holland we went to Belgium, and made a hasty trip through that country, stopping at Brussels, where we visited the battlefield of Waterloo. From Belgium we went direct to Paris, where we found that Mr. Theodore Stanton, the son of Mrs. Elizabeth Cady Stanton, had kindly provided accommodations for us. We had barely got settled in Paris before an invitation came to me from the University Club of Paris to be its guest at a banquet which was soon to be given. The other guests were ex-President Benjamin Harrison and Archbishop Ireland, who were in Paris at the time. The American Ambassador, General Horace Porter, presided at the banquet. My address on this occasion seemed to give satisfaction to those who heard it. General Harrison kindly devoted a large portion of his remarks at dinner to myself and to the influence of the work at Tuskegee on the American race question. After my address at this banquet other invitations came to me, but I declined the most of them, knowing that if I accepted them all, the object of my visit would be defeated. I did, however, consent to deliver an address in the American chapel the following Sunday morning, and at this meeting General Harrison, General Porter, and other distinguished Americans were present.

Later we received a formal call from the American Ambassador, and were invited to attend a reception at his residence. At this reception we met many Americans, among them Justices Fuller and

Harlan, of the United States Supreme Court. During our entire stay of a month in Paris, both the American Ambassador and his wife, as well as several other Americans, were very kind to us.

While in Paris we saw a good deal of the now rather famous American Negro painter, Mr. Henry O. Tanner, whom we had formerly known in America. It was very satisfactory to find how well known Mr. Tanner was in the field of art, and to note the high standing which all classes accorded to him. When we told some Americans that we were going to the Luxembourg Palace to see a painting by an American Negro, it was hard to convince them that a Negro had been thus honoured. I do not believe that they were really convinced of the fact until they saw the picture for themselves. My acquaintance with Mr. Tanner reënforced in my mind the truth which I am constantly trying to impress upon our students at Tuskegee—and on our people throughout the country, as far as I can reach them with my voice—that any man, regardless of colour, will be recognized and rewarded just in proportion as he learns to do something well—learns to do it better than some one else—however humble the thing may be. As I have said, I believe that my race will succeed in proportion as it learns to do a common thing in an uncommon manner; learns to do a thing so thoroughly that no one can improve upon what it has done; learns to make its services of indispensable value. This was the spirit that inspired me in my first effort at Hampton, when I was given the opportunity to sweep and dust that schoolroom. In a degree I felt that my whole future life depended upon the thoroughness with which I cleaned that room, and I was determined to do it so well that no one could find any fault with the job. Few people ever stopped, I found, when looking at his pictures, to inquire whether Mr. Tanner was a Negro painter, a French painter, or a German painter. They simply knew that he was able to produce something which the world wanted—a great painting—and the matter of his colour did not enter into their minds. When a Negro girl learns to cook, to wash dishes, to sew, to write a book, or a Negro boy learns to groom horses, or to grow sweet potatoes, or to produce butter, or to build a house, or to be able to practise medicine, as well or better than some one else, they will be rewarded regardless of race or colour. In the long run, the world is going to have the best, and any difference in race, religion, or previous history will not long keep the world from what it wants.

I think that the whole future of my race hinges on the question as to whether or not it can make itself of such indispensable value that the people in the town and the state where we reside will feel that our presence is necessary to the happiness and well-being of the community. No man who continues to add something to the material, intellectual, and moral well-being of the place in which he lives is long left without proper reward. This is a great human law which cannot be permanently nullified.

The love of pleasure and excitement which seems in a large measure to possess the French people impressed itself upon me. I think they are more noted in this respect than is true of the people of my own race. In point of morality and moral earnestness I do not believe that the French are ahead of my own race in America. Severe competition and the great stress of life have led them to learn to do things more thoroughly and to exercise greater economy; but time, I think, will bring my race to the same point. In the matter of truth and high honour I do not believe that the average Frenchman is ahead of the American Negro; while so far as mercy and kindness to dumb animals go, I believe that my race is far ahead. In fact, when I left France, I had more faith in the future of the black man in America than I had ever possessed.

From Paris we went to London, and reached there early in July, just about the height of the London social season. Parliament was in session, and there was a great deal of gaiety. Mr. Garrison and other friends had provided us with a large number of letters of introduction, and they had also sent letters to other persons in different parts of the United Kingdom, apprising these people of our coming. Very soon after reaching London we were flooded with invitations to attend all manner of social functions, and a great many invitations came to me asking that I deliver public addresses. The most of these invitations I declined, for the reason that I wanted to rest. Neither were we able to accept more than a small proportion of the other invitations. The Rev. Dr. Brooke Herford and Mrs. Herford, whom I had known in Boston, consulted with the American Ambassador, the Hon. Joseph Choate, and arranged for me to speak at a public meeting to be held in Essex Hall. Mr. Choate kindly consented to preside. The meeting was largely attended. There were many distinguished persons present, among them several members of Parliament, including Mr. James Bryce, who spoke at the meeting. What the American Ambassador said in introducing me, as well as a synopsis of what I said, was widely published in England and in the American papers at the time. Dr. and Mrs. Herford gave Mrs. Washington and myself a reception, at which we had the privilege of meeting some of the best people in England. Throughout our stay in London Ambassador Choate was most kind and attentive to us. At the Ambassador's reception I met, for the first time, Mark Twain.

We were the guests several times of Mrs. T. Fisher Unwin, the daughter of the English statesman, Richard Cobden. It seemed as if both Mr. and Mrs. Unwin could not do enough for our comfort and happiness. Later, for nearly a week, we were the guests of the daughter of John Bright, now Mrs. Clark, of Street, England. Both Mr. and Mrs. Clark, with their daughter, visited us at Tuskegee the next year. In Birmingham, England, we were the guests for several days of Mr. Joseph Sturge, whose father was a great abolitionist and friend of Whittier and Garrison. It was a great privilege to meet throughout England those who had known and honoured the late William Lloyd Garrison, the Hon. Frederick Douglass, and other abolitionists. The English abolitionists with whom we came in contact never seemed to tire of talking about these two Americans. Before going to England I had had no proper conception of the deep interest displayed by the abolitionists of England in the cause of freedom, nor did I realize the amount of substantial help given by them.

In Bristol, England, both Mrs. Washington and I spoke at the Women's Liberal Club. I was also the principal speaker at the Commencement exercises of the Royal College for the Blind. These exercises were held in the Crystal Palace, and the presiding officer was the late Duke of Westminster, who was said to be, I believe, the richest man in England, if not in the world. The Duke, as well as his wife and their daughter, seemed to be pleased with what I said, and thanked me heartily. Through the kindness of Lady Aberdeen, my wife and I were enabled to go with a party of those who were attending the International Congress of Women, then in session in London, to see Queen Victoria, at Windsor Castle, where, afterward, we were all the guests of her Majesty at tea. In our party was Miss Susan B. Anthony, and I was deeply impressed with the fact that one did not often get an opportunity to see, during the same hour, two women so remarkable in different ways as Susan B. Anthony and Queen Victoria.

In the House of Commons, which we visited several times, we met Sir Henry M. Stanley. I talked with him about Africa and its relation to the American Negro, and after my interview with him I became more convinced than ever that there was no hope of the American Negro's improving his condition by emigrating to Africa.

On various occasions Mrs. Washington and I were the guests of Englishmen in their country homes, where, I think, one sees the Englishman at his best. In one thing, at least, I feel sure that the English are ahead of Americans, and that is, that they have learned how to get more out of life. The home life of the English seems to me to be about as perfect as anything can be. Everything moves like clockwork. I was impressed, too, with the deference that the servants show to their "masters" and "mistresses,"—terms which I suppose would not be tolerated in America. The English servant expects, as a rule, to be nothing but a servant, and so he perfects himself in the art to a degree that no class of servants in America has yet reached. In our country the servant expects to become, in a few years, a "master" himself. Which system is preferable? I will not venture an answer.

Another thing that impressed itself upon me throughout England was the high regard that all classes have for law and order, and the ease and thoroughness with which everything is done. The Englishmen, I found, took plenty of time for eating, as for everything else. I am not sure if, in the long run, they do not accomplish as much or more than rushing, nervous Americans do.

My visit to England gave me a higher regard for the nobility than I had had. I had no idea that they were so generally loved and respected by the masses, nor had I any correct conception of how much time and money they spent in works of philanthropy, and how much real heart they put into this work. My impression had been that they merely spent money freely and had a "good time."

It was hard for me to get accustomed to speaking to English audiences. The average Englishman is so serious, and is so tremendously in earnest about everything, that when I told a story that would have made an American audience roar with laughter, the Englishmen simply looked me straight in the face without even cracking a smile.

When the Englishman takes you into his heart and friendship, he binds you there as with cords of steel, and I do not believe that there are many other friendships that are so lasting or so satisfactory. Perhaps I can illustrate this point in no better way than by relating the following incident. Mrs. Washington and I were invited to attend a reception given by the Duke and Duchess of Sutherland, at Stafford House—said to be the finest house in London; I may add that I believe the Duchess of Sutherland is said to be the most beautiful woman in England. There must have been at least three hundred persons at this reception. Twice during the evening the Duchess sought us out for a conversation, and she asked me to write her when we got home, and tell her more about the work at Tuskegee. This I did. When Christmas came we were surprised and delighted to receive her photograph with her autograph on it. The correspondence has continued, and we now feel that in the Duchess of Sutherland we have one of our warmest friends.

After three months in Europe we sailed from Southampton in the steamship *St. Louis*. On this steamer there was a fine library that had been presented to the ship by the citizens of St. Louis, Mo. In this library I found a life of Frederick Douglass, which I began reading. I became especially interested in Mr. Douglass's description of the way he was treated on shipboard during his first or second visit to England. In this description he told how he was not permitted to enter the cabin, but had to confine himself to the deck of the ship. A few minutes after I had finished reading this description I was waited on by a committee of ladies and gentlemen with the request that I deliver an address at a concert which was to be given the following evening. And yet there are people who are bold enough to say that race feeling in America is not growing less intense! At this concert the Hon. Benjamin B. Odell, Jr., the present governor of New York, presided. I was never given a more cordial hearing anywhere. A large proportion of the passengers were Southern people. After the concert some of the passengers proposed that a subscription be raised to help the work at Tuskegee, and the money to support several scholarships was the result.

While we were in Paris I was very pleasantly surprised to receive the following invitation from the citizens of West Virginia and of the city near which I had spent my boyhood days:—

CHARLESTON, W. VA., MAY 16, 1899.
PROFESSOR BOOKER T. WASHINGTON, PARIS, FRANCE:

DEAR SIR: Many of the best citizens of West Virginia have united in liberal expressions of admiration and praise of your worth and work, and desire that on your return from Europe you should favour them with your presence and with the inspiration of your words. We most sincerely indorse this move, and on behalf of the citizens of Charleston extend to you our most cordial invitation to have you come to us, that we may honour you who have done so much by your life and work to honour us.

  We are,   Very truly yours,

THE COMMON COUNCIL OF THE CITY OF CHARLESTON,

        By W. HERMAN SMITH, Mayor.

This invitation from the City Council of Charleston was accompanied by the following:—

PROFESSOR BOOKER T. WASHINGTON, PARIS, FRANCE:

DEAR SIR: We, the citizens of Charleston and West Virginia, desire to express our pride in you and the splendid career that you have thus far accomplished, and ask that we be permitted to show our pride and interest in a substantial way.

Your recent visit to your old home in our midst awoke within us the keenest regret that we were not permitted to hear you and render some substantial aid to your work, before you left for Europe.

In view of the foregoing, we earnestly invite you to share the hospitality of our city upon your return from Europe, and give us the opportunity to hear you and put ourselves in touch with your work in a way that will be most gratifying to yourself, and that we may receive the inspiration of your words and presence.

An early reply to this invitation, with an indication of the time you may reach our city, will greatly oblige,

       Yours very respectfully,

  The Charleston *Daily Gazette*, The *Daily Mail-Tribune*; G. W. Atkinson, Governor; E. L. Boggs, Secretary to Governor; Wm. M. O. Dawson, Secretary of State; L. M. La Follette, Auditor; J. R. Trotter, Superintendent of Schools; E. W. Wilson, ex-Governor; W. A. MacCorkle, ex-Governor; John Q. Dickinson, President Kanawha Valley Bank; L. Prichard, President Charleston National Bank; Geo. S. Couch, President

Kanawha National Bank; Ed. Reid, Cashier Kanawha National Bank; Geo. S. Laidley, Superintendent City Schools; L. E. McWhorter, President Board of Education; Chas. K. Payne, wholesale merchant; and many others.

This invitation, coming as it did from the City Council, the state officers, and all the substantial citizens of both races of the community where I had spent my boyhood, and from which I had gone a few years before, unknown, in poverty and ignorance, in quest of an education, not only surprised me, but almost unmanned me. I could not understand what I had done to deserve it all.

I accepted the invitation, and at the appointed day was met at the railway station at Charleston by a committee headed by ex-Governor W. A. MacCorkle, and composed of men of both races. The public reception was held in the Opera-House at Charleston. The Governor of the state, the Hon. George W. Atkinson, presided, and an address of welcome was made by ex-Governor MacCorkle. A prominent part in the reception was taken by the coloured citizens. The Opera-House was filled with citizens of both races, and among the white people were many for whom I had worked when a boy. The next day Governor and Mrs. Atkinson gave me a public reception at the State House, which was attended by all classes.

Not long after this the coloured people in Atlanta, Georgia, gave me a reception at which the Governor of the state presided, and a similar reception was given me in New Orleans, which was presided over by the Mayor of the city. Invitations came from many other places which I was not able to accept.

CHAPTER XVII

Last Words

Before going to Europe some events came into my life which were great surprises to me. In fact, my whole life has largely been one of surprises. I believe that any man's life will be filled with constant, unexpected encouragements of this kind if he makes up his mind to do his level best each day of his life—that is, tries to make each day reach as nearly as possible the high-water mark of pure, unselfish, useful living. I pity the man, black or white, who has never experienced the joy and satisfaction that come to one by reason of an effort to assist in making some one else more useful and more happy.

Six months before he died, and nearly a year after he had been stricken with paralysis, General Armstrong expressed a wish to visit Tuskegee again before he passed away. Notwithstanding the fact that he had lost the use of his limbs to such an extent that he was practically helpless, his wish was gratified, and he was brought to Tuskegee. The owners of the Tuskegee Railroad, white men living in the town, offered to run a special train, without cost, out to the main station—Chehaw, five miles away—to meet him. He arrived on the school grounds about nine o'clock in the evening. Some one had suggested that we give the General a "pine-knot torchlight reception." This plan was carried out, and the moment that his carriage entered the school grounds he began passing between two lines of lighted and waving "fat pine" wood knots held by over a thousand students and teachers. The whole thing was so novel and surprising that the General was completely overcome with happiness. He remained a guest in my home for nearly two months, and, although almost wholly without the use of voice or limb, he spent nearly every hour in devising ways and means to help the South. Time and time again he said to me, during this visit, that it was not only the duty of the country to assist in elevating the Negro of the South, but the poor white man as well. At the end of his visit I resolved anew to devote myself more earnestly than ever to the cause which was so near his heart. I said that if a man in his condition was willing to think, work, and act, I should not be wanting in furthering in every possible way the wish of his heart.

The death of General Armstrong, a few weeks later, gave me the privilege of getting acquainted with one of the finest, most unselfish, and most attractive men that I have ever come in contact with. I refer to the Rev. Dr. Hollis B. Frissell, now the Principal of the Hampton Institute, and General Armstrong's successor. Under the clear, strong, and almost perfect leadership of Dr. Frissell, Hampton has had a career of prosperity and usefulness that is all that the General could have wished for. It seems to be the constant effort of Dr. Frissell to hide his own great personality behind that of General Armstrong—to make himself of "no reputation" for the sake of the cause.

More than once I have been asked what was the greatest surprise that ever came to me. I have little hesitation in answering that question. It was the following letter, which came to me one Sunday morning when I was sitting on the veranda of my home at Tuskegee, surrounded by my wife and three children:—

HARVARD UNIVERSITY, CAMBRIDGE, MAY 28, 1896.

PRESIDENT BOOKER T. WASHINGTON,

MY DEAR SIR: Harvard University desires to confer on you at the approaching Commencement an honorary degree; but it is our custom to confer degrees only on gentlemen who are present. Our Commencement occurs this year on June 24, and your presence would be desirable from about noon till about five o'clock in the afternoon. Would it be possible for you to be in Cambridge on that day?

Believe me, with great regard,

Very truly yours,
CHARLES W. ELIOT.

This was a recognition that had never in the slightest manner entered into my mind, and it was hard for me to realize that I was to be honoured by a degree from the oldest and most renowned university in America. As I sat upon my veranda, with this letter in my hand, tears came into my eyes. My whole former life—my life as a slave on the plantation, my work in the coal-mine, the times when I was without food and clothing, when I made my bed under a sidewalk, my struggles for an education, the trying days I had had at Tuskegee, days when I did not know where to turn for a dollar to continue the work there, the ostracism and sometimes oppression of my race,—all this passed before me and nearly overcame me.

I had never sought or cared for what the world calls fame. I have always looked upon fame as something to be used in accomplishing good. I have often said to my friends that if I can use whatever prominence may have come to me as an instrument with which to do good, I am content to have it. I care for it only as a means to be used for doing good, just as wealth may be used. The more I come into contact with wealthy people, the more I believe that they are growing in the direction of looking upon their money simply as an instrument which God has placed in their hand for doing good with. I never go to the office of Mr. John D. Rockefeller, who more than once has been generous to Tuskegee, without being reminded of this. The close, careful, and minute investigation that he always makes in order to be sure that every dollar that he gives will do the most good—an investigation that is just as searching as if he were investing money in a business enterprise—convinces me that the growth in this direction is most encouraging.

At nine o'clock, on the morning of June 24, I met President Eliot, the Board of Overseers of Harvard University, and the other guests, at the designated place on the university grounds, for the purpose of being escorted to Sanders Theatre, where the Commencement exercises were to be held and degrees conferred. Among others invited to be present for the purpose of receiving a degree at this time were General Nelson A. Miles, Dr. Bell, the inventor of the Bell telephone, Bishop Vincent, and the Rev. Minot J. Savage. We were placed in line immediately behind the President and the Board of Overseers, and directly afterward the Governor of Massachusetts, escorted by the Lancers, arrived and took his place in the line of march by the side of President Eliot. In the line there were also various other officers and professors, clad in cap and gown. In this order we marched to Sanders Theatre, where, after the usual Commencement exercises, came the conferring of the honorary degrees. This, it seems, is always considered the most interesting feature at Harvard. It is not known, until the individuals appear, upon whom the honorary degrees are to be conferred, and those receiving these honours are cheered by the students and others in proportion to their popularity. During the conferring of the degrees excitement and enthusiasm are at the highest pitch.

When my name was called, I rose, and President Eliot, in beautiful and strong English, conferred upon me the degree of Master of Arts. After these exercises were over, those who had received honorary degrees were invited to lunch with the President. After the lunch we were formed in line again, and were escorted by the Marshal of the day, who that year happened to be Bishop William Lawrence, through the grounds, where, at different points, those who had been honoured were called by name and received the Harvard yell. This march ended at Memorial Hall, where the alumni dinner was served. To see over a thousand strong men, representing all that is best in State, Church, business, and education, with the glow and enthusiasm of college loyalty and college pride,—which has, I think, a peculiar Harvard flavour,—is a sight that does not easily fade from memory.

Among the speakers after dinner were President Eliot, Governor Roger Wolcott, General Miles, Dr. Minot J. Savage, the Hon. Henry Cabot Lodge, and myself. When I was called upon, I said, among other things:—

It would in some measure relieve my embarrassment if I could, even in a slight degree, feel myself worthy of the great honour which you do me to-day. Why you have called me from the Black Belt of the South, from among my humble people, to share in the honours of this occasion, is not for me to explain; and yet it may not be inappropriate for me to suggest that it seems to me that one of the most vital questions that touch our American life is how to bring the strong, wealthy, and learned into helpful touch with the poorest, most ignorant, and humblest, and at the same time make one appreciate the vitalizing, strengthening influence of the other. How shall we make the mansions on yon Beacon Street feel and see the need of the spirits in the lowliest cabin in Alabama cottonfields or Louisiana sugar-bottoms? This problem Harvard University is solving, not by bringing itself down, but by bringing the masses up.

* * * * *

If my life in the past has meant anything in the lifting up of my people and the bringing about of better relations between your race and mine, I assure you from this day it will mean doubly more. In the economy of God there is but one standard by which an individual can succeed—there is but one for a race. This country demands that every race shall measure itself by the American standard. By it a race must rise or fall, succeed or fail, and in the last analysis mere sentiment counts for little. During the next half-century and more, my race must continue passing through the severe American crucible. We are to be tested in our patience, our forbearance, our perseverance, our power to endure wrong, to withstand temptations, to economize, to acquire and use skill; in our ability to compete, to succeed in commerce, to disregard the superficial for the real, the appearance for the substance, to be great and yet small, learned and yet simple, high and yet the servant of all.

As this was the first time that a New England university had conferred an honorary degree upon a Negro, it was the occasion of much newspaper comment throughout the country. A correspondent of a New York paper said:—

When the name of Booker T. Washington was called, and he arose to acknowledge and accept, there was such an outburst of applause as greeted no other name except that of the popular soldier patriot, General Miles. The applause was not studied and stiff, sympathetic and condoling; it was enthusiasm and admiration. Every part of the audience from pit to gallery joined in, and a glow covered the cheeks of those around me, proving sincere appreciation of the rising struggle of an ex-slave and the work he has accomplished for his race.

A Boston paper said, editorially:—

In conferring the honorary degree of Master of Arts upon the Principal of Tuskegee Institute, Harvard University has honoured itself as well as the object of this distinction. The work which Professor Booker T. Washington has accomplished for the education, good citizenship, and popular enlightenment in his chosen field of labour in the South entitles him to rank with our national benefactors. The university which can claim him on its list of sons, whether in regular course or *honoris causa,* may be proud.

It has been mentioned that Mr. Washington is the first of his race to receive an honorary degree from a New England university. This, in itself, is a distinction. But the degree was not conferred because Mr. Washington is a coloured man, or because he was born in slavery, but because he has shown, by his work for the elevation of the people of the Black Belt of the South, a genius and a broad humanity which count for greatness in any man, whether his skin be white or black.

Another Boston paper said:—

It is Harvard which, first among New England colleges, confers an honorary degree upon a black man. No one who has followed the history of Tuskegee and its work can fail to admire the courage, persistence, and splendid common sense of Booker T. Washington. Well may Harvard honour the ex-slave, the value of whose services, alike to his race and country, only the future can estimate.

The correspondent of the New York *Times* wrote:—

All the speeches were enthusiastically received, but the coloured man carried off the oratorical honours, and the applause which broke out when he had finished was vociferous and long-continued.

Soon after I began work at Tuskegee I formed a resolution, in the secret of my heart, that I would try to build up a school that would be of so much service to the country that the President of the United States would one day come to see it. This was, I confess, rather a bold resolution, and for a number of years I kept it hidden in my own thoughts, not daring to share it with any one.

In November, 1897, I made the first move in this direction, and that was in securing a visit from a member of President McKinley's Cabinet, the Hon. James Wilson, Secretary of Agriculture. He came to deliver an address at the formal opening of the Slater-Armstrong Agricultural Building, our first large building to be used for the purpose of giving training to our students in agriculture and kindred branches.

In the fall of 1898 I heard that President McKinley was likely to visit Atlanta, Georgia, for the purpose of taking part in the Peace Jubilee exercises to be held there to commemorate the successful close of the Spanish-American war. At this time I had been hard at work, together with our teachers, for eighteen years, trying to build up a school that we thought would be of service to the Nation, and I determined to make a direct effort to secure a visit from the President and his Cabinet. I went to Washington, and I was not long in the city before I found my way to the White House. When I got there I found the waiting rooms full of people, and my heart began to sink, for I feared there would not be much chance of my seeing the President that day, if at all. But, at any rate, I got an opportunity to see Mr. J. Addison Porter, the secretary to the President, and explained to him my mission. Mr. Porter kindly sent my card directly to the President, and in a few minutes word came from Mr. McKinley that he would see me.

How any man can see so many people of all kinds, with all kinds of errands, and do so much hard work, and still keep himself calm, patient, and fresh for each visitor in the way that President McKinley does, I cannot understand. When I saw the President he kindly thanked me for the work which we were doing at Tuskegee for the interests of the country. I then told him, briefly, the object of my visit. I impressed upon him the fact that a visit from the Chief Executive of the Nation would not only encourage our students and teachers, but would help the entire race. He seemed interested, but did not make a promise to go to Tuskegee, for the reason that his plans about going to Atlanta were not then fully made; but he asked me to call the matter to his attention a few weeks later.

By the middle of the following month the President had definitely decided to attend the Peace Jubilee at Atlanta. I went to Washington again and saw him, with a view of getting him to extend his trip to Tuskegee. On this second visit Mr. Charles W. Hare, a prominent white citizen of Tuskegee, kindly volunteered to accompany me, to reënforce my invitation with one from the white people of Tuskegee and the vicinity.

Just previous to my going to Washington the second time, the country had been excited, and the coloured people greatly depressed, because of several severe race riots which had occurred at different points in the South. As soon as I saw the President, I perceived that his heart was greatly burdened by reason of these race disturbances.

Although there were many people waiting to see him, he detained me for some time, discussing the condition and prospects of the race. He remarked several times that he was determined to show his interest and faith in the race, not merely in words, but by acts. When I told him that I thought that at that time scarcely anything would go farther in giving hope and encouragement to the race than the fact that the President of the Nation would be willing to travel one hundred and forty miles out of his way to spend a day at a Negro institution, he seemed deeply impressed.

While I was with the President, a white citizen of Atlanta, a Democrat and an ex-slaveholder, came into the room, and the President asked his opinion as to the wisdom of his going to Tuskegee. Without hesitation the Atlanta man replied that it was the proper thing for him to do. This opinion was reënforced by that friend of the race, Dr. J. L. M. Curry. The President promised that he would visit our school on the 16th of December.

When it became known that the President was going to visit our school, the white citizens of the town of Tuskegee—a mile distant from the school—were as much pleased as were our students and teachers. The white people of the town, including both men and women, began arranging to decorate the town, and to form themselves into committees for the purpose of coöperating with the officers of our school in order that the distinguished visitor might have a fitting reception. I think I never realized before this how much the white people of Tuskegee and vicinity thought of our institution. During the days when we were preparing for the President's reception, dozens of these people came to me and said that, while they did not want to push themselves into prominence, if there was anything they could do to help, or to relieve me personally, I had but to intimate it and they would be only too glad to assist. In fact, the thing that touched me almost as deeply as the visit of the President itself was the deep pride which all classes of citizens in Alabama seemed to take in our work.

The morning of December 16th brought to the little city of Tuskegee such a crowd as it had never seen before. With the President came Mrs. McKinley and all of the Cabinet officers but one; and most of them brought their wives or some members of their families. Several prominent generals came, including General Shafter and General Joseph Wheeler, who were recently returned from the Spanish-American war. There was also a host of newspaper correspondents. The Alabama Legislature was in session at Montgomery at this time. This body passed a resolution to adjourn for the purpose of visiting Tuskegee. Just before the arrival of the President's party the Legislature arrived, headed by the governor and other state officials.

The citizens of Tuskegee had decorated the town from the station to the school in a generous manner. In order to economize in the matter of time, we arranged to have the whole school pass in review before the President. Each student carried a stalk of sugar-cane with some open bolls of cotton fastened to the end of it. Following the students the work of all departments of the school passed in review, displayed on "floats" drawn by horses, mules, and oxen. On these floats we tried to exhibit not only the present work of the school, but to show the contrasts between the old methods of doing things and the new. As an example, we showed the old method of dairying in contrast with the improved methods, the old methods of tilling the soil in contrast with the new, the old methods of cooking and housekeeping in contrast with the new. These floats consumed an hour and a half of time in passing.

In his address in our large, new chapel, which the students had recently completed, the President said, among other things:—

> To meet you under such pleasant auspices and to have the opportunity of a personal observation of your work is indeed most gratifying. The Tuskegee Normal and Industrial Institute is ideal in its conception, and has already a large and growing reputation in the country, and is not unknown abroad. I congratulate all who are associ-

ated in this undertaking for the good work which it is doing in the education of its students to lead lives of honour and usefulness, thus exalting the race for which it was established.

Nowhere, I think, could a more delightful location have been chosen for this unique educational experiment, which has attracted the attention and won the support even of conservative philanthropists in all sections of the country.

To speak of Tuskegee without paying special tribute to Booker T. Washington's genius and perseverance would be impossible. The inception of this noble enterprise was his, and he deserves high credit for it. His was the enthusiasm and enterprise which made its steady progress possible and established in the institution its present high standard of accomplishment. He has won a worthy reputation as one of the great leaders of his race, widely known and much respected at home and abroad as an accomplished educator, a great orator, and a true philanthropist.

The Hon. John D. Long, the Secretary of the Navy, said in part:—

I cannot make a speech to-day. My heart is too full—full of hope, admiration, and pride for my countrymen of both sections and both colours. I am filled with gratitude and admiration for your work, and from this time forward I shall have absolute confidence in your progress and in the solution of the problem in which you are engaged.

The problem, I say, has been solved. A picture has been presented to-day which should be put upon canvas with the pictures of Washington and Lincoln, and transmitted to future time and generations—a picture which the press of the country should spread broadcast over the land, a most dramatic picture, and that picture is this: The President of the United States standing on this platform; on one side the Governor of Alabama, on the other, completing the trinity, a representative of a race only a few years ago in bondage, the coloured President of the Tuskegee Normal and Industrial Institute.

God bless the President under whose majesty such a scene as that is presented to the American people. God bless the state of Alabama, which is showing that it can deal with this problem for itself. God bless the orator, philanthropist, and disciple of the Great Master—who, if he were on earth, would be doing the same work—Booker T. Washington.

Postmaster General Smith closed the address which he made with these words:—

We have witnessed many spectacles within the last few days. We have seen the magnificent grandeur and the magnificent achievements of one of the great metropolitan cities of the South. We have seen heroes of the war pass by in procession. We have seen floral parades. But I am sure my colleagues will agree with me in saying that we have witnessed no spectacle more impressive and more encouraging, more inspiring for our future, than that which we have witnessed here this morning.

Some days after the President returned to Washington I received the letter which follows:—

EXECUTIVE MANSION, WASHINGTON, DEC. 23, 1899.

DEAR SIR: By this mail I take pleasure in sending you engrossed copies of the souvenir of the visit of the President to your institution. These sheets bear the autographs of the President and the members of the Cabinet who accompanied him on the trip. Let me take this opportunity of congratulating you most heartily and sincerely upon the great success of the exercises provided for and entertainment furnished us under your auspices during our visit to Tuskegee. Every feature of the programme was perfectly executed and was viewed or participated in with the heartiest satisfaction by every visitor present. The unique exhibition which you gave of your pupils engaged in their industrial vocations was not only artistic but thoroughly impressive. The tribute paid by the President and his Cabinet to your work was none too high, and forms a most encouraging augury, I think, for the future prosperity of your institution. I cannot close without assuring you that the modesty shown by yourself in the exercises was most favourably commented upon by all the members of our party.

With best wishes for the continued advance of your most useful and patriotic undertaking, kind personal regards, and the compliments of the season, believe me, always,

Very sincerely yours,
JOHN ADDISON PORTER,
Secretary to the President.

To PRESIDENT BOOKER T. WASHINGTON, Tuskegee Normal and Industrial Institute, Tuskegee, Ala.

Twenty years have now passed since I made the first humble effort at Tuskegee, in a broken-down shanty and an old hen-house, without owning a dollar's worth of property, and with but one teacher and thirty students. At the present time the institution owns twenty-three hundred acres of land, over seven hundred of which are under cultivation each year, entirely by student labour. There are now upon the grounds, counting large and small, forty buildings; and all except four of these have been almost wholly erected by the labour of our students. While the students are at work upon the land and in erecting buildings, they are taught, by competent instructors, the latest methods of agriculture and the trades connected with building.

There are in constant operation at the school, in connection with thorough academic and religious training, twenty-eight industrial departments. All of these teach industries at which our men and women can find immediate employment as soon as they leave the institution. The only difficulty now is that the demand for our graduates from both white and black people in the South is so great that we cannot supply more than one-half the persons for whom applications come

Here, in 1906, with Mr. and Mrs. Washington and some Tuskegee faculty and staff, are two of the school's most ardent supporters, Andrew Carnegie (seated at Washington's left) and an early trustee of Hampton Institute, businessman Robert C. Ogden (seated at Margaret Washington's right).

to us. Neither have we the buildings nor the money for current expenses to enable us to admit to the school more than one-half the young men and women who apply to us for admission.

In our industrial teaching we keep three things in mind: first, that the student shall be so educated that he shall be enabled to meet conditions as they exist *now*, in the part of the South where he lives—in a word, to be able to do the thing which the world wants done; second, that every student who graduates from the school shall have enough skill, coupled with intelligence and moral character, to enable him to make a living for himself and others; third, to send every graduate out feeling and knowing that labour is dignified and beautiful—to make each one love labour instead of trying to escape it. In addition to the agricultural training which we give to young men, and the training given to our girls in all the usual domestic employments, we now train a number of girls in agriculture each year. These girls are taught gardening, fruit-growing, dairying, bee-culture, and poultry-raising.

While the institution is in no sense denominational, we have a department known as the Phelps Hall Bible Training School, in which a number of students are prepared for the ministry and other forms of Christian work, especially work in the country districts. What is equally important, each one of these students works half of each day at some industry, in order to get skill and the love of work, so that when he goes out from the institution he is prepared to set the people with whom he goes to labour a proper example in the matter of industry.

The value of our property is now over $300,000. If we add to this our endowment fund, which at present is $215,000, the value of the total property is now nearly half a million dollars. Aside from the need for more buildings and for money for current expenses, the endowment fund should be increased to at least $500,000. The annual current expenses are now about $80,000. The greater part of this I collect each year by going from door to door and from house to house. All of our property is free from mortgage, and is deeded to an undenominational board of trustees who have the control of the institution.

From thirty students the number has grown to eleven hundred, coming from twenty-seven states and territories, from Africa, Cuba, Porto Rico, Jamaica, and other foreign countries. In our departments there are eighty-six officers and instructors; and if we add the families of our instructors, we have a constant population upon our grounds of not far from fourteen hundred people.

I have often been asked how we keep so large a body of people together, and at the same time keep them out of mischief. There are two answers: that the men and women who come to us for an education are in earnest; and that everybody is kept busy. The following outline of our daily work will testify to this:—

5 A.M., rising bell; 5.50 A.M., warning breakfast bell; 6 A.M., breakfast bell; 6.20 A.M., breakfast over; 6.20 to 6.50 A.M., rooms are cleaned; 6.50, work bell; 7.30, morning study hour; 8.20, morning school bell; 8.25, inspection of young men's toilet in ranks; 8.40, devotional exercises in chapel; 8.55, "five minutes with the daily news;" 9 A.M., class work begins; 12, class work closes; 12.15 P.M., dinner; 1 P.M., work bell; 1.30 P.M., class work begins; 3.30 P.M., class work ends; 5.30 P.M., bell to "knock off" work; 6 P.M., supper; 7.10 P.M., evening prayers; 7.30 P.M., evening study hours; 8.45 P.M., evening study hour closes; 9.20 P.M., warning retiring bell; 9.30 P.M., retiring bell.

We try to keep constantly in mind the fact that the worth of the school is to be judged by its graduates. Counting those who have finished the full course, together with those who have taken enough training to enable them to do reasonably good work, we can safely say that at least three thousand men and women from Tuskegee are now at work in different parts of the South; men and women who, by their own example or by direct effort, are showing the masses of our

A Tuskegee instructor and three graduates. The caption to this photograph in The Outlook *informed readers that "these men have gone to Africa, under the auspices of the German Government, to teach cotton-raising to the natives of Togoland. Ancestors of two of these men came from this part of Africa."*

race how to improve their material, educational, and moral and religious life. What is equally important, they are exhibiting a degree of common sense and self-control which is causing better relations to exist between the races, and is causing the Southern white man to learn to believe in the value of educating the men and women of my race. Aside from this, there is the influence that is constantly being exerted through the mothers' meeting and the plantation work conducted by Mrs. Washington.

Wherever our graduates go, the changes which soon begin to appear in the buying of land, improving homes, saving money, in education, and in high moral character are remarkable. Whole communities are fast being revolutionized through the instrumentality of these men and women.

Ten years ago I organized at Tuskegee the first Negro Conference. This is an annual gathering which now brings to the school eight or nine hundred representative men and women of the race, who come to spend a day in finding out what the actual industrial, mental, and moral conditions of the people are, and in forming plans for improvement. Out from this central Negro Conference at Tuskegee have grown numerous state and local conferences which are doing the same kind of work. As a result of the influence of these gatherings, one delegate reported at the last annual meeting that ten families in his community had bought and paid for homes. On the day following the annual Negro Conference, there is held the "Workers' Conference." This is composed of officers and teachers who are engaged in educational work in the larger institutions in the South. The Negro Conference furnishes a rare opportunity for these workers to study the real condition of the rank and file of the people.

In the summer of 1900, with the assistance of such prominent coloured men as Mr. T. Thomas Fortune, who has always upheld my hands in every effort, I organized the National Negro Business League, which held its first meeting in Boston, and brought together for the first time a large number of the coloured men who are engaged in various lines of trade or business in different parts of the

United States. Thirty states were represented at our first meeting. Out of this national meeting grew state and local business leagues.

In addition to looking after the executive side of the work at Tuskegee, and raising the greater part of the money for the support of the school, I cannot seem to escape the duty of answering at least a part of the calls which come to me unsought to address Southern white audiences and audiences of my own race, as well as frequent gatherings in the North. As to how much of my time is spent in this way, the following clipping from a Buffalo (N.Y.) paper will tell. This has reference to an occasion when I spoke before the National Educational Association in that city.

Booker T. Washington, the foremost educator among the coloured people of the world, was a very busy man from the time he arrived in the city the other night from the West and registered at the Iroquois. He had hardly removed the stains of travel when it was time to partake of supper. Then he held a public levee in the parlours of the Iroquois until eight o'clock. During that time he was greeted by over two hundred eminent teachers and educators from all parts of the United States. Shortly after eight o'clock he was driven in a carriage to Music Hall, and in one hour and a half he made two ringing addresses, to as many as five thousand people, on Negro education. Then Mr. Washington was taken in charge by a delegation of coloured citizens, headed by the Rev. Mr. Watkins, and hustled off to a small informal reception, arranged in honour of the visitor by the people of his race.

Nor can I, in addition to making these addresses, escape the duty of calling the attention of the South and of the country in general, through the medium of the press, to matters that pertain to the interests of both races. This, for example, I have done in regard to the evil habit of lynching. When the Louisiana State Constitutional Convention was in session, I wrote an open letter to that body pleading for justice for the race. In all such efforts I have received

The Booker T. Washington Monument, unveiled on April 5, 1922, now the centerpiece of Tuskegee University's campus. It bears the inscription: "He lifted the veil of ignorance from his people and pointed the way to progress through education and industry." Not seen in this photograph is the anvil on which the former slave sits, the plow by his side, and the book on his knees.

warm and hearty support from the Southern newspapers, as well as from those in all other parts of the country.

Despite superficial and temporary signs which might lead one to entertain a contrary opinion, there was never a time when I felt more hopeful for the race than I do at the present. The great human law that in the end recognizes and rewards merit is everlasting and universal. The outside world does not know, neither can it appreciate, the struggle that is constantly going on in the hearts of both the Southern white people and their former slaves to free themselves from racial prejudice; and while both races are thus struggling they should have the sympathy, the support, and the forbearance of the rest of the world.

As I write the closing words of this autobiography I find myself—not by design—in the city of Richmond, Virginia: the city which only a few decades ago was the capital of the Southern Confederacy, and where, about twenty-five years ago, because of my poverty I slept night after night under a sidewalk.

This time I am in Richmond as the guest of the coloured people of the city; and came at their request to deliver an address last night to both races in the Academy of Music, the largest and finest audience room in the city. This was the first time that the coloured people had ever been permitted to use this hall. The day before I came, the City Council passed a vote to attend the meeting in a body to hear me speak. The state Legislature, including the House of Delegates and the Senate, also passed a unanimous vote to attend in a body. In the presence of hundreds of coloured people, many distinguished white citizens, the City Council, the state Legislature, and state officials, I delivered my message, which was one of hope and cheer; and from the bottom of my heart I thanked both races for this welcome back to the state that gave me birth.

OTHER
EARLY BLACK
NARRATIVES

Editor's Note: Numbered footnotes throughout *The History of Mary Prince, a West Indian Slave* are reproduced from the original 1831 publication, and are the work of a contemporary editor.

F R O M

The History of Mary Prince, a West Indian Slave

by Mary Prince

I was born at Brackish-Pond, in Bermuda, on a farm belonging to Mr. Charles Myners. My mother was a household slave; and my father, whose name was Prince, was a sawyer belonging to Mr. Trimmingham, a ship-builder at Crow-Lane. When I was an infant, old Mr. Myners died, and there was a division of the slaves and other property among the family. I was bought along with my mother by old Captain Darrel, and given to his grandchild, little Miss Betsey Williams. Captain Williams, Mr. Darrel's son-in-law, was master of a vessel which traded to several places in America and the West Indies, and he was seldom at home long together.

Mrs. Williams was a kind-hearted good woman, and she treated all her slaves well. She had only one daughter, Miss Betsey, for whom I was purchased, and who was about my own age. I was made quite a pet of by Miss Betsey, and loved her very much. She used to lead me about by the hand, and call me her little nigger. This was the happiest period of my life; for I was too young to understand rightly my condition as a slave, and too thoughtless and full of spirits to look forward to the days of toil and sorrow.

My mother was a household slave in the same family. I was under her own care, and my little brothers and sisters were my play-fellows and companions. My mother had several fine children after she came to Mrs. Williams,—three girls and two boys. The tasks given out to us children were light, and we used to play together with Miss Betsey, with as much freedom almost as if she had been our sister.

My master, however, was a very harsh, selfish man; and we always dreaded his return from sea. His wife was herself much afraid of him; and, during his stay at home, seldom dared to shew her usual kindness to the slaves. He often left her, in the most distressed circumstances, to reside in other female society, at some place in the West Indies of which I have forgot the name. My poor mistress bore his ill-treatment with great patience, and all her slaves loved and pitied her. I was truly attached to her, and, next to my own mother, loved her better than any creature in the world. My obedience to her commands was cheerfully given: it sprung solely from the affection I felt for her, and not from fear of the power which the white people's law had given her over me.

I had scarcely reached my twelfth year when my mistress became too poor to keep so many of us at home; and she hired me out to Mrs. Pruden, a lady who lived about five miles off, in the adjoining parish, in a large house near the sea. I cried bitterly at parting with my dear mistress and Miss Betsey, and when I kissed my mother and brothers and sisters, I thought my young heart would break, it pained me so. But there was no help; I was forced to go. Good Mrs. Williams comforted me by saying that I should still be near the home I was about to quit, and might come over and see her and my kindred whenever I could obtain leave of absence from Mrs. Pruden. A few hours after this I was taken to a strange house, and found myself among strange people. This separation seemed a sore trial to me then; but oh! 'twas light, light to the trials I have since endured!— 'twas nothing—nothing to be mentioned with them; but I was a child then, and it was according to my strength.

I knew that Mrs. Williams could no longer maintain me; that she was fain to part with me for my food and clothing; and I tried to submit myself to the change. My new mistress was a passionate woman; but yet she did not treat me very unkindly. I do not remember her striking me but once, and that was for going to see Mrs. Williams when I heard she was sick, and staying longer than she had given me leave to do. All my employment at this time was nursing a sweet baby, little Master Daniel; and I grew so fond of my nursling that it was my greatest delight to walk out with him by the sea-shore, accompanied by his brother and sister, Miss Fanny and Master James.—Dear Miss Fanny! She was a sweet, kind young lady, and so fond of me that she wished me to learn all that she knew herself; and her method of teaching me was as follows:—Directly she had said her lessons to her grandmamma, she used to come running to me, and make me repeat them one by one after her; and in a few months I was able not only to say my letters but to spell many small words. But this happy state was not to last long. Those days were too pleasant to last. My heart always softens when I think of them.

At this time Mrs. Williams died. I was told suddenly of her death, and my grief was so great that, forgetting I had the baby in my arms, I ran away directly to my poor mistress's house; but reached it only in time to see the corpse carried out. Oh, that was a day of sorrow,— a heavy day! All the slaves cried. My mother cried and lamented her sore; and I (foolish creature!) vainly entreated them to bring my dear mistress back to life. I knew nothing rightly about death then, and it seemed a hard thing to bear. When I thought about my mistress I felt as if the world was all gone wrong; and for many days and weeks I could think of nothing else. I returned to Mrs. Pruden's; but my sorrow was too great to be comforted, for my own dear mistress was always in my mind. Whether in the house or abroad, my thoughts were always talking to me about her.

I staid at Mrs. Pruden's about three months after this; I was then sent back to Mr. Williams to be sold. Oh, that was a sad sad time! I recollect the day well. Mrs. Pruden came to me and said, "Mary, you will have to go home directly; your master is going to be married, and he means to sell you and two of your sisters to raise money for the wedding." Hearing this I burst out a crying,—though I was then far from being sensible of the full weight of my misfortune, or of the misery that waited for me.

. . . The black morning at length came; it came too soon for my poor mother and us. Whilst she was putting on us the new osnaburgs in which we were to be sold, she said, in a sorrowful voice, (I shall never forget it!) "See, I am *shrouding* my poor children; what a task for a mother!"—She then called Miss Betsey to take leave of us. "I am going to carry my little chickens to market," (these were her very words,) "take your last look of them; may be you will see them no more." "Oh, my poor slaves! my own slaves!" said dear Miss Betsey, "you belong to me; and it grieves my heart to part with you."—Miss Betsey kissed us all, and, when she left us, my mother called the rest of the slaves to bid us good bye. One of them, a woman named Moll, came with her infant in her arms. "Ay!" said my mother, seeing her turn away and look at her child with the tears in her eyes, "your turn will come next." The slaves could say nothing to comfort us; they could only weep and lament with us. When I left my dear little brothers and the house in which I had been brought up, I thought my heart would burst.

Our mother, weeping as she went, called me away with the children Hannah and Dinah, and we took the road that led to Hamble Town, which we reached about four o'clock in the afternoon. We followed my mother to the market-place, where she placed us in a row against a large house, with our backs to the wall and our arms folded across our breasts. I, as the eldest, stood first, Hannah next to me, then Dinah; and our mother stood beside, crying over us. My heart throbbed with grief and terror so violently, that I pressed my hands quite tightly across my breast, but I could not keep it still, and it continued to leap as though it would burst out of my body. But who cared for that? Did one of the many by-standers, who were looking at us so carelessly, think of the pain that wrung the hearts of the negro woman and her young ones? No, no! They were not all

"At length the vendue master, who was to offer us for sale like sheep or cattle, arrived, and asked my mother which was the eldest. She said nothing, but pointed to me."

bad, I dare say, but slavery hardens white people's hearts towards the blacks; and many of them were not slow to make their remarks upon us aloud, without regard to our grief—though their light words fell like cayenne on the fresh wounds of our hearts. Oh those white people have small hearts who can only feel for themselves.

At length the vendue master, who was to offer us for sale like sheep or cattle, arrived, and asked my mother which was the eldest. She said nothing, but pointed to me. He took me by the hand, and led me out into the middle of the street, and, turning me slowly round, exposed me to the view of those who attended the vendue. I was soon surrounded by strange men, who examined and handled me in the same manner that a butcher would a calf or a lamb he was about to purchase, and who talked about my shape and size in like words—as if I could no more understand their meaning than the dumb beasts. I was then put up to sale. The bidding commenced at a few pounds, and gradually rose to fifty-seven, (Bermuda currency; about £38 sterling) when I was knocked down to the highest bidder; and the people who stood by said that I had fetched a great sum for so young a slave. . . .

My new master was a Captain I————, who lived at Spanish Point. After parting with my mother and sisters, I followed him to his store, and he gave me into the charge of his son, a lad about my own age, Master Benjy, who took me to my new home. I did not know where I was going, or what my new master would do with me. My heart was quite broken with grief, and my thoughts went back continually to those from whom I had been so suddenly parted. "Oh, my mother! my mother!" I kept saying to myself, "Oh, my mammy and my sisters and my brothers, shall I never see you again!"

Oh, the trials! the trials! they make the salt water come into my eyes when I think of the days in which I was afflicted—the times that are gone; when I mourned and grieved with a young heart for those whom I loved.

It was night when I reached my new home. The house was large, and built at the bottom of a very high hill; but I could not see much of it that night. I saw too much of it afterwards. The stones and the timber were the best things in it; they were not so hard as the hearts of the owners.

Before I entered the house, two slave women, hired from another owner, who were at work in the yard, spoke to me, and asked who I belonged to? I replied, "I am come to live here." "Poor child, poor child!" they both said; "you must keep a good heart, if you are to live here."—When I went in, I stood up crying in a corner. Mrs. I——— came and took off my hat, a little black silk hat Miss Pruden made for me, and said in a rough voice, "You are not come here to stand up in corners and cry, you are come here to work." She then put a child into my arms, and, tired as I was, I was forced instantly to take up my old occupation of a nurse.—I could not bear to look at my mistress, her countenance was so stern. She was a stout tall woman with a very dark complexion, and her brows were always drawn together into a frown. I thought of the words of the two slave women when I saw Mrs. I———, and heard the harsh sound of her voice.

The person I took the most notice of that night was a French Black called Hetty, whom my master took in privateering from another vessel, and made his slave. She was the most active woman I ever saw, and she was tasked to her utmost. A few minutes after my arrival she came in from milking the cows, and put the sweet-potatoes on for supper. She then fetched home the sheep, and penned them in the fold; drove home the cattle, and staked them about the pond side;[1] fed and rubbed down my master's horse, and gave the hog and the fed cow[2] their suppers; prepared the beds, and undressed the children, and laid them to sleep. I liked to look at her and watch all her doings, for hers was the only friendly face I had as yet seen, and I felt glad that she was there. She gave me my supper of potatoes

---

[1] The cattle on a small plantation in Bermuda are, it seems, often thus staked or tethered, both night and day, in situations where grass abounds.
[2] A cow fed for slaughter.

and milk, and a blanket to sleep upon, which she spread for me in the passage before the door of Mrs. I———'s chamber.

I got a sad fright, that night. I was just going to sleep, when I heard a noise in my mistress's room; and she presently called out to inquire if some work was finished that she had ordered Hetty to do. "No, Ma'am, not yet," was Hetty's answer from below. On hearing this, my master started up from his bed, and just as he was, in his shirt, ran down stairs with a long cow-skin[3] in his hand. I heard immediately after, the cracking of the thong, and the house rang to the shrieks of poor Hetty, who kept crying out, "Oh, Massa! Massa! me dead. Massa! have mercy upon me—don't kill me outright."— This was a sad beginning for me. I sat up upon my blanket, trembling with terror, like a frightened hound, and thinking that my turn would come next. At length the house became still, and I forgot for a little while all my sorrows by falling fast asleep.

The next morning my mistress set about instructing me in my tasks. She taught me to do all sorts of household work; to wash and bake, pick cotton and wool, and wash floors, and cook. And she taught me (how can I ever forget it!) more things than these; she caused me to know the exact difference between the smart of the rope, the cart-whip, and the cow-skin, when applied to my naked body by her own cruel hand. And there was scarcely any punishment more dreadful than the blows I received on my face and head from her hard heavy fist. She was a fearful woman, and a savage mistress to her slaves.

There were two little slave boys in the house, on whom she vented her bad temper in a special manner. One of these children was a mulatto, called Cyrus, who had been bought while an infant in his mother's arms; the other, Jack, was an African from the coast of Guinea, whom a sailor had given or sold to my master. Seldom a day passed without these boys receiving the most severe treatment, and

---

[3] A thong of hard twisted hide, known by this name in the West Indies.

often for no fault at all. Both my master and mistress seemed to think that they had a right to ill-use them at their pleasure; and very often accompanied their commands with blows, whether the children were behaving well or ill. I have seen their flesh ragged and raw with licks.—Lick—lick—they were never secure one moment from a blow, and their lives were passed in continual fear. My mistress was not contented with using the whip, but often pinched their cheeks and arms in the most cruel manner. My pity for these poor boys was soon transferred to myself; for I was licked, and flogged, and pinched by her pitiless fingers in the neck and arms, exactly as they were. To strip me naked—to hang me up by the wrists and lay my flesh open with the cow-skin, was an ordinary punishment for even a slight offence. My mistress often robbed me too of the hours that belong to sleep. She used to sit up very late, frequently even until morning; and I had then to stand at a bench and wash during the greater part of the night, or pick wool and cotton; and often I have dropped down overcome by sleep and fatigue, till roused from a state of stupor by the whip, and forced to start up to my tasks.

Poor Hetty, my fellow slave, was very kind to me, and I used to call her my Aunt; but she led a most miserable life, and her death was hastened (at least the slaves all believed and said so,) by the dreadful chastisement she received from my master during her pregnancy. It happened as follows. One of the cows had dragged the rope away from the stake to which Hetty had fastened it, and got loose. My master flew into a terrible passion, and ordered the poor creature to be stripped quite naked, notwithstanding her pregnancy, and to be tied up to a tree in the yard. He then flogged her as hard as he could lick, both with the whip and cow-skin, till she was all over streaming with blood. He rested, and then beat her again and again. Her shrieks were terrible. The consequence was that poor Hetty was brought to bed before her time, and was delivered after severe labour of a dead child. She appeared to recover after her confinement, so far that she was repeatedly flogged by both master and mistress afterwards; but her former strength never returned to her. Ere long her body and

limbs swelled to a great size; and she lay on a mat in the kitchen, till
the water burst out of her body and she died. All the slaves said that
death was a good thing for poor Hetty; but I cried very much for her
death. The manner of it filled me with horror. I could not bear to
think about it; yet it was always present to my mind for many a day.

After Hetty died all her labours fell upon me, in addition to my
own. I had now to milk eleven cows every morning before sunrise,
sitting among the damp weeds; to take care of the cattle as well as the
children; and to do the work of the house. There was no end to my
toils—no end to my blows. I lay down at night and rose up in the
morning in fear and sorrow; and often wished that like poor Hetty I
could escape from this cruel bondage and be at rest in the grave. But
the hand of that God whom then I knew not, was stretched over me;
and I was mercifully preserved for better things. It was then, however, my heavy lot to weep, weep, weep, and that for years; to pass
from one misery to another, and from one cruel master to a worse.
But I must go on with the thread of my story.

One day a heavy squall of wind and rain came on suddenly, and
my mistress sent me round the corner of the house to empty a large
earthen jar. The jar was already cracked with an old deep crack that
divided it in the middle, and in turning it upside down to empty it, it
parted in my hand. I could not help the accident, but I was dreadfully
frightened, looking forward to a severe punishment. I ran crying to
my mistress, "O mistress, the jar has come in two." "You have
broken it, have you?" she replied; "come directly here to me." I
came trembling: she stripped and flogged me long and severely with
the cow-skin; as long as she had strength to use the lash, for she did
not give over till she was quite tired.—When my master came home
at night, she told him of my fault; and oh, frightful! how he fell a
swearing. After abusing me with every ill name he could think of,
(too, too bad to speak in England,) and giving me several heavy
blows with his hand, he said, "I shall come home to-morrow morning at twelve, on purpose to give you a round hundred." He kept his
word—Oh sad for me! I cannot easily forget it. He tied me up upon

a ladder, and gave me a hundred lashes with his own hand, and master Benjy stood by to count them for him. When he had licked me for some time he sat down to take breath; then after resting, he beat me again and again, until he was quite wearied, and so hot (for the weather was very sultry), that he sank back in his chair, almost like to faint. While my mistress went to bring him drink, there was a dreadful earthquake. Part of the roof fell down, and every thing in the house went—clatter, clatter, clatter. Oh I thought the end of all things near at hand; and I was so sore with the flogging, that I scarcely cared whether I lived or died. The earth was groaning and shaking; every thing tumbling about; and my mistress and the slaves were shrieking and crying out, "The earthquake! the earthquake!" It was an awful day for us all.

During the confusion I crawled away on my hands and knees, and laid myself down under the steps of the piazza, in front of the house. I was in a dreadful state—my body all blood and bruises, and I could not help moaning piteously. The other slaves, when they saw me, shook their heads and said, "Poor child! poor child!"—I lay there till the morning, careless of what might happen, for life was very weak in me, and I wished more than ever to die. But when we are very young, death always seems a great way off, and it would not come that night to me. The next morning I was forced by my master to rise and go about my usual work, though my body and limbs were so stiff and sore, that I could not move without the greatest pain.— Nevertheless, even after all this severe punishment, I never heard the last of that jar; my mistress was always throwing it in my face.

Some little time after this, one of the cows got loose from the stake, and ate one of the sweet-potato slips. I was milking when my master found it out. He came to me, and without any more ado, stooped down, and taking off his heavy boot, he struck me such a severe blow in the small of my back, that I shrieked with agony, and thought I was killed; and I feel a weakness in that part to this day. The cow was frightened at his violence, and kicked down the pail and spilt the milk all about. My master knew that this accident was his own fault, but he was so enraged that he seemed glad of an excuse to go on with his ill usage. I cannot remember how many licks he gave me then, but he beat me till I was unable to stand, and till he himself was weary.

[After this beating, Mary runs away to her mother, who hides her in a cavern, bringing her food every night after all in the Darrel household have gone to bed. Mary's sanctuary comes to an end when her father, still living in Crow's Lane, decides that in the long run it would be better for his daughter to return to Captain I. "I entreat you, for the love of God," says Mary's father to Captain I., "to forgive her for running away, and that you will be a kind master to her in the future." Mary endures another five years with Captain and Mrs. I. "and almost daily received the same harsh treatment." Hope for a less brutal bondage comes when Captain I. ships Mary off to Turk's Island for sale to a Mr. D. —Ed.]

My new master was one of the owners or holders of the salt ponds, and he received a certain sum for every slave that worked upon his premises, whether they were young or old. This sum was allowed him out of the profits arising from the salt works. I was immediately sent to work in the salt water with the rest of the slaves. This work was perfectly new to me. I was given a half barrel and a shovel, and had to stand up to my knees in the water, from four o'clock in the morning till nine, when we were given some Indian corn boiled in water, which we were obliged to swallow as fast as we could for fear the rain should come on and melt the salt. We were then called again to our tasks, and worked through the heat of the day; the sun flaming upon our heads like fire, and raising salt blisters in those parts which were not completely covered. Our feet and legs, from standing in the salt water for so many hours, soon became full of dreadful boils, which eat down in some cases to the very bone, afflicting the sufferers with great torment. We came home at twelve; ate our corn soup, called *blawly,* as fast as we could, and went back to our employment till dark at night. We then shovelled up the salt in large heaps, and went down to the sea, where we washed the pickle from our limbs, and cleaned the barrows and shovels from the salt. When we returned to the house, our master gave us each our allowance of raw Indian corn, which we pounded in a mortar and boiled in water for our suppers.

We slept in a long shed, divided into narrow slips, like the stalls used for cattle. Boards fixed upon stakes driven into the ground, without mat or covering, were our only beds. On Sundays, after we had washed the salt bags, and done other work required of us, we went into the bush and cut the long soft grass, of which we made trusses for our legs and feet to rest upon, for they were so full of the salt boils that we could get no rest lying upon the bare boards.

Though we worked from morning till night, there was no satisfying Mr. D———. I hoped, when I left Capt. I———, that I should have been better off, but I found it was but going from one butcher to another. There was this difference between them: my former master used to beat me while raging and foaming with passion; Mr. D——— was usually quite calm. He would stand by and give orders for a slave to be cruelly whipped, and assist in the punishment, without moving a muscle of his face; walking about and taking snuff with the greatest composure. Nothing could touch his hard heart—neither sighs, nor tears, nor prayers, nor streaming blood; he was deaf to our cries, and careless of our sufferings.—Mr. D——— has often stripped me naked, hung me up by the wrists, and beat me with the cow-skin, with his own hand, till my body was raw with gashes. Yet there was nothing very remarkable in this; for it might serve as a sample of the common usage of the slaves on that horrible island.

Owing to the boils in my feet, I was unable to wheel the barrow fast through the sand, which got into the sores, and made me stumble at every step; and my master, having no pity for my sufferings from this cause, rendered them far more intolerable, by chastising me for not being able to move so fast as he wished me. Another of our employments was to row a little way off from the shore in a boat, and dive for large stones to build a wall round our master's house. This was very hard work; and the great waves breaking over us continually, made us often so giddy that we lost our footing, and were in danger of being drowned.

Ah, poor me!—my tasks were never ended. Sick or well, it was work—work—work!—After the diving season was over, we were sent to the South Creek, with large bills, to cut up mangoes to burn lime with. Whilst one party of slaves were thus employed, another were sent to the other side of the island to break up coral out of the sea.

When we were ill, let our complaint be what it might, the only medicine given to us was a great bowl of hot salt water, with salt mixed with it, which made us very sick. If we could not keep up with the rest of the gang of slaves, we were put in the stocks, and severely flogged the next morning. Yet, not the less, our master expected, after we had thus been kept from our rest, and our limbs rendered stiff and sore with ill usage, that we should still go through the ordinary tasks of the day all the same.—Sometimes we had to work all night, measuring salt to load a vessel; or turning a machine to draw water out of the sea for the salt-making. Then we had no sleep—no rest— but were forced to work as fast as we could, and go on again all next day the same as usual. Work—work—work—Oh that Turk's Island was a horrible place! The people in England, I am sure, have never found out what is carried on there. Cruel, horrible place!

Mr. D——— had a slave called old Daniel, whom he used to treat in the most cruel manner. Poor Daniel was lame in the hip, and could not keep up with the rest of the slaves; and our master would order him to be stripped and laid down on the ground, and have him beaten with a rod of rough briar till his skin was quite red and raw. He would then call for a bucket of salt, and fling upon the raw flesh till the man writhed on the ground like a worm, and screamed aloud with agony. This poor man's wounds were never healed, and I have often seen them full of maggots, which increased his torments to an intolerable degree. He was an object of pity and terror to the whole gang of slaves, and in his wretched case we saw, each of us, our own lot, if we should live to be as old.

Oh the horrors of slavery!—How the thought of it pains my heart! But the truth ought to be told of it; and what my eyes have seen I think it is my duty to relate; for few people in England know what slavery is. I have been a slave—I have felt what a slave feels, and I know what a slave knows; and I would have all the good people in England to know it too, that they may break our chains, and set us free.

Mr. D———— had another slave called Ben. He being very hungry, stole a little rice one night after he came in from work, and cooked it for his supper. But his master soon discovered the theft; locked him up all night; and kept him without food till one o'clock the next day. He then hung Ben up by his hands, and beat him from time to time till the slaves came in at night. We found the poor creature hung up when we came home; with a pool of blood beneath him, and our master still licking him. But this was not the worst. My master's son was in the habit of stealing the rice and rum. Ben had seen him do this, and thought he might do the same, and when master found out that Ben had stolen the rice and swore to punish him, he tried to excuse himself by saying that Master Dickey did the same thing every night. The lad denied it to his father, and was so angry with Ben for informing against him, that out of revenge he ran and got a bayonet, and whilst the poor wretch was suspended by his hands and writhing under his wounds, he run it quite through his foot. I was not by when he did it, but I saw the wound when I came home, and heard Ben tell the manner in which it was done.

I must say something more about this cruel son of a cruel father.—He had no heart—no fear of God; he had been brought up by a bad father in a bad path, and he delighted to follow in the same steps. There was a little old woman among the slaves called Sarah, who was nearly past work; and, Master Dickey being the overseer of the slaves just then, this poor creature, who was subject to several bodily infirmities, and was not quite right in her head, did not wheel the barrow fast enough to please him. He threw her down on the ground, and after beating her severely, he took her up in his arms and flung her among the prickly-pear bushes, which are all covered over with sharp venomous prickles. By this her naked flesh was so grievously wounded, that her body swelled and festered all over, and she died a few days after. In telling my own sorrows, I cannot pass by those of my fellow-slaves—for when I think of my own griefs, I remember theirs.

I think it was about ten years I had worked in the salt ponds at Turk's Island, when my master left off business, and retired to a house he had in Bermuda, leaving his son to succeed him in the island. He took me with him to wait upon his daughters; and I was joyful, for I was sick, sick of Turk's Island, and my heart yearned to see my native place again, my mother, and my kindred.

I had seen my poor mother during the time I was a slave in Turk's Island. One Sunday morning I was on the beach with some of the slaves, and we saw a sloop come in loaded with slaves to work in the salt water. We got a boat and went aboard. When I came upon the deck I asked the black people, "Is there any one here for me?" "Yes," they said, "your mother." I thought they said this in jest—I could scarcely believe them for joy; but when I saw my poor mammy my joy was turned to sorrow, for she had gone from her senses. "Mammy," I said, "is this you?" She did not know me. "Mammy," I said, "what's the matter?" She began to talk foolishly, and said that she had been under the vessel's bottom. They had been overtaken by a violent storm at sea. My poor mother had never been on the sea before, and she was so ill, that she lost her senses, and it was long before she came quite to herself again. She had a sweet child with her—a little sister I had never seen, about four years of age, called Rebecca. I took her on shore with me, for I felt I should love her directly; and I kept her with me a week. Poor little thing! hers has been a sad life, and continues so to this day. My mother worked for some years on the island, but was taken back to Bermuda some time before my master carried me again thither.[4]

After I left Turk's Island, I was told by some negroes that came over from it, that the poor slaves had built up a place with boughs and leaves, where they might meet for prayers, but the white people pulled it down twice, and would not allow them even a shed for prayers. A flood came down soon after and washed away many houses, filled the place with sand, and overflowed the ponds: and I do think that this was for their wickedness; for the Buckra men[5] there were very wicked. I saw and heard much that was very very bad at that place.

I was several years the slave of Mr. D———— after I returned to my native place. Here I worked in the grounds. My work was planting and hoeing sweet-potatoes, Indian corn, plaintains, bananas, cabbages, pumpkins, onions, &c. I did all the household work, and attended upon a horse and cow besides,—going also upon all errands. I had to curry the horse—to clean and feed him—and sometimes to ride him a little. I had more than enough to do—but still it was not so very bad as Turk's Island.

My old master often got drunk, and then he would get in a fury with his daughter, and beat her till she was not fit to be seen. I remember on one occasion, I had gone to fetch water, and when I was coming up the hill I heard a great screaming; I ran as fast as I could to the house, put down the water, and went into the chamber, where I found my master beating Miss D———— dreadfully. I strove with all my strength to get her away from him; for she was all black

---

[4] Of the subsequent lot of her relatives she can tell but little. She says, her father died while she and her mother were at Turk's Island; and that he had been long dead and buried before any of his children in Bermuda knew of it, they being slaves on other estates. Her mother died after Mary went to Antigua. Of the fate of the rest of her kindred, seven brothers and three sisters, she knows nothing further than this—that the eldest sister, who had several children to her master, was taken by him to Trinidad; and that the youngest, Rebecca, is still alive, and in slavery in Bermuda. Mary herself is now about forty-three years of age.

[5] Negro term for white people.

and blue with bruises. He had beat her with his fist, and almost killed her. The people gave me credit for getting her away. He turned round and began to lick me. Then I said, "Sir, this is not Turk's Island." I can't repeat his answer, the words were too wicked—too bad to say. He wanted to treat me the same in Bermuda as he had done in Turk's Island.

He had an ugly fashion of stripping himself quite naked, and ordering me then to wash him in a tub of water. This was worse to me than all the licks. Sometimes when he called me to wash him I would not come, my eyes were so full of shame. He would then come to beat me. One time I had plates and knives in my hand, and I dropped both plates and knives, and some of the plates were broken. He struck me so severely for this, that at last I defended myself, for I thought it was high time to do so. I then told him I would not live longer with him, for he was a very indecent man—very spiteful, and too indecent; with no shame for his servants, no shame for his own flesh. So I went away to a neighbouring house and sat down and cried till the next morning, when I went home again, not knowing what else to do.

After that I was hired to work at Cedar Hills, and every Saturday night I paid the money to my master. I had plenty of work to do there—plenty of washing; but yet I made myself pretty comfortable. I earned two dollars and a quarter a week, which is twenty pence a day.

During the time I worked there, I heard that Mr. John Wood was going to Antigua. I felt a great wish to go there, and I went to Mr. D———, and asked him to let me go in Mr. Wood's service. Mr. Wood did not then want to purchase me; it was my own fault that I came under him, I was so anxious to go. It was ordained to be, I suppose; God led me there. The truth is, I did not wish to be any longer the slave of my indecent master.

Mr. Wood took me with him to Antigua, to the town of St. John's, where he lived. This was about fifteen years ago. He did not then know whether I was to be sold; but Mrs. Wood found that I could work, and she wanted to buy me. Her husband then wrote to my master to inquire whether I was to be sold? Mr. D———— wrote in reply, "that I should not be sold to any one that would treat me ill." It was strange he should say this, when he had treated me so ill himself. So I was purchased by Mr. Wood for 300 dollars, (or £100 Bermuda currency.)[6]

My work there was to attend the chambers and nurse the child, and to go down to the pond and wash clothes. But I soon fell ill of the rheumatism, and grew so very lame that I was forced to walk with a stick. I got the Saint Anthony's fire, also, in my left leg, and became quite a cripple. No one cared much to come near me, and I was ill a long long time; for several months I could not lift the limb. I had to lie in a little old out-house, that was swarming with bugs and other vermin, which tormented me greatly; but I had no other place to lie in. I got the rheumatism by catching cold at the pond side, from washing in the fresh water; in the salt water I never got cold. The person who lived in next yard, (a Mrs. Greene,) could not bear to hear my cries and groans. She was kind, and used to send an old slave woman to help me, who sometimes brought me a little soup. When the doctor found I was so ill, he said I must be put into a bath of hot water. The old slave got the bark of some bush that was good for the pains, which she boiled in the hot water, and every night she came and put me into the bath, and did what she could for me: I don't know what I should have done, or what would have become of me, had it not been for her.—My mistress, it is true, did send me a little food; but no one from our family came near me but the cook, who used to shove my food in at the door, and say, "Molly, Molly, there's your dinner." My mistress did not care to take any trouble about me; and if the Lord had not put it into the hearts of the neighbours to be kind to me, I must, I really think, have lain and died.

[6] About £67. 10s. sterling.

It was a long time before I got well enough to work in the house. Mrs. Wood, in the meanwhile, hired a mulatto woman to nurse the child; but she was such a fine lady she wanted to be mistress over me. I thought it very hard for a coloured woman to have rule over me because I was a slave and she was free. Her name was Martha Wilcox; she was a saucy woman, very saucy; and she went and complained of me, without cause, to my mistress, and made her angry with me. Mrs. Wood told me that if I did not mind what I was about, she would get my master to strip me and give me fifty lashes: "You have been used to the whip," she said, "and you shall have it here." This was the first time she threatened to have me flogged; and she gave me the threatening so strong of what she would have done to me, that I thought I should have fallen down at her feet, I was so vexed and hurt by her words. The mulatto woman was rejoiced to have power to keep me down. She was constantly making mischief; there was no living for the slaves—no peace after she came.

I was also sent by Mrs. Wood to be put in the Cage one night, and was next morning flogged, by the magistrate's order, at her desire; and this all for a quarrel I had about a pig with another slave woman. I was flogged on my naked back on this occasion: although I was in no fault after all; for old Justice Dyett, when we came before him, said that I was in the right, and ordered the pig to be given to me. This was about two or three years after I came to Antigua.

When we moved from the middle of the town to the Point, I used to be in the house and do all the work and mind the children, though still very ill with the rheumatism. Every week I had to wash two large bundles of clothes, as much as a boy could help me to lift; but I could give no satisfaction. My mistress was always abusing and fretting after me. It is not possible to tell all her ill language.—One day she followed me foot after foot scolding and rating me. I bore in silence a great deal of ill words: at last my heart was quite full, and I told her that she ought not to use me so;—that when I was ill I might have lain and died for what she cared; and no one would then come near me to nurse me, because they were afraid of my mistress. This was a great affront. She called her husband and told him what I had said. He flew into a passion: but did not beat me then; he only abused and swore at me; and then gave me a note and bade me go and look for an owner. Not that he meant to sell me; but he did this to please his wife and to frighten me. I went to Adam White, a cooper, a free black, who had money, and asked him to buy me. He went directly to Mr. Wood, but was informed that I was not to be sold. The next day my master whipped me.

[Mary tries several more times to obtain a new owner, but to no avail; and her miseries continue. One blessing to befall her during this time is an invitation from another enslaved woman to attend a Methodist prayer meeting in Date Hill, where Mary has accompanied the D. family for their "change of air." The prayer meeting has a powerful effect on Mary, and when the D. family returns to town she joins the Moravian church. Another bright spot in her life is her marriage "about Christmas 1826" to a self-employed carpenter and cooper, a freedman named Daniel James.

Not long after Mary's marriage (for which she was beaten), the Woods make a trip to England, taking Mary along. In England, there is no abatement in the abuse, and it is exacerbated by the Woods' frequent threat to throw Mary out into the street to fend for herself and "be d———d." After the fourth such threat Mary, aware that she is legally free in England, takes the Woods up on their offer.

After getting succor from the Moravian Missionaries and shelter from a "shoe-black" named Mash and his wife, Mary eventually makes her way to the Anti-Slavery Society, where she inquires "if they could get me my freedom, and send me back to the West Indies." —Ed.]

The gentlemen of the Society took me to a lawyer, who examined very strictly into my case; but told me that the laws of England could do nothing to make me free in Antigua.[7] However they did all they could for me: they gave me a little money from time to time to keep me from want; and some of them went to Mr. Wood to try to persuade him to let me return a free woman to my husband; but though they offered him, as I have heard, a large sum for my freedom, he was sulky and obstinate, and would not consent to let me go free.

This was the first winter I spent in England, and I suffered much from the severe cold, and from the rheumatic pains, which still at times torment me. However, Providence was very good to me, and I got many friends—especially some Quaker ladies, who hearing of my case, came and sought me out, and gave me good warm clothing and money. Thus I had great cause to bless God in my affliction.

When I got better I was anxious to get some work to do, as I was unwilling to eat the bread of idleness. Mrs. Mash, who was a laundress, recommended me to a lady for a charwoman. She paid me very handsomely for what work I did, and I divided the money with Mrs. Mash; for though very poor, they gave me food when my own money was done, and never suffered me to want.

In the spring, I got into service with a lady, who saw me at the house where I sometimes worked as a charwoman. This lady's name was Mrs. Forsyth. She had been in the West Indies, and was accustomed to Blacks, and liked them. I was with her six months, and went with her to Margate. She treated me well, and gave me a good character when she left London.[8]

After Mrs. Forsyth went away, I was again out of place, and went to lodgings, for which I paid two shillings a week, and found coals and candle. After eleven weeks, the money I had saved in service was all gone, and I was forced to go back to the Anti-Slavery office to ask a supply, till I could get another situation. I did not like to go back—I did not like to be idle. I would rather work for my living than get it

---

[7] She came first to the Anti-Slavery Office in Aldermanbury, about the latter end of November 1828; and her case was referred to Mr. George Stephen to be investigated.

[8] She refers to a written certificate which will be inserted afterwards.

for nothing. They were very good to give me a supply, but I felt shame at being obliged to apply for relief whilst I had strength to work.

At last I went into the service of Mr. and Mrs. Pringle, where I have been ever since, and am as comfortable as I can be while separated from my dear husband, and away from my own country and all old friends and connections. My dear mistress teaches me daily to read the word of God, and takes great pains to make me understand it. I enjoy the great privilege of being enabled to attend church three times on the Sunday; and I have met with many kind friends since I have been here, both clergymen and others. The Rev. Mr. Young, who lives in the next house, has shown me much kindness, and taken much pains to instruct me, particularly while my master and mistress were absent in Scotland. Nor must I forget, among my friends, the Rev. Mr. Mortimer, the good clergyman of the parish, under whose ministry I have now sat for upwards of twelve months. I trust in God I have profited by what I have heard from him. He never keeps back the truth, and I think he has been the means of opening my eyes and ears much better to understand the word of God. Mr. Mortimer tells me that he cannot open the eyes of my heart, but that I must pray to God to change my heart, and make me to know the truth, and the truth will make me free.

I still live in the hope that God will find a way to give me my liberty, and give me back to my husband. I endeavour to keep down my fretting, and to leave all to Him, for he knows what is good for me better than I know myself. Yet, I must confess, I find it a hard and heavy task to do so.

I am often much vexed, and I feel great sorrow when I hear some people in this country say, that the slaves do not need better usage, and do not want to be free.[9] They believe the foreign people,[10] who deceive them, and say slaves are happy. I say, Not so. How can

---

[9] The whole of this paragraph especially, is given as nearly as was possible in Mary's precise words.

[10] She means West Indians.

slaves be happy when they have the halter round their neck and the whip upon their back? and are disgraced and thought no more of than beasts?—and are separated from their mothers, and husbands, and children, and sisters, just as cattle are sold and separated? Is it happiness for a driver in the field to take down his wife or sister or child, and strip them, and whip them in such a disgraceful manner?—women that have had children exposed in the open field to shame! There is no modesty or decency shown by the owner to his slaves; men, women, and children are exposed alike. Since I have been here I have often wondered how English people can go out into the West Indies and act in such a beastly manner. But when they go to the West Indies, they forget God and all feeling of shame, I think, since they can see and do such things. They tie up slaves like hogs—moor[11] them up like cattle, and they lick them, so as hogs, or cattle, or horses never were flogged;—and yet they come home and say, and make some good people believe, that slaves don't want to get out of slavery. But they put a cloak about the truth. It is not so. All slaves want to be free—to be free is very sweet. I will say the truth to English people who may read this history that my good friend, Miss S————, is now writing down for me. I have been a slave myself—I know what slaves feel—I can tell by myself what other slaves feel, and by what they have told me. The man that says slaves be quite happy in slavery—that they don't want to be free—that man is either ignorant or a lying person. I never heard a slave say so. I never heard a Buckra man say so, till I heard tell of it in England. Such people ought to be ashamed of themselves. They can't do without slaves, they say. What's the reason they can't do without slaves as well as in England? No slaves here—no whips—no stocks—no punishment, except for wicked people. They hire servants in England; and if they don't like them, they send them away: they can't lick them. Let them work ever so hard in England, they are far

---

[11] A West Indian phrase: to fasten or tie up.

better off than slaves. If they get a bad master, they give warning and go hire to another. They have their liberty. That's just what *we* want. We don't mind hard work, if we had proper treatment, and proper wages like English servants, and proper time given in the week to keep us from breaking the Sabbath. But they won't give it: they will have work—work—work, night and day, sick or well, till we are quite done up; and we must not speak up nor look amiss, however much we be abused. And then when we are quite done up, who cares for us, more than for a lame horse? This is slavery. I tell it, to let English people know the truth; and I hope they will never leave off to pray God, and call loud to the great King of England, till all the poor blacks be given free, and slavery done up for evermore.

FROM

The Life of Josiah Henson, Formerly a Slave, Now an Inhabitant of Canada, as Narrated by Himself

by Josiah Henson

I was born, June 15, 1789, in Charles County, Maryland, on a farm belonging to Mr. Francis N., about a mile from Port Tobacco. My mother was the property of Dr. Josiah McP., but was hired by Mr. N., to whom my father belonged. The only incident I can remember, which occurred while my mother continued on N.'s farm, was the appearance of my father one day, with his head bloody and his back lacerated. He was in a state of great excitement, and though it was all a mystery to me at the age of three or four years, it was explained at a later period, and I understood that he had been suffering the cruel penalty of the Maryland law for beating a white man. His right ear had been cut off close to his head, and he had received a hundred lashes on his back. He had beaten the overseer for a brutal assault on my mother, and this was his punishment. Furious at such treatment, my father became a different man, and was so morose, disobedient, and intractable, that Mr. N. determined to sell him. He accordingly parted with him, not long after, to his son, who lived in Alabama; and neither my mother nor I, ever heard of him again. He was naturally, as I understood afterwards from my mother and other persons, a man of amiable temper, and of considerable energy of character; but it is not strange that he should be essentially changed by such cruelty and injustice under the sanction of law.

After the sale of my father by N., and his leaving Maryland for Alabama, Dr. McP. would no longer hire out my mother to N. She returned, therefore, to the estate of the doctor, who was very much kinder to his slaves than the generality of planters, never suffering them to be struck by any one. He was, indeed, a man of good natural impulses, kind-hearted, liberal, and jovial. The latter quality was so much developed as to be his great failing; and though his convivial excesses were not thought of as a fault by the community in which he lived, and did not even prevent his having a high reputation for goodness of heart, and an almost saint-like benevolence, yet they were, nevertheless, his ruin. My mother, and her young family of three girls and three boys, of which I was the youngest, resided on this estate for two or three years, during which my only recollections are of being rather a pet of the doctor's, who thought I was a bright child, and of being much impressed with what I afterwards recognized as the deep piety and devotional feeling and habits of my mother. I do not know how, or where she acquired her knowledge of God, or her acquaintance with the Lord's prayer, which she so frequently repeated and taught me to repeat. I remember seeing her often on her knees, endeavoring to arrange her thoughts in prayers appropriate to her situation, but which amounted to little more than constant ejaculation, and the repetition of short phrases, which were within my infant comprehension, and have remained in my memory to this hour.

After this brief period of comparative comfort, however, the death of Dr. McP. brought about a revolution in our condition, which, common as such things are in slave countries, can never be imagined by those not subject to them, nor recollected by those who have been, without emotions of grief and indignation deep and ineffaceable. The doctor was riding from one of his scenes of riotous excess, when, falling from his horse, in crossing a little run, not a foot deep, he was unable to save himself from drowning.

In consequence of his decease, it became necessary to sell the estate and the slaves, in order to divide the property among the heirs; and we were all put up at auction and sold to the highest bidder, and scattered over various parts of the country. My brothers and sisters were bid off one by one, while my mother, holding my hand, looked on in an agony of grief, the cause of which I but ill understood at first, but which dawned on my mind, with dreadful clearness, as the sale proceeded. My mother was then separated from me, and put up in her turn. She was bought by a man named Isaac R., residing in Montgomery county, and then I was offered to the assembled purchasers. My mother, half distracted with the parting forever from all her children, pushed through the crowd, while the bidding for me was going on, to the spot where R. was standing. She fell at his feet, and clung to his knees, entreating him in tones that a mother only could command, to buy her *baby* as well as herself, and spare to her one of her little ones at least. Will it, can it be believed that this man, thus appealed to, was capable not merely of turning a deaf ear to her supplication, but of disengaging himself from her with such violent blows and kicks, as to reduce her to the necessity of creeping out of his reach, and mingling the groan of bodily suffering with the sob of a breaking heart? Yet this was one of my earliest observations of men; an experience which has been common to me with thousands of my race, the bitterness of which its frequency cannot diminish to any individual who suffers it, while it is dark enough to overshadow the whole after-life with something blacker than a funeral pall.—I was bought by a stranger.—Almost immediately, however, whether my childish strength, at five or six years of age, was overmastered by such scenes and experiences, or from some accidental cause, I fell sick, and seemed to my new master so little likely to recover, that he proposed to R., the purchaser of my mother, to take me too at such a trifling rate that it could not be refused. I was thus providentially restored to my mother; and under her care, destitute as she was of the proper means of nursing me, I recovered my health, and grew up to be an uncommonly vigorous and healthy boy and man.

The character of R., the master whom I faithfully served for many years, is by no means an uncommon one in any part of the world; but it is to be regretted that a domestic institution should anywhere put it in the power of such a one to tyrannize over his fellow beings, and inflict so much needless misery as is sure to be produced by such a man in such a position. Coarse and vulgar in his habits, unprincipled and cruel in his general deportment, and especially addicted to the vice of licentiousness, his slaves had little opportunity for relaxation from wearying labor, were supplied with the scantiest means of sustaining their toil by necessary food, and had no security for personal rights. The natural tendency of slavery is, to convert the master into a tyrant, and the slave into the cringing, treacherous, false, and thieving victim of tyranny. R. and his slaves were no exception to the general rule, but might be cited as apt illustrations of the nature of the case.

My earliest employments were, to carry buckets of water to the men at work, to hold a horse-plough, used for weeding between the rows of corn, and as I grew older and taller, to take care of master's saddle-horse. Then a hoe was put into my hands, and I was soon required to do the day's work of a man; and it was not long before I could do it, at least as well as my associates in misery.

The every-day life of a slave on one of our southern plantations, however frequently it may have been described, is generally little known at the North; and must be mentioned as a necessary illustration of the character and habits of the slave and the slave-holder, created and perpetuated by their relative position. The principal food of those upon my master's plantation consisted of corn meal, and salt herrings; to which was added in summer a little buttermilk, and the few vegetables which each might raise for himself and his family, on the little piece of ground which was assigned to him for the purpose, called a truck patch. The meals were two, daily. The first, or breakfast, was taken at 12 o'clock, after laboring from daylight; and the other when the work of the remainder of the day was over. The only dress was of tow cloth, which for the young, and often even for those who had passed the period of childhood, consisted of a single garment, something like a shirt, but longer, reaching to the ankles; and for the older, a pair of pantaloons, or a gown, according to the sex; while some kind of round jacket, or overcoat, might be added in winter, a wool hat once in two or three years, for the males, and a pair of coarse shoes once a year. Our lodging was in log huts, of a single small room, with no other floor than the trodden earth, in which ten or a dozen persons—men, women, and children—might sleep, but which could not protect them from dampness and cold, nor permit the existence of the common decencies of life. There were neither beds, nor furniture of any description—a blanket being the only addition to the dress of the day for protection from the chillness of the air or the earth. In these hovels were we penned at night, and fed by day; here were the children born, and the sick—neglected. Such were the provisions for the daily toil of the slave.

Notwithstanding this system of management, however, I grew to be a robust and vigorous lad, and at fifteen years of age, there were few who could compete with me in work, or in sport—for not even the condition of a slave can altogether repress the animal spirits of the young negro. I was competent to all the work that was done upon the farm, and could run faster and farther, wrestle longer, and jump higher, than anybody about me. My master and my fellow slaves used to look upon me, and speak of me, as a wonderfully smart fellow, and prophecy the great things I should do when I became a man. A casual word of this sort, sometimes overheard, would fill me with a pride and ambition which some would think impossible in a negro slave, degraded, starved, and abused as I was, and had been, from my earliest recollection. But the love of superiority is not confined to kings and emperors; and it is a positive fact, that pride and ambition were as active in my soul as probably they ever were in that of the greatest soldier or statesman. The objects I pursued, I must admit, were not just the same as theirs. Mine were to be first in the field, whether we were hoeing, mowing, or reaping; to surpass those of my own age, or indeed any age, in athletic exercises; and to obtain, if possible, the favorable regard of the petty despot who ruled over us. This last was an exercise of the understanding, rather than of the affections; and I was guided in it more by what I supposed would be effectual, than by a nice judgment of the propriety of the means I used.

I obtained great influence with my companions, as well by the superiority I showed in labor and in sport, as by the assistance I yielded them, and the favors I conferred upon them, from impulses which I cannot consider as wrong, though it was necessary for me to conceal sometimes the act as well as its motive. I have toiled, and induced others to toil, many an extra hour, in order to show my master what an excellent day's work had been accomplished, and to win a kind word, or a benevolent deed from his callous heart. In general, indifference, or a cool calculation of my value to him, were my reward, chilling those hopes of an improvement in my condition, which was the ultimate object of my efforts. I was much more easily moved to compassion and sympathy than he was; and one of the means I took to gain the good-will of my fellow sufferers, was by taking from him some things that he did not give, in part payment of my extra labor. The condition of the male slave is bad enough, Heaven knows; but that of the female, compelled to perform unfit labor, sick, suffering, and bearing the burdens of her own sex un-pitied and unaided, as well as the toils which belong to the other, has often oppressed me with a load of sympathy. And sometimes, when I have seen them starved, and miserable, and unable to help them-selves, I have helped them to some of the comforts which they were denied by him who owned them, and which my companions had not the wit or the daring to procure. Meat was not a part of our regular food; but my master had plenty of sheep and pigs, and sometimes I have picked out the best one I could find in the flock, or the drove, carried it a mile or two into the woods, slaughtered it, cut it up, and distributed it among the poor creatures, to whom it was at once food, luxury, and medicine. Was this wrong? I can only say that, at this distance of time, my conscience does not reproach me for it, and that then I esteemed it among the best of my deeds.

By means of the influence thus acquired, the increased amount of work done upon the farm, and by the detection of the knavery of the overseer, who plundered his employer for more selfish ends, and through my watchfulness was caught in the act and dismissed, I was promoted to be superintendent of the farm work, and managed to raise more than double the crops, with more cheerful and willing labor, than was ever seen on the estate before.

Previous to my attaining this important station, however, an incident occurred of so powerful an influence on my intellectual development, my prospect of improvement in character, as well as condition, my chance of religious culture, and in short, on my whole nature, body and soul, that it deserves especial notice and commemoration. There was a person living at Georgetown, a few miles only from R's plantation, whose business was that of a baker, and whose character was that of an upright, benevolent, Christian man. He was noted especially for his detestation of slavery, and his resolute avoidance of the employment of slave labor in his business. He would not even hire a slave, the price of whose toil must be paid to his master, but contented himself with the work of his own hands, and with such free labor as he could procure. His reputation was high, not only for this almost singular abstinence from what no one about him thought wrong, but for his general probity and excellence. This man occasionally served as a minister of the Gospel, and preached in a neighborhood where preachers were somewhat rare at that period. One Sunday when he was to officiate in this way, at a place three or four miles distant, my mother persuaded me to ask master's leave to go and hear him; and although such permission was not given freely or often, yet his favor to me was shown for this once by allowing me to go, without much scolding, but not without a pretty distinct intimation of what would befall me, if I did not return immediately after the close of the service. I hurried off, pleased with the opportunity, but

without any definite expectations of benefit or amusement; for up to
this period of my life, and I was then eighteen years old, I had never
heard a sermon, nor any discourse or conversation whatever, upon
religious topics, except what had been impressed upon me by my
mother, of the responsibility of all to a Supreme Being. When I
arrived at the place of meeting, the services were so far advanced that
the speaker was just beginning his discourse, from the text, Hebrews
ii. 9; "That he, by the grace of God, should taste of death for every
man." This was the first text of the Bible to which I had ever listened, knowing it to be such. I have never forgotten it, and scarce a
day has passed since, in which I have not recalled it, and the sermon
that was preached from it. The divine character of Jesus Christ, his
life and teachings, his sacrifice of himself for others, his death and
resurrection were all alluded to, and some of the points were dwelt
upon with great power,—great, at least, to me, who heard of these
things for the first time in my life. I was wonderfully impressed, too,
with the use which the preacher made of the last words of the text,
"for every man." He said the death of Christ was not designed for the
benefit of a select few only, but for the salvation of the world, for the
bond as well as the free; and he dwelt on the glad tidings of the
Gospel to the poor, the persecuted, and the distressed, its deliverance
to the captive, and the liberty wherewith Christ has made us free, till
my heart burned within me, and I was in a state of the greatest
excitement at the thought that such a being as Jesus Christ had been
described should have died for me—for *me* among the rest, a poor,
despised, abused slave, who was thought by his fellow creatures fit
for nothing but unrequited toil and ignorance, for mental and bodily
degradation. I immediately determined to find out something more
about "Christ and him crucified;" and revolving the things which I
had heard in my mind as I went home, I became so excited that I
turned aside from the road into the woods, and prayed to God for
light and for aid with an earnestness, which, however unenlightened,
was at least sincere and heartfelt; and which the subsequent course of
my life has led me to imagine might not have been unacceptable to

Him who heareth prayer. At all events, I date my conversion, and my awakening to a new life—a consciousness of superior powers and destiny to any thing I had before conceived of—from this day, so memorable to me. I used every means and opportunity of inquiry into religious matters; and so deep was my conviction of their superior importance to every thing else, so clear my perception of my own faults, and so undoubting my observation of the darkness and sin that surrounded me, that I could not help talking much on these subjects with those about me; and it was not long before I began to pray with them, and exhort them, and to impart to the poor slaves those little glimmerings of light from another world, which had reached my own eye. In a few years I became quite an esteemed preacher among them, and I will not believe it is vanity which leads me to think I was useful to some.

[Here, Henson moves forward to when he is about twenty, and recounts a chilling incident that spiraled out of his effort to protect his drunk owner, who had gotten into a fight with his brother's overseer, a Mr. L., who was likewise whiskeyed up. When Henson came to his owner's aid, he accidentally knocked down Mr. L. As happened with his father, he would not be forgiven for hitting a white man. About a week later, while on an errand for his owner, Henson was ambushed by Mr. L. With the aid of a stick, and then a fence stake "six or seven feet long" and the strength of three black men in his charge, Mr. L. subjected Henson to a beating that left him with severe wounds to the head, a broken right arm, and shattered shoulder blades. Henson would not be able to work for five months, and never again be able to raise his hands above his head. After recounting his owner's unsuccessful attempt to have Mr. L. prosecuted "for abusing and maiming his slave," Henson continues his narrative. —Ed.]

My situation, as overseer, I retained, together with the especial favor of my master, who was not displeased either with saving the expense of a large salary for a white superintendent, or with the superior crops I was able to raise for him. I will not deny that I used his property more freely than he would have done himself, in supplying his people with better food; but if I cheated him in this way, in small matters, it was unequivocally for his own benefit in more important ones; and I accounted, with the strictest honesty, for every dollar I received in the sale of the property entrusted to me. Gradually the disposal of every thing raised on the farm, the wheat, oats, hay, fruit, butter, and whatever else there might be, was confided to me, as it was quite evident that I could, and did sell for better prices than any one else he could employ, and he was quite incompetent to attend to the business himself. For many years I was his factotum, and supplied him with all his means for all his purposes, whether they were good or bad. I had no reason to think highly of his moral character, but it was my duty to be faithful to him, in the position in which he placed me; and I can boldly declare, before God and man, that I was so. I forgave him the causeless blows and injuries he had inflicted on me in childhood and youth, and was proud of the favor he now showed me, and of the character and reputation I had earned by strenuous and persevering efforts.

When I was about twenty-two years of age, I married a very efficient, and, for a slave, a very well-taught girl, belonging to a neighboring family, reputed to be pious and kind, whom I first met at the chapel I attended; and during nearly forty years that have since elapsed, I have had no reason to regret the connection, but many, to rejoice in it, and be grateful for it. She has borne me twelve children, eight of whom survive, and promise to be the comfort of my declining years.

Things remained in this condition for a considerable period; my occupations being to superintend the farming operations, and to sell the produce in the neighboring markets of Washington and Georgetown. Many respectable people, yet living there, may possibly have some recollection of " 'Siah," or "Si," (as they used to call me,) as their market-man; but if they have forgotten me, I remember them with an honest satisfaction.

After passing his youth in the manner I have mentioned in a general way, and which I do not wish more particularly to describe, my master, at the age of forty-five, or upwards, married a young woman of eighteen, who had some little property, and more thrift. Her economy was remarkable, and was certainly no addition to the comfort of the establishment. She had a younger brother, Francis, to whom R. was appointed guardian, and who used to complain—not without reason, I am confident—of the meanness of the provision made for the household; and he would often come to me, with tears in his eyes, to tell me he could not get enough to eat. I made him my friend for life, by sympathizing in his emotions, and satisfying his appetite, sharing with him the food I took care to provide for my own family.

[Despite the thrift of his wife, Mr. R.'s finances go from bad to worse. Believing that seizure of his human property is imminent, Mr. R. entrusts his good and faithful servant 'Siah with escorting his slaves, eighteen in all, to a brother in Kentucky, with the understanding that he and his household will soon follow.

The Negro caravan sets out from Maryland in February 1825. When they arrive in Ohio, a free state, they are urged by more than a few people to seize the day and take their liberty. As Henson tells his reader, freedom was more than a notion: "From my earliest recollection, freedom had been the object of my ambition, a constant motive to exertion, an ever-present stimulus to gain and to save. No other means of obtaining it, however, had occurred to me, but purchasing myself of my master. The idea of running away was not one that I had ever indulged." And it is not one that he indulges in Ohio: "I had promised that man to take his property to Kentucky, and deposit it with his brother; and this, and this only, I resolved to do." True to his word, in the middle of April 1825, Henson delivers himself and the others to Mr. R.'s brother, possessor of a large plantation with, Henson estimates, eighty to one hundred slaves.

Henson's owner never comes to Kentucky. Three years pass before news arrives that because his wife refuses to move, Mr. R. is staying put. Henson also finds out that Mr. R. has made plans to sell all his slaves save Henson and his family.

Eventually, with the encouragement and aid of a white Methodist preacher, Henson decides to return to Maryland in order to persuade his owner to let him buy his freedom.

When Henson arrives in Maryland he does so with a substantial down payment on himself ($350), money raised from preaching and speaking engagements as well as donations while en route to Maryland. Mr. R. agrees to manumission; however, after he has Henson's money in hand, he not only reneges on the deal, but also plots to sell Henson down the river, literally.

Henson is about to leave for New Orleans, under the pretext of accompanying Mr. R.'s nephew on a journey, when his narrative continues. —Ed.]

My wife and children accompanied me to the landing, where I bade them an adieu, which might be for life, and then stepped into the boat, which I found manned by three white men, who had been hired for the trip. Mr. Amos and myself were the only other persons on board. The load consisted of beef-cattle, pigs, poultry, corn, whiskey, and other articles from the farm, and from some of the neighboring estates, which were to be sold as we dropped down the river, wherever they could be disposed of to the greatest advantage. It was a common trading voyage to New Orleans, in which I was embarked, the interest of which consisted not in the incidents that occurred, not in storms, or shipwreck, or external disaster of any sort; but in the storm of passions contending within me, and the imminent risk of the shipwreck of my soul, which was impending over me nearly the whole period of the voyage. One circumstance, only, I will mention, illustrating, as other events of my life have often done, the counsel of the Saviour, "He that will be chief among you, let him be your servant."

We were, of course, all bound to take our trick at the helm in turn, sometimes under direction of the captain, and sometimes on our own responsibility, as he could not be always awake. In the daytime there was less difficulty than at night, when it required some one who knew the river, to avoid sand-bars and snags, and the captain was the only person on board who had this knowledge. But whether by day or by night, as I was the only negro on the boat, I was made to stand at least three tricks to any other person's one; so that from being much with the captain, and frequently thrown upon my own exertions, I learnt the art of steering and managing the boat far better than the rest. I watched the manœuvres necessary to shoot by a sawyer, to land on a bank, or avoid a snag, or a steamboat, in the rapid current of the Mississippi, till I could do it as well as the captain. After a while the captain had a disease of the eyes, by which they became very much inflamed and swollen. He was soon rendered totally blind, and unable to perform his share of duty. This disorder is not an infrequent consequence of exposure to the intense light of the sun, doubled as it is by the reflection from the river. I was the person who could best take his place, and I was, in fact, master of the boat from that time till our arrival at New Orleans.

After the captain became blind, we were obliged to lie by at night, as none of the rest of us had been down the river before; and it was necessary to keep watch all night, to prevent depredations by the negroes on shore, who used frequently to attack such boats as ours, for the sake of the provisions on board. As I paced backwards and forwards on the deck, during my watch, it may well be believed I revolved many a painful and passionate thought. After all that I had done for Isaac and Amos R., after all the regard they professed for me, and the value they could not but put upon me, such a return as this for my services, such an evidence of their utter inattention to my claims upon them, and the intense selfishness with which they were ready to sacrifice me, at any moment, to their supposed interest, turned my blood to gall and wormwood, and changed me from a lively, and I will say, a pleasant-tempered fellow, into a savage, morose, dangerous slave. I was going not at all as a lamb to the slaughter, but I felt myself becoming more ferocious every day; and as we approached the place where this iniquity was to be consummated, I became more and more agitated with an almost uncontrollable fury. I had met, on the passage, with some of my Maryland acquaintance who had been sold off to this region; and their haggard and wasted appearance told a piteous story of excessive labor and insufficient food. I said to myself, "If this is to be my lot, I cannot survive it long. I am not so young as these men, and if it has brought them to such a condition, it will soon kill me. I am to be taken by my masters and owners, who ought to be my grateful friends, to a place and a condition where my life is to be shortened, as well as made more wretched. Why should I not prevent this wrong, if I can, by shortening their lives, or those of their agents in accomplishing such detestable injustice? I can do the last easily enough. They have no suspicion of me, and they are at this moment under my control, and in my power. There are many ways in which I can despatch them and escape, and I feel that I should be justified in availing myself of the first good opportunity." These were not thoughts which just flitted across my mind's eye, and then disappeared. They fashioned themselves into shapes which grew larger, and seemed firmer, every time they presented themselves; and at length my mind was made up to convert the phantom shadow into a positive reality. I resolved to kill my four companions, take what money there was in the boat, then to scuttle the craft, and escape to the north. It was a poor plan, may-be, and would very likely have failed; but it was as well contrived, under the circumstances, as the plans of murderers usually are; and blinded by passion, and stung to madness as I was, I could not see any difficulty about it. One dark, rainy night, within a few days of New Orleans, my hour seemed to have come. I was alone on the deck; Mr. Amos and the hands were all asleep below, and I crept down noiselessly, got hold of an axe, entered the cabin, and looking by the aid of

272 ◆ JOSIAH HENSON

the dim light there for my victims, my eye fell upon Master Amos, who was nearest to me; my hand slid along the axe-handle, I raised it to strike the fatal blow,—when suddenly the thought came to me, "What! commit *murder!* and you a Christian?" I had not called it murder before. It was self-defence,—it was preventing others from murdering me,—it was justifiable, it was even praiseworthy. But now, all at once, the truth burst upon me that it was a crime. I was going to kill a young man, who had done nothing to injure me, but obey commands which he could not resist; I was about to lose the fruit of all my efforts at self-improvement, the character I had acquired, and the peace of mind which had never deserted me. All this came upon me instantly, and with a distinctness which made me almost think I heard it whispered in my ear; and I believe I even turned my head to listen. I shrunk back, laid down the axe, crept up on deck again, and thanked God, as I have done every day since, that I had not committed murder.

My feelings were still agitated, but they were changed. I was filled with shame and remorse for the design I had entertained, and with the fear that my companions would detect it in my face, or that a careless word would betray my guilty thoughts. I remained on deck all night, instead of rousing one of the men to relieve me, and nothing brought composure to my mind, but the solemn resolution I then made to resign myself to the will of God, and take with thankfulness, if I could, but with submission, at all events, whatever he might decide should be my lot. I reflected that if my life were reduced to a brief term, I should have less to suffer, and that it was better to die with a Christian's hope, and a quiet conscience, than to live with the incessant recollection of a crime that would destroy the value of life, and under the weight of a secret that would crush out the satisfaction that might be expected from freedom and every other blessing.

It was long before I recovered my self-control and serenity; but I believe no one but those to whom I have told the story myself, ever suspected me of having entertained such thoughts for a moment.

This portrait was the frontispiece to the 1858 version of Henson's life story, Truth Stranger Than Fiction: Father Henson's Story of His Own Life.

In a few days after this tremendous crisis we arrived in New Orleans, and the little that remained of our cargo was soon sold, the men were discharged, and nothing was left but to dispose of me, and break up the boat, and then Mr. Amos would take passage on a steamboat, and go home. There was no longer any disguise about the purpose of selling me. Mr. Amos acknowledged that such were his instructions, and he set about fulfilling them. Several planters came to the boat to look at me; and I was sent of some hasty errand, that they might see how I could run. My points were canvassed as those of a horse would have been; and doubtless some account of my human faculties was thrown into the discussion of the bargain, that my value as a domestic animal might be enhanced. Amos had talked, with apparent kindness, about getting me a good master, who would employ me as a coachman, or as a house-servant; but as time passed on I could discern no particular effort of the kind. At length every thing was wound up but this single affair. The boat was to be sold, and I was to be sold, the next day, and Amos was to set off on his return, at six o'clock in the afternoon. I could not sleep that night, which seemed long enough to me, though it was one of the shortest in the year. The slow way in which we had come down had brought us to the long days and the heat of June; and everybody knows what the climate of New Orleans is at that time of the year.

A little before daylight master Amos awoke indisposed. His stomach was disordered, but he lay down again, thinking it would pass off. In a little while he was up again, and felt more sick than before, and it was soon evident that the river fever was upon him. He became rapidly worse, and by eight o'clock in the morning he was utterly prostrate; his head was on my lap, and he was begging me to help him, to do something for him, to save him. The tables were turned. He was now rather more dependent upon me than I had been upon him the day before. He entreated me to despatch matters, to sell the flat boat, in which we two had been living by ourselves for some days, and to get him and his trunk, containing the proceeds of the trip, on board the steamer as quick as possible, and especially not to desert him so long as he lived, nor to suffer his body, if he died, to be thrown into the river. I attended to all his requests, and by twelve o'clock that day, he was in one of the cabins of the steamer appropriated to sick passengers.

All was done which could be done for the comfort and relief of any one in such a desperate condition. But he was reduced to extremity. He ceased to grow worse after a day or two, and he must speedily have died, if he had not; but his strength was so entirely gone, that he could neither speak, nor move a limb; and could only indicate his wish for a teaspoonful of gruel, or something to moisten his throat, by a feeble motion of his lips. I nursed him carefully and constantly. Nothing else could have saved his life. It hung by a thread for a long time. We were as much as twelve days in reaching home, for the water was low at that season, particularly in the Ohio river; and when we arrived at our landing he was still unable to speak, and could only be moved on a sheet, or a litter. Something of this sort was soon fixed up at the landing, on which he could be carried to the house, which was five miles off; and I got a party of the slaves belonging to the estate to form relays for the purpose. As we approached the house, the surprise at seeing me back again, and the perplexity to imagine what I was bringing along, with such a party, were extreme; but the discovery was soon made which explained the strange appearance; and the grief of father and mother, and brothers and sisters, made itself seen and heard. Loud and long were the lamentations over poor Amos; and when the family came a little to themselves, great were the commendations bestowed upon me, for my care of him and of the property.

[Henson suspects that his owner's gratitude will be short-lived and that he will soon lay new plans to sell him away from his family. And so, he determines to "make my escape to Canada."

They will be a party of six: father, mother, two teenage (?) boys, and two tots. So that they might make utmost haste during their escape, Henson has his wife make a large knapsack in which to carry the two small children. As part of the preparation for their journey, after a day's work Henson would often "pack the little ones on my back . . . and trot around the cabin with them, and go some little distance from it, in order to accustom both of them and myself to the task before us." —Ed.]

At length the eventful night came. I went up to the house to ask leave to take Tom home with me, that he might have his clothes mended. No objection was made, and I bade Master Amos "good night" for the last time. It was about the middle of September, and by nine o'clock in the evening all was ready. It was a dark, moonless night, and we got into the little skiff in which I had induced a fellow-slave to take us across the river. It was an agitating and solemn moment. The good fellow who was rowing us over, said this affair might end in his death; "but," said he, "you will not be brought back alive, will you?" "Not if I can help it," I answered. "And if you are overpowered and return," he asked, "will you conceal my part of the business?" "That I will, so help me God," I replied. "Then I am easy," he answered, "and wish you success." We landed on the Indiana shore, and I began to feel that I was my own master. But in what circumstances of fear and misery still! We were to travel by night, and rest by day, in the woods and bushes. We were thrown absolutely upon our own poor and small resources, and were to rely on our own strength alone. The population was not so numerous as now, nor so well disposed to the slave. We dared look to no one for help. But my courage was equal to the occasion, and we trudged on cautiously and steadily, and as fast as the darkness, and the feebleness of my wife and boys would allow.

It was nearly a fortnight before we reached Cincinnati; and a day or two previous to getting there, our provisions were used up, and I had the misery to hear the cry of hunger and exhaustion from those I loved so dearly. It was necessary to run the risk of exposure by daylight upon the road; so I sprung upon it boldly from our hiding place one morning, and turned towards the south, to prevent the suspicion of my going the other way. I approached the first house I saw, and asked if they would sell me a little bread and meat. No, they had nothing for black fellows. At the next I succeeded better, but had to make as good a bargain as I could, and that was not very successful, with a man who wanted to see how little he could give me for my quarter of a dollar. As soon as I had succeeded in making a purchase, I followed the road, still towards the south, till I got out of sight of the house, and then darted into the woods again, and returned northward, just out of sight of the road. The food which I bought, such as it was, put new life and strength into my wife and children when I got back to them again, and we at length arrived safe at Cincinnati. There we were kindly received and entertained for several days, my wife and little ones were refreshed, and then we were carried on our way thirty miles in a wagon.

We followed the same course as before, of travelling by night, and resting by day, till we arrived at the Scioto, where we had been told we should strike the military road of General Hull, in the last war with Great Britain, and might then safely travel by day. We found the road, accordingly, by the large sycamore and elm which marked its beginning, and entered upon it with fresh spirits early in the day. Nobody had told us that it was cut through the wilderness, and I had neglected to provide any food, thinking we should soon come to some habitation, where we could be supplied. But we travelled on all day without seeing one, and laid down at night, hungry and weary enough. I thought I heard the howling of wolves, and the terror inspired by this, and the exertions I used to keep them off, by making as much noise as I could, took away all power of sleeping, till daylight, and rendered a little delay inevitable. In the morning we were as hungry as ever, but had nothing to relieve our appetites but a little piece of dried beef. I divided some of this all round, and then started for a second day's trip in the wilderness. It was a hard trial, and this day is a memorable one in my life. The road was rough, of course, being neglected, and the logs lying across it constantly; the underbrush was somewhat cleared away, and that was about all to mark the track. As we went wearily on, I was a little ahead of my wife and the boys, when I heard them call to me, and, turning round, saw that my wife had fallen over a log, and was prostrate on the ground. "Mother's dying," cried Tom; and when I reached her, it seemed really so. She had fainted. I did not know but it might be fatal, and was half distracted with the fear and the uncertainty. In a few minutes, however, she recovered sufficiently to take a few mouthfuls of the beef, and this, with a little rest, revived her so much that she bravely set out once more.

We had not gone far, and I suppose it was about three o'clock in the afternoon, when we discerned some persons approaching us at no great distance. We were instantly on the alert, as we could hardly expect them to be friends. The advance of a few paces showed me they were Indians, with packs on their shoulders; and they were so near that if they were hostile, it would be useless to try to escape. So I walked along boldly, till we came close upon them. They were bent down with their burdens, and had not raised their eyes till now; and when they did so, and saw me coming towards them, they looked at me in a frightened sort of way for a moment, and then, setting up a peculiar howl, turned round, and ran as fast as they could. There were three or four of them, and what they were afraid of I could not imagine, unless they supposed I was the devil, whom they had perhaps heard of as black. But even then one would have thought my wife and children might have reassured them. However, there was no doubt they were well frightened, and we heard their wild and prolonged howl, as they ran, for a mile or more. My wife was alarmed too, and thought they were merely running back to collect more of a party, and then to come and murder us, and she wanted to turn back. I told her they were numerous enough to do that, if they wanted to, without help; and that as for turning back, I had had quite too much of the road behind us, and that it would be a ridiculous thing that both parties should run away. If they were disposed to run, I would follow. We did follow on, and soon the noise was stopped; and, as we advanced, we could discover Indians peeping at us from behind the trees, and dodging out of our sight, if they thought we were looking at them. Presently we came upon their wigwams, and saw a fine looking, stately Indian, with his arms folded, waiting for us to approach. He was apparently the chief, and, saluting us civilly, he soon discovered that we were human beings, and spoke to his young men, who were scattered about, and made them come in, and give up their foolish fears. And now curiosity seemed to prevail. Each one wanted to touch the children, who were shy as partridges, with their long life in the woods; and as they shrunk away, and uttered a little cry of alarm, the Indian would jump back too, as if he thought they would bite him. However, a little while sufficed to make them understand what we were, and whither we were going, and what we needed; and as little, to set them about supplying our wants, feeding us bountifully, and giving us a comfortable wigwam for our night's rest. The next day we resumed our march, and found, from the Indians, that we were only about twenty-five miles from the lake. They sent some of their young men to point out the place where we were to turn off, and parted from us with as much kindness as possible.

In passing over the part of Ohio near the lake, where such an extensive plain is found, we came to a spot overflowed by a stream, across which the road passed. I forded it first, with the help of a sounding-pole, and then taking the children on my back, first, the two little ones, and then the others, one at a time, and, lastly, my wife, I succeeded in getting them all safely across, where the ford was one hundred to one hundred and fifty yards wide, and the deepest part perhaps four feet deep. At this time the skin was worn from my back to an extent almost equal to the size of my knapsack.

[Soon, the family is in a "wide plain" southwest of Sandusky city, and then, near water. After hiding his family in some bushes, Henson ventures toward a ship loading cargo. When asked if he is looking for work, Henson says yes. While working, he asks around about the best way to reach Canada. His inquiry is made known to the ship's captain, a "Scotchman" by the name of Burnham, who, "by his frank look and manner soon induced me to acknowledge my condition and purpose."

Passage to Buffalo is what comes of Henson's conversation with Captain Burnham. When the ship drops anchor at Black Rock, this good captain, as Henson fondly recalls, "put us on board the ferry-boat to Waterloo, paid the passage money, and gave me a dollar in parting." Soon, the Henson family is free, at last. —Ed.]

When I got on the Canada side, on the morning of the 28th of October, 1830, my first impulse was to throw myself on the ground, and giving way to the riotous exultation of my feelings, to execute sundry antics which excited the astonishment of those who were looking on. A gentleman of the neighborhood, Colonel Warren, who happened to be present, thought I was in a fit, and as he inquired what was the matter with the poor fellow, I jumped up and told him *I was free*. "O," said he, with a hearty laugh, "is that it? I never knew freedom make a man roll in the sand before." It is not much to be wondered at, that my certainty of being free was not quite a sober one at the first moment; and I hugged and kissed my wife and children all round, with a vivacity which made them laugh as well as myself. There was not much time to be lost, though, in frolic, even at this extraordinary moment. I was a stranger, in a strange land, and had to look about me at once, for refuge and resource. I found a lodging for the night; and the next morning set about exploring the interior for the means of support. I knew nothing about the country, or the people; but kept my eyes and ears open, and made such inquiries as opportunity afforded. I heard, in the course of the day, of a Mr. Hibbard, who lived some six or seven miles off, and who was a rich man, as riches were counted there, with a large farm, and several small tenements on it, which he was in the habit of letting to his laborers. To him I went, immediately, though the character given him by his neighbors was not, by any means, unexceptionably good. But I thought he was not probably any worse than those I had been accustomed to serve, and that I could get along with him, if honest and faithful work would satisfy him. In the afternoon I found him, and soon struck a bargain with him for employment. I asked him if there was any house where he would let me live. He said yes, and led the way to an old two story sort of shanty, into the lower story of which the pigs had broken, and had apparently made it their resting-place for some time. Still, it was a house, and I forthwith expelled the pigs, and set about cleaning it for the occupancy of a better sort of tenants. With the aid of hoe and shovel, hot-water and a mop, I got the floor into a tolerable condition by midnight, and only then did I rest from my labor. The next day I brought the rest of the Hensons to *my house,* and though there was nothing there but bare walls and floors, we were all in a state of great delight, and my old woman laughed and acknowledged that it was worth while, and that it was better than a log-cabin with an earth-floor. I begged some straw of Mr. Hibbard, and confining it by logs in the corners of the room, I made beds of it three feet thick, upon which we reposed luxuriously after our long fatigues.

[In time, the Hensons settle down into a relatively good life. One high point is when the oldest son, Tom, gets a little school-ing, and then one day proposes to teach his father to read. Hen-son's touch of education fills him with a deep desire to help lift other black people out of "the terrible abyss of ignorance." It is a yearning without shape or form—but not forever. —Ed.]

After about three years had passed, I improved my condition again by taking service with a gentleman by the name of Riseley, whose residence was only a few miles distant, and who was a man of more elevation of mind than Mr. Hibbard, and of superior abilities. At his place I began to reflect, more and more, upon the circum-stances of the blacks, who were already somewhat numerous in this region. I was not the only one who had escaped from the States, and had settled on the first spot in Canada which they had reached.

Several hundreds of colored persons were in the neighborhood; and in the first joy of their deliverance, were going on in a way which, I could see, led to little or no progress in improvement. They were content to have the proceeds of their labor at their own command, and had not the ambition for, or the perception of what was within their easy reach, if they did but know it. They were generally working for hire upon the lands of others, and had not yet dreamed of becoming independent proprietors themselves. It soon became my great object to awaken them to a sense of the advantages which offered themselves to their grasp; and Mr. Riseley, seeing clearly the justness of my views, and willing to coöperate with me in the attempt to make them generally known among the blacks, permitted me to call meetings, at his house, of those who were known to be among the most intelligent and successful of our class. At these meetings we considered and discussed the subject, till we were all of one mind; and it was agreed, among the ten or twelve of us who assembled at them, that we would invest our earnings in land, and undertake the task, which, though no light one certainly, would yet soon reward us for our effort, of settling upon wild lands which we could call our own; and where every tree which we felled, and every bushel of corn we raised, would be for ourselves; in other words, where we could secure all the profits of our own labor.

The advantages of this course need not be dwelt upon in a country which is every day exemplifying it, and has done so for two hundred years and more; and has, by this very means, acquired an indestructible character for energy, enterprise, and self-reliance. It was precisely the Yankee spirit which I wished to instill into my fellow-slaves, if possible; and I was not deterred from the task by the perception of the immense contrast in all the habits and character generated by long ages of freedom and servitude, activity and sloth, independence and subjection. My associates agreed with me, and we resolved to select some spot among the many offered to our choice, where we would colonize and raise our own crops, eat our own bread, and be, in short, our own masters. I was deputed to explore the country, and find a place to which I would be willing to migrate myself; and they all said they would go with me whenever such a one should be found. I set out accordingly in the autumn of 1834, and travelled on foot all over the extensive region between lakes Ontario, Erie, and Huron. When I came to the territory east of Lake St. Clair and Detroit River, I was strongly impressed with its fertility, its convenience, and, indeed, its superiority, for our purposes, to any other spot I had seen. I determined this should be the place; and so reported, on my return, to my future companions. They were wisely cautious, however, and sent me off again in the summer, that I might see it at the opposite seasons of the year, and be better able to judge of its advantages. I found no reason to change my opinion, but upon going further towards the head of Lake Erie, I discovered an extensive tract of government land, which, for some years, had been granted to a Mr. McCormick upon certain conditions, and which he had rented out to settlers upon such terms as he could obtain. This land being already cleared, offered some advantages for the immediate raising of crops, which were not to be overlooked by persons whose resources were so limited as ours; and we determined to go there first, for a time, and with the proceeds of what we could earn there, to make our purchases in Dawn afterwards. This plan was followed, and some dozen or more of us settled upon these lands the following spring, and accumulated something by the crops of wheat and tobacco we were able to raise.

I discovered, before long, that McCormick had not complied with the conditions of his grant, and was not, therefore, entitled to the rent he exacted from settlers. I was advised by Sir John Cockburn, to whom I applied on the subject, to appeal to the legislature for relief. We did so; and though McCormick was able, by the aid of his friends, to defeat us for one year, yet we succeeded the next, upon a second appeal, and were freed from all rent, thereafter, so long as we remained. Still, this was not our own land. The government, though it demanded no rent, might set up the land for sale at any time, and then we should, probably, be driven off by wealthier purchasers, with the entire loss of all our improvements, and with no retreat provided. It was manifest that it was altogether better for us to purchase before competition was invited; and we kept this fully in mind during the time we staid here. We remained in this position six or seven years; and all this while the colored population was increasing rapidly around us, and spreading very fast into the interior settlements and the large towns. The immigration from the United States was incessant, and some, I am not unwilling to admit, were brought hither with my knowledge and connivance. I was glad to help such of my old friends as had the spirit to make the attempt to free themselves; and I made more than one trip, about this time, to Maryland and Kentucky, with the expectation, in which I was not disappointed, that some might be enabled to follow in my footsteps. I knew the route pretty well, and had much greater facilities for travelling than when I came out of that Egypt for the first time.

I did not find that our prosperity increased with our numbers. The mere delight the slave took in his freedom, rendered him, at first, contented with a lot far inferior to that which he might have attained. Then his ignorance led him to make unprofitable bargains, and he would often hire wild land on short terms, and bind himself to clear a certain number of acres; and by the time they were cleared and fitted for cultivation his lease was out, and his landlord would come in, and raise a splendid crop on the new land; and the tenant would, very likely, start again on just such another bargain, and be no better off at the end of ten years than he was at the beginning. Another way in which they lost the profits of their labor, was by raising nothing but tobacco, the high price of which was very tempting, and the cultivation of which was a monopoly in their hands, as no white man understood it, or could compete with them at all. The consequence was, however, that they had nothing but tobacco to sell; there was rather too much of it in the market, and the price of wheat rose, while their commodity was depressed; and they lost all they should have saved, in the profit they gave the trader for his corn and stores. I saw the effect of these things so clearly that I could not help trying to make my friends and neighbors see it too; and I set seriously about the business of lecturing upon the subject of crops, wages, and profits, as if I had been brought up to it. I insisted on the necessity of their raising their own crops, saving their own wages, and securing the profits of their own labor, with such plain arguments as occurred to me, and were as clear to their comprehension as to mine. I did this very openly; and, frequently, my audience consisted in part of the very traders whose inordinate profits upon individuals I was trying to diminish, but whose balance of profit would not be ultimately lessened, because they would have so many more persons to trade with who would be able to pay them a reasonable advance in cash, or its equivalent, on all their purchases. The purse is a tender part of the system; but I handled it so gently, that the sensible portion of my natural opponents were not, I believe, offended; while those whom I wished to benefit, saw, for the most part, the propriety of my advice, and took it. At least, there are now great numbers of settlers, in this region of Canada, who own their farms, and are training up their children in true independence, and giving them a good elementary education, who had not taken a single step towards such a result before I began to talk to them.

[With the assistance of a Congregationalist minister and his Quaker friend, Henson's community receives funds to help them continue to help themselves. Land in the town of Dawn and a school are the first priorities. As part of his contribution to his community's buildup, Henson goes on speaking engagements in the northeast. It is with special mention of donations from Boston that enable the settlement to construct a sawmill and thus clear the land in order to plant and harvest cash and keep crops—and thus support their school—that Josiah Henson brings his narrative to a close. —Ed.]

I could give here a great many particulars, which would amuse and interest the reader, if they did not instruct him. But it is better not to indulge the inclination; and I will conclude my narrative by simply recording my gratitude, heartfelt and inexpressible, to God, and to many of my fellow-men, for the vast improvement in my condition, both physical and mental; for the great degree of comfort with which I am surrounded; for the good I have been enabled to effect; for the light which has risen upon me; for the religious privileges I enjoy, and the religious hopes I am permitted to cherish; for the prospects opening to my children, so different from what they might have been; and, finally, for the cheering expectation of benefiting not only the present, but many future generations of my race.

F R O M

Running a Thousand Miles for Freedom: Or, the Escape of William and Ellen Craft from Slavery

by William and Ellen Craft

[William and Ellen Craft of Macon, Georgia, came up with a most ingenious plan of escape, the critical element of which was Ellen's masquerade as William's "master." To this end, Ellen, who was a light-skinned quadroon, cut her hair short and donned clothes befitting a Southern gentleman: black trousers, a black cloak, a white dress shirt, an ascot, a beaver stovepipe hat. To further disguise her feminine features as well as discourage conversation, Ellen came up with the idea of a poultice in a white handkerchief "to be worn under the chin, up the cheeks, and to tie over the head." To excuse her from any writing, she'd put her right hand in a sling.

With Ellen thus disguised and William readied for his role as "William Johnson's" manservant, the Crafts made their break for freedom on December 21, 1848. —Ed.]

When the time had arrived for us to start, we blew out the lights, knelt down, and prayed to our Heavenly Father mercifully to assist us, as he did his people of old, to escape from cruel bondage; and we shall ever feel that God heard and answered our prayer. Had we not been sustained by a kind, and I sometimes think special, providence, we could never have overcome the mountainous difficulties which I am now about to describe.

After this we rose and stood for a few moments in breathless silence,—we were afraid that some one might have been about the cottage listening and watching our movements. So I took my wife by the hand, stepped softly to the door, raised the latch, drew it open, and peeped out. Though there were trees all around the house, yet the foliage scarcely moved; in fact, everything appeared to be as still as death. I then whispered to my wife, "Come my dear, let us make a desperate leap for liberty!" But poor thing, she shrank back, in a state of trepidation. I turned and asked what was the matter; she made no reply, but burst into violent sobs, and threw her head upon my breast. This appeared to touch my very heart, it caused me to enter into her feelings more fully than ever. We both saw the many mountainous difficulties that rose one after the other before our view, and knew far too well what our sad fate would have been, were we caught and forced back into our slavish den. Therefore on my wife's fully realizing the solemn fact that we had to take our lives, as it were, in our hands, and contest every inch of the thousand miles of slave territory over which we had to pass, it made her heart almost sink within her, and, had I known them at that time, I would have repeated the following encouraging lines, which may not be out of place here—

> *"The hill, though high, I covet to ascend,*
> *The* difficulty will not me offend;
> *For I perceive the way to life lies here:*
> *Come, pluck up heart, let's neither faint nor fear;*
> *Better, though difficult, the right way to go,—*
> *Than wrong, though easy, where the end is woe."*

However, the sobbing was soon over, and after a few moments of silent prayer she recovered her self-possession, and said, "Come,

William, it is getting late, so now let us venture upon our perilous journey."

We then opened the door, and stepped as softly out as "moonlight upon the water." I locked the door with my own key, which I now have before me, and tiptoed across the yard into the street. I say tiptoed, because we were like persons near a tottering avalanche, afraid to move, or even breathe freely, for fear the sleeping tyrants should be aroused, and come down upon us with double vengeance, for daring to attempt to escape in the manner which we contemplated.

We shook hands, said farewell, and started in different directions for the railway station. I took the nearest possible way to the train, for fear I should be recognized by some one, and got into the negro car in which I knew I should have to ride; but my *master* (as I will now call my wife) took a longer way round, and only arrived there with the bulk of the passengers. He obtained a ticket for himself and one for his slave to Savannah, the first port, which was about two hundred miles off. My master then had the luggage stowed away, and stepped into one of the best carriages.

But just before the train moved off I peeped through the window, and, to my great astonishment, I saw the cabinet-maker with whom I had worked so long, on the platform. He stepped up to the ticket-seller, and asked some question, and then commenced looking rapidly through the passengers, and into the carriages. Fully believing that we were caught, I shrank into a corner, turned my face from the door, and expected in a moment to be dragged out. The cabinet-maker looked into my master's carriage, but did not know him in his new attire, and, as God would have it, before he reached mine the bell rang, and the train moved off.

I have heard since that the cabinet-maker had a presentiment that we were about to "make tracks for parts unknown;" but, not seeing me, his suspicions vanished, until he received the startling intelligence that we had arrived safely in a free State.

As soon as the train had left the platform, my master looked round in the carriage, and was terror-stricken to find a Mr. Cray—an old friend of my wife's master, who dined with the family the day before, and knew my wife from childhood—sitting on the same seat.

The doors of the American railway carriages are at the ends. The passengers walk up the aisle, and take seats on either side; and as my master was engaged in looking out of the window, he did not see who came in.

My master's first impression, after seeing Mr. Cray, was, that he was there for the purpose of securing him. However, my master thought it was not wise to give any information respecting himself, and for fear that Mr. Cray might draw him into conversation and recognise his voice, my master resolved to feign deafness as the only means of self-defence.

After a little while, Mr. Cray said to my master, "It is a very fine morning, sir." The latter took no notice, but kept looking out of the window. Mr. Cray soon repeated this remark, in a little louder tone, but my master remained as before. This indifference attracted the attention of the passengers near, one of whom laughed out. This, I suppose, annoyed the old gentleman; so he said, "I will make him hear;" and in a loud tone of voice repeated, "It is a very fine morning, sir."

My master turned his head, and with a polite bow said, "Yes," and commenced looking out of the window again.

One of the gentlemen remarked that it was a very great deprivation to be deaf. "Yes," replied Mr. Cray, "and I shall not trouble that fellow any more." This enabled my master to breathe a little easier, and to feel that Mr. Cray was not his pursuer after all.

. . . We arrived at Savannah early in the evening, and got into an omnibus, which stopped at the hotel for the passengers to take tea. I stepped into the house and brought my master something on a tray to the omnibus, which took us in due time to the steamer, which was bound for Charleston, South Carolina.

Soon after going on board, my master turned in; and as the captain and some of the passengers seemed to think this strange, and also questioned me respecting him, my master thought I had better get out the flannels and opodeldoc which we had prepared for the rheumatism, warm them quickly by the stove in the gentleman's saloon, and bring them to his berth. We did this as an excuse for my master's retiring to bed so early.

While at the stove one of the passengers said to me, "Buck, what have you got there?" "Opodeldoc, sir," I replied. "I should think it's opo-*devil,*" said a lanky swell, who was leaning back in a chair with his heels upon the back of another, and chewing tobacco as if for a wager; "it stinks enough to kill or cure twenty men. Away with it, or I reckon I will throw it overboard!"

It was by this time warm enough, so I took it to my master's berth, remained there a little while, and then went on deck and asked the steward where I was to sleep. He said there was no place provided for coloured passengers, whether slave or free. So I paced the deck till a late hour, then mounted some cotton bags, in a warm place near the funnel, sat there till morning, and then went and assisted my master to get ready for breakfast.

He was seated at the right hand of the captain, who, together with all the passengers, inquired very kindly after his health. As my master had one hand in a sling, it was my duty to carve his food. But when I went out the captain said, "You have a very attentive boy, sir; but you had better watch him like a hawk when you get on to the North. He seems all very well here, but he may act quite differently there. I know several gentlemen who have lost their valuable niggers among them d———d cut-throat abolitionists."

Before my master could speak, a rough slave-dealer, who was sitting opposite, with both elbows on the table, and with a large piece of broiled fowl in his fingers, shook his head with emphasis, and in a deep Yankee tone, forced through his crowded mouth the words, "Sound doctrine, captain, very sound." He then dropped the chicken into the plate, leant back, placed his thumbs in the armholes of his fancy waistcoat, and continued, "I would not take a nigger to the North under no consideration. I have had a deal to do with niggers in my time, but I never saw one who ever had his heel upon free soil that was worth a d———n." "Now stranger," addressing my master, "if you have made up your mind to sell that ere nigger, I am your man; just mention your price, and if it isn't out of the way, I will pay for him on this board with hard silver dollars." This hard-featured, bristly-bearded, wire-headed, red-eyed monster, staring at my master as the serpent did at Eve, said, "What do you say, stranger?" He replied, "I don't wish to sell, sir; I cannot get on well without him."

"You will have to get on without him if you take him to the North," continued this man; "for I can tell ye, stranger, as a friend, I am an older cove than you, I have seen lots of this ere world, and I reckon I have had more dealings with niggers than any man living or dead. I was once employed by General Wade Hampton, for ten years, in doing nothing but breaking 'em in; and everybody knows that the General would not have a man that didn't understand his business. So I tell ye, stranger, again, you had better sell, and let me take him down to Orleans. He will do you no good if you take him across Mason's and Dixon's line; he is a keen nigger, and I can see from the cut of his eye that he is certain to run away." My master said, "I think not, sir; I have great confidence in his fidelity." "Fi*devil,*" indignantly said the dealer, as his fist came down upon the edge of the saucer and upset a cup of hot coffee in a gentleman's lap. (As the scalded man jumped up the trader quietly said, "Don't disturb yourself, neighbour; accidents will happen in the best of families.") "It always makes me mad to hear a man talking about fidelity in niggers. There isn't a d———d one on 'em who wouldn't cut sticks, if he had half a chance."

[Ellen goes up on deck only to have the slave trader follow and continue his harangue, which sends Ellen back into the cabin. —Ed.]

On my master entering the cabin he found at the breakfast-table a young southern military officer, with whom he had travelled some distance the previous day.

After passing the usual compliments the conversation turned upon the old subject,—niggers.

The officer, who was also travelling with a man-servant, said to my master, "You will excuse me, Sir, for saying I think you are very likely to spoil your boy by saying 'thank you' to him. I assure you, sir, nothing spoils a slave so soon as saying, 'thank you' and 'if you please' to him. The only way to make a nigger toe the mark, and to keep him in his place, is to storm at him like thunder, and keep him trembling like a leaf. Don't you see, when I speak to my Ned, he darts like lightning; and if he didn't I'd skin him."

Just then the poor dejected slave came in, and the officer swore at him fearfully, merely to teach my master what he called the proper way to treat me.

After he had gone out to get his master's luggage ready, the officer said, "That is the way to speak to them. If every nigger was drilled in this manner, they would be as humble as dogs, and never dare to run away.

The gentleman urged my master not to go to the North for the restoration of his health, but to visit the Warm Springs in Arkansas.

My master said, he thought the air of Philadelphia would suit his complaint best; and, not only so, he thought he could get better advice there.

The boat had now reached the wharf. The officer wished my master a safe and pleasant journey, and left the saloon.

There were a large number of persons on the quay waiting the arrival of the steamer: but we were afraid to venture out for fear that some one might recognize me; or that they had heard that we were gone, and had telegraphed to have us stopped. However, after remaining in the cabin till all the other passengers were gone, we had our luggage placed on a fly, and I took my master by the arm, and with a little difficulty he hobbled on shore, got in and drove off to the best hotel, which John C. Calhoun, and all the other great southern fire-eating statesmen, made their head-quarters while in Charleston.

On arriving at the house the landlord ran out and opened the door: but judging, from the poultices and green glasses, that my master was an invalid, he took him very tenderly by one arm and ordered his man to take the other.

My master then eased himself out, and with their assistance found no trouble in getting up the steps into the hotel. The proprietor made me stand on one side, while he paid my master the attention and homage he thought a gentleman of his high position merited.

[After an anxious respite in the hotel, the Crafts head to the Custom-house Office to arrange passage on a steamer bound for Wilmington, North Carolina. —Ed.]

When we reached the building, I helped my master into the office, which was crowded with passengers. He asked for a ticket for himself and one for his slave to Philadelphia. This caused the principal officer—a very mean-looking, cheese-coloured fellow, who was sitting there—to look up at us very suspiciously, and in a fierce tone of voice he said to me, "Boy, do you belong to that gentleman?" I quickly replied, "Yes, sir" (which was quite correct). The tickets were handed out, and as my master was paying for them the chief man said to him, "I wish you to register your name here, sir, and also the name of your nigger, and pay a dollar duty on him."

My master paid the dollar, and pointing to the hand that was in the poultice, requested the officer to register his name for him. This seemed to offend the "high-bred" South Carolinian. He jumped up, shaking his head; and, cramming his hands almost through the bottom of his trousers pockets, with a slave-bullying air, said, "I shan't do it."

This attracted the attention of all the passengers. Just then the young military officer with whom my master travelled and conversed on the steamer from Savannah stepped in, somewhat the worse for brandy; he shook hands with my master, and pretended to know all about him. He said, "I know his kin (friends) like a book;" and as the officer was known in Charleston, and was going to stop there with friends, the recognition was very much in my master's favour.

The captain of the steamer, a good-looking jovial fellow, seeing that the gentleman appeared to know my master, and perhaps not wishing to lose us as passengers, said in an off-hand sailor-like manner, "I will register the gentleman's name, and take the responsibility upon myself." He asked my master's name. He said, "William Johnson." The names were put down, I think, "Mr. Johnson and slave."

. . . We reached Wilmington the next morning, and took the train for Richmond, Virginia. I have stated that the American railway carriages (or cars, as they are called), are constructed differently to those in England. At one end of some of them, in the South, there is a little apartment with a couch on both sides for the convenience of families and invalids; and as they thought my master was very poorly, he was allowed to enter one of these apartments at Petersburg, Virginia, where an old gentleman and two handsome young ladies, his daughters, also got in, and took seats in the same carriage. But before the train started, the gentleman stepped into my car, and questioned me respecting my master. He wished to know what was the matter with him, where he was from, and where he was going. I told him where he came from, and said that he was suffering from a complication of complaints, and was going to Philadelphia, where he thought he could get more suitable advice than in Georgia.

The gentleman said my master could obtain the very best advice in Philadelphia. Which turned out to be quite correct, though he did not receive it from physicians, but from kind abolitionists who understood his case much better. The gentleman also said, "I reckon your master's father hasn't any more such faithful and smart boys as you." "O, yes, sir, he has," I replied, "lots on 'em." Which was literally true. This seemed all he wished to know. He thanked me, gave me a ten-cent piece, and requested me to be attentive to my good master. I promised that I would do so, and have ever since endeavoured to keep my pledge. During the gentleman's absence, the ladies and my master had a little cosy chat. But on his return, he said, "You seem to be very much afflicted, sir." "Yes, sir," replied the gentleman in the poultices. "What seems to be the matter with you, sir; may I be allowed to ask?" "Inflammatory rheumatism, sir." "Oh! that is very bad, sir," said the kind gentleman: "I can sympathise with you; for I know from bitter experience what the rheumatism is." If he did, he knew a good deal more than Mr. Johnson.

The gentleman thought my master would feel better if he would lie down and rest himself; and as he was anxious to avoid conversation, he at once acted upon this suggestion. The ladies politely rose, took their extra shawls, and made a nice pillow for the invalid's head. My master wore a fashionable cloth cloak, which they took and covered him comfortably on the couch. After he had been lying a little while the ladies, I suppose, thought he was asleep; so one of them gave a long sigh, and said, in a quiet fascinating tone, "Papa, he seems to be a very nice young gentleman." But before papa could speak, the other lady quickly said, "Oh! dear me, I never felt so much for a gentleman in my life!" To use an American expression, "they fell in love with the wrong chap."

[The young ladies and their father continue to fuss over the "very nice young gentleman" until they reach their destination, Richmond, Virginia.

One of Ellen's new carriage mates is an elderly woman who upon first seeing William takes him to be her Ned who took his liberty eighteen months earlier. Ellen swiftly convinces the woman that she is mistaken, but she can do little but endure the ensuing debate about slavery and emancipation among the passengers. The elderly woman has just gotten off the train when *Running a Thousand Miles for Freedom* continues. —Ed.]

For the purpose of somewhat disguising myself, I bought and wore a very good second-hand white beaver, an article which I had never indulged in before. So just before we arrived at Washington, an uncouth planter, who had been watching me very closely, said to my master, "I reckon, stranger, you are *'spiling'* that ere nigger of yourn, by letting him wear such a devilish fine hat. Just look at the quality on it; the President couldn't wear a better. I should just like to go and kick it overboard." His friend touched him, and said, "Don't speak so to a gentleman." "Why not?" exclaimed the fellow. He grated his short teeth, which appeared to be nearly worn away by the incessant chewing of tobacco, and said, "It always makes me itch all over, from head to toe, to get hold of every d———d nigger I see dressed like a white man. Washington is run away with *spiled* and free niggers. If I had my way I would sell every d———d rascal of 'em way down South, where the devil would be whipped out on 'em."

This man's fierce manner made my master feel rather nervous, and therefore he thought the less he said the better; so he walked off without making any reply. In a few minutes we were landed at Washington, where we took a conveyance and hurried off to the train for Baltimore.

We left our cottage on Wednesday morning, the 21st of December, 1848, and arrived at Baltimore, Saturday evening, the 24th (Christmas Eve). Baltimore was the last slave port of any note at which we stopped.

On arriving there we felt more anxious than ever, because we knew not what that last dark night would bring forth. It is true we were near the goal, but our poor hearts were still as if tossed at sea; and, as there was another great and dangerous bar to pass, we were afraid our liberties would be wrecked, and, like the ill-fated *Royal Charter*, go down for ever just off the place we longed to reach.

They are particularly watchful at Baltimore to prevent slaves from escaping into Pennsylvania, which is a free State. After I had seen my master into one of the best carriages, and was just about to step into mine, an officer, a full-blooded Yankee of the lower order, saw me. He came quickly up, and, tapping me on the shoulder, said in his unmistakable native twang, together with no little display of his authority, "Where are you going, boy?" "To Philadelphia, sir," I humbly replied. "Well, what are you going there for?" "I am travelling with my master, who is in the next carriage, sir." "Well, I calculate you had better get him out; and be mighty quick about it, because the train will soon be starting. It is against my rules to let any man take a slave past here, unless he can satisfy them in the office that he has a right to take him along."

The officer then passed on and left me standing upon the platform, with my anxious heart apparently palpitating in the throat. At first I scarcely knew which way to turn. But it soon occurred to me that the good God, who had been with us thus far, would not forsake us at the eleventh hour. So with renewed hope I stepped into my master's carriage, to inform him of the difficulty. I found him sitting at the farther end, quite alone. As soon as he looked up and saw me, he smiled. I also tried to wear a cheerful countenance, in order to break the shock of the sad news. I knew what made him smile. He was aware that if we were fortunate we should reach our destination at five o'clock the next morning, and this made it the more painful to communicate what the officer had said; but, as there was no time to lose, I went up to him and asked him how he felt. He said "Much better," and that he thanked God we were getting on so nicely. I then said we were not getting on quite so well as we had anticipated. He anxiously and quickly asked what was the matter. I told him. He started as if struck by lightning, and exclaimed, "Good Heavens! William, is it possible that we are, after all, doomed to hopeless bondage?" I could say nothing, my heart was too full to speak, for at first I did not know what to do. However we knew it would never do to turn back to the "City of Destruction," like Bunyan's *Mistrust* and *Timorous,* because they saw lions in the narrow way after ascending the hill Difficulty; but press on, like noble *Christian* and *Hopeful,* to the great city in which dwelt a few "shining ones." So, after a few moments, I did all I could to encourage my companion, and we stepped out and made for the office: but how or where my master obtained sufficient courage to face the tyrants who had power to blast all we held dear, heaven only knows! Queen Elizabeth could not have been more terror-stricken, on being forced to land at the traitors' gate leading to the Tower, than we were on entering that office. We felt that our very existence was at stake, and that we must either sink or swim. But, as God was our present and mighty helper in this as well as in all former trials, we were able to keep our heads up and press forwards.

On entering the room we found the principal man, to whom my master said, "Do you wish to see me, sir?" "Yes," said this eagle-eyed officer; and he added, "It is against our rules, sir, to allow any person to take a slave out of Baltimore into Philadelphia, unless he can satisfy us that he has a right to take him along." "Why is that?" asked my master," with more firmness than could be expected. "Because, sir," continued he, in a voice and manner that almost chilled our blood, "if we should suffer any gentleman to take a slave past here into Philadelphia; and should the gentleman with whom the slave might be travelling turn out not to be his rightful owner; and should the proper master come and prove that his slave escaped on our road, we shall have him to pay for; and, therefore, we cannot let any slave pass here without receiving security to show, and to satisfy us, that it is all right."

This conversation attracted the attention of the large number of bustling passengers. After the officer had finished, a few of them said, "Chit, chit, chit;" not because they thought we were slaves endeavouring to escape, but merely because they thought my master was a slaveholder and invalid gentleman, and therefore it was wrong to detain him. The officer, observing that the passengers sympathised with my master, asked him if he was not acquainted with some gentleman in Baltimore that he could get to endorse for him, to show that I was his property, and that he had a right to take me off. He said, "No;" and added, "I bought tickets in Charleston to pass us through to Philadelphia, and therefore you have no right to detain us here." "Well, sir," said the man, indignantly, "right or no right, we shan't let you go." These sharp words fell upon our anxious hearts like the crack of doom, and made us feel that hope only smiles to deceive.

For a few moments perfect silence prevailed. My master looked at me, and I at him, but neither of us dared to speak a word, for fear of making some blunder that would tend to our detection. We knew that the officers had power to throw us into prison, and if they had done so we must have been detected and driven back, like the vilest felons, to a life of slavery, which we dreaded far more than sudden death.

We felt as though we had come into deep waters and were about being overwhelmed, and that the slightest mistake would clip asunder the last brittle thread of hope by which we were suspended, and let us down for ever into the dark and horrible pit of misery and degradation from which we were straining every nerve to escape. While our hearts were crying lustily unto Him who is ever ready and able to save, the conductor of the train that we had just left stepped in. The officer asked if we came by the train with him from Washington; he said we did, and left the room. Just then the bell rang for the train to leave; and had it been the sudden shock of an earthquake it could not have given us a greater thrill. The sound of the bell caused every eye to flash with apparent interest, and to be more steadily fixed upon us than before. But, as God would have it, the officer all at once thrust his fingers through his hair, and in a state of great agitation said, "I really don't know what to do; I calculate it is all right." He then told the clerk to run and tell the conductor to "let this gentleman and slave pass;" adding, "As he is not well, it is a pity to stop him here. We will let him go." My master thanked him, and stepped out and hobbled across the platform as quickly as possible. I tumbled him unceremoniously into one of the best carriages, and leaped into mine just as the train was gliding off towards our happy destination. . . .

We left Baltimore about eight o'clock in the evening; and not being aware of a stopping-place of any consequence between there and Philadelphia, and also knowing that if we were fortunate we should be in the latter place early the next morning, I thought I might indulge in a few minutes' sleep in the car; but I, like Bunyan's Christian in the arbour, went to sleep at the wrong time, and took too long a nap. So, when the train reached Havre de Grace, all the first-class passengers had to get out of the carriages and into a ferryboat, to be ferried across the Susquehanna river, and take the train on the opposite side.

The road was constructed so as to be raised or lowered to suit the tide. So they rolled the luggage-vans on to the boat, and off on the other side; and as I was in one of the apartments adjoining a baggage-car, they considered it unnecessary to awaken me, and tumbled me over with the luggage. But when my master was asked to leave his seat, he found it very dark, and cold, and raining. He missed me for the first time on the journey. On all previous occasions, as soon as the train stopped, I was at hand to assist him. This caused many slaveholders to praise me very much: they said they had never before seen a slave so attentive to his master: and therefore my absence filled him with terror and confusion; the children of Israel could not have felt more troubled on arriving at the Red Sea. So he asked the conductor if he had seen anything of his slave. The man being somewhat of an abolitionist, and believing that my master was really a slaveholder, thought he would tease him a little respecting me. So he said, "No, sir; I haven't seen anything of him for some time: I have no doubt he has run away, and is in Philadelphia, free, long before now." My master knew that there was nothing in this; so he asked the conductor if he would please to see if he could find me. The man indignantly replied, "I am no slave-hunter; and as far as I am concerned everybody must look after their own niggers." He went off and left the confused invalid to fancy whatever he felt inclined. My master at first thought I must have been kidnapped into slavery by some one, or left, or perhaps killed on the train. He also thought of stopping to see if he could hear anything of me, but he soon remembered that he had no money. That night all the money we had was consigned to my own pocket, because we thought, in case there were any pickpockets about, a slave's pocket would be the last one they would look for. However, hoping to meet me some day in a land of liberty, and as he had the tickets, he thought it best upon the whole to enter the boat and come off to Philadelphia, and endeavour to make his way alone in this cold and hollow world as best he could. The time was now up, so he went on board and came across with feelings that can be better imagined than described.

After the train had got fairly on the way to Philadelphia, the guard came into my car and gave me a violent shake, and bawled out at the same time, "Boy, wake up!" I started, almost frightened out of my wits. He said, "Your master is scared half to death about you." That frightened me still more—I thought they had found him out; so I anxiously inquired what was the matter. The guard said, "He thinks you have run away from him." This made me feel quite at ease. I said, "No, sir; I am satisfied my good master doesn't think that." So off I started to see him. He had been fearfully nervous, but on seeing me he at once felt much better. He merely wished to know what had become of me.

On returning to my seat, I found the conductor and two or three other persons amusing themselves very much respecting my running away. So the guard said, "Boy, what did your master want?"[1] I replied, "He merely wished to know what had become of me." "No," said the man, "that was not it; he thought you had taken French leave, for parts unknown. I never saw a fellow so badly scared about losing his slave in my life. Now," continued the guard, "let me give you a little friendly advice. When you get to Philadelphia, run away and leave that cripple, and have your liberty." "No, sir," I indifferently replied, "I can't promise to do that." "Why

---

[1] I may state here that every man slave is called boy till he is very old, then the more respectable slaveholders call him uncle. The women are all girls till they are aged, then they are called aunts. This is the reason why Mrs. Stowe calls her characters Uncle Tom, Aunt Chloe, Uncle Tiff, &c.

not?" said the conductor, evidently much surprised; "don't you want your liberty?" "Yes, sir," I replied; "but I shall never run away from such a good master as I have at present."

One of the men said to the guard, "Let him alone; I guess he will open his eyes when he gets to Philadelphia, and see things in another light." After giving me a good deal of information, which I afterwards found to be very useful, they left me alone.

I also met with a coloured gentleman on this train, who recommended me to a boarding-house that was kept by an abolitionist, where he thought I would be quite safe, if I wished to run away from my master. I thanked him kindly, but of course did not let him know who we were. Late at night, or rather early in the morning, I heard a fearful whistling of the steam-engine; so I opened the window and looked out, and saw a large number of flickering lights in the distance, and heard a passenger in the next carriage—who also had his head out of the window—say to his companion, "Wake up, old horse, we are at Philadelphia!"

The sight of those lights and that announcement made me feel almost as happy as Bunyan's Christian must have felt when he first caught sight of the cross. I, like him, felt that the straps that bound the heavy burden to my back began to pop, and the load to roll off. I also looked, and looked again, for it appeared very wonderful to me how the mere sight of our first city of refuge should have all at once made my hitherto sad and heavy heart become so light and happy. As the train speeded on, I rejoiced and thanked God with all my heart and soul for his great kindness and tender mercy, in watching over us, and bringing us safely through.

As soon as the train had reached the platform, before it had fairly stopped, I hurried out of my carriage to my master, whom I got at once into a cab, placed the luggage on, jumped in myself, and we drove off to the boarding-house which was so kindly recommended to me. On leaving the station, my master—or rather my wife, as I may now say—who had from the commencement of the journey borne up in a manner that much surprised us both, grasped me by the hand, and said, "Thank God, William, we are safe!" then burst into tears, leant upon me, and wept like a child. The reaction was fearful. So when we reached the house, she was in reality so weak and faint that she could scarcely stand alone. However, I got her into the apartments that were pointed out, and there we knelt down, on this Sabbath, and Christmas-day,—a day that will ever be memorable to us,—and poured out our heartfelt gratitude to God, for his goodness in enabling us to overcome so many perilous difficulties, in escaping out of the jaws of the wicked.

FROM

The Narrative of Bethany Veney, a Slave Woman

by Bethany Veney

I have but little recollection of my very early life. My mother and her five children were owned by one James Fletcher, Pass Run, town of Luray, Page County, Virginia. Of my father I know nothing.

The first thing I remember with any distinctness was when, about seven years old, I was, with other children, knocking apples from a tree, when we were surprised by my young mistress, Miss Nasenath Fletcher, calling to us, in a loud and threatening tone, demanding what we were doing. Without waiting for reply, she told us to follow her; and, as she led the way down to a blackberry pasture not far off, she endeavored, in a very solemn manner, to impress us with the importance of always telling the truth. "If asked a question," she said, "we must answer directly, yes or no." I asked her "what we must say if asked something which we did not know." She answered, "Why, you must say you don't know, of course." I said, "I shall say, 'Maybe 'tis, and maybe 'tain't.'" I remember well how the children laughed at this; and then Miss Nasenath went on to tell us that *some time* all this world that we saw would be burned up,—that the moon would be turned into blood, the stars would fall out of the sky, and everything would melt away with a great heat, and that everybody, *every little child* that had told a lie, would be cast into a lake of fire and brimstone, and would burn there for ever and ever, and, what was more, though they should burn for ever and ever, they would never be burned up.

I was dreadfully frightened; and, as soon as I could get away, I ran to my mammy, and, repeating what mistress had said, begged to know if it could be true. To my great sorrow, she confirmed it all, but added what Miss Nasenath had failed to do; namely, that those who told the truth and were good would always have everything they should want. It seemed to me then there was nothing so good as molasses and sugar; and I eagerly asked, "Shall I have all the molasses and sugar I want, if I tell the truth?" "Yes," she replied, "*if you are good;* but remember, if you tell lies, you will be burned in the lake that burns for ever and ever."

This made a very strong impression upon me. I can never forget my mammy's manner at the time. I believed every word she said, and from that day to this I have never doubted its truth.

Though my conception of what constituted the truth was very dim, my fear of what should befall me, if I were to tell a lie, was very great. Still, I was only a young child, and could not, long at a time, be very unhappy.

My old master, who at times was inclined to be jolly, had a way of entertaining his friends by my singing and dancing. Supper over, he would call me into his room, and, giving me to understand what he wanted of me, I would, with all manner of grotesque grimaces, gestures, and positions, dance and sing:—

> *"Where are you going, Jim?*
> *Where are you going, Sam?*
> *To get a proper larning,*
> *To jump Jim Crow."*
>
> or
>
> *"David the king was grievit and worrit,*
> *He went to his chamber—*
> *His chamber and weppit;*

> *And, as he went, he weppit and said,*
> *'O my son, O my son!*
> *Would to God I had died*
> *For thee, O Absalom,*
> *My son, my son,' "—*

and many other similar songs, of the meaning of which I had of course no idea, and I have since thought neither he nor his friends could have had any more than I. . . .

Year after year rolled on. Master Jonas Mannyfield lived seven miles from us, on the other side of the Blue Ridge; and he owned a likely young fellow called Jerry. We had always known each other, and now he wanted to marry me. Our masters were both willing; and there was nothing to hinder, except that there was no minister about there to marry us. "No matter for that," Kibbler said to Jerry. "If you want Bett, and she wants you, that's the whole of it." But I didn't think so. I said, "No: never till somebody comes along who can marry us." So it happened, one day, there was a colored man—a pedler, with his cart—on the road, and Jerry brought him in, and said he was ready to be minister for us. He asked us a few questions, which we answered in a satisfactory manner, and then he declared us husband and wife. I did not want him to make us promise that we would always be true to each other forsaking all others, as the white people do in their marriage service, because I knew that at any time our masters could compel us to break such a promise; and I had never forgotten the lesson learned, so many years before, in the blackberry pasture.

So Jerry and I were happy as, under all the circumstances we could well be. When he asked his master's consent to our marriage, he told him he had had thoughts of removing to Missouri, in which case he should take him with him, and we would have to be separated; but, if he chose to run the risk, he had nothing to say. Jerry did not think there was any danger, and we were not dissuaded; for hearts that love are much the same in bond or free, in white or black.

Eight or ten months passed on, when one night my brother Stephen, who lived on the Blue Ridge, near Master Mannyfield, came to see me, and, as we talked of many things, he spoke of Jerry in a way that instantly roused my suspicion. I said: "Tell me what is the matter? I know there is something. Is Jerry dead? Is he sold? Tell me what it is." I saw he dreaded to speak, and that frightened me the more.

At last, he said: " 'Tis no use, Betty. You have got to know it. Old Look-a-here's people are all in jail for debt." "Old Look-a-here" was the nickname by which Mannyfield was known by the colored people far and near, because he had a way of saying, when he was about to whip one of his slaves, "Now look-a-here, you black rascal," or "you black wench."

The next day was Saturday, and I hurried to complete my task in the corn-field, and then asked my master if I could go to see Jerry. He objected at first, but at last gave me a pass to see my brother, and be gone until Monday morning.

The sun might have been two hours high when I started; but, before I was half over the mountain, night had closed round me its deepest gloom. The vivid flashes of lightning made the carriage path plain at times, and then I could not see a step before me; and the rolling thunder added to my fear and dread. I was dripping wet when, about nine o'clock, I reached the house. It had been my plan to get Stephen to go on with me to Jerry's mother's, and stay the night there; but his mistress, who was sister to my Miss Lucy, declared we must not go on in the storm, and, giving me supper, brought bedding, that I might lie on the kitchen floor and rest me there. In the morning, after a good breakfast, she started us off, with a bag of biscuits to eat by the way. Jerry's mother was glad to go with us; and we hurried along to Jerry, in jail at Little Washington, where he with his fellow-slaves was confined, like sheep or oxen, shut up in stalls, to be sold to pay their owner's debts.

Jerry saw us, as we came along the road, through the prison bars; and the jailer allowed us to talk together there, not, however, without a witness to all we might say. We had committed no offence against God or man. Jerry had not; and yet, like base criminals, we were denied even the consolation of privacy. This was a necessary part of the system of American slavery. Neither wife nor mother could intervene to soften its rigors one jot.

Several months passed, and Mannyfield was still unable to redeem his property; and they were at last put up at auction, and sold to the highest bidder. Frank White, a slave-trader, bought the entire lot, and proceeded at once to make up a gang for the Southern market.

Arrangements were made to start Friday morning; and on Thursday afternoon, chained together, the gang were taken across the stream, and encamped on its banks. White then went to Jerry, and, taking the handcuffs from his wrists, told him to go and stay the night with his wife, and see if he could persuade her to go with him. If he could, he would buy her, and so they need not be separated. He would pass that way in the morning, and see. Of course, Jerry was only too glad to come; and, at first, I thought I would go with him. Then came the consciousness that this inducement was only a sham, and that, once exposed for sale in a Southern market, the bidder with the largest sum of money would be our purchaser singly quite as surely as together; and, if separated, what would I do in a strange land? No: I would not go. It was far better for me to stay where, for miles and miles, I knew every one, and every one knew me. Then came the wish to secrete ourselves together in the mountains, or elsewhere, till White should be gone; but, to do this, detection was sure. Then we remembered that White had trusted us, in letting him come to me, and we felt ashamed, for a moment, as if we had tried to cheat; but what *right* had White to carry him away, or even to own him at all? Our poor, ignorant reasoning found it hard to understand his rights or our own; and we at last decided that, as soon as it was light, Jerry should take to the mountains, and, when White was surely gone, either I would join him there, and we would make for the North together, or he would come back, go to White's mother, who lived a few miles distant, and tell her he would work for her and obey her, but he would never go South to be worked to death in the rice-swamps or cotton-fields.

We talked late into the night; and at last, in the silence and dread, worn out with sorrow and fear, my head on his shoulder, we both dropped asleep.

Daylight was upon us when we waked. The sad consciousness of our condition, and our utter helplessness, overpowered us. I opened the door, and there was my mistress, with pail in hand, going to the spring for water. "Oh, what shall I do? Where shall I go?" cried Jerry, as he saw her. "Have no fear," I said. "Go right along. I know mistress will never betray you." And, with a bound, he was over the fence, into the fields, and off to the mountains.

In a very short time, White and his poor, doomed company came along, and called for Jerry. I had taken my pail to milk the cows; and, seeing me, he sung out, "Woman, where is Jerry, I say?" "I don't know where Jerry is," I answered. Then, turning to Kibbler, who, hearing the outcry, now came out, he said, "You told me that woman wouldn't lie; and you know well enough she is lying now, when she says she don't know where that ———— rascal is." Kibbler answered very slowly and thoughtfully, "I never knowed her to lie; but may be this time,—may be this time." White then turned to me, and said, "I took off his handcuffs, and let him go to you, and you had no business to serve me so."

It was true I did not know where Jerry was at that time. We had agreed that we would meet that night near the blacksmith's old shop, on the other side of the run; and that was all I knew of his where-abouts, though he had not been gone long enough to be far away. It was true he had trusted us, and I felt very badly; but what else *could* we have done? Kind reader, *what* think you?

I then told him that Jerry had said he was willing to work, and would go to his mother's and serve her, but *never*, if he could help it, would he be carried South.

Then White tried to bargain with Kibbler for my purchase, say-ing he would give any price he should name for me, because he knew

I would then find Jerry. But it was no use. Kibbler had a kind spot in his heart, and would not consent to let me go. So the slave-trader moved on with his human cattle.

Five miles on the road lived David McCoy, another slave-trader. When White reached his house, it was agreed by them that, if McCoy could find Jerry within two days, he should bring him on, and they would meet at Stanton, Va. . . .

The place where I was to meet Jerry was, as I have said, across the run, in a corn-field, near the blacksmith's shop, the time Friday night.

It had rained hard all day, and the stream was swollen, and pouring and rushing at a fearful rate. I waited till everybody was in bed and asleep, when I lighted my pine knot, and started for the Pass. It was still raining, and the night was very dark. Only by my torch could I see a step before me; and, when I attempted to wade in, as I did in many different places, I found it was no use. I should surely be drowned if I persisted. So, disappointed and grieved, I gave up and went home. The next morning I was able to get over on horseback to milk the cows, but I neither heard nor saw anything of Jerry.

Saturday night came. I knew well that, if not caught by White, Jerry would be round. At last, every one was in bed, and all was still. I waited and listened. I listened and waited. Then I heard his step at the door. I hurriedly opened it, and he came in. His clothes were still damp and stiff from the rain of yesterday. He was frightened and uneasy. He had been hiding around in different places, constantly fearing detection. He had seen me from behind the old blacksmith's shop when I had tried the night before, with my pine knot, to ford the stream; and he was glad, he said, when he saw me go back, for he knew I should be carried down by the current and be drowned, if I had persisted. I went to my mistress's bedroom, and asked her if I might go to the cellar. She knew at once what I meant, and whispered softly, "Betty, has Jerry come?" then, without waiting for reply, added, "get him some milk and light bread and butter." I was not long in doing so; and the poor fellow ate like one famishing.

Then he wanted to know all that had happened, and what White had said when he found he was gone. We talked a long time, and tried to devise some plans for our mutual safety and possible escape from slavery altogether; but, every way we looked, the path was beset with danger and exposure. We were both utterly disheartened. But sleep came at last and, for the time being, relieved us of our fears.

In the morning, which was Sunday, we had our breakfast together, and, as the hours passed, began to feel a little comforted. After dinner, we walked out to the field and strolled about for some time; and, when ready to go back to the house, we each took an armful of fodder along for the horses. As we laid it down and turned to go into the house, David McCoy rode up on horseback. He saw Jerry at once, and called him to come to the fence. The excitement of the last days—the fasting and the fear—had completely cowed and broken whatever of manhood, or even of brute courage, a slave might by any possibility be presumed at any time to be possessed of, and the last remains of these qualities in poor Jerry were gone. He mutely obeyed; and when, with an oath, McCoy commanded him to mount the horse behind him, he mutely seated himself there. McCoy then called to me to go to the house and bring Jerry's clothes. "Never,"—I screamed back to him,—"never, not to save your miserable life." But Jerry said: "O Betty, 'tis no use. We can't help it." I knew this was so. I stifled my anger and my grief, brought his little bundle, into which I tucked a testament and catechism some one had given me, and shook hands "good-by" with him. So we *parted forever,* in this world.

[In the opening lines of the next chapter Veney informs readers: "Several months passed, and I became a mother." —Ed.]

FROM

Memories of Childhood's Slavery Days

by Annie L. Burton

The memory of my happy, care-free childhood days on the plantation, with my little white and black companions, is often with me. Neither master nor mistress nor neighbors had time to bestow a thought upon us, for the great Civil War was raging. That great event in American history was a matter wholly outside the realm of our childish interests. Of course we heard our elders discuss the various events of the great struggle, but it meant nothing to us.

On the plantation there were ten white children and fourteen colored children. Our days were spent roaming about from plantation to plantation, not knowing or caring what things were going on in the great world outside our little realm. Planting time and harvest time were happy days for us. How often at the harvest time the planters discovered cornstalks missing from the ends of the rows, and blamed the crows! We were called the "little fairy devils." To the sweet potatoes and peanuts and sugar cane we also helped ourselves.

Those slaves that were not married served the food from the great house, and about half-past eleven they would send the older children with food to the workers in the fields. Of course, I followed, and before we got to the fields, we had eaten the food nearly all up.

When the workers returned home they complained, and we were whipped.

The slaves got their allowance every Monday night of molasses, meat, corn meal, and a kind of flour called "dredgings" or "shorts." Perhaps this allowance would be gone before the next Monday night, in which case the slaves would steal hogs and chickens. Then would come the whipping-post. Master himself never whipped his slaves; this was left to the overseer.

We children had no supper, and only a little piece of bread or something of the kind in the morning. Our dishes consisted of one wooden bowl, and oyster shells were our spoons. This bowl served for about fifteen children, and often the dogs and the ducks and the peafowl had a dip in it. Sometimes we had buttermilk and bread in our bowl, sometimes greens or bones.

Our clothes were little homespun cotton slips, with short sleeves. I never knew what shoes were until I got big enough to earn them myself.

If a slave man and woman wished to marry, a party would be arranged some Saturday night among the slaves. The marriage ceremony consisted of the pair jumping over a stick. If no children were born within a year or so, the wife was sold.

At New Year's, if there was any debt or mortgage on the plantation, the extra slaves were taken to Clayton and sold at the court house. In this way families were separated.

When they were getting recruits for the war, we were allowed to go to Clayton to see the soldiers.

I remember, at the beginning of the war, two colored men were hung in Clayton; one, Cæsar King, for killing a blood hound and biting off an overseer's ear; the other, Dabney Madison, for the murder of his master. Dabney Madison's master was really shot by a man named Houston, who was infatuated with Madison's mistress, and who had hired Madison to make the bullets for him. Houston escaped after the deed, and the blame fell on Dabney Madison, as he was the only slave of his master and mistress. The clothes of the two victims were hung on two pine trees, and no colored person would touch them. Since I have grown up, I have seen the skeleton of one of these men in the office of a doctor in Clayton.

After the men were hung, the bones were put in an old deserted house. Somebody that cared for the bones used to put them in the sun in bright weather, and back in the house when it rained. Finally the bones disappeared, although the boxes that had contained them still remained.

At one time, when they were building barns on the plantation, one of the big boys got a little brandy and gave us children all a drink, enough to make us drunk. Four doctors were sent for, but nobody could tell what was the matter with us, except they thought we had eaten something poisonous. They wanted to give us some castor oil, but we refused to take it, because we thought that the oil was made from the bones of the dead men we had seen. Finally, we told about the big white boy giving us the brandy, and the mystery was cleared up.

Young as I was then, I remember this conversation between master and mistress, on master's return from the gate one day, when he had received the latest news: "William, what is the news from the seat of war?" "A great battle was fought at Bull Run, and the Confederates won," he replied. "Oh, good, good," said mistress, "and what did Jeff Davis say?" "Look out for the blockade. I do not know what the end may be soon," he answered. "What does Jeff Davis mean by that?" she asked. "Sarah Anne, I don't know, unless he means that the niggers will be free." "O, my God, what shall we do?" "I presume," he said, "we shall have to put our boys to work and hire help." "But," she said, "what will the niggers do if they are free? Why, they will starve if we don't keep them." "Oh, well," he said, "let them wander, if they will not stay with their owners. I don't doubt that many owners have been good to their slaves, and they would rather remain with their owners than wander about without home or country."

My mistress often told me that my father was a planter who

owned a plantation about two miles from ours. He was a white man, born in Liverpool, England. He died in Lewisville, Alabama, in the year 1875.

I will venture to say that I only saw my father a dozen times, when I was about four years old; and those times I saw him only from a distance, as he was driving by the great house of our plantation. Whenever my mistress saw him going by, she would take me by the hand and run out upon the piazza, and exclaim, "Stop there, I say! Don't you want to see and speak to and caress your darling child? She often speaks of you and wants to embrace her dear father. See what a bright and beautiful daughter she is, a perfect picture of yourself. Well, I declare, you are an affectionate father." I well remember that whenever my mistress would speak thus and upbraid him, he would whip up his horse and get out of sight and hearing as quickly as possible. My mistress's action was, of course, intended to humble and shame my father. I never spoke to him, and cannot remember that he ever noticed me, or in any way acknowledged me to be his child.

My mother and my mistress were children together, and grew up to be mothers together. My mother was the cook in my mistress's household. One morning when master had gone to Eufaula, my mother and my mistress got into an argument, the consequence of which was that my mother was whipped, for the first time in her life. Whereupon, my mother refused to do any more work, and ran away from the plantation. For three years we did not see her again.

Our plantation was one of several thousand acres, comprising large level fields, upland, and considerable forests of Southern pine. Cotton, corn, sweet potatoes, sugar cane, wheat, and rye were the principal crops raised on the plantation. It was situated near the P——— River, and about twenty-three miles from Clayton, Ala.

One day my master heard that the Yankees were coming our way, and he immediately made preparations to get his goods and valuables out of their reach. The big six-mule team was brought to the smoke-house door, and loaded with hams and provisions. After being loaded, the team was put in the care of two of the most trustworthy and valuable slaves that my master owned, and driven away. It was master's intention to have these things taken to a swamp, and there concealed in a pit that had recently been made for the purpose. But just before the team left the main road for the by-road that led to the swamp, the two slaves were surprised by the Yankees, who at once took possession of the provisions, and started the team toward Clayton, where the Yankees had headquarters. The road to Clayton ran past our plantation. One of the slave children happened to look up the road, and saw the Yankees coming, and gave warning. Whereupon, my master left unceremoniously for the woods, and remained concealed there for five days. The niggers had run away whenever they got a chance, but now it was master's and the other white folks' turn to run.

The Yankees rode up to the piazza of the great house and inquired who owned the plantation. They gave orders that nothing must be touched or taken away, as they intended to return shortly and take possession. My mistress and the slaves watched for their return day and night for more than a week, but the Yankees did not come back.

One morning in April, 1865, my master got the news that the Yankees had left Mobile Bay and crossed the Confederate lines, and that the Emancipation Proclamation had been signed by President Lincoln. Mistress suggested that the slaves should not be told of their freedom; but master said he would tell them, because they would soon find it out, even if he did not tell them. Mistress, however, said she could keep my mother's three children, for my mother had now been gone so long.

All the slaves left the plantation upon the news of their freedom, except those who were feeble or sickly. With the help of these, the crops were gathered. My mistress and her daughters had to go to the kitchen and to the washtub. My little half-brother, Henry, and myself had to gather chips, and help all we could. My sister, Caroline, who was twelve years old, could help in the kitchen.

After the war, the Yankees took all the good mules and horses from the plantation, and left their old army stock. We children chanced to come across one of the Yankees' old horses, that had "U. S." branded on him. We called him "Old Yank" and got him fattened up. One day in August, six of us children took "Old Yank" and went away back on the plantation for watermelons. Coming home, we thought we would make the old horse trot. When "Old Yank" commenced to trot, our big melons dropped off, but we couldn't stop the horse for some time. Finally, one of the big boys went back and got some more melons, and left us eating what we could find of the ones that had been dropped. Then all we six, with our melons, got on "Old Yank" and went home. We also used to hitch "Old Yank" into a wagon and get wood. But one sad day in the fall, the Yankees came back again, and gathered up their old stock, and took "Old Yank" away.

One day mistress sent me out to do some churning under a tree. I went to sleep and jerked the churn over on top of me, and consequently got a whipping.

My mother came for us at the end of the year 1865, and demanded that her children be given up to her. This, mistress refused to do, and threatened to set the dogs on my mother if she did not at once leave the place. My mother went away, and remained with some of the neighbors until supper time. Then she got a boy to tell Caroline to come down to the fence. When she came, my mother told her to go back and get Henry and myself and bring us down to the gap in the fence as quick as she could. Then my mother took Henry in her arms, and my sister carried me on her back. We climbed fences and crossed fields, and after several hours came to a little hut which my mother had secured on a plantation. We had no more than reached the place, and made a little fire, when master's two sons rode up and demanded that the children be returned. My mother refused to give us up. Upon her offering to go with them to the Yankee headquarters to find out if it were really true that all negroes had been made free, the young men left, and troubled us no more.

The cabin that was now our home was made of logs. It had one door, and an opening in one wall, with an inside shutter, was the only window. The door was fastened with a latch. Our beds were some straw.

There were six in our little family; my mother, Caroline, Henry, two other children that my mother had brought with her upon her return, and myself.

The man on whose plantation this cabin stood, hired my mother as cook, and gave us this little home. We children used to sell blueberries and plums that we picked. One day the man on whom we depended for our home and support, left. Then my mother did washing by the day, for whatever she could get. We were sent to get cold victuals from hotels and such places. A man wanting hands to pick cotton, my brother Henry and I were set to help in this work. We had to go to the cotton field very early every morning. For this work, we received forty cents for every hundred pounds of cotton we picked.

Caroline was hired out to take care of a baby.

In 1866, another man hired the plantation on which our hut stood, and we moved into Clayton, to a little house my mother secured there. A rich lady came to our house one day, looking for some one to take care of her little daughter. I was taken, and adopted into this family. This rich lady was Mrs. E. M. Williams, a music teacher, the wife of a lawyer. We called her "Mis' Mary." . . .

SUGGESTIONS FOR FURTHER READING

ABOUT BOOKER T. WASHINGTON

DU BOIS, W. E. B. "Of Mr. Booker T. Washington and Others," in *The Souls of Black Folk: Essays and Sketches*. Chicago: A. C. McClurg, 1903.

FRANKLIN, JOHN HOPE and MEIER, AUGUST, eds. *Black Leaders of the Twentieth Century*. Urbana and Chicago: University of Illinois Press, 1982. In addition to a fine essay by Louis R. Harlan, "Booker T. Washington and the Politics of Accommodation," this book also contains insightful essays on many of his friends and foes, including T. Thomas Fortune, Mary McLeod Bethune, Ida B. Wells, and W. E. B. Du Bois.

HARLAN, LOUIS R. *Booker T. Washington: The Making of a Black Leader, 1856–1901*. New York: Oxford University Press, 1972, and *Booker T. Washington: The Wizard of Tuskegee, 1901–1915*. New York: Oxford University Press, 1983. This thoughtful, exhaustive study of Washington has no rival.

HAWKINS, HUGH, ed. *Booker T. Washington and His Critics: Black Leadership in Crisis*. 2nd ed. Lexington, Mass.: D. C. Heath, 1974. This book gathers excerpts of Washington's writings and speeches and a wide array of commentary. A second edition was published in 1974 with the subtitle "Black Leadership in Crisis."

MEIER, AUGUST. *Negro Thought in America, 1880–1915: Racial Ideologies in the Age of Booker T. Washington*. Ann Arbor: University of Michigan Press, 1963. According to Washington's biographer, Louis R. Harlan, this book "provides the best analysis of Washington's relationship with the black ideologies and race movements of his day."

MILLER, KELLY. "Radicals and Conservatives" in *Radicals and Conservatives and Other Essays on the Negro in America*. New York: Schocken, 1968 (first published in 1908 under title *Race Adjustment: Essays on the Negro in America*). This essay by a leading black thinker from the first third of the century is perhaps the finest comparison of Washington to his most famous black predecessor, Frederick Douglass.

BY BOOKER T. WASHINGTON

———. *Character Building: Being Addresses Delivered on Sunday Evenings to the Students of Tuskegee Institute*. New York: Doubleday, Page & Company, 1902.

——— with S. LAING WILLIAMS. *Frederick Douglass*. Philadelphia: G. W. Jacobs, 1907.

———. *The Future of the American Negro*. Boston: Small, Maynard & Company, 1899. A collection of Washington's essays and speeches.

———. *The Man Farthest Down: A Record of Observation and Study in Europe*. New York: Doubleday, Page & Company, 1912. Washington's comparative analysis of poor Europeans and black Americans based on his visit to Europe in late summer–early fall 1910. Washington's collaborator on this book was Robert E. Park, his chief ghostwriter and in-house editor from 1905 to 1912.

———. *My Larger Education, Being Chapters from My Experience*. New York: Doubleday, Page & Company, 1911. Still another memoir, published four years before his death.

———. *The Negro in Business*. Boston and Chicago: Hertel, Jenkins & Co., 1907.

———. *The Story of My Life and Work* (with illustrations by Frank Beard). Naperville, Ill.: J. L. Nichols and Company, 1900. Washington's first autobiography, a revised edition of which was published in 1901 as *An Autobiography by Booker T. Washington: The Story of My Life*, with an updated edition released shortly after Washington's death in 1915 under the title *Booker T. Washington's Own Story of His Life and Work*.

————. *The Story of the Negro: The Rise of the Race from Slavery*, vols. I & II. 1909. Gloucester, Mass.: Peter Smith, 1969. In 1940 this study was published by Washington's favorite publisher, only now without Walter Hines Page, Doubleday, Doran & Company.

————. *Tuskegee and Its People: Their Ideals and Achievements*. New York: D. Appleton and Company, 1905.

————. *Up from Slavery: An Autobiography*. New York: Doubleday, Page & Company, 1901. First edition. Originally published serially in *The Outlook*, November 3, 1900–February 23, 1901.

————. *Working with the Hands*. New York: Doubleday, Page & Company, 1904. A sequel to *Up from Slavery*, with photographs by Frances Benjamin Johnson.

OF RELATED INTEREST

ANDREWS, WILLIAM L. *To Tell a Free Story: The First Century of Afro-American Autobiography, 1760–1865*. Urbana: University of Illinois Press, 1986.

FOSTER, FRANCES SMITH. *Witnessing Slavery: The Development of Antebellum Slave Narratives*. Westport, Conn.: Greenwood Press, 1979.

GATES, HENRY LOUIS, JR., general ed. *The Schomburg Library of Nineteenth-Century Black Women Writers*. New York: Oxford University Press, 1988, 1991, 35 volumes. This landmark series contains a rich assortment of long and short works of nonfiction and fiction, as well as poetry. Among the volumes of particular value for anyone wanting a deeper encounter with early black women's autobiography are: *Incidents in the Life of a Slave Girl* by Harriet Jacobs; *Six Women's Slave Narratives; Collected Black Women's Narratives; Spiritual Narratives;*

and *Behind the Scenes: Or, Thirty Years a Slave, and Four Years in the White House* by Elizabeth Keckley.

WOODWARD, C. VANN. *Origins of the New South, 1877–1913.* Baton Rouge: Louisiana State University Press, 1951. One of the best general histories of the South during "The Age of Booker T. Washington."

◆ ◆ ◆ ◆ ◆ ◆ ◆ ◆ ◆ ◆ ◆ ◆ ◆ ◆ ◆ ◆ ◆ ◆ ◆

CHECKLIST OF ILLUSTRATIONS

All of the illustrations in this edition are from The New York Public Library's Schomburg Center for Research in Black Culture.

Frontispiece: Photograph of Booker T. Washington in the 1880s, photographer unknown.
Photographs and Prints Division

Pages xv, 106, 121: Photographic illustrations from *The Story of My Life and Work* by Booker T. Washington (Naperville, Ill.: J. L. Nichols, 1900).
Manuscripts, Archives and Rare Books Division

Page xvi: Title page from the pamphlet of Booker T. Washington's Atlanta address on September 18, 1895. N.d. n.p.
Manuscripts, Archives and Rare Books Division

Pages xx, 154: Letters from Booker T. Washington to Emily Howland dated February 28, 1901, and September 6, 1895.
Manuscripts, Archives and Rare Books Division

Pages xxii–xxiii: Portrait of Booker T. Washington by Alfred Houghton Clark and the first page of the first installment of *Up from Slavery* from *The Outlook*, November 3, 1900.
Manuscripts, Archives and Rare Books Division

Page xxvii: Photograph of Booker T. Washington toward the end of his life, n.d., photographer unknown.
Photographs and Prints Division

Pages xxxiv–xxxvii: From the first edition of *Up from Slavery* (New York: Doubleday, Page & Company, 1901): Photograph of Booker T. Washington, with credit "Photographed for *The World's Work* by Gertrude Käsebier"; title page; Booker T. Washington's autograph dated May 31, 1902; and inscription from inside front cover of book, "Gift—For exhibition purposes," by Arturo Alfonso Schomburg.
Manuscripts, Archives and Rare Books Division

Pages 9, 43, 58, 88, 93, 113, 118, 128, 129, 187, 226: Photographic illustrations for *Up from Slavery* from *The Outlook*, November 3, 1900–February 23, 1901.
Manuscripts, Archives and Rare Books Division

Page 24: "Making Salt, at Saltville, Virginia," lithograph (?), artist unknown, n.d.
Photographs and Prints Division

Page 34: Rendering of Hampton Normal and Agricultural Institute, medium unknown.
Photographs and Prints Division

Pages 47, 195: Photographs of Booker T. Washington and his residence at Tuskegee, The Oaks, used in 50th anniversary edition of *Up from Slavery* (New York: Doubleday, Page & Company, 1951).
General Research and Reference Division

Page 60: Engraving of "two members of the Ku Klux Klan in their disguises" from the December 19, 1868, edition of *Harper's Weekly*, with the caption "engraved from a photograph, representing two members of the Ku Klux Klan order captured in a recent riot at Huntsville, Alabama, in 1868."
Photographs and Prints Division

Page 137: Page of fundraising brochure for Tuskegee Institute, ca. 1889–1899.
Manuscripts, Archives and Rare Books Division

Page 193: Photograph of Margaret Murray Washington, photographer unknown, n.d.
Photographs and Prints Division

Page 223: Detail of group photograph including Booker T. Washington, his wife Margaret Murray Washington, and benefactors, by Frances Benjamin Johnston, 1906.
Photographs and Prints Division

Page 229: Photograph of the Booker T. Washington Monument on the campus of Tuskegee University by Otis Finley, Jr., n.d.
Photographs and Prints Division

Page 237: "A slave-pen at New Orleans—Before the auction. A sketch of the past," from the January 24, 1863, issue of *Harper's Weekly*.
Photographs and Prints Division

Page 273: Portrait of Josiah Henson used as frontispiece for *Truth Stranger Than Fiction: Father Henson's Story of His Own Life* (Boston: John P. Jewett and Company, 1858).
Manuscripts, Archives and Rare Books Division